Shadow Prowler

Shadow Prowler

ALEXEY PEHOV

TRANSLATION BY ANDREW BROMFIELD

A TOM DOHERTY ASSOCIATES BOOK
NEW YORK

This is a work of fiction. All of the characters, organizations, and events portrayed in this novel are either products of the author's imagination or are used fictitiously.

SHADOW PROWLER

Copyright © 2002 by Aleksey Pehov

English translation copyright © 2010 by Aleksey Pehov

Originally published as КРАДУЩИЙСЯ В ТЕНИ by Alfa-Book in Moscow, Russia

A Tor Book
Published by Tom Doherty Associates, LLC
175 Fifth Avenue
New York, NY 10010

www.tor-forge.com

Tor® is a registered trademark of Tom Doherty Associates, LLC.

Library of Congress Cataloging-in-Publication Data

Pehov, Alexey.
    [Kradushchiisia v teni. English]
    Shadow prowler / Alexey Pehov. — 1st ed.
        p. cm.
    "A Tom Doherty Associates Book."
    ISBN 978-0-7653-2403-0
    I. Title.
    PG3492.94.E39K7313 2010
    891.73'5—dc22
                                        2009041231

First Edition: February 2010

Printed in the United States of America

0 9 8 7 6 5 4 3 2 1

Acknowledgments

I would like to thank Robert Gottlieb, my agent, for arranging the publication of my novel in the United States. I would also like to thank Olga Gottlieb for her invaluable assistance, Andrew Bromfield for his excellent translation of my novel from Russian to English, Patrick LoBrutto for incredible text editing, Zamir Gotta for help, the great team of Trident Media Group for professionalism, and, of course, my wife, Elena, for creative vision and all her support.

Shadow Prowler

1

NIGHT

Night is the best time for my kind. When I appear in the street, ordinary people have long been asleep in their warm, soft beds. Old drunks out drinking late won't brave the city's impenetrable darkness. No, they would rather spend an uncomfortable night in a tavern.

Night. Silence. Only the hollow echo of the municipal guard patrol's footsteps bounce off the walls of the old houses and ripple on along Avendoom's dark streets, dead and empty until morning.

The soldiers hurry along, walking quickly. In the darkest alleyways they break into a run. I can easily understand how these valiant servants of the law feel: no, it's not people they're afraid of—any madcaps who might summon up the impudence to attack the guardians of public order will be given short shrift with their heavy battle-axes. What makes them afraid is something else. There are other creatures lurking in the shadows of the stone buildings. Creatures that creep out into the open at this uneasy hour for their nocturnal hunt. And may Sagot help the men of the watch if those vile beasts are feeling hungry.

The shades of night are a refuge for all: for the good townsfolk, fearfully hiding themselves away from dangerous men; for the petty thieves whose one wish is to clean out the respectable citizens' purses as quickly as possible; for the robbers just waiting for a chance to make use of their knives. And, of course, for the demons living in those dark shades, who are only too happy to prey on good citizens, petty thieves, and robbers alike.

Fortunately, I have yet to run into the demons who have appeared in the city since the Nameless One began stirring in the Desolate Lands after centuries of calm. And that's why I'm still alive.

Shortly after they pass me, the watchmen's footsteps fade into silence on the next street.

On the orders of Baron Frago Lanten, the head of Avendoom's municipal guard, all patrols have been tripled in strength. The rumor is that the artifact that has until now held the Nameless One in the Desolate Lands is weakening, and soon he will burst through into our world from that icy desert covered with eternal snow. War is approaching, no matter how hard the Order of Magicians and the multitudes of priests try to put it off. It's simply a matter of time. Six months, or perhaps a year— and then all those things they used to frighten us with when we were children will be upon us. The Nameless One will gather together an army and come to us from behind the Needles of Ice, and the horror will begin. Even here, in the capital, you sometimes come across devotees of the Nameless One. And I'm far from certain that the Wild Hearts of the Lonely Giant Fortress will be able to hold back the hordes of ogres and giants. . . .

Once again I have gone unnoticed. My thanks to the shadow of night. The shadow is my helpmate, my lover, my companion. I hide inside her, I live with her, and she is the only one always ready to shelter me, to save me from the arrows, from the swords that flash balefully in the moonlit night, and the bloodthirsty, golden eyes of the demons. No one else cares for Harold . . . maybe Brother For.

"Shadow is the sister of darkness," says Brother For, Sagot's kindly priest. And where there is darkness, the Nameless One is never far away.

What absolute nonsense! The Nameless One and the shadow? Entirely different things. You might as well compare an ogre and a giant. The shadow is life, freedom, money, and reputation. Shadow Harold knows about such things firsthand. For a shadow to appear there has to be at least a scintilla of light, and to compare it with darkness is stupid, to say the least. But of course, I don't tell my old teacher that. You don't go teaching your grandmother to suck eggs.

It's quiet. So quiet you can hear the moths scrabbling at the coolness of the night with their fragile little wings. It's a long time now since the watch patrol passed me and it's high time for me to be going about my business, but somehow I'm feeling extracautious tonight. . . . Some premonition makes me remain in cover, beside the wall of the building that is submerged in gloom.

There were no suspicious sounds to be heard in that narrow little street with the old stone houses that could remember the old Quiet Times. Nothing but a painted tin sign above the baker's shop creaking in the faint wind. The slow-stirring grayish yellow mist for which our capital is famous lay thick across the rough stone paving of the road, chipped and battered by the cart wheels. They say the mist was a trick played by some half-trained wizard back in the distant past. But ever since then not one of the kingdom's archmagicians has been able to rid the city of the consequences of his innocent prank.

The silence alarms me. The only place that is ever this quiet is a rich man's vault after a visit from one of the city's bands of petty thieves.

The signboard creaks, the light wind swirls merrily, clouds drift lazily across the night sky. But I stand there, fused with the shadow of the building, trying not to move a muscle. My intuition and my experience of life compel me to listen to the night silence of the city. No street, not even the most deserted, could be as dead as this.

There should be sounds in the night. Rats rustling in the garbage. A drunk snoring away beside them, his pockets cleaned out by thieves who are already sheltering for the night in some dark, narrow hidey-hole. The sound of snoring from the windows of the gray houses. A dirty dog sneaking through the darkness. The heavy breathing of a novice thief lying in wait for his victim, clutching his knife in a palm sweaty from excitement. Sounds from the shops and workshops—even at night the laborious work continues in some of them. But there was none of this in the dark little street wreathed in its shroud of mist. There was nothing but silence, gloom, and a thickening atmosphere of danger.

The carefree, roistering wind ruffled my hair affectionately, but I didn't dare raise my hood. Some insistent hand seemed to hold me back.

Sagot! What is happening on this quiet little street of artisans?

In answer to my prayer the glorious god of all thieves seemed to make my hearing keener.

Footsteps. Hasty footsteps that even the creeping yellow-gray froth of the mist had failed to deaden. In a recess in the wall of the house opposite, I spotted a momentary flicker in the darkness.

Had someone else decided to hide here?

I peered hard into the ink-black night. No. I'd imagined it. I was too much on edge, anticipating nonexistent problems. I must be getting old.

Meanwhile the footsteps grew louder and louder. The sounds came from the street into which the municipal guard patrol had turned only a few minutes earlier. I froze and tried to merge even deeper into the shadow, while the phantom of danger circled indolently above my head.

A man came round the bend at a fast walk, almost a run, and made straight for me. He had to be a fool or a brave man to be roaming through the darkness alone. Most likely a fool. Brave men don't live long in our world. But then, neither do fools, unless they work as jesters for our glorious king.

The stranger was coming closer. Tall and well dressed, even wealthy looking, his hand resting on the hilt of a rather good sword.

Once again clouds crept across the sky, covering the stars, and the gloom that was already total became absolutely impenetrable. Even when he drew level with me, I couldn't make out the stranger's face, although he was so close that if I'd wanted, I could have reached out my hand and lifted the bulging purse off his belt. But I'm no small-time pickpocket, I won't stoop to that—the impetuous years of my youth are long since over and gone, and in any case my instinct has already hinted that this is the wrong moment to twitch a single muscle, or even take a deep breath.

In the niche opposite me the darkness began swirling again, eddying chaotically and welling up into a dark flower of death, and ice-cold terror froze me to the spot. From out of the gloom, Darkness burst forth in the form of a winged demon with a horned skull for a head, and fell on its victim like an avalanche from the Mountains of the Dwarves, pinning him down with its prodigious weight.

The man let out a screech like a wounded cat and grabbed vainly at his useless sword, trying to draw it, but the Darkness crumpled up the nocturnal wayfarer, sucked him in, and devoured him, and then the creature, whatever it was, soared up into the sky, bearing away its fresh meat, and perhaps a soul as well. I slid slowly down the wall, trying to calm my breathing. My heart was pounding like a mad thing.

The demon hadn't noticed me, although I was directly opposite it all the time. But if I had made just the slightest movement! If I had even started breathing a little more loudly. . . . Then I was the one who would have been his prey.

I had been lucky. Once again I had been very lucky. A thief's luck is a fickle wench, she can turn her back on him at any moment, but as long as she is with me, I can carry on plying my trade.

In a dark corner of the next building a rat squeaked, followed by another. Up in the sky a bat flew past, hunting the late June moths. The danger had passed, now I could carry on along my way. I detached myself from the wall and set off, trying to stick to the darkest sections of the street.

Moving rapidly, but with my boots making no sound, I dashed from building to building, from shadow to shadow. I left the Street of the Bakers behind me, turning into the alleyway on the right. The mist was thicker here, it welcomed me into the soft embrace of its clammy paws, deadening my footsteps, concealing me from the eyes of humans and nonhumans alike.

The dark alleyway came to an end, and the dark walls of the houses that had seen so much joy and sorrow in this life suddenly parted sharply. The wind scattered the clouds and the sky was transformed into a tablecloth across which some rich man had scattered bright coins. Hundreds and thousands of stars started twinkling at me out of the cold summer night.

On Grok Square there were occasional street lamps burning. After all, it is one of the large central squares, and even if they were afraid, the lamplighters had to do their job. Encased in its glass armor, each flame cast a spot of flickering light around itself, and chaotic shadows danced in silence on the walls of the sullen buildings.

I wish the wind would drive its herd of gray, fluffy sheep back out across the sky, but for the time being I'll have to stick to the shadow, huddling against the walls of the tall buildings. Only the shadow has turned pale and timid from all the light all around.

Grok himself stared at me mutely with his all-seeing eyes. I think he was a general who saved our kingdom from an invasion by orcs, or some royal adviser back in the hoary old days of antiquity. And there, right behind the plinth of his pedestal, is the goal of my nocturnal outing. A large house, surrounded by a wall with battlements, built out of immense blocks of stone quarried in the Mountains of the Dwarves in the times when that race was still on friendly terms with our kingdom. To my mind the building is in barbarously bad taste, but the Duke Patin who lives here would hardly be interested in my opinion. A cousin of the king who is in charge of the treasury is a very big wheel, and so people turn a blind eye to his whimsical taste in architecture.

The king tolerates his relative's other caprices; rich aristocrats can get away with almost anything. But rumor has it that just recently he discovered a certain sum of money missing from the treasury. And that means that heads are bound to roll, since His Majesty is not very well disposed to individuals who expend the state's money too liberally. Fine by me; one less fat cat.

The high wall of the house was buttressed at each end by a tower with a truncated pinnacle. In the left tower there was a gateway seven yards wide with heavy wooden gates clad in iron sheeting. Four horsemen could easily enter it riding abreast. But that grand formal entrance was only for the invited, and it would be best for me to forget about it.

I ran quickly across the illuminated square and took cover in the shadow of the columns of the Royal Library—a place of pilgrimage for magicians of the Order and for historians. Sometimes even nobles came here to improve their store of wisdom, although more often the so-called gentlemen preferred to go straight to Ranneng—the city of learning—for their studies.

From my shelter I have a clear view of the duke's residence. It is as if the house has died. I can't see any guards at the gates or on the walls. They must be huddling in the watch house with their teeth chattering. I can understand them; I would be hidden away in my den myself, if not for the Commission. A certain individual made me a generous offer— he was interested in a rare little item in the duke's collection. The fee offered was excellent, and all I had to do was get into the house, take the trinket, and leave. Not too difficult, especially if you bore in mind the fact that His Lordship and his retinue had gone off hunting deer in the forests around the city and there would only be a very small number of menials left in the house.

Of course, the risk of stirring up a hornets' nest was considerable. But by the time the hornets realized what was what, I would be long gone.

I ran my hands carefully over my equipment and clothing, checking for the hundredth time that night to make sure I had brought everything I needed to carry out my plan. A dark gray jerkin with a hood, gray gloves, black trousers and boots. A large double-edged knife, firmly secured to my thigh by two leather straps so that it would not hinder my movements. That knife had cost me a whole stack of gold coins. It was a little less than a cubit in length, almost a short sword, and the mounting of the blade was covered with a strip of silver, so if you wished you could even risk a fight with someone who had risen from the dead. I could quite easily be lucky enough to walk away from such a skirmish, even if my arm had been torn off. And with the same knife, or rather, its heavy handle, I could easily knock out any idiot who couldn't sleep at night and happened to get under my feet. The master thief is not the one who slits the throat of the watchman roused by the alarm, but the one who enters silently, takes what he wants, and makes a quiet exit, leaving behind the smallest possible number of clues, including dead bodies.

Hanging behind my shoulder I had a miniature crossbow that fitted comfortably into one hand without hindering my movements. It fired short, thick bolts with heads that had four barbs, and with the necessary skill this little toy could hit a man's eye at seventy paces.

The small calfskin bag hanging on my belt contained several phials for use in extreme circumstances. For them a certain dwarf merchant of my acquaintance had stripped me of all my earnings from a robbery at a reception in the home of one of the city's notorious rakes. But the effectiveness of those magic baubles more than justified the price I had paid for them.

That was all. No more time for delay. I went dashing toward the duke's house, all the time keeping as close as possible to wall of the library. If anyone had taken it into his head to look down, he would have seen nothing but the gray stones and the wind-shredded mist playing tag with the shadows in the square. I ran fast, close to the right side of the house, with the gray crenellated wall flashing past my eyes in a blur. There it was, almost invisible to people passing by on the street: the small wicket gate for servants that led into His Lordship's inner sanctum.

As ill luck would have it, there was a street lamp burning opposite the gate and there was no cover—I might have been standing on Sagot's palm. The light fell directly on the wall, and there was not a trace of shadow. Fortunately, the narrow street was empty and the patrol was not due to pass by there for another two minutes or so. I had enough time.

Reaching inside my belt, I took out a set of lock picks made by dwarves to my own specifications. Only ignorant philistines think that being a master thief is easy and cheap. That's rubbish. If you want to steal anything worth stealing, the most important thing is your equipment (I maintain a modest silence on the subject of experience and talent—you can't steal much without them).

Completely absorbed in scrabbling with my pick, I felt for the spring of the lock. Aha! A quiet click. The first line of defense had been overcome.

But just at that moment there was the sound of hoofbeats at the end of the narrow street and I started working faster.

A click. The second secret solved. I spun my pick in desperation, feeling for that final spring. That's it! No more time left!

I jerked the pick out of the lock—all the springs were already free— and dashed across to the other side of the winding street. Into the refuge of the shadow.

Just in time.

A group of horsemen appeared from round the bend. Two, three, five, seven. Oho! Thirteen of them! A lucky number. They were riding tall horses of the Doralissian breed. Dark silhouettes against the gray background of the night. I squatted down, pulled the hood over my face, and screwed up my eyes, hoping that they hadn't glinted in the light from the stars.

Ten of the soldiers were wearing the gray and blue uniform of the royal guard. The eleventh turned out to be a woman with her face concealed by a dense veil. But even beneath that veil, I could see the sparkle of her eyes. Hmmm, I thought, isn't that something, sparkling eyes. The two men riding on either side of her had their faces hidden under the hoods of their cloaks.

I wonder what the king's guardsmen and a mysterious lady are doing out in the street at night? I think it's none of my business.

Only three minutes after the strange cavalcade, another detachment of horsemen came galloping by. They were dressed in ordinary uniforms, not gray and blue, but I spotted a purple stripe on the sleeve of the last man.

Oho! Wild Hearts! Just how do they happen to be so far away from the Lonely Giant?

I waited until the riders disappeared into the next street, loitered for a few more minutes, and went back to the wicket gate.

The courtyard was quiet, dark, and deserted. In the whole of the duke's grand nest, only two windows were lit up: one in the kitchen and one under the roof. The grass that was shrinking from the chill of the June night completely muffled my steps. It was too cold for the crickets, and the heavy hand of silence hung over the inner yard.

There was the door into the kitchen. The timid, trembling flame of a torch was blackening the wall beside the door. I turned the bronze handle, and I was inside.

The stoves and fireplaces in the kitchen were long since cold. The tables were stacked with dirty dishes and there was a young scullion sleeping on the floor. I stopped in a corner and began checking everything against the plan that I was carrying in the most reliable place of all—my head. That door over there will take me into a dining hall with a high marble staircase leading to the second floor. But I don't need to risk the hall, there's another way round. The oak door on the right leads into the servants' wing, and from there I can get to the second floor, avoiding the guard. Of course the hour is late and the guardsmen, if I know anything about their kind, have been asleep for a long time, but even so, there's no point in asking for trouble.

I set off, treading carefully (the dry floorboards creaked under my feet). In the dark corridor only every second torch was lit. From behind a door on the left I heard the snoring of someone in good health and clearly well satisfied with life. That was definitely a guard—no one else could be so recklessly carefree.

Chuckling to myself, I moved on.

Forward! And quietly! The most important thing is not to hurry.

I walked to the staircase leading from the servants' wing to the ducal apartments. Climbing the steps took no time at all, and there in front of me were the heavy double doors of oak. Locked, of course, but we can deal with that.

The corridor was as gloomy and deserted as the rest of the building. But I could see that from that point on the floor was cunningly paved with slabs of Isilian marble, which makes footsteps sound unnaturally loud and clear. A deaf man at the other side of the city could hear them. And I had to walk the full length of the corridor to the bedchamber at the far end.

Curses! If only I could fly!

But I can't. And so I shall have to use every ounce of the skill that Sagot has granted me in order not to make any noise.

Suddenly I heard a menacing growl behind me. I shuddered and froze, with my foot suspended above the black-and-white marble slabs. I turned my head gingerly, and there was a garrinch, devouring me with the insane glare of its white eyes.

A shudder ran right through me. That swindler Gozmo—when he gave me the Commission there wasn't a word about the duke having one of these brutes in the house.

Garrinches live far away in the south, in the Steppes of Ungava, almost on the borders of the hot Sultanate. The creatures are magnificent watchdogs, especially useful against lads like me. Getting hold of a live garrinch cub is incredibly difficult, almost impossible, because the price is simply sky-high. They say the king's treasure house is guarded by two of the beasts.

What a garrinch resembles most of all is a huge rat, the size of a well-fattened calf, covered with snake's scales instead of fur, with a magnificent set of teeth that can saw straight through a knight in armor, and two white gimlets for eyes. Killing one is extremely difficult—unless, of course, you happen to be a magician.

The creature snorted and stared alertly, probing the shadow where I had thought it best to hide. There was nothing I could do but pray to Sagot to protect his humble servant. I was drenched in cold sweat. After thinking for about a minute, it began growling again. It sensed a trick, but it couldn't understand where I could have gone, so it was trying to flush me out.

Eventually the beast abandoned its thoughts of an easy supper and set off at a slow, pigeon-toed waddle toward the open door leading into the servants' wing. I realized that one reason the door was usually locked was so that the brute that was let out to guard the second floor wouldn't eat anyone. But I had nonchalantly left the door wide open. What fun and games there would be in the morning when someone discovered a couple of servants were missing!

I caught my breath and took my finger off the trigger of the crossbow. The danger had passed. But I had to be on the alert; the creature could come back at any time.

There was a narrow strip of light showing under the door of the duke's bedchamber. Strange. Could there possibly be someone inside?

I set my ear to the keyhole.

"Nonsense! I am loyal to the Master!" a harsh, shrill voice exclaimed.

The duke? Why in the name of darkness was he at home and not out hunting?

"Loyal?" The second voice sent cold shivers down my spine—it was pure malice, without a single drop of life in it: a blend of baleful mockery and the chill of the grave. "Strange. If that is so, then why has the king still not abandoned his foolish plans for the Horn?"

"That's all because of his accursed guard and Alistan Markauz. The king is watched round the clock. The captain suspects something. I'm not able to speak to His Majesty in private."

"My Master is not accustomed to his orders not being carried out."

"And I am not accustomed to not getting what I was promised long ago!" The man's voice broke into a shout. "You're all despicable, lying scum! I want nothing more to do with you."

"Very well. Now you will receive your payment," the dead voice said after pausing for a moment, as if its owner were listening carefully to some new instruction.

"Wait, wait, I was jok— Aaaagh!"

There was a repulsive squelching sound on the other side of the door, then something fell and the shutters slammed against the wall as they were thrown open.

I swore under my breath and peeked warily into the duke's bedchamber.

The flame in the hearth was flickering feebly, too faint to illuminate the gigantic room and only picking a few spots out of the darkness, but I had an excellent view of Duke Patin sitting bolt upright in his armchair with his face contorted in terror and his throat ripped out. Blood was gushing from the ragged wound in jolly, rhythmical spurts.

I spotted the nocturnal visitor's winged silhouette against the open window. For one instant I looked into those yellow eyes that gazed at me in cold disdain, with the arrogance of death itself, and then my finger squeezed the trigger of its own accord. The bowstring gave a dry twang and the heavy crossbow bolt struck the creature in the back just as it turned and leapt from the window with its wings outspread. There was a dull thud, as if the dwarf-made steel had struck a wet tree trunk, not living flesh. The creature melted away into the night without a sound. I don't think it was bothered at all by the bolt in its back.

Time to run for it. There was nothing I could do to help the duke, and if they caught me beside the body, they would pin the murder on me. A serious crime against the crown like that means long, slow conversations in the torture chambers of the Gray Stones.

I dashed over to the shelves, grabbed what I needed—a gold statuette of a dog—and ran back out of the door.

The garrinch appeared again at the far end of the corridor. We spotted each other at the same moment.

The brute let out a roar of joy and came hurtling toward this new promise of supper, taking immense bounds. Still moving, I tossed the crossbow back over my shoulder, stuck my hand into my bag, and pulled out a phial of phosphorescent blue liquid. The most important thing in our business is to keep your nerve. When the garrinch was only two bounds away, I dashed the contents of the phial straight into its fearsome grin.

The brute's face was shrouded in a cloud of blue mist. It pulled up sharply, sneezed in astonishment, and then, completely forgetting about me, started rubbing its front paws hard over its face in furious desperation. I ran past it as quickly as I could, in my heart wishing the loathsome creature deliverance from the magical itching—in perhaps two or three hundred years.

Tomorrow the whole city will be in an uproar, and I need to be noticed as little as possible. Behind my back the newly deceased duke's abode is already no bigger than a doll's house. Once I get the money, I'll lie low for a couple of months. I've completed the Commission and now I can go back to my den, praying to Sagot that I won't meet anyone on my way. . . .

2

UNEXPECTED ENCOUNTERS

Evening twilight descends on bustling Avendoom, obliging the towns-folk to make haste, with humans and nonhumans alike hurrying to complete their business before the onset of night. In the cramped quarters and winding alleyways of the Port City the citizens strive to make the best use of every minute before the darkness sends them all scurrying back to their homes.

There goes a group of women running by, clutching baskets containing unsold food. There goes a pair of young noblemen, the arrogant bastards blind drunk, hurtling past on their fiery steeds, throwing up the mud and forcing passersby to squeeze back against the walls, leaving them waving their fists furiously at the riders' receding backs. There's a fat shopkeeper cuffing his boy apprentice round the ear to make him get on with closing the shop's shutters.

The Port City guard turns a blind eye to everything, even to a man with the outline of a crossbow clearly visible under his cloak. To be quite honest, it was illegal for ordinary citizens to carry such a weapon within the city limits, and if I had been noticed by the guard of the Inner City, it would have cost me more than just a simple smile. In fact, it would have taken at least two gold pieces to make the guardians of public order forget my face until the next time we met.

I keep saying "Port City" and "Inner City," but these names only mean something to someone who lives in Avendoom.

For reasons lost to history the capital city sprang up on the shoreline of the Cold Sea, in the north of the kingdom of Valiostr. From the height of a dragon's flight it has the form of a huge triangle, with its base thrust against the inclement, leaden-gray waters of the Cold Sea and its two other sides enclosed by a high, forbidding wall with mighty guard towers built into it at regular intervals.

There are eight city gates—four on each of the two landward sides of the triangle—and on the side facing the sea the city is protected against the enemy by a powerful fort armed with cannon made by the dwarves' ancient enemies, the gnomes. Gnomes are not very fond of the sea, but in this case their liking for gold proved stronger than their dislike of saltwater. And now the fort provides Avendoom with secure protection on the seaward side, and the Miranuehans in their leaky tubs no longer dare to attack the massive gray bastion and its cannon.

They say that not a single gate ever fell during the three assaults on the capital city that have taken place during the last three hundred years. But who can tell what will happen if the army of the Nameless One gathers its forces together and emerges from its centuries-long exile in the Desolate Lands to test our capital's valor with an onslaught of ogres and giants? And the lads from the Crayfish Dukedom won't just sit back and watch, they'll be sure to help our enemies. Well, only time will tell for sure. Extending around the outer wall are the Suburbs. Immediately inside the gates, in the so-called Outer City, stand houses belonging to moderately prosperous citizens. Beyond them lies the Inner City, which is surrounded by an additional wall. (On one or two occasions I have been obliged to climb over it, when an especially zealous patrol decided to test how fast old Harold could run.)

The Inner City consists entirely of houses belonging to aristocrats, big wheels, and magicians. There are good pickings here, but the chances of coming unstuck are pretty good, too. This is where the king's palace is located.

The Artisans' City and the Magicians' Quarter slice into the Inner City from the seaward side. Shops, smithies, tanneries, bakeries, little magic stalls, libraries, shrines to the gods, and so forth. The Port City runs along the very edge of the sea. Ships from all over the world visit the port. And in this district of the capital there are also streets which it is best not to enter without chain mail and reliable guards. Especially at night.

All these things I'm telling you are only a small part of the overall picture, a mere drop of wine in an ocean of mud, because our capital contains a hundred other districts and areas. Some are inhabited entirely by wizards, others by the dwarves who did not fall out completely with men after we concluded a pact with the gnomes. And there is also the Secret Territory (or Forbidden Territory, or Stain, as it is also known), a district surrounded by a high wall impregnated with defensive magic. No one knows what goes on there.

The Secret Territory, which is adjacent to the Port City, came into being about three hundred years ago as the result of a curse. The magicians of the kingdom were unable to cope with it and decided to seal off the cursed section of the city from the others with a wall. There have always been rumors about the terrible creatures inhabiting the Forbidden Territory, but no reckless daredevils who are prepared to check these stories have ever been found.

All right, that's enough! If I start going through all the places of interest in our beloved city, I'll still be listing them off when night falls.

I stopped outside an old, entirely unremarkable building like many others in the Port City. The only thing that distinguished it from its peers was a signboard: THE KNIFE AND AX. There were a huge knife and an immense ax made of tin hanging there, too. I suspect that even a thick-witted Doralissian would understand just what kind of men gather in this establishment. I pushed open the wooden door and plunged into the loud hubbub of the crowd.

Unlike other establishments, this inn, the refuge of rogues and thieves, would be working all night. Old Gozmo, the owner of this fleapit, knew how to rake in the cash all right.

I nodded to the two bouncers standing at the entrance with their cudgels at the ready, and set off toward the bar.

Several individuals cast malicious glances after me and I heard whispering behind my back. This world is far from perfect; it contains plenty of envious people who have reason to resent my dexterity. Let them grumble. They won't dare go any further than muttering behind my back.

I finally made my way through all the tables and nodded to Gozmo, who was standing behind his own bar today. The stooped old rascal, who was once fond of strolling into the homes of the rich residents of Avendoom during the night hours, had settled down now and opened this establishment, where individuals who were not entirely respectable and whose hands were not exactly clean could feel relatively at ease. This was where the lads in my profession relaxed as they looked for their next job, for buyers and clients. "Aaah ... Harold," he greeted me warmly. Gozmo was always glad to see his clients—it came with his new profession. "Haven't seen you in quite a while. Seems like years since you last visited your old friend."

"I've been busy, you know the way it is," I said, shoving the bundle with the statuette across the bar into the round-shouldered innkeeper's hand.

Gozmo provided good information, and he was the one who had passed on the Commission for a trip to the town house of the recently deceased Duke Patin. The innkeeper deftly caught the bundle and, with a movement as inconspicuous as my own, dispatched into my hand a purse containing the promised twenty pieces of gold. The goods were immediately seized by one of the inn's serving men, who shoved them into a dirty canvas bag and bore them off to the client.

I counted out five coins from what I had received.

"Now, that's why I'm so very fond of you, my boy, you always settle your debts," the old rogue said merrily, and I frowned.

Of course, I steal other people's property, but I have to pay the informant out of my own pocket, with the gold I receive for the sale of those items. I'm not exactly a skinflint, but even so, being left with fifteen gold pieces instead of twenty is rather annoying. However, I still owed the old swindler for my last job, so he had a perfect right to take the amount owed to him.

"Have you heard that milord Patin up and died all of a sudden two days ago?" Gozmo asked apropos of nothing as he wiped the beer mugs. He seemed not to notice my sullen expression.

"Really?" I said, expressing my seemingly genuine amazement at the unexpected departure from this life of the duke, who had the strength of all the plow horses in Valiostr and Zagorie combined.

"Yes, yes. They found him with his throat torn out. And the garrinch that guarded his treasure was scratching itself and taking no notice of anybody."

"Really?" I asked again, completely astonished. "Who would ever have thought there was a garrinch in there? Nobody ever mentioned that to me."

The innkeeper turned a deaf ear to my rebuke. He knew how to pretend to be absolutely stone deaf, and I must say that sometimes he managed it superbly.

"The usual for you, is it?"

"Yes. Is my table free?"

Gozmo nodded, and I set off past some drunken crooks who were bawling and yelling about something or other, past the seminaked girl singing on the stage, toward the far corner of the large room. I sat down with my back to the wall, facing the entrance to the establishment. Well, I can't help it, it's a habit developed over the years.

Immediately, as if by magic, a mug of porter and a plate of meat appeared in front of me. I should tell you that Gozmo's chef was sometimes visited by genuine inspiration, and at those moments he cooked every bit as well as the lads in the aristocrats' kitchens. The food and drink were brought by a delightful little serving wench, who winked merrily at me but, catching sight of my perpetual scowl, she snorted and retreated to the kitchen, wiggling her backside angrily and drawing admiring glances from the crooks sitting at the neighboring tables.

I, however, had no time for her undeniable charms right now. The whole city was seething. It was time for me to lie low.

A peasant could live well on fifteen gold pieces for almost a whole year, but it wasn't a very large sum for me, and I really had to give up working for the next few months. If I was unlucky, someone might just link the duke's death to the disappearance of the statuette, and the hunt would be on for all thieves everywhere in Avendoom. And then they might haul me in with all the rest. If they could catch me, of course. I had my doubts about the abilities of Frago Lanten's subordinates. In fact, I didn't think too highly of the guards in general.

Before I could even take a sip from my mug of thick black beer, a skinny, pale individual suddenly appeared and sat down on the chair facing me without so much as a by-your-leave. I'd never even seen the lad before.

I took an instant dislike to the fellow. His pallor and thinness prompted the thought that he might be a vampire, but of course I was mistaken there. Vampires don't exist. My uninvited guest was a man. And judging from all appearances, a very dangerous one. Not a single superfluous or unnecessary movement and a chilling gaze of cold appraisal. It wasn't my first time out in the street, I'd seen plenty of his type before.

I very nearly reached for my crossbow, but stopped myself. Who could tell? Perhaps he simply wanted to chat about the weather.

"I don't think I asked anyone to join me, did I?" I asked as indifferently as possible.

But my brief moment of tension had not escaped my uninvited guest and he gave a crooked grin.

"Are you Harold?"

"Anything's possible." I shrugged and took a gulp of beer.

"I've been told to let you know that Markun is not happy."

"Since when do hired assassins pass on messages from the head of the Guild of Thieves?" I asked sharply, setting my mug down on the table.

"That, Harold, is none of your business," said Paleface, not in the least put out that I had guessed what he was. "Markun is asking you one last time to join the guild and pay your dues."

Ah, the guilds, the guilds! The king turns a blind eye to the Guild of Thieves and the Guild of Assassins. For the time being, at least. The official authorities don't touch these dubious organizations as long as they don't overreach themselves and they pay their taxes. And it must be admitted that the sums of money paid into the treasury are huge. Almost half of the earnings of the night brethren. And that's why I'm not in the guild. Why should I make a present to anyone of the gold pieces earned by my almost honest labor?

"I am sorry to disappoint him," I said, and laughed as loathsomely as I could manage.

Shadow Harold, legendary master thief of Avendoom, who has never once been taken by the guards, does not wish to join the guild.

"I'm a free hunter. And I don't intend to knuckle under to a fat-bellied pickpocket."

"Very well." Paleface was not at all perturbed by my refusal and carried on staring indifferently into my eyes. "Is that your final word?"

I nodded, indicating that the conversation was at an end. A deafening silence suddenly descended on the Knife and Ax. The girl stopped singing, the drunken laughter and lively conversations came to a sudden halt. A genuine graveyard, with Gozmo as the cadaver-in-chief. I looked in the direction of the door, and my eyes must have turned square in amazement if even a professional like Paleface did what no experienced assassin should ever do: Forgetting about me, he turned round to see what had happened back there.

A detachment of the municipal guard was standing at the entrance to the inn, clutching their halberds and crossbows in their hands. And no one had even the slightest doubt that the lads were ready to put them to good use at the first glint of a knife anywhere. It was clear that these were no Port City wasters, but soldiers of the Inner City. They were too well fed and well groomed. Definitely not to be provoked. And even the bouncers, whose mothers might have been accused of intimate relations with trolls, moved aside to allow the uninvited guests into the inner sanctum of the world of thieves.

Something very important was about to happen if the guardsmen, whom Gozmo paid off regularly so that they wouldn't even notice his little establishment and the public that frequented it, had actually come here.

Standing at the head of the orange and black horde was none other than the commander of the municipal guard himself, Baron Frago Lanten. The baron probed the silent room with a short-sighted gaze that eventually picked me out, then he nodded to himself and set off straight toward me.

"Wine," he growled as he walked past the pale-faced Gozmo, who had finally left the perfectly clean beer mugs in peace.

"Straight away, Your Grace. The very best of everything," the innkeeper replied obsequiously, recovering slightly from the shock. After all, a man like Lanten doesn't often visit the modest rats' holes where thieves gather. The serving wenches immediately started scurrying about, and the general hubbub in the room started up again, but you could feel the apprehensive tension hovering in the air. The girl on the stage started singing again in a trembling voice, squinting sideways at the baron. Dozens of pairs of eyes followed the short man as he walked to my table. At any moment, if he felt like it he could stick anyone who chose not to live according to the law in the Gray Stones—the grimmest and harshest prison in the northern kingdoms.

A few men couldn't stand it any longer and started moving toward the door. The guard didn't try to stop them.

"Don't start celebrating yet," hissed Paleface. "I'll get another chance to have a long conversation with you, Harold."

Then he disappeared, simply evaporating into the gloom as if he had never been there at all.

I breathed out quietly and rubbed my sweaty palms together.

"Harold?" the baron asked, stopping in front of me.

I gazed intently at the short, muscular man in the uniform of the Avendoom guard. His doublet was a lot richer than an ordinary soldier's. To my mind there was rather too much velvet in it. But that slim, elegant blade from Filand was very much to my liking. For that you could easily buy three establishments every bit as good as the Knife and Ax.

There was no point in denying anything, and I pointed to the chair on which Paleface had just been sitting.

"Have a seat, Your Grace."

Gozmo came hurrying over, delivering a bottle of the finest wine, glasses, and hors d'oeuvres in person. Milord waited in silence until it was all on the table and said quietly, "And now clear off. Get under my feet and I'll see you rot in jail."

Gozmo left, with repeated bows and assurances concerning his own honesty, almost stumbling into a table as he went.

Without speaking, Frago poured a glass of the red wine made far away in the south, where the Crest of the World meets the steppes of Ungava, and drained it in a single gulp. Then he gave a grunt of satisfaction and set about studying my face. Though we were, so to speak, at daggers drawn and had reason to resent each other, I respected this man. May Sagot strike me dead if I lied.

The baron was honest. He never used underhand stealth, he never humiliated his subordinates, although he kept a tight grip on them. The baron was devoted to the king and he had earned his position for his genuine efforts, not because of money or family ties.

Avendoom had benefited greatly from this man's appointment as head of the guard, even though it meant hard times for us thieves. The number of crimes was not reduced, of course, but now the cutthroats looked around carefully before setting out on their dark business, to make sure that His Grace was nowhere near at hand. A small, but nonetheless real victory in the eternal battle between the law and crime.

"I can't say that I'm pleased to meet you," the baron growled, glaring at me from under his thick, bushy eyebrows. "I'd be delighted to ship you off to the Gray Stones."

I said nothing. I did have a certain appropriate phrase right there on the tip of my tongue, but I decided to hold it in reserve for later. That evening, at least, I didn't really want to go to prison.

"Let's go, Harold."

"Where to, Your Grace?" I asked. The man had shocked me. "Not to those beloved Gray Stones of yours?"

"No. Not yet anyway." He glanced at me. "A certain . . . individual wants to have a word with you. I have to deliver you to him."

Although I tried not to, I couldn't help casting a glance at the bored guardsmen loitering by the door. I couldn't handle them. Too many. And there were probably just as many at the back door.

"All the exits are closed off." The baron seemed to have heard what I was thinking.

I pushed my chair back without speaking and stood up, wrapping myself in my cloak.

"Well, that's good," the commander of the guard said quietly and, picking up the unpaid-for bottle of expensive wine in his left hand, he set off toward the door. I followed him, feeling the curious glances of every eye in the inn boring into my back.

3

THE COMMISSION

Standing outside the inn, engulfed by the twilight as thick as cream, was a large carriage, harnessed to a foursome of ash-gray horses of the Doralissian breed. The horses were squinting sideways at the guardsmen and snorting nervously. Humans weren't the only ones who wanted to spend the night behind the protection of secure walls.

I suddenly noticed that the windows of the carriage were blocked off with thick planks of wood.

An expensive carriage. Not the kind everyone can afford. And a four-in-hand of Doralissian horses cost an incredible amount of money.

We set off along the dark streets, and the only time I bounced was when the wheel ran over a cobblestone jutting out especially high from the surface of the road. The baron didn't say anything, merely casting occasional gloomy glances in my direction, and I was left with nothing to do but listen to the clip-clopping of hooves from the mounted guardsmen escorting us and try to guess where they were taking me.

Who is it that wants to meet me? It's obvious straightaway that whoever the lad might be, he must have plenty of influence—since he sent Frago Lanten himself to fetch me. I wonder what this unidentified individual wants from me? Payment for some inconvenience that I've caused him? I just hope he isn't one of the magicians. I don't want to spend the rest of my days in the skin of a toad or a Doralissian.

I chuckled quietly to myself, attracting the baron's surly glance. It was hard to say which was worse, the body of a toad or the body of a goat-man. I would probably have chosen the former, because in Avendoom they were less fond of Doralissians than they were of toads. Suddenly the driver stopped the carriage and a pair of zealous guards swung the door open. The cool breath of night struck me in the face. Even in summer it is rather cool in Avendoom—since it is quite close to the Desolate Lands, the blessed heat only visits the city in August, and even then only for a couple of weeks, until the wind from the Cold Sea brings the rains. Valiostr is the most northerly kingdom of Siala, so the weather here leaves a lot to be desired.

"What's this, then? A brief recreational stroll?" I asked the baron, trying to maintain my presence of mind.

"Stop wrangling with me, Harold. Just do as you're told and all will be love and affection between us."

I shrugged and jumped down onto the stone road and surveyed the surroundings. The little street was empty and the dark houses on one side hung over us like the Zam-da-Mort. There was a high wall running along the other side of the street. Right then. That meant we were somewhere on the edge of the Inner City.

Thin, tentative tongues of grayish yellow mist were already creeping out of the municipal drainage system. It was still timid, pressing low against the surface of the street, not yet daring to rise higher. But in a few hours' time a thick blanket of the mist would cover the city, just as it did every night in June, and hang there until the morning.

On this occasion the darkness in the street was impenetrable, clouds covered the sky with their heavy carcasses, and the only light radiated from the guards' torches and the oil lamps hanging on the carriage. The guards were peering hard into the darkness, holding their crossbows at the ready.

"Is he clean? No weapons?" Frago asked.

The guards hastily patted me down once again, took the lock picks out of the secret pocket on my belt, then extracted a slim razor from the top of my boot and nodded.

"Clean, Your Grace. Clean as a Doralissian on his way home after a business meeting with a dwarf. Yargi knows the thieves' tricks."

The guards on the horses burst into laughter. "Enough of that!" Lanten barked irritably. "Blindfold him and let's get going."

The guard who called himself Yargi took a strip of heavy, dark cloth out of his pocket and blindfolded me with it. Hands took hold of me by the arms, shoved me into the carriage, slammed the door shut, and the carriage set off again. I raised my hands to ease the pressure of the cloth against my eyes.

"I wouldn't do that if I were you, Harold," the baron said straight into my ear, speaking very politely.

"Where are you taking me, Your Grace? Or is it a secret?"

"A state secret, you could say. But for now keep quiet and be patient. Don't make me angry."

"I beg your pardon, Your Grace, but what will happen if I make you angry?"

The darkness had made me talkative and sharpened my tongue.

"If you don't come to an agreement with the man we're going to see, then you'll find yourself in my hands. . . . And I'll be angry."

I decided it was better to be patient and say nothing for a while. It would be no problem for me to jump out of the carriage that was dashing through the streets and try to escape. I would have a few precious moments before the guards realized what had happened. But I didn't really want to risk playing tag with crossbow bolts.

Meanwhile the carriage was bowling through the city at an excellent speed. The driver was evidently very skillful and he did not wish to spare the carriage, the horses, or the passengers. Now my entire backside took a battering on the potholes. But the baron wasn't complaining. That must mean there was a good reason for all the hurry, and I gritted my teeth and tried to sit up straight when we heeled over on the bends. Actually, just once I did allow myself the pleasure of giving way, allowing inertia to throw me against Frago, and lifting the purse off his belt. I must say there wasn't much in it, though.

Eventually we arrived. I was taken out and handed over to some men who took a tight grip on my elbows. Then they led me off somewhere. There was nothing I could do but move my feet, stumbling every time there were steps up or down.

All the time the baron was snorting behind me. Corridors, stairways, rooms, halls. Sounds. My feet walked across a bare stone floor, raising a hollow, resonant echo from the slabs of Isilian marble; they stamped across squeaking wooden floorboards. I had long ago lost count of the number of steps and stairways and bends in the countless corridors of the huge building through which I was being led. Torches hissed and sputtered close to my ear; sometimes we met someone as we walked along, but I could hear them hastily move aside, making way for us.

Finally a door opened and I felt the dense pile of a carpet under my feet. Without seeing it, I couldn't say how much it was worth, but it had probably been made in the Sultanate, and that certainly meant a fair amount of money.

"Remove his blindfold."

Frago, who was standing behind me, removed the damned rag from my eyes. For a brief moment I squeezed them shut against the bright light coming from a fireplace and dozens of candles and torches burning in the small room.

Then I studied the room critically, evaluating at a glance the Sultanate carpets, the candlesticks, the costly furniture made of timber found in the Forests of I'alyala, right beside the Crest of the World, the complete set of knight's armor made by dwarf master craftsmen, which was standing in the farthest corner of the room. Not to mention the goblets and the tableware, which I think were all made of gold. Mmm. I could really cut loose if only I could have this place to myself for just a few minutes.

Only instead of one person, I saw several.

The little old man sitting in an armchair beside the hearth, muffled in a thick woolen blanket, was clutching a silvery staff encrusted with ivory in his right hand. A magician, as far as I could judge. An archmagician, in fact, bearing in mind that his staff bore four silver rings of rank. Or even more precisely, a master, since he had a small black bird sitting on the top of his staff instead of the usual stone.

The old man appeared small and puny. He looked like an old, fragile hazelnut, and he was shuddering in annoyance, as if the heat from the fireplace right beside him could not warm his ancient bones. It seemed that if you just prodded the magician with your finger, or a strong wind blew on him, he would simply fall to pieces.

A deceptive impression. A none-too-pleasant end lay in store for anyone who prodded Artsivus, archmagician and master, the head of the Order of Magicians. This man was one of the most influential figures in the kingdom and the king's first adviser, although many, seeing the puny old man for the first time, might have doubts about the soundness of his reason.

The person sitting in the armchair opposite Artsivus and elegantly cradling a goblet of white wine was a woman, wearing the very expensive, magnificent, lightblue dress of a female inhabitant of Mirangrad. A rather risky choice of garment in our kingdom, especially since the war with Miranueh had not actually ended, but was only lying dormant for the time being while the two sides recovered from the bloody battles that had broken off five years earlier. Miranuehans are liked no better than the Nameless One in Avendoom, but I could see that the lady was not concerned about that.

The female stranger's face was covered by a veil that completely concealed it from my curious gaze. And those golden eyes, though covered by the veil, still sparkled. Amazing. I had encountered this unknown noblewoman two days earlier, on that memorable night when I had a little job to do in Duke Patin's town house. Judging from her jewelry, she must be the same woman who had ridden along the narrow street, surrounded by the king's personal guards.

Standing by the wall was a man armed with a sword of Canian forgework. This gentleman examined my humble person with disdainful curiosity, as if what he was looking at were, in the very best case, a rat. Although it was he who was the Rat. That was what his foes called him. Count Alistan Markauz, captain of the king's personal guards, who had chosen a gray rat as his crest. He could always be recognized from his heavy knightly armor with the rodent's head engraved on the breastplates and the helmet, which itself was in the form of a rat's head. Vicious tongues had it that the Rat even slept and washed in his armor, but I believe this assertion was not entirely correct.

Alistan was the finest swordsman of the kingdom, the rock on which our most dear king relied. He was the head of the security service and a man of honor, defined in terms that only he understood, who hated and exterminated all who plotted evil against his glorious lord. His whole life was military routine, skirmishes with ogres and giants beside the Lonely Giant fortress, war with the orcs of Zagraba, and a couple of border wars with Miranueh when their king felt like moving on to bigger things after a few skirmishes with the western clans of the Zagraban orcs.

Having survived all these battles, Alistan Markauz had become the man he was at that moment—the king's right arm and a bulwark of the throne. The soldier looked at me with his steely gray eyes, chewing on his luxuriant, dangling mustache, styled in the manner of the inhabitants of Lowland. I responded to his narrow-eyed gaze with a sour look and transferred my attention to the fourth person in the room.

Well, of course, when I say "person," that's something of an exaggeration. There, staring at me with arctic blue eyes, was a green-skinned goblin. The genuine article. One of those who live somewhere in the Forests of Zagraba, side by side with orcs and elves.

The goblins are an unfortunate and downtrodden race. They are no taller than the smallest of gnomes. That is, they come up to about my navel, no higher than that. From the dawn of time men, confusing things in the way they always do, believed that goblins were the orcs' allies, and for century after century attempted to exterminate this universally persecuted tribe of Siala.

The systematic extermination of the race of goblins was so successful that this once multitudinous, peaceful race, which had suffered from the scimitars of the orcs as well as the swords and pikes of men, was almost completely wiped out. And when men finally realized the truth (that is, when they swallowed their pride and asked the elves), there were only a few small tribes left, hiding in the remotest thickets of Zagraba with the help of their shamans' magic.

And so, we had even begun taking them into service. They proved to be very intelligent and resourceful, their little claret-colored tongues could be very sharp, and they were adroit and nimble, therefore perfectly suited for service as messengers and spies.

And in addition, the Order of Magicians was very interested in goblin shamanism, which derived from the rites of the orcs and the dark elves.

Shamanism, for anyone who doesn't know, is the most ancient form of wizardry in this world. It appeared in Siala together with the ogres, the most ancient race. And therefore the magicians of men are tremendously curious about the primordial source, which was borrowed from the ogres by the orcs, then the elves, and then the goblins.

By the way, the little green-skinned lad on the carpet in front of me happened to be a jester. That was clear from his cap with little bells, his jester's leotard in red and blue squares, and the jester's mace that he was clutching in his green hand. The goblin was sitting there with his funny little legs crossed, occasionally turning his head, so that his little bells tinkled in a gay melody.

Noticing me studying him in astonishment, he laughed, with a bright flash of teeth as sharp as needles. He sniffed through his long, hooked nose, winked his blue eye, and showed me his claret-colored tongue. Magnificent! That was all I needed to really make my day!

I transferred my gaze to the final stranger in the room, sitting in the armchair in front of which the goblin had positioned himself. To look at, this man was very much like a prosperous innkeeper. Fat and short, with a bald head and neat, tidy hands. And his clothes were more than modest: the spacious brown trousers worn by ordinary guardsmen, and simple thick sweater of sheep's wool, very suitable for the frosts of January—the kind knitted by the peasants who live beside the Lonely Giant fortress. I wondered if he felt hot in it.

All in all, the man in front of me was entirely gray and undistin-guished. Especially if you failed to notice the thick gold ring with an enormous ruby on his right hand, and his eyes. Those brown eyes were full of intelligence, steel, and power. The power of a king.

I bowed low and froze.

"Just so," Stalkon the Ninth said in a deep, resonant voice.

It was the voice I had heard when they led me into the room.

"So this is the thief famous throughout the whole of Avendoom? Shadow Harold?"

"Yes indeed, Your Majesty," Baron Lanten, who was standing beside me, replied obsequiously.

"Well now." The king patted the seated jester on the head and the jester purred in pleasure, imitating a cat. "You found him quickly, Frago. Far more quickly than I was expecting. I thank you."

The baron lowered his head modestly and pressed his hand to his heart, although any fool could see that he was absolutely delighted to be praised.

"Wait outside the door, baron, if you would be so kind," Archmagi-cian Artsivus said from his chair with a cough.

The commander of the guard bowed once more and went out, clos-ing the door firmly behind him.

"I have heard a lot about you, Harold," the king said, looking intently into my eyes.

"I did not think my reputation was so great, Your Majesty." I felt awkward in the company of the leading figures of the state.

"Ah, but he's bold," the jester declared squeakily, pulling yet another face at me and turning his eyes in toward his nose.

"And modest," the mysterious woman said with a laugh, running the finger of a gloved hand along the edge of her crystal goblet. You always hear about women whose laughter sounds like music in all those silly love songs. I always thought it was just the bards singing through their hats. I never imagined it was true. And fancy hearing it in this company. She would bear watching, this one. Oh, not because Harold is so taken with a pretty lady. I like ladies enough—in their place. No, no, this lady was commanding, dangerous . . . different. You could tell just by her demeanor that she was the equal of anyone in the room—even the king. And they all knew it, too. Let us not say that cranky old Harold was suspicious . . . no, not suspicious, exactly . . . but she would bear watching, this one.

I felt like a cow at market, being discussed by two peasant buyers.

"Have a seat, Harold," said the king, gesturing graciously in my direction, and I sat down in an armchair with a tall, carved back depicting some episode from the battle that took place on the Field of Sorna.

"With your permission?" the king asked casually, picking my crossbow up off the little table standing beside his armchair.

The knife, lock picks, and razor were lying there, too.

"Made by dwarves?"

Without even giving me time to nod, His Majesty aimed the weapon at the ancient suit of armor standing in the farthest corner of the room and pressed the trigger. The string twanged and the bolt whined as it flew straight in through the eye slit of the knight's helmet.

The jester clapped his hands in a caricature of applause. Stalkon knew how to fire a weapon. In general there were many things he was good at. Especially maintaining a firm grip on the kingdom. The simple people adored him, although he had ruthlessly repressed the rebellions that had flared up several times during the spring famine. And everybody also knew that, in addition to the crown, His Majesty had inherited knowledge from his father, grandfather, and great-grandfather. The great intellect of the dynasty of Stalkon was legendary throughout the land.

He hadn't raised taxes excessively, but neither had he reduced them to paltry levels. He had loosened the traders' and merchants' leashes, but arranged things so that if they wanted to trade in Valiostr, then they paid taxes. He also took money from the guilds of thieves and assassins. He did not oppress the other races that were friendly to men, and they repaid him, if not with friendship, then at least with tolerance toward humans, and they obeyed the laws of the kingdom.

The king's only mistake, or so his enemies whispered, was the idea of an alliance with the gnomes: When it was concluded the dwarves fell out with Valiostr and locked themselves away in their mountains. Of course, a small community of dwarves had remained in Avendoom, basically the most greedy of them, dreaming of raking in a little more gold from the sale of expensive craftwork, although even they disapproved of the fact that men had come to terms with the gnomes, the enemies of all dwarves. In this matter, however, I was on the king's side. If the choice was between the swords that dwarves made for the richest inhabitants of the kingdom and the cannon that the gnomes made, naturally you had to choose what was more effective in battle and cheaper—the cannon.

"An interesting toy. But we're not here now to talk about your crossbow," the king said, setting the discharged weapon back down on the small table. "Could you tell me, thief, how you came by this item?"

The delighted jester took out a gold statuette of a dog from behind the armchair and showed it to me. My back was instantly bathed in cold, sticky sweat. Although I managed to hold my face in a mask of polite respect, a note of panic appeared in my voice. There in the goblin's hands was the trinket from the duke's house. So that was where Gozmo's man had taken it. Good old Gozmo! If we happen to meet again, there's a very unpleasant conversation in store for him.

So now all the clues pointed to me. Now I was implicated in a crime against the crown. The quartering they would administer would be regarded as the grace of the gods and the mercy of the king's court. If only they didn't do anything worse to me! I decided I had better say nothing and listen.

"Clever and cautious. Rare qualities," said the woman, surveying me from behind her dense veil.

The jester giggled quietly at some joke only he understood, and scuttled round the room. Then, still clutching the statuette in his hand, he stood beside Alistan, copied his pose and serious expression, and froze, setting his hand on the head of the golden dog and transforming it into an improvised sword. I almost burst out laughing. It really was just like the Rat and very funny. The goblin certainly earned his pay.

"It was on our instructions, Harold, that you found yourself in the home of my most dear departed cousin. Before deciding if you were suited to a certain job, we had to test you. And a setting more ideal than my cousin's town house, with a garrinch roaming around freely at night, is hard to imagine. Don't you agree?"

"The royal treasure house would be even more ideal," I blurted out.

Shadow Harold had nothing more to lose. It was obvious anyway that in the morning I would be taking the journey to the Gray Stones. I reminded myself once again to have a word with Gozmo when I got the chance—to thank him for palming off this "Commission" on me.

"Oho! Shadow Harold has a sweet tooth!" the goblin squeaked.

I cast a caustic glance at him, but he only laughed mockingly and stuck his tongue out again.

"I know that, Kli-Kli," Stalkon replied to the jester, then he picked up my knife, drew it out of its scabbard and, as he studied it, asked casually, "What happened in the house that night? How did he die?"

I swallowed the spittle that had thickened in my mouth and launched into my story under the gaze of five watchful pairs of eyes. No one interrupted me, Archmagician Artsivus seemed to be dozing in his chair and, remarkably enough, the goblin's face was thoughtful and troubled. When I finished my story, an oppressive silence filled the room, with only the fire crackling quietly in the hearth.

"I told you, Your Majesty, not to trust the duke," Alistan blurted out angrily. For some reason he had believed my story straightaway, and now his eyes were glittering with fury. "I'll double the guard."

The king stroked his chin thoughtfully, studying me intently for a while without saying anything. Then he nodded his head abruptly, clearly having made up his mind.

"We'll talk about my safety later, good friend Alistan. But first I have a proposition for our guest. Harold, do you know who the Nameless One is?" Stalkon asked, taking me by surprise.

"He is evil and darkness." The question had perplexed me.

The Nameless One, the Nameless One. The one they used to frighten you with in your distant childhood, when you wouldn't go to bed on time.

Alistan snorted, as if he had expected no more from a thief.

"That depends on how you understand the word," the monarch said. "Evil. Hmm . . . But are you aware that, outside of Valiostr, the Nameless One is known only in the Border Kingdom, and then only because the orcs attack those lands with his name on their lips? Well, and perhaps also in Isilia, and somewhat in Miranueh, but there the Nameless One is no more than a terrible fairy tale. He is actually not entirely black evil, and far from being darkness, merely a very powerful wizard who settled in the Desolate Lands and has been dreaming for a long, long time of seeing Valiostr reduced to ruins."

"By your leave . . . ," said the archmagician, breaking his silence and butting into the conversation for the first time. "Young man, let me tell you a legend that is really not a legend at all, but the plain truth. . . . Five hundred years or so ago, when our kingdom was not yet so great and powerful, two brothers lived in Avendoom. One of them was a magnificent general, the other a talented magician who studied the various aspects of shamanism. At that time magic was still a mysterious art to men—it was constantly being improved, we were still learning, borrowing from the experience of the dark elves, orcs, and goblins. Later we added a little something of our own to produce what we have now. Unfortunately the stone magic of the gnomes and dwarves is beyond us. Hmm . . . But I digress. . . . It happened in the final year of the Quiet Times, as that period is now known. The general Grok . . . I hope you know that name?"

I nodded. Everyone knew Grok Square and the general's statue. The old man grunted approval, fidgeting in an effort to make himself more comfortable in his chair, and then went on with his story:

"In the final year of the Quiet Times an army of orcs attacked our city and attempted to take it by storm. The famous Avendoom walls did not yet exist then and Grok, in command of only a few thousand weary soldiers who were still alive after a number of battles, was holding back the onslaught of the enemy who had emerged from the Forests of Zagraba. Mmm . . . His brother did not come to support him. I do not know why, unfortunately history is silent on that question. A quarrel, envy, illness, some stupid accident—whatever it was, the most powerful magician of the time failed to come to the aid of the embattled warriors.

But even so, Grok and his men held out. They stood their ground until the arrival of the dark elves. By which time the army of Valiostr had been reduced first to a thousand men, and then to something less than four hundred. After the victory the magician was seized and executed for treason."

The old man stopped speaking and stared at the fire with his weepy eyes.

"What was that magician called?" I asked, intrigued.

"He bore the same name as his twin brother—Grok. It was a disgrace for the Order of Magicians. A terrible disgrace. We struck out the name of the reprobate from all the annals. After that he became known as the Nameless One. But he managed to survive. Or rather, his spirit survived. During his lifetime the wizard had studied Kronk-a-Mor, the forbidden sorcery of the ogres. The use of this form of shamanism can enable the spirit of a man who has died to live for a certain time without any physical body, and then inhabit a new one. And that is what happened. He went far away to the north, deep into the Desolate Lands, nurturing plans of vengeance. The power of the Kronk-a-Mor was so great that ogres, giants, and some orcs recognized the Nameless One as their lord and master. Although, to be honest, I have serious doubts concerning the orcs. As a race they are too cunning and independent; most likely it is simply convenient to make themselves out to be cruel barbarians and appeal to the Nameless One when they attack their enemies. High politics, the elfin houses call it! But as for the ogres, giants, and some individual humans, they are devoted, body and soul, to the Nameless One. These enemies of Valiostr would long ago have left their own lands to wage war against us, if they were not held back by the Lonely Giant fortress. And even though the Nameless One has acquired eternal life, so far he has not dared to invade Valiostr, because we were canceling out his power. That is, until the equilibrium was disrupted."

"Well, all right . . . ," I began—there was something that didn't quite add up in my mind. "Ogres, orcs, giants. What about those vile brutes that hunt in the streets of the capital at night? Do they also obey the Nameless One? And what about the mysterious Master that the duke mentioned?"

"I do not know," said the magician, frowning. "Perhaps they are servants of the Nameless One, perhaps of someone else, and they escaped from the depths when the equilibrium of the magical source was disrupted."

"By the way," the king interrupted, "how much longer will my subjects have to put up with these repulsive beasts?"

"The council is doing absolutely everything possible, Your Majesty. We have prepared a spell, and by the end of the week not a single creature of the night will be able to enter our city. At least, that is my hope."

"Why doesn't the Order of Magicians destroy the Nameless One?" I asked, bringing the conversation back to its original subject.

"The Kronk-a-Mor gives the reprobate secure protection. Unfortunately, we understand nothing about the shamanism of the ogres. And we are unlikely ever to learn now. The Nameless One has waited for centuries, building up his power and gathering his army. Only the Rainbow Horn, a mighty artifact of the past, which was given to Grok by the elves who took it from the ogres in ancient times, has held the Nameless One and his army behind the Mountains of Despair. The elves say that the ogres themselves created this artifact to counter their own magic, to neutralize it if the Kronk-a-Mor should suddenly escape their control. The Rainbow Horn is the one single reason why the Nameless One has never dared to make war against us. In some way the Horn completely neutralizes his magic—" Artsivus began coughing.

"It is only while the Horn retains its power that the Nameless One dare not venture to pass the Lonely Giant. What can he do without his magic? This wizard should not be regarded as darkness," the king continued. "He is simply a very talented magician who has made good use of his knowledge and now wants to take his revenge for being executed. Regard him as merely a little unbalanced by his hatred. And now that the power of the Horn has weakened over the centuries, the Nameless One is raising his head. I am certain that the enemy will soon strike a blow against our kingdom."

"He is on the very point of striking," Alistan said quietly. "Elfin scouts report that the Nameless One is preparing his army for a campaign. Thousands of giants, ogres, and other creatures are gathering from all across the Desolate Lands. In the Crayfish Dukedom they are forging weapons night and day. By next spring, or perhaps sooner, the

Nameless One and his forces will be at the walls of the city. The Lonely Giant will not hold out, and I cannot even send them reinforcements."

Stalkon nodded. "The orcs would immediately get wind of it. They would attack from the rear, and Miranueh is not in a peaceful mood just at the moment, either. The only possible help could come from the dark elves and the Border Kingdom, but if the orcs decide to attack, then they will attack the Borderland as well. The Nameless One is unlikely to enter any other lands, and so we cannot expect help from Garrak, or the Empire, or Filand. Isilia, as always, will remain neutral and sit things out without interfering. Miranueh will merely rub its hands in glee. We shall have to manage with our own forces."

"And it is not only the Nameless One who has become active recently," said the magician. "The orcs are raising their heads in the Forests of Zagraba, in the mountains trolls have starting attacking the dwarves' settlements, a dragon has been seen on the southern borders. A dragon! It is more than two hundred years since the last one approached the borders of our kingdom. The world is teetering on the threshold of war. A terrible war."

"I have begun gathering an army," the king said with a frown. "By the end of the year I hope to put at least fifty thousand men in the field against the Nameless One. Some will have to be left on the borders with Zagraba and Miranueh. And there is also the militia, but that is merely a gesture of despair. We need to announce a levy, but I am afraid that there will be a panic, the prices of goods will shoot sky-high, and we shall have refugees. Thank the gods we have the dark elves on our side, as well as the gnomes and their cannon."

"I beg your pardon, Your Majesty, I . . . I have no doubts concerning the gnomes—dump a sackful of gold pieces in front of them, and they'll make war on their own grandmother—but the elves . . . Are you sure about them?"

"We have no need to lie," said the woman, throwing back her veil. "I myself have seen the army of the Nameless One preparing for war beyond the Needles of Ice."

My jaw dropped. The person gazing at me was an elfess. A genuine dark elfess.

The bewitching charm of the elves. It was invented by the same storyteller who thought up the goblins' thirst for blood. It is only in fairy tales that elves are beautiful, only in fairy tales that they are immortal, only in fairy tales do they have golden hair, green eyes, melodic voices, and a light, floating step. And only in fairy tales are elves wise, truthful, just, and chivalrous. In real life . . .

In real life anyone who knew no better could take an elf from the forests of Zagraba and I'alyala for an orc. Because the fairy-tale beauty of the elves lauded to the heavens by drunken storytellers in the taverns simply doesn't exist.

Well of course, there are some attractive faces even among this race, but they're certainly no paragon of beauty. Elves look like people, except for their swarthy skin, yellow eyes, black lips, and ash-gray hair. And those protruding fangs put a real scare into the unsophisticated philistine and the lover of old wives' tales.

Don't believe in the kindheartedness of the elves. One day, if you are unlucky, you may be present at an elfin torture session, when they apply the Green Leaf to their closest relatives, the orcs.

That's right. Orcs and elves appeared in Siala in the very same year. But the orcs arrived here just a little before the elves, for which the ashen-haired ones can never forgive them. And, apart from the ogres, the elves and the orcs were the first to be brought to Siala by the gods. The race of orcs was granted pride and fury, and the elves cunning and guile. But both of them received yet another gift—hatred. To this day they still make war, slaying each other in large numbers in the thousands upon thousands of bloody battles that take place in the boundless Forests of Zagraba.

The gnomes and the dwarves, Doralissians and men, centaurs and giants, and the multitude of other races that inhabit Siala only appeared later. But the first arrivals were the unsuccessful children—the orcs and elves. Afterward the elves divided into dark and light, although the only difference between them is that the dark elves employ shamanism, and the light elves use wizardry.

The dark and light elves are not hostile to each other; they simply regard each other with a considerable degree of contempt. Even now the dark elves cannot understand why their relatives use an alien magic, not original to their race. About two thousand years ago they found themselves unable to live together, and so they separated. The dark elves remained in the Forests of Zagraba, while the light elves moved away to the Forests of I'alyala, which lie beside the Crest of the World.

"Allow me to introduce you, Harold," said the king, indicating the elfess. "This is Lady Miralissa from the House of the Black Moon."

I bowed with restraint. A name with the ending *ssa* indicated that the elfess was from the Supreme Family of the house. In simple worlds, a personage of the royal blood. Well now, this was beginning to add up. Harold has a sharp eye.

"Pleased to make your acquaintance, milady."

"Likewise."

"The pleasantries can wait," the king declared. "We have very little time and you, Harold, will have to help us."

"To stop the Nameless One?" I asked skeptically.

If that's it, then the king or his advisers really have lost their grip.

"Yes," said the archmagician.

Then everybody in this room is definitely deranged!

Alistan was observing me closely, trying to discover any sign of mockery of his king. I refrained. It was hard, certainly, but I refrained. The jester didn't, though. The goblin burst into laughter and fell on the carpet, clutching at his stomach.

"The life of the kingdom is in the hands of a thief! Watch out that he doesn't filch it!"

I personally didn't find that at all funny.

"Quiet, Kli-Kli," Alistan said sternly, keeping his eyes fixed intently on me.

"All right, I hold my tongue, I repent, I die." The goblin flung his arms out in a tragic gesture.

"Of course, I am flattered by such an honor," I began cautiously, trying not to provoke the lunatics. "But does it not seem to you that I have rather less power and experience than the Order and the Wild Hearts, and it will be rather difficult to stop this wizard single-handedly?"

The goblin tittered and collapsed onto the carpet again. "Oh, Harold!" said the jester, wiping away genuine tears. "Not only are you clever and bold, you are cocksure, too."

"Then what does my task consist of, Your Majesty?" I carried on playing the fool, waiting for the moment when they might let me go.

And then I'll run for it. I don't give a damn where, anywhere will do, even the Sultanate, just as long as it's as far away as possible. To lands where there are no insane kings, crazy jesters, and senile geriatric wizards.

"We need the Rainbow Horn," the elfess said. "It is the only thing that can halt the Nameless One. I fear that even the army will not be able to stand against the full battle host of the Desolate Lands."

"The Rainbow Horn?" I echoed stupidly. "What has it got to do with this?"

"I have already explained," Artsivus said with a frown of annoyance. "Is your fear beginning to affect your hearing?"

"Understand this, Harold. The magic of the ogres is not ideal and in many ways it is crude, even though it is very powerful, but the law of equilibrium . . ." The elfess pursed her black lips ironically, exposing her fangs even more. And still she possessed an exotic beauty. "As time passes, the Horn loses its magical properties. It has to be . . ."

"Reactivated," the archmagician prompted, staring into the flames that were merrily consuming the wood in the hearth.

"Yes, magically charged after a certain period of time. Otherwise nothing will remain of its special properties. The Horn is weakening at this moment, that is why the Nameless One has begun to stir beyond the Needles of Ice. We need you to get the artifact for the Order."

"You mean you don't have it?" I asked, astounded.

"That is precisely the point. We don't," the Rat exclaimed furiously. "And all thanks to the stupidity of the Order."

"The Order acted out of the very best of motives!" the archmagician retorted sharply.

"Well, we're certainly paying for them now!"

"Your job, milord Alistan, is to protect the king's life and brandish that piece of ironmongery you carry, not to interfere in the business of the Order!" The old man was simply seething with indignation and his beard wagged in a way that reminded me of a Doralissian whose favorite horse has been stolen.

"That's enough!" the king roared furiously. He didn't seem anything like a good-natured innkeeper now. "Explain the thief's task to him."

"About three hundred years ago," Artsivus began, speaking in a dull voice and casting a hostile glance at the captain of the guard from under his thick gray eyebrows, "the Council of the Order decided to use the Horn to annihilate the Kronk-a-Mor that binds the Nameless One to this world. We . . . we did not quite manage it. . . ."

Alistan snorted loudly.

"We ought to send Your Magicship to Miranueh as a diplomat! Perhaps we would get the disputed lands then? *Not quite* . . ." The jester giggled, savoring those two words, but then his eyes met the magician's stern gaze, and he shut up.

"Yes . . . Nothing came of our attempt. We tried to control the magic of the ogres, about which we knew absolutely nothing. A power flow was shorted out at the wrong point or an operon was shifted several degrees off the fifth astral position. . . . Mmm, yes . . ." Artsivus realized that he had wandered into tangled thickets that were absolutely impenetrable to anyone but himself. "It was all out of control, and the sudden surge of magic struck Avendoom. Or rather, part of it. The part that is now known as the Secret Territory."

"So that's how it appeared . . . ," I drawled.

"Do you realize how grateful the inhabitants of the glorious capital of Valiostr would be if they only knew who was responsible for putting the Stain on the map?" The goblin opened his eyes wide, transforming them into two small blue lakes.

The archmagician sighed heavily—evidently I was not the only one already weary of the jester—and continued:

"The Order decided to put the Horn as far out of harm's way as possible. They charged it, then took it to Grok's sepulchre and left it there. And that, in effect, is the entire story."

"And you want me to get the Horn out of the grave?" I asked in amazement. "But what do you need me for? Any gravedigger with a spade could manage a simple little job like that! And by the way, where is Grok buried?"

A tense, oppressive silence filled the little room. The elfess and Artsivus exchanged astonished glances. The Count of the Rat gave a crooked smile and looked at me disdainfully. I will pass over the jester and his drooping jaw in polite silence. The king was the only one who carried on as before, twirling my knife in his hands, sometimes glancing at me and trying to figure out if I was deliberately playing the fool.

"Hm-hmm. Young man, do you know any history at all?" the magician asked cautiously.

"It would be about as much use to me as a h'san'kor. I'm a thief, not a learned old maid." I was getting seriously tired of this buffoonery.

These lads certainly know how to wind up a man's nerves.

"Why, he probably doesn't even know how to read," the goblin declared with a pompous air.

I ignored that.

"The Horn is buried with Grok in the Palaces of Bone, Harold," the elfess said in a quiet voice, and she shuddered as if her swarthy skin had been touched by a cold wind from beyond the Mountains of Despair.

That was when I burst into laughter, realizing that these five lunatics were hoaxing me.

"He's gone crazy," the jester said in response to my laughter, shaking his green head dismally so that the little bells on his cap jangled sadly.

"They're joking, aren't they, Your Majesty? They must be! Why Hrad Spein? Wouldn't it be easier for me to draw up a new Vastar's Bargain and invite dragons to protect our beloved homeland? Or tame a h'san'kor for you? Believe me, I could manage that far more easily and much more quickly than an excursion to Hrad Spein!"

"They are not joking," the king said in a serious voice, and the next burst of laughter stuck in my throat.

Isn't that just wonderful! All I have to do is go down into Hrad Spein to retrieve some stupid magical whistle. . . .

"We need that Horn, Master Harold," said the elfess, speaking to me tenderly, as if I were a capricious little child. "And we need it urgently. Before the onset of winter."

"But why me?"

"Because only a tricky and cunning man will pass where a large troop of soldiers or magicians will get stuck in the mire. The finest thief in the kingdom, for instance. Yes, yes. Don't try to be modest. We know far more about you than you think."

"Does this mean others have already tried to get the Horn?"

"A hundred thousand demons! Yes!" Alistan clenched and unclenched his fists several times. "Do you really think we would have turned to a thief if there were any other way of getting into the damned catacombs? We sent the first expedition in winter. Of those who went down underground, none returned, and those who waited up above were cut down by orcs. The second party set out in early spring. In view of the failure of the first expedition, we sent an expedition of more than a hundred men. Experienced soldiers, eight magicians of the Order, plus support from the dark elves, who acted as our guides in the Forests of Zagraba.... And, may the demons take me, nothing came of it! Eighty men went down into the burial sites, and only one came back out, as white-haired as a snow owl and completely insane. The remnants of the second expedition arrived in Avendoom a week ago. All eight magicians were left behind, underground. With seventy-one other men, more than half of whom were my soldiers!"

"And now you've decided a thief will be able to do what a hundred men couldn't," I summed up.

Wonderful, the big shots have failed to do the impossible and now they want a lowly thief to do their bidding. I wonder which brilliant mind came up with this idea?

"Can I refuse?" This was a purely rhetorical question, as Brother For likes to say.

"Yes, Baron Lanten is still outside the door. You can take a ride to the Gray Stones with him," Alistan laughed.

I get it. So that's the way it is. Either take your chances in Hrad Spein or rot in the Gray Stones—and who knows which is better? If it was up to me, I'd choose the Gray Stones, but I can probably risk it and try to trick the whole Council of Lunatics.

"I accept," I said, nodding, and got up out of my armchair. "Can I go now? To carry out my mission?"

At least it seemed like I had a real chance to cut and run before they really had me on the hook.

"Of course," the king said with a feeble wave of his hand, and his immense ring glinted as it caught the light of a candle. "You accept the Commission?"

At that point I sat back down in the armchair. I'd thought I was going to trick them all, thought I was the most slippery eel there, but they were the ones who had tricked me.

When a master thief performs a task for a client, he accepts a Commission, which renders the agreement between thief and client stronger than any amount of gold could. In accepting a Commission, a thief undertakes to carry it out (or, if he is unsuccessful, to return the initial pledge, together with interest on the total value of the deal), and the client commits himself to paying in full when the task has been completed.

The Commission is an inviolable contract between the master thief and the client. And it cannot be violated, torn up, or put aside without the agreement of both parties. As the masters say, you can cheat and break a contract even with darkness, but not with Sagot. The punishment will follow immediately—something like falling into the firm grip of the guards at the scene of the crime, finding yourself in prison, or running into a knife in a perfectly safe alleyway. Luck will simply turn her back on the night hunter. And the client will not flourish if he refuses to pay, without good reason. The patron of thieves turns a blind eye to the doings of footpads and petty criminals, but not to those of master thieves following sound and reliable leads.

To refuse the Commission meant confessing to my recent lie about being willing to cooperate and being sent to the most uncomfortable cell in the Gray Stones, with a grand view of the Cold Sea. To accept meant that I couldn't make a run for it, because the Commission wouldn't let me go. There was no way I could pull out of it. "What are the terms?" I asked Stalkon hopelessly.

"You must deliver the Rainbow Horn to the capital before the beginning of January."

"The payment?"

"Fifty thousand pieces of gold."

"As the pledge?" I tried to keep my voice steady.

Fifty thousand . . . well, of course, it's not half the kingdom or the hand of the princess from the fairy tale, but it offers plenty of scope. . . . Several generations could live well on that amount of money. The fortunes of certain barons and counts are no more than a third of the sum proposed.

"How much do you want?"

I thought for a moment, hesitating.

"A hundred will do."

"You'll get the money as you leave the palace. By the way, don't forget your toys. Is that all?"

"I request you to pronounce the official formula. That is, of course, if Your Majesty is familiar with it."

"I request Shadow Harold to accept my Commission," said the king, speaking the official formulation of a contract between a thief and a client.

"I accept the Commission," I sighed.

"It has been heard," the elfess said with a flash of her fangs, and threw the veil over her face.

There was no thunder and no lightning. Simply, somewhere Sagot remembered what had been said, and now he would watch carefully to make sure the conditions of the contract were observed. Or if not him, then his servants would watch. The important thing was that the Commission would have to be carried out. If it cost me my life, I had to do it, because there is no running away from fate. And not to carry out the Commission was absolutely impossible. I couldn't go off to Hrad Spein, hide somewhere near the entrance, and then say: Sorry, I gave it a try but it didn't work out. They were right when they said Stalkon was clever; he had closed off all the escape routes and loopholes by offering a huge sum of money. And if I didn't manage to pull it off, I would have to return the pledge and a huge amount of interest on the total sum of the deal. I didn't have that kind of money, so that meant the terms of the Commission would be violated.

"Congrotolations, Harold!" Kli-Kli bowed elegantly in my direction. "Now you're the king's man."

"I have questions."

The words "Your Majesty" were set aside now until afterward. Now there was only a client, a master thief, and Sagot observing us from heaven, or wherever it is that he lives.

"Yes?"

"Am I going there alone?"

The thought flashed swiftly through my head that if I went alone, I'd certainly never get there. I'd either lose my way in the Forests of Zagraba or get clubbed to death somewhere along the way.

"No, but we have decided that this time the expedition should be small and it must travel in secret. Someone had eyes following the first expeditions. Servants of the Nameless One or someone else, we never found the informers."

"How small a detachment?" I asked with a frown.

"Lady Miralissa and two of her compatriots will be your guides in the forest and will protect you with magic."

"Stop!" It didn't bother me in the slightest that I had interrupted a king. Alistan frowned, but I couldn't give a damn. In the face of a Commission all are equal. "You mentioned magic. . . . How many magicians of the Order will go with us?"

"Not one," snapped Artsivus, suddenly emerging from his contemplations.

I paused for a moment, ruffled up my hair with a nervous gesture, and said, "I thought I just heard you say—"

"Not one," the archmagician repeated just as firmly. "We've already lost eight of our best in those cursed Palaces of Bone as it is. All the magicians will be needed on the walls of the city if your undertaking ends in failure."

Worse and worse. Why not just throw us into the orcs' labyrinth? It'll be easier on our nerves. There's absolutely no point going into the Forests of Zagraba, and especially to Hrad Spein, without a good magician.

"In addition to your elves, you will also be accompanied by the ten Wild Hearts who escorted the Lady Miralissa from the Lonely Giant. And also milord Alistan. He will command the expedition."

Alistan gave me a sour look. He clearly did not relish the thought of traveling in the company of a thief. The Rat and the Wild Hearts would make up a small, concentrated force capable of fighting off a small detachment of attackers if we ran into any along the way. So how many of us were there? Fifteen was the number. "Good. When do we set out?"

"The sooner the better."

"Then at the end of the week," I said, counting the days.

"What?" Alistan took a step in my direction. "You're mocking us!"

"Me? Absolutely not." I shook my head, making it clear to the knight that I didn't have the slightest intention of mocking. "I need to buy equipment and make thorough preparations for the trek; I personally wish to come back alive from Hrad Spein. It's a month's riding, maybe two, to the Forests of Zagraba, and let's say a month, allowing a huge safety margin, at Hrad Spein, and the same amount of time to get back to Avendoom. We can reasonably expect to be back here in November or December. Provided we don't run into trouble, naturally. Your Majesty, I need access to the Royal Library."

I can read perfectly well.

"What on earth for?" the old magician asked, astonished.

"I don't want to go blundering into Hrad Spein like some incompetent idiot. The Nameless One himself could lose his way in there. I need plans and old maps. At least for what they call the human section. Grok isn't buried in the lower levels, is he?"

"No, his grave is on the eighth level."

I breathed a quiet sigh of relief. That was one little piece of good news at least. Trying to enter the levels of the ogres was simple suicide. There was no way I would ever reach them alive. I'd be gobbled up somewhere along the way. But I could risk going down as far as the eighth level.

"That's good. I think there must be old plans in the library?"

"Yes, there are," said Artsivus with a nod, then hesitated for a moment before adding: "Only, Grok's grave isn't shown on them, I'm certain of that."

"Why not?" Miralissa asked in amazement, distracted from her contemplation of the fragile goblet of wine.

"The eighth level may not be the twenty-eighth, but it was still not built by men. Or for men. No one must know who lives there and what dangers await."

"I can't believe the magicians of the Order left absolutely no records of Grok's grave and the booby traps in Hrad Spein," I said, starting to feel nervous. "They must be somewhere, surely?"

"They are." The old man nodded and wrapped the woolen blanket around himself even more tightly.

"Where, then?"

Would you believe it! First they insist that I carry out a Commission and then they make things difficult by keeping secrets of their own.

"In the old Tower of the Order."

"And where is the old Tower of the Order?" I had to drag every word out of the old man with red-hot pincers.

"Somewhere in the Forbidden Territory of the city."

That was when the fanfare sounded in my head, announcing that now I was in a right royal fix.

4

'd promised the king I would go back to the palace after a week, so now I had an entire seven days to prepare for the dubious undertaking of a journey to Hrad Spein. Very first thing the following morning I set out for the Royal Library on Grok Square.

Naturally, to go in through the central entrance would be an act of great insolence and an open challenge to every nobleman in the kingdom, and so I maneuvered through the bustling stream of townsfolk who were already up and hurrying about their business and made my way to the right side of the gray building, were there was a separate entrance for employees.

I walked up to the cast-iron door and knocked loudly. But as always happens, my modest personage was ignored in the most shameless fashion. After waiting for a couple of minutes, I hammered again, with redoubled strength. Silence again. Has everybody in there gone to sleep, then? I can easily believe it, there are never many visitors, especially since entrance is restricted to nobles, priests, and members of the Order. Simple folk have no need of books, they're happy if they can manage to feed their families. I waited for a while and then knocked yet again, so loudly that the racket frightened the pigeons on the nearby roofs, and the startled flock went soaring up into the cloudless June sky.

Eventually a lock clicked, a bolt squeaked, the door opened a crack, and an old man peered out at me with a short-sighted, angry expression.

"What's all the racket about, you hooligan?"

I didn't say a word, just held out the king's ring before the old man had time to slam the door in my face. He screwed up his eyes and peered closely at the circle of gold, then opened the door and stepped aside.

"Why didn't you say so straightaway? Come in then, if you've nothing better to do at home."

There was no point in arguing, so I walked into the library, and the old man rapidly slammed the door behind me.

"They're always trying to get me! But I'm too smart for them!" The old man giggled and grinned gleefully, exposing the worn stumps of yellow teeth.

"Who are *they*?" I asked in an effort to patch things up with the caretaker.

"Ogres!"

Well, how about that? The old man's touched. He's gone completely round the bend hidden away in here among all these books.

The old man nodded a few times, and then shuffled off along a narrow corridor into the depths of the building. I had no option but to go after him.

"What have you come for, then? To increase your stock of knowledge?" the old man asked querulously.

"Uh-huh."

"A magician's apprentice, I suppose."

"Yes."

"Oh, sure," the old-timer chortled, not believing a single word.

For a minute we walked on in total silence along service corridors with dim light streaming in through narrow little steel-barred windows. Specks of dust glittered and sparkled as they drifted through the rays of sunlight.

"So tell me, apprentice, what the hell are you doing with that wasp hidden under your cloak?" the old man suddenly asked in a cunning voice, stopping and looking me straight in the eyes.

"I see you're sharp-sighted," I said, amazed. "How do you know about the wasp?"

"How do I know?" the old man muttered, walking on. "I served thirty years as a scout in the Wild Hearts. So I ought to be able to spot a lousy little crossbow, even if it is hidden."

"The Wild Hearts? A scout? Thirty years?"

"Sure."

Well now, how about that! The old-timer's a genuine hero, a walking legend! But then what's he doing in a place like this? Over their period of service the wild ones put together a fair-sized fortune, so they can relax and live out the rest of their lives in their own little houses with no worries or cares, and no need to slave away day and night, choking on old dust.

"You're not lying?" Somehow it was hard to believe I was face-to-face with a genuine Wild Heart, even a retired one.

The old man snorted angrily and rolled up the sleeve of his greasy, moth-eaten, light green shirt to reveal a tattoo on his forearm. A small purple heart, the kind that lovers draw on walls, only this one had teeth.

The Wild Heart. And below it the title of his unit: BRIAR.

So the old-timer isn't lying. No fool on earth would be stupid enough to tattoo himself with the symbol of the Wild Hearts, let alone the name of a reconnaissance unit. The Hearts would simply slice the rogue's arm off, tattoo and all. And they wouldn't bother about his age.

I whistled.

"Oho! And how many missions?"

"Forty-three," the old man muttered modestly. "I got as far as the Needles of Ice with my detachment."

I almost stumbled and fell. Forty-three missions beyond the Lonely Giant? That was impressive. This old-timer deserved a little respect.

"Was it tough?"

"You bet it was," the old man replied, thawing a little. "We're here."

We left the dark, narrow little corridor behind us and entered an immense hall that seemed to go on forever. The vast numbers of tables and chairs for visitors were all empty, except for one, where a youth wearing the robes of the Order was sitting. He was leafing through a thick, dusty book, blowing his nose into a handkerchief every second. The snot-nosed juvenile took no notice of us.

An entire lifetime would be far too short to read everything that had accumulated in the library over the centuries. The huge shelves of black Zagraban oak soared way up high into the space under the domed ceiling, their tops hidden in darkness that not even the light streaming in through the tall lancet windows could dispel. There were thousands of books—hundreds of thousands—standing on the shelves, preserving the knowledge of thousands of generations of Siala on their yellowed pages.

There were narrow balconies winding around the walls of the library, so that visitors could climb all the way up to the ceiling to get the book they needed. There were books here that had been written by half-blind priests sitting beside a candle with its flame flickering in the wind: ancient tomes of the elves, who had created their manuscripts when the full moon shone and the black waters of the Iselina reflected the heavenly lamp of night as they flowed between the roots of gigantic trees. There were books here by the gnomes—written first on clay tablets, and later on thin sheets of metal, and finally printed on the printing press they invented, which was stored away somewhere safe in the Steel Mines. Scrolls written by human magicians; books created by the finest minds of Siala; books produced by nonentities and mediocrities. Learning of all kinds: history, culture, war, peace, magic, shamanism, life, and death. Legends of the gods, men, elves, heroes, stories of hundreds of animals and other creatures, of thousands of stars, and Sagot only knows what else. All the knowledge of the world was gathered together in this ancient library, which was based on the library at Ranneng, built almost nine hundred years earlier.

"Oho!" I exclaimed admiringly, throwing my head back to look up at the ceiling and trying to make out exactly where in the gloom the walls of learning came to an end.

I'd never been in any libraries before. Except for a few private ones, where I'd borrowed a couple of rare volumes from the owners for other, equally passionate lovers of literature.

"Oho's about right!" the old man said as proudly as if he'd written everything in the place himself. "So what are you after, hooligan?"

"Are there any old plans of the city here?"

"There are a few, all right," he mumbled.

"I need plans of the Stain. And plans of Hrad Spein—in fact, everything you have on the place."

The old man whistled, pursed his lips, and snapped his fingers a couple of times as he gazed thoughtfully over my shoulder, then he fixed the gaze of his watery eyes directly on me. "So that's the lay of the land, is it, my old mate? Why not ask for a map that shows the treasures of the dwarves or the gnomes while you're at it? If you didn't have that ring, I'd throw you out on your ear. I get all sorts in here asking about documents proscribed by the Order. No end to them these days. Pah! Right, let's go . . ." The old man turned his back on me and started wandering through the shelves toward the mysterious inner depths of the library.

"No end to them?" I questioned him cautiously. "Who?"

"You, for instance. Why the hell can't you all stay at home with the girls?"

"And who else?"

"There was one here yesterday," the old-timer muttered angrily without turning round as he led me into a narrow little room with a wrought-metal door in the wall.

"He looked like you. Gray and tight-lipped he was, just like you. Came in the evening. And he stuck a ring under my nose, too. A bit different from yours, but it had just as much authority, you mark my words. Old man, he said, give me the plans of the Stain, he said. At least he hadn't completely lost his senses, like you. He didn't ask any questions about Hrad Spein. We're here. Hang on, I'll unlock the door."

The old man began fiddling with a massive bundle of keys and swearing as he opened the squeaky old locks.

I was thinking hard. Who else has suddenly decided he needs maps of the forbidden district of the city? Has the king hired someone else to do the job as well as me? Doesn't he trust me? Or are these people working for someone else? The Nameless One, for instance?

"What's your name, pops?" I asked amiably, bending down to duck under the ceiling of a gray corridor that led deep under the ground, into darkness.

"Bolt," the old-timer muttered, lighting the torch lying ready near at hand. "Crossbow Bolt, that's my name. Mind you don't break your legs, the steps are steep. All the forbidden books are kept in an underground depository. Let's get what you want, then you can go back up to read it, otherwise I'll freeze to death here."

"I heard that the forbidden books couldn't be taken out of the depository."

"Hmm . . . I'd like to tell the Order where to stick their stupid rules. Those fat bloated wizards don't understand a thing. If they'd ever fought ogres, like me, they'd soon drop all that stupid nonsense. Who needs this old junk? When you've read everything you want, I'll bring them back. Careful, the step's broken here."

Hm. Bolt. I knew that in the Wild Hearts many soldiers were given nicknames to replace their real names. The nickname described the man, and men earned them for the specific quality of their service, actions, knowledge, or character. The Wild Hearts took pride in their new names.

Crossbow Bolt. So in former times the old man must have been a good shot.

We walked down into a dark hall that was small, but even so the torchlight was too feeble to illuminate it fully. The old man reached out one hand into the darkness, there was a loud click somewhere up above our heads, and the room was flooded with blinding sunlight. I squeezed my eyes tightly shut in sudden surprise.

"Aha, frightened, eh?" The old man giggled with delight. "Come on now, don't be afraid. Come on, open those peepers."

I slowly got used to the bright light. Like the large hall up above, this small one was crammed absolutely full of books and scrolls on metal shelves. And hanging from the high ceiling there was a blindingly bright round sphere, like a little sun.

"The dwarves invented it. Did you think they run around in the dark in those caves of theirs, smashing their foreheads against the walls? Oho noo . . . They put up magic lamps like this. Magic! Our Order's never even come close to anything like it. The charlatans! But the dwarves put one of these candles in here, and about ten of them in the basements of the royal palace. Of course, I've got no idea how much money they took for it. But it's handy all right."

I nodded.

"Right, then. Stay here, and don't touch anything or stick your nose into anything. I'll go and get what you want." The old man gave me a menacing look to make sure I understood what he'd said.

As soon as he was gone, I instantly shed my harmless pose and started strolling about, looking at the titles of the old volumes. My eyes slid along until they suddenly came to rest on a small shelf of magic scrolls. The following words were written in immense, ornate letters on the wall

beside the shelf: BATTLE SPELLS! RUNE MAGIC. THESE SCROLLS MAY ONLY
BE USED BY ARCHMAGICIANS OF THE ORDER, WHEN PERMISSION HAS
BEEN GRANTED BY THE COUNCIL!

I couldn't understand why rune-magic battle spells would be lying
there so openly, entirely unprotected. Any light-fingered rogue—like
me, for instance—could easily make off with these rolled-up sheets of
parchment.

Carelessness will destroy the world yet. Just you mark my words!

I glanced round quickly, grabbed one scroll, with a black ribbon, out
of the dusty heap and stuck it inside my shirt. Then I moved away, to
wait for the old man. I'd acted like a petty thief, but I thought to myself
that no one else was going to need the scroll for a long time, and it
might come in handy in Hrad Spein.

The trouble with scrolls is that you can only use them once. After
you've chanted the formula and worked the spell, you can simply throw
the useless parchment away. The magic destroys the words, erasing them
from the scroll and from the reader's memory. But at least you don't have
to be a magician to work magic that has been written down on paper.
You only need to know how to read.

I heard Bolt coughing somewhere behind the shelves, and then he
himself appeared, carrying two books in his hands. One was huge and
thick, in a brown buffalo-skin binding with worn gold embossing, the
other was small and so old that I thought it would crumble to dust under his fingers.

"An ogre almost grabbed me back there," the old man muttered, handing me the books I wanted. "The brute was hiding under the shelves. I
had to give it a couple of kicks to frighten it off. Well, why are you just
standing there like a block of wood?"

"Is that all?" I asked Bolt in amazement as I looked at the two books.
I'd been expecting more.

"That's enough cheek from you. The big one is plans of Avendoom,
drawn four hundred years ago, and the little one's about Hrad Spein.
Written quite recently, but it's in a terrible state. The other books are in
orcish. You don't happen to savvy their spiel, do you. Right! Then quit
your moaning."

The old man turned out the dwarves' sun, took the torch out of its
bracket, and started climbing up the steps. We walked all the way back

in silence. Then, still without speaking, the custodian locked the iron door and showed me to a table, only not in the large hall. It was in a little cubbyhole, surrounded by books. Then he walked off, muttering something to himself.

I began my research with what was simplest and easiest. Setting aside the little book, I pulled over the weighty tome composed of maps of the city bound together into a single volume.

The pages of fine parchment rustled quietly under my fingers as I turned them in search of the part of Avendoom that interested me. The maps in the book were astoundingly precise and detailed. It was obvious at first glance that this was the painstaking handiwork of dwarves. Only those large but meticulous hands could possibly have traced the lines so precisely and lovingly.

As the pages flashed past my eyes, so did the streets of Avendoom and the city's history. I found what I was looking for quite quickly. The Forbidden Territory. Of course, drawn at a time when the magicians of the Order had not yet combined forces with the Rainbow Horn to transform five whole streets into a cursed spot that was walled off from the rest of the city.

Well then, getting into the Forbidden Territory would be fairly easy. Only what was waiting for me in there? Three roads left the Port City, running in parallel toward the Artisans' City: the Street of the Sleepy Cat, the Street of Men, and Graveyard Street. The last of these ran into the old graveyard that was still in use at that time.

Running at right angles to the Street of the Sleepy Cat was the Street of the Magicians, which opened out into the square where the old Tower of the Order stood. On the other side of the square the Street of the Roofers began. As I had expected, all these streets occupied a substantial chunk of the city, a lot more than I had been counting on, in fact. It was going to be a tricky business. But if I wanted to find Grok's grave, I would have to get into the old Tower of the Order somehow. I couldn't understand how the two previous expeditions could have set out for Hrad Spein without knowing where to look for the Horn. What had they been counting on?

I tried to memorize all the roads, buildings, and side streets. Call me a fool, if you like, but I never copy plans down onto parchment. What do I have a head for?

Round about midday I leaned back in my chair, exhausted, then slammed the large volume shut and pushed it aside. I stretched and yawned. I would tackle the little book on Hrad Spein next. Hrad Spein, the very worst haunted house ever, filled with the shades of demons, orcs, ogres, and elves. Well, at least we would have an elf with us. What a curious, rare beauty she was, although not a conventional beauty by any means. Not that she was my type—what a match that would be! Ho-ho. Mysterious though, fascinating secrets there. She would bear watching.

My stomach was quite shamelessly reminding me that it was feeling rather hungry. Bolt went by, and I asked him if he could bring me something to eat or go and buy something. The only answer I got was a furious glance and a stern lecture that I should stuff my belly at an inn, not a depository of learning.

Deciding to try a different approach, I took out a silver coin and set it spinning on the table. Before the coin even came to a stop, Bolt grabbed it and disappeared into the walls of books and scrolls. A little while later he came back with a huge amount of food and four bottles of sour red wine: he'd been generous with my money and bought enough drink for an entire squadron.

We dined right there, on the table. In half a day not a single other person had come to visit the library building, and as I gnawed on a tough, unappetizing chicken leg, I realized how lonely and miserable the old man must feel here. Meanwhile, Bolt reserved most of his attention for the wine. After my snack, I told the custodian to go away and let me get on with my work, and he picked up the bottles and the remaining food and left.

I pulled over the little book, which bore a title in black letters: *Hrad Spein. A nocturnal mystery, shrouded in death. A history with conjectures. The scholarly work of the magician Dalistus of the Snow, the Order of Aven-doom.*

Well, at least it would make interesting reading.

Ornate letters and engravings, maps, drawings of mysterious, inconceivable creatures. The terrible tale took a grip on me, plunging me into an age of ancient mysteries.

"Hrad Spein" is a ogric name. Translated into the language of men it means "Palaces of Bone." But the dark elves say that the human tongue is incapable of expressing the universal horror that the ogres invested in those two words. No one knows who created Hrad Spein, and in which age, whose thought and strength it was that bit so deep into the bones of the earth, creating those immense caves and caverns that were later transformed into the architectural wonders of the northern world and, later still, into a world of darkness and horror.

The first to discover Hrad Spein were the ogres, before they withdrew into the Desolate Lands. There were no orcs yet then, not to mention human beings. The ogres spent a long time exploring Hrad Spein, a very long time. That was where they solved the mysteries of the Kronk-a-Mor. Nothing is known about the origin of the ogres, but they appeared in Siala a lot later than the time when unknown builders first laid the foundations of the Palaces of Bone. They say that the potency of the ogres' magic came from ageless catacombs, where they discovered the ancient writings of an unknown race that lived in Siala long before the ogres arrived.

Deep, deep under the ground the ogres came across gigantic halls and caves. They started using Hrad Spein as their graveyard, leaving their dead and placing terrible curses on the burial sites. Later, when the ogres moved away to the north, it was the bones of orcs and elves that found their final resting place in Hrad Spein. While constantly warring with each other above the ground, they also found time to create magnificent palaces below it, palaces of a beauty that stunned their contemporaries. And thousands of thousands were interred there, in the ancient burial grounds.

Exquisitely elegant ceilings, columns, frescoes, halls, statues, and corridors—that was Hrad Spein in those times. The orcs and the elves worked together. It was the only place where there was an effective truce between the feuding relatives. Neither side intruded on the lower levels of the ogres. Both races realized that nothing good could be expected from the ogres' magic, and the upper layers of the palaces provided more than enough space for them.

But eventually the bloodlust of the orcs and the hatred of the elves had their effect, and blood was spilt in this place that was sacred to both races. Both of them started installing traps in their own territory to catch their enemies. The underground halls crackled with dark shamanic energy and were drowned in blood. In the end, neither orcs nor elves could feel safe in these places any longer. The Palaces of Bone were abandoned and subsequently the secret knowledge of the locations of traps and labyrinths in the lower levels was lost.

Hrad Spein became like a gigantic underground layer cake tens of leagues deep and wide. The levels of the ogres, the levels of the orcs and the elves. Halls, corridors, and caves. Burial sites, treasure chambers, and magical rooms. Everything in the Palaces of Bone became wound up tight into one gigantic, inextricable tangle. By the time the orcs and elves left the place, men had appeared in the world of Siala and they found their way to Hrad Spein.

They too did not dare go down to the lower levels. Amazing as it might seem, our race had the wits not to do that. Men took over the upper three levels for burying their warriors. Hrad Spein became legendary as the greatest burial ground in the Northern Lands. Only brave soldiers who had fallen in battle were considered worthy to be buried in Hrad Spein, and, of course, aristocrats.

But then, something happened. Nobody ever knew what it was exactly, or why it happened. In Hrad Spein the evil of the ogres' bones awoke, protected by the dark shamanism that had lain dormant all these centuries on the lower levels of the underground regions. It awoke, rousing the dead—and someone else as well. And it rose to the very upper level, but did not emerge from the bounds of Hrad Spein, settling forever in the ancient palaces, and no one dared to go down to those places. Except for the magicians carrying the Horn to Grok's grave.

Time went by, and the Forests of Zagraba swallowed up the entrances to this underground country, concealing the horror of night forever beneath the green crowns of their trees. Over the centuries the dreadful tales about Hrad Spein acquired even greater depths of horror and darkness. Only once, about forty years ago, did dark elves venture down into those places to leave there forever the head of the House of the Black Rose, but they were only able to carry the body of the warrior who had fallen in battle with the orcs as far as the fourth level. They abandoned his body there, amid the darkness and the horror, and retreated upward, fighting off the creatures of the night and losing soldiers as they went. In the end only a pitiful remnant of the elves managed to escape back into the sunlight.

And now I must set out to go to this dark place. With no help to rely on, no precise maps of the levels and the halls, no knowledge of where the traps are positioned, or even how to find Grok's grave, which was not built by the overzealous magicians on the levels of men, but on the eighth level, one that was used by the elves. I just hope that Artsivus is right and in the old Tower of the Order I'll be able to find at least some maps and a plan showing the location of the Horn.

When I was about halfway through studying the work of the magician Dalistus of the Snow, Bolt came back, after having taken on board a full load of wine, and joined me at my table. He started telling me about his life and how he served in the Lonely Giant fortress. About the battles with orcs and svens when he used to fire his trusty crossbow. I didn't really listen to his drunken tale-telling, just nodded mechanically sometimes as I carried on studying the history of Hrad Spein. It was already evening before the old man, evidently weary already of his own stories and with nothing else left to say, asked if he could look at my crossbow. I tore myself away from the book and looked up at him in amazement.

"Well, what are you looking at me like that for? Are you afraid I'm drunk and I'll hurt myself? Why, I was using a crossbow before you were even born, you snot-nose! Give me it, nothing will happen."

I hesitated for a moment, then took the miniature weapon out from under my cloak and held it out to Bolt, after first checking that the safety catch was on, so that the metal arrow couldn't be fired if the trigger was pressed accidentally.

The old-timer grabbed the crossbow out of my hands, clicked his tongue in satisfaction, weighed the weapon in his hands, and aimed it at something behind my back. He found the safety catch very quickly and immediately released it. I began regretting that I hadn't disarmed the weapon. Then the custodian, apparently tired of playing with the crossbow, put it down beside him, poured a fresh glass of wine, and clinked it against the weapon. And now that he had a new and probably more appreciative listener, he went on with the story of his life at the Lonely Giant. I immersed myself in the book again and only emerged from my reverie late in the evening, when Bolt yelled piercingly right in my ear:

"An ogre!"

The old man's howl was so unexpected and so loud, that I fell backward, together with my chair, and struck my head painfully against the wooden floor. Through the flash of pain I saw a heavy arrow bury itself in the table, after punching right through the book about Hrad Spein.

Bolt grabbed the crossbow and fired upward at something without even taking aim. I heard a cry of pain, fury, and amazement and flung my head back, expecting to see a genuine ogre for the first time in my life. But all I saw was my old friend Paleface standing there, his left hand clutching his right shoulder, which had a crossbow bolt jutting out of it.

I jumped to my feet, forgetting all about the pain in my head, grabbed the crossbow out of the drunken old-timer's hands, and dashed across to the steps leading up to the balcony. Reloading the weapon on the run, I thought to myself that Bolt certainly deserved his nickname. Anyone who could hit the target at that distance, even in the shoulder, and without really taking aim, when he was as drunk as a lord, was a real master.

Meanwhile Paleface went dashing away from me into one of the dimly lit corridors on the second floor. I rushed after him.

The assassin was gone. One of the second-floor windows was wide open. I reloaded my weapon, walked up to the opening, and cautiously leaned out, ready to pull back at any moment if Paleface hadn't run away, only hidden. But the night street was deserted, with only a few lamps burning, and I hastily slammed the window frames shut so that nothing else could stick its head in from out of the darkness. After expressing aloud my wish that the son of a bitch Paleface would be eaten by some especially hungry brutish creature that very night, I went back down the steps.

"Did the ogre get away?" asked Bolt, throwing up his arms.

He had already pulled the arrow out of the book, and now he was showering choice expletives on the entire tribe of ogres for damaging the old manuscript.

"He won't get far. You winged him," I reassured the old man.

Apparently Markun had given up waiting for Harold to join the guild and had decided to dispatch him to Sagot, to make sure the others wouldn't rebel.

"Yes, I got him good," the old-timer said with a solemn nod of his head, hiccupping and swaying in the gusts of an invisible wind.

"Thanks, Bolt, you've been a great help. It's getting late, I'll be going home."

I've found out everything I needed and now, before I take my trip to the forbidden part of the city, I have to get a good night's sleep.

"Come round again, old buddy," said the ancient custodian.

I thrust a gold piece into the old man's hand, hoping that none of the city's petty rogues would ever learn of my shameful generosity, and went out into the night.

5

Question: What can be worse than an enraged Doralissian? Answer: The only thing worse than an enraged Doralissian is a bunch of enraged Doralissians. And there were an entire dozen of those half men, half goats howling furiously as they pursued me through the dark night streets of Avendoom, yelling with all the power of their far from feeble lungs.

As soon as I got back from the Royal Library and opened the door of my new and—dare I say it?—secret lair, the Doralissians came at me in a rush out of the darkness, bleating balefully and holding their spiked cudgels at the ready. I was saved only by my own naturally rapid reactions and the stupidity of my attackers: the goat-men tried to push each other aside in the hope of being the first to get at my unfortunate head. As a result a jam formed in the doorway, and I was out of there.

And now, exhausted, furious, and short of sleep, I had been trying for twenty minutes to shake off my pursuers, but the brutes were still yelling and bleating somewhere behind me.

No one leapt out at me from the dark gateways of the city, demanding my purse. All the drunks and midnight ramblers who hadn't managed to take refuge at home before the onset of night had spotted the chase and the roads had cleared as if by magic. Even the creatures of the night had heard the furious cries of my pursuers and decided not to emerge into the light, for fear of attracting the hot-tempered goats' attention.

The Port City came to an end, and I plunged into the network of narrow streets in the Artisans' City, skirting round the magicians' districts. Magicians are a capricious and cantankerous crowd. The first thing they'd do would be to zap the howling mob that had woken them up with some heavy-duty spell, and then they'd start figuring out who was to blame, and what to do about the wall of that house over there that had been damaged accidentally by the magic, and whether they ought to clean off the ashes that were all that was left of the screeching stampede.

So that I could run more easily, I gave a sharp tug on the string of the cloak covering my shoulders and the black material slid off, falling onto the road. I really felt like dumping the crossbow and the knife, too, but the thought of how valuable they were prevented me from committing an act of financial stupidity in order to save myself.

If I'd stopped, of course, I could have brought down a couple of goatmen with the crossbow, but the others would still have caught up with me and given me a drubbing. So there was nothing else for it but to run. I heard gleeful, surprised bleating behind me: The beasts had obviously found my cloak and stopped to wonder where I could have got to. Fortunately for me, Doralissians are not good runners, despite the fact that they have hooves. And they are also quite incredibly stupid. The only real reason these quarrelsome creatures were tolerated was for their horses.

Horses of the Doralissian breed had more stamina and speed than any others in the world. Buyers in the Sultanate and the elfin noble houses paid really big money for them.

On the Street of the Butchers I came to a sharp halt and caught my breath. I thought I'd heard the creatures shout something as I entered my den. Something like: "Give us back our horse!" Their brains must have completely turned to mush. I'm a master thief, I don't steal horses. Either this was simply a woeful mistake, or someone had set me up. But exactly which ill-wisher could it be, out of the hundreds of possible candidates? From round the corner I heard bleating and the clatter of hooves drawing closer. The Doralissians must finally have realized that I couldn't be hiding in the cloak, and continued the pursuit. Should I try to conceal myself in the shadow? I would have done it long before, if not for the goats' excellent sense of smell.

But this can't go on for much longer—I'll run out of steam soon, and the brutes will grab me, alive but weakened. Or those wild howls will attract unwanted attention to my humble person. From the creatures of the night, for instance. I'll have to resort to extreme measures. I stuck my hand inside my shirt and tugged out the scroll with the battle spell that I had recently borrowed from the library. Ah, and I'd been planning to hold on to it until the Palaces of Bone and use it there.

I hastily ripped off the black ribbon and unrolled the scroll. I didn't know how the spell worked, but I had to hurry. The howls of the Doralissians were drawing closer now. Screwing up my eyes to make out the small, fancy letters of the spell by the light of the moon, I began reading:

"*Laosto s'ha f'nadra koli set! I'hna azh zhazakh'ida!*"

My tongue twisted around desperately in my mouth, attempting to pronounce the unpronounceable. After the magical phrases I gestured theatrically in the direction of the approaching Doralissians.

Nothing happened.

That is, absolutely nothing. I was left standing there like an idiot in the middle of the dark street, with my arm flung out and my jaw hanging loose in astonishment. The rune magic hadn't worked! Maybe I hadn't read the incantation right?

Okay, try again! I glanced at the scroll, swore, and flung it away. The ink had disappeared and the letters of the spell were gone. Obviously I had pronounced the accursed words correctly after all, but then why in the name of Darkness weren't they having any effect?

Realizing that while I just stood there thinking I offered a fine target, I decided I'd better get moving.

A few minutes later, with the bitter sweat flooding my eyes and my lungs whistling like a blacksmith's bellows, I realized very clearly just how bad things were. As ill luck would have it, there wasn't a single guardsman anywhere in sight. That's always the way. When you need them, they're nowhere to be found. The goat-men might not run as fast as men can, but there's no denying their sheer stubbornness.

It was all over! I had no more strength to run. Another minute, and I was going to collapse on the road, come what may!

I pressed myself against the wall of a house that cast a thick black shadow. My nose was assaulted by the rank odor of rotten fish. An appalling smell, I must say. But there was one good thing about it—the brutes might smell the fish instead of Harold. I froze, trying to breathe through my mouth in order not to collapse in a faint from that appalling aroma.

They appeared about fifteen seconds later, puffing and panting as they plodded along in single file, glancing around and clutching their barbed cudgels in their hands.

"Whe-e-re cou-ould he have go-o-one?" one of them bleated clumsily in human language, striking his club against the wall of the house beside him in confirmation of his less than positive feelings concerning a certain Harold.

Chips of stone were sent flying.

"He-e-e's got ahea-ea-ead of us," one of the crowd of volunteer executioners snorted. "Run i-i-into the i-i-inner ci-i-ity of humans."

"He took our ho-orse! Our ho-orse!"

"Ye-es! Ye-es! Our ho-orse! We have to ca-atch up with hi-im!" they all started howling together.

As I listened to the sound of clattering hooves moving away, I made a sincerely heartfelt wish that my new friends would run into trouble on their nighttime run through the dark city. I waited a little longer, just to make quite sure that I wouldn't run into another group of nighttime enthusiasts again.

There wasn't a sound. Nothing but the bats that had appeared in the city from somewhere in the south, soaring through the starry sky.

I wondered what the Doralissians wanted from me. And why did they seem to think that I'd stolen their horse? What would Harold want with a horse? Surely they could have figured that out, even with their goat brains? I listened intently to the silence. Seems like I could get moving again. First I ought to go home for a moment, collect all my important and valuable things, and move to a new lair. I was just about to take a step out of the shadow when someone grabbed hold of me very firmly by the chest and lifted me three yards off the ground with incredible ease.

I was taken completely by surprise. I was scared. I opened my mouth to yell. I raised the crossbow, which was still in my hand, and prepared to shoot. And it was only then that I looked at my attacker.

The howl stuck somewhere in the region of my belly, and I gulped with a quiet gurgle.

Well then . . . There I was, suspended three yards above the ground, flailing my feet about in a hopeless attempt to locate some support, and held tight in the grip of . . . Well, it was probably a demon.

The immense torso seemed to grow straight out of the gray wall of the building. The monster's body merged smoothly into the shadow. Two immense hands held me in their firm grasp. The head ... well, it looked like a demon's head. The standard collection of huge teeth that could slice straight through a knight in armor and his armored steed; foul, stinking breath that must have killed every rat for a league in all directions; scarlet slits for eyes, with pupils like a snake's.

"H-hi there," I said as politely and calmly as I could manage, although any townsfolk who weren't asleep yet could have heard the pounding of my heart. "I'm Harold. Who are you?"

The creature narrowed its eyes even further and shook me like a cat shaking a mouse, but it spoke:

"Vukhdjaaz—the clever demon."

Brrrr. That breath! The stench of rotten fish had been far more pleasant! "Really?" I said with polite surprise, and the demon gave me another ominous glance. "Ah, yes! Of course, of course! The cleverest of all the demons."

I had evidently succeeded in flattering the monster, and for a while he forgot about his gastronomic preferences.

"Yes. Vukhdjaaz is clever. He was waiting. Watching. Clever." The creature nodded its horned head. "When someone read the Spell of Return, Vukhdjaaz managed to hide."

"Wow!" I said admiringly, and earned a glance of approval from the beast.

Bang! This time the demon didn't jolt me quite so hard. It didn't even rattle my teeth.

"All the demons went back into the Darkness, but I stayed." Another jolt.

"Why?" I asked, puzzled.

"There's a lot of food here." His eyes narrowed again and glinted as they stared at me.

H'san'kor! The wrong question.

"I was wondering about something else. Why did all the other demons go back into the Darkness?" I said hastily to distract the hungry creature from bad thoughts about my own humble person.

"Ah," said the beast, after considering the word "wondering" for a long moment. That was fair enough; it never does any harm to increase your vocabulary. "Some mortal read a spell that ended the freedom of demons in this anthill of men. I'm going to catch him and suck the marrow out of his bones. You haven't seen anyone round here, have you?"

I shook my head desperately. I thought I knew which particular mortal we were talking about here.

"And who released Vukhdjaaz from the Darkness?" I asked, desperately seeking a way out of this unpleasant situation.

"The Master." Another jolt.

"The Nameless One?"

The demon only snorted and seared me once again with that hungry glance. This creature had a really great talent for making me feel nervous. Just what was it he saw in me?

"Vukhdjaaz is hungry."

"Yes?" I squealed, setting my finger on the trigger of the crossbow.

Of course, shooting at a demon with an ordinary crossbow bolt is like pricking an ogre with a pin. It only annoys them even more. But what else could I do?

"Yes. And Vukhdjaaz needs help, too."

"Perhaps Harold can help you?"

"He can." Vukhdjaaz inhaled my odor and a sticky thread of saliva dripped out of the corner of his mouth.

"No, with your business!" I wailed despairingly.

"Ah?" The demon seemed a little upset, but he moved his toothy face away from me. "Vukhdjaaz wants to stay in this world. The food is not so good in the Darkness. Harold will help Vukhdjaaz."

"Of course, what do I have to do?"

"Soon I'll be drawn into the Darkness. No matter how well I hide."

The sooner the better, I thought, putting on the polite expression of an attentive listener.

"But if I can find something first, I'll stay here for a long time. I can sense the thing. It's here in the city. Vukhdjaaz is clever," the demon reminded me yet again.

"What is this thing?"

"A horse."

Well, naturally. There's more meat on a horse than on a man. And this demon's so big. And so hungry.

"All right." It wasn't really a very tricky job. "Tomorrow I'll get you a horse. Which breed do you prefer?"

"You're stupid," the demon hissed, prodding me with a clawed finger. The prod sent me staggering back several steps. "Not a live horse, *the* Horse."

"Aaah. *That* horse, why didn't you explain straightaway?" I decided that stupidity was the quickest way into Vukhdjaaz's stomach, and it was much safer to be clever, even if I didn't understand a thing.

"I give you four days. Vukhdjaaz is clever. Get me the Horse." The demon looked at me, waiting for an answer.

"Of course, of course. I'll do everything." I still hadn't understood the point of the conversation, but I was really keen to get rid of this creature that found it so easy to appear out of walls and hide inside them.

"I'll be watching." The demon impaled me with its scarlet eyes. "Do as I order, or I'll suck the marrow out of your bones. Vukhdjaaz is clever. You can't trick him."

The demon took a step toward the gray wall and dissolved into it. I stood there for a while, trying to calm the rapid pounding of my heart, which was about to tear itself out of my chest.

What do I make of all this? First a group of crazed Doralissians pursues me, demanding that I give back their horse, then I chant a spell that has been lying in the depository at the library for Sagot only knows how many centuries, and do what the entire Order was unable to do: I drive all the demons back into the Darkness. Or almost all. Then a ravenously hungry demon, the most stupid in the entire world, picks me up like a little kitten and also demands a horse. I wonder if Vukhdjaaz and the Doralissians are looking for different horses or the same one? Maybe I should introduce them to each other, and they can make their own deal about horses? Maybe horse-breeding was coming into fashion in a big way?

I walked home—and got my cloak—without making any attempt to hide, in the complete certainty that not a single creature of the night could get me, apart from the extremely clever Vukhdjaaz. I didn't bother to change my lair, just set all my troubles aside until the morning, dropped onto the bed, and instantly fell asleep.

There were exactly six days left until the expedition to Hrad Spein.

6

DAYTIME SURPRISES

Bang! Bang! Bang!

The unceremonious hammering on the door made me leap up off the old cracked wooden bedstead and start fumbling around for my weapon. "Harold? Are you there? Open up! In the name of the Order!" a loud, deep voice shouted.

What could the Order want with me at this early hour? I glanced out through the dirty windowpane. The sun was already quite high.

"Harold! Open the door, or I'll break it in!"

Okay, try. Although, if he really is a magician of the Order, he won't need to try very hard. He'll only need to spit and half the house will be reduced to splinters. I began thinking seriously about taking a stroll through the window.

"Harold, His Magicness Artsivus requests you to come. Urgently!"

Artsivus? Why didn't he say straightaway that he was from Artsivus, instead of threatening to shatter the door?

"Just a moment. Wait," I shouted, feeling at my cloak. It was a little dirty and there were hoofprints on it, but it was perfectly wearable.

I opened the lock, drew the bolt, and took a step back. But I didn't put the crossbow away—after all, anyone could be hiding behind the name of an archmagician of the Order.

"Come in."

The door opened and there in front of me was a harmless-looking young man in a blue robe that dangled like a sack from his narrow shoulders. I would never have thought this young lad could hammer on the door so hard.

"Are you Harold? On the—" My visitor spotted the crossbow trained on him, turned gray in the face, and stopped talking.

I put the weapon away behind my back—there's no point in frightening children.

"Yes, I'm Harold."

"Master Harold. His Magicship, the head of the Order, Master Artsivus, asks you to come to him without delay."

"I see. What's happened?"

"I don't know."

"All right. Wait."

Without hurrying, I took the bag containing the magic ingredients and the gold I had received from the king out of its secret hiding place. I'm not usually so stupid as to keep my money all in one heap, especially at home. It's simpler to pass it on to a few reliable people and make the gold work for you. In a gnome bank, for instance. The money's always reliably protected by traps, locks, magic, and furious mattockmen. But I was going to need the king's gold pieces today.

"Where's the carriage?"

"Eeeh . . . ," said the apprentice, embarrassed. "I'm on foot."

"Magnificent! Then tell me, apprentice, how come you're still alive after walking all the way through the Port City to reach me? Round here they leave naïve children like you floating under the pier. Or maybe you weren't lying when you said you would break in the door, and you know how to shoot fireballs?"

The lad became even more embarrassed, and blushed.

"Well," he mumbled, "just a little."

"Okay, lead on," I sighed.

Why on earth Artsivus would take on such an awkward child as an apprentice was beyond me.

Noon. The central street of the Port City was packed solid with people. There was everybody here—from idly wandering revelers to traders in all sorts of everything.

I spotted an elderly pickpocket with two of his apprentices training under his supervision right there in the crowd. They were cutting the strings of the idle onlookers' purses. One apprentice evidently felt

my gaze on him, and gave me a tense look, but then, realizing that
I was on no closer terms with the law than himself, he winked gaily. I
winked back.

In wonderful times of long ago I also began my career with the pockets of the idle public on the Market Square. Many years have passed
since then. Nowadays no one remembers Harold the Flea, a skinny,
eternally hungry young lad roaming round the squares and streets of
the city in search of nourishment and a place to spend the night in a
dirty alley or a barracks. Those times came to an end, Harold the Flea
disappeared, and Shadow Harold appeared in Avendoom.

"Oi!" my guide shouted when someone in the crowd stepped on his
foot.

"Wake up," I whispered in his ear. "We have to get out of this crush.
Keep left, along the wall."

The torrent of people was thinner here, and we could stop jostling
with our elbows.

The crowd of humans and nonhumans was seething with gossip.
Groups of gossipmongers sprang up spontaneously first in one spot,
then another.

Rumors, rumors, rumors.

"Did you know the Nameless One is already on the march?"

"What's the king doing?"

"No, that's rubbish. There is no Nameless One!"

"Oh yes, there is! My granny told me about him, may she live in the
light!"

"What's the king doing? He's gathering an army. Taxes will go shooting up again, and the poor people will suffer."

"Hey!" I called to Artsivus's apprentice.

"Yes?"

"We've got a long, long walk to the Tower of the Order. Wouldn't it
be better to turn off onto the Street of the Bedbugs? There's no crush
there."

"Mmmm . . . ," the lad said hesitantly. "Milord Artsivus said you have
no business in the Tower of the Order. He asked me to take you to one
of the houses near here."

"All right then, let's go."

Does Artsivus think a thief will defile his holy magical sanctuary?

The number of people in the streets could be explained in the first instance by the incredibly fine weather for June. At this time of year in north Valiostr—which means in Avendoom, too—it was usually still cool, more reminiscent of early April somewhere on the southern boundaries of the kingdom. What else could you expect, with the Desolate Lands so close? But the situation right now was rather different. The sun was blazing away with all its strength. I was streaming with sweat. And I wasn't the only one. A citizen of the Border Kingdom walked past us with his apprentice. He was frying and smoking in his chain mail. The Borderland men never took their armor off, no matter where they were. It was a habit that came from living beside the Forests of Zagraba.

If this weather holds out until the end of August, then half the city will simply die of the heat. I've already heard people saying that it's a new trial visited on us by the Nameless One.

"Harold! Hey, Harold!"

I turned toward the shout. There, standing outside the Knife and Ax, waving desperately to me, was the owner of said establishment, a good fellow and my "dearest friend" Gozmo.

What does he want with me? I already have a Commission. And what a Commission! Suicidally profitable, you could say. But all the same I gave a sharp tug on the sleeve of Artsivus's apprentice and nodded for him to follow me. The lad opened his mouth to object that His Magicship was far more important than some innkeeper, but I turned my back on him and crossed to the other side of the street. The young magician had no choice but to follow me.

"What is it, Gozmo?" I asked none too amiably. "Why shout and let the whole city know that I'm Harold?

"Ah. Eer . . ." The stoop-shouldered innkeeper gave my companion an inquiring look.

"Will you stand me a beer?" I asked, nodding significantly toward the door. "We can talk in there."

"Come on in."

The inn was empty, which was only to be expected. Customers would start to appear as evening came on, in the twilight. The empty tables and benches looked strange and lonely. The fire was out. There were stools heaped up on the tables closest to the doors, with their legs sadly up toward the ceiling. Beside them the singer of the establishment, now playing the role of cleaning lady, was scrubbing away diligently with a rag. One of the bouncers was helping her. Yes, Gozmo's staff were certainly masters of all trades.

"Come over to the bar, Harold, and your friend can take a seat at that table over there. What will you have to drink, young man?"

"Water." The magician's apprentice obviously felt awkward—his face was set in an expression of astonishment that he could possibly have entered such a dubious place of his own free will.

Gozmo pulled a sour face and looked at me. "Who's your new friend?"

I shrugged, and Gozmo took a glass of water over to the apprentice's table, then came and stood facing me, behind the bar, and poured a full mug of beer from a barrel hidden underneath it. He drank that beer himself and rarely shared it with anyone. I took a large gulp and gave Gozmo an appreciative nod. It was genuinely magnificent porter, just as I had expected. My old mate Gozmo didn't poison his own innards with the rubbish that he poured for most of his regulars without any pangs of conscience.

The former thief wasn't drinking right now, though. He was shifting nervously from one foot to the other and casting wary glances in my direction. Why would that be? But he didn't say anything, and I've never been unduly curious, so I simply sipped the beer, waiting for the innkeeper to explain why he had called me over.

"So, why did you call me, my old friend?" I asked impatiently. "That's a fine beer you've stood me, of course, but what's the reason for it?"

"You know, Harold," Gozmo said nervously, giving me another wary glance. "I wanted to apologize for what happened. Believe me, I'm very sorry, if I'd known it would all turn out like that, I would never have—"

"You mean the garrinch in the duke's house?" I interrupted, playing ignorant and forgetting to mention the incident with Lanten and the fact that I knew perfectly well who the client had been.

I'm going to keep that conversation for a more appropriate moment.

"The garrinch? Ah, yes. That's what I mean," Gozmo said uncertainly, in a slightly surprised voice. He sat down on a chair, relieved to realize that I didn't intend to declare war and spill blood. "I just wanted you to know that I had absolutely no idea."

"Calm down, will you, Gozmo! What's got you so nervous all of a sudden?" I said, waving my hand magnanimously. "After all, nothing terrible happened, did it? No one got hurt. I've got other business to attend to, so I'd better be going."

"So you accept my apology?" Gozmo asked in relief.

He looked as if the full weight of the Zam-da-Mort itself had fallen from his shoulders. It was all very strange—good old Gozmo wasn't usually tormented much by his conscience. And even the fact that he hadn't told me the client was the king shouldn't be making him this nervous. In any case, Gozmo had the right to conceal the name of the client.

"Forget it," I said, and the young lad and I walked back out into the street.

"What did that man want from you?" he asked after we had walked in silence for a minute.

"Do you have a name?" I said, answering a question with a question as I watched a guard patrol go by.

"Roderick."

"Well then, Roderick, do we have much farther to go?"

"We're almost there—we go through that lane," he muttered.

"Are you certain that's our way?" I asked the young magician, jabbing my finger toward a dark, foul-smelling corridor formed by two buildings huddling close to each other. "To the Street of the Apples?"

"Yes."

I shrugged, nodded to Roderick to go first, and followed him, taking my crossbow out from under my cloak. What could I expect from this youngster who knew nothing about the customs of the Port City?

More people die in dark, smelly alleyways like this than on the border in battles with orcs and Miranuehans. But the alley turned out to be empty. When the way out onto the Street of the Apples was already close and we only had another twenty yards to go before we broke free of this narrow trench, I relaxed. And so, Roderick and I came face-to-face with five rather unfriendly-looking thugs who had appeared from the Street of the Sleepy Dog, shutting us in the narrow alley.

"What do these men want?" Roderick whispered in alarm.

I recognized the third man in the group from the Street of the Apples. "We've got serious trouble here."

"Haven't you g-got any m-money?" Roderick asked in a frightened voice.

"I wouldn't exactly say that. Only it's not money they've come for."

"F-for what, then?" asked Artsivus's apprentice, growing even more frightened.

"For my life. And I think they'll dispatch you to the next world for good measure. When I make a move, you attack the ones behind us."

"B-but I don't know how," Roderick protested. "I haven't even got a weapon."

"Then we'll die."

His only answer was a loud gulp.

Four of the men were clutching short, heavy armored-infantry swords, the kind used by the soldiers of the Border Kingdom. The most efficient weapon in confined spaces or dense ranks, where you can't turn with a long blade. The fifth man, whose right shoulder was bandaged, hung back behind the others.

"How's your health, Paleface?" I asked politely when they walked up and stopped five yards away from us.

"Better than yours will be in a moment," the assassin replied.

"Kill them!"

My crossbow gave a click and the hulk that Paleface was hiding behind started tumbling backward with a bolt in his forehead. The second ugly brute yelled and raised his sword above his head, and then there was a roar behind me and I felt the searing heat as a ball of fire the size of a good horse's head went flying past me straight at the killers. I abandoned everything, dropped down onto my belly, and put my arms over my head.

A loud boom struck my ears, I felt the earth shake, and crumbs of stone came showering down on me. Someone howled. What's the advantage of wizardry over shamanism? Wizardry takes effect instantly, while shamanism is an entire ritual. Goblins dance, orcs sing. That's why shamanism acts a lot more slowly, but the shamans don't lose any strength after they use it, unlike magicians.

The fireball, that weapon so beloved of all novice magicians, had transformed one attacker into a heap of ash, then struck the wall of the building and exploded.

Paleface was howling and yelling somewhere beside the end of the alley. I could see that his face was burned, and bloodied by small splinters of stone. A hole big enough to drive the royal carriage through had appeared in the house to the left of us. Roderick certainly hadn't been stingy with his spell.

Tearing my eyes away from Paleface, I turned toward the magician's apprentice. The young lad, totally drained of strength, was half sitting, half lying, propped up against the wall, and the two remaining thugs were staring at him in amazement.

"Let's run for it!" howled one of the killers, throwing away his sword. In his fright he obviously hadn't realized that Roderick couldn't hurt a fly right now.

They ran off in the same direction they'd just come from, stomping their feet and howling in terror. Of course, I didn't bother to follow them. I was more interested in Paleface, but he had vanished without a trace.

"Lucky bastard," I said, shaking my head in admiration.

I went across to Roderick.

"Are you alive?"

He nodded feebly, but his eyes were glowing. "I did it! That's the first time I've made that spell work!"

"Oh yes! I almost got roasted. Thanks for the help. Now let me help you up. Or the guards will come running in a moment."

Roderick gave a brief nod of his light-haired head. I helped him get up off the ground, then supported him as I led him toward the deserted Street of the Apples.

7

DISCOVERIES

The look on the face of His Magicship, Master of the Order of Valiostr, Archmagician Artsivus boded no good to my own humble personage. The old dodderer received me in his own home, located in the Inner City, right beside the king's palace. The archmagician was seated in a deep armchair and swaddled in a heap of woolen blankets that would have warmed a dead man in the very fiercest of winters, but that was still not enough for his frostbitten bones. "Harold, may you be torn limb from limb!" the old man screeched. "What have you done? Have you completely lost your mind?"

"What's happened, Your Magicship?" I really didn't understand.

"Hmm." Artsivus cast another keen glance at me. "So you don't know anything. You're as innocent as Jock the Winter-Bringer? Hmm . . ."

The old man drummed his fingers on the little table while he pondered something and then asked abruptly, "What were you doing yesterday? Mind, think before you answer me; I shall recognize a lie."

I wonder what it is I'm suspected of now? Should I confess to stealing the magical scroll? After all, it was lying there unwanted for all those years.

Years?

I strained my memory, trying to remember what the magical spell had looked like. I seemed to recall it was the only one not covered with a thick layer of dust. That was why I'd chosen it from among all the others. But if it wasn't dusty, that meant it had been put there quite recently. . . .

I began my story in a very roundabout fashion. The archmagician, however, showed no signs of impatience and didn't interrupt me. He

simply knitted his bushy eyebrows whenever I started throwing in unnecessary details or long descriptions in an attempt to divert him. Then
I decided to tell him about the scroll after all, and then about the unexpected effect it had when I took a chance and tried the spell on the Doralissians. Surprisingly enough, the old man wasn't even interested, as if
it wasn't me that had driven all the demons out of the city. The archmagician was only concerned about the Doralissians.

"Say that again, what was it they were shouting?"

"Well, something like: 'Give us back our horse.'"

"Did you hear anything else about horses last night?"

"No," I lied, deciding not to mention Vukhdjaaz, although he had
harped on about some horse or other as well. I was interested to see if
the archmagician would notice my lie.

"Good." Artsivus didn't spot my fib. "The scroll is very interesting,
especially since I'm sure that no one in the Order has ever heard of any
such spell."

The old man squirmed in his chair, adjusted the edge of a blanket
that had slipped off onto the floor, and looked at me thoughtfully again.

"So where is the Horse?" he suddenly cooed in a sweet voice.

Only there was nothing sweet about the look in his eyes.

"What would I want with a horse? What would I do with it?"

The archmagician knitted his brows and said nothing for a moment,
but a hint of doubt appeared in his eyes. "You mean it wasn't you who
stole the Horse from Archmagician O'Stand's house last night?"

"He must be raving mad, if he keeps a horse in his house!" I exclaimed in amazement.

"What horse are you talking about, thief? Yesterday a magical stone—
the Horse of Shadows—was stolen by persons unknown from the house
of Archmagician O'Stand, who came here from Filand. We were planning to use it to drive the demons back into the Darkness. But now it
has disappeared!"

"But the demons have gone. I pronounced that spell."

"Yes, they've gone." The archmagician nodded. "And it worries me
very much that you did what the entire Order couldn't do. How did that
scroll, which no one knew about, come to be where it was? Who else
paid a visit to this Bolt of yours and asked about plans of the forbidden
zone? Who is the Master? Why did the killers attack you and Roderick?

Who wanted the Stone, and how could anyone have found out about it?"

"But why did you immediately suspect me, Your Magicship?" I asked, squinting at a nearby armchair.

"Sit down, you might as well," said the archmagician, spotting my glance. "Who else could have pulled off a trick like that, Harold? Not a single magical trap was activated, the Stone simply disappeared. Any fool can see it was the work of a master."

"Well, I'm not the only thief in the city. There are at least two more men in the capital who are capable of doing a job like that. But what does O'Stand himself say?"

"Nothing. He's dead." The archmagician closed his eyes wearily. "The servants found him with his throat cut. He was killed like some drunk on a spree at Stark's Stables. An archmagician of Filand! It's more than just a political scandal, it's a serious blow to the prestige of the Order of Valiostr!"

"Did he come here especially because of this Horse?"

"Yes. We summoned him as soon as the creatures of night appeared in the city. Filand owns—used to own—the Stone, a great relic that can be used to drive demons into the Darkness."

"Are you concerned that the dark creatures might reappear?"

"I'm by no means certain that they have gone anywhere," Artsivus muttered. "What makes you think that the spell worked correctly? Perhaps that demon simply lied to you?"

Actually, it was me who had lied to Artsivus, when I told him that after I read the scroll I saw a demon appear, yell that the spell was dragging him into the Darkness, and then disappear. Of course, nothing of the sort had happened, but I didn't want any magicians who specialized in demons scurrying about after me in an attempt to capture Vukhdjaaz.

Of course, he had to be exterminated, but right now I had to take a necessary risk, otherwise the magicians would shut me away somewhere behind a hundred locks just in order to lure a real live demon into their clutches.

Demons, as everyone knows, are immune to almost all kinds of magic, and therefore represent a substantial and dangerous mystery. A mystery that many generations of magicians have puzzled over. After all, there's nothing a battle magician would like more than to acquire immunity to his enemy's spells. And if the Order had a real live demon, then it would do everything in its power to discover the secret of invulnerability to magic. It takes very special objects like the Stones to set the demons trembling. And, of course, demons can also be trapped using the spells on scrolls written by anonymous know-it-alls or the demonologists of the Order.

"How should I know?" I asked, shrugging and raising my honest glance to Artsivus's face. "That brute disappeared. And what difference does it make now who has this Horse?"

"It can be used, not just to drive demons away, but also to summon them," the archmagician said wearily, and started coughing again.

"But what have the Doralissians got to do with all this?"

"Well, it happens to be their artifact. The Filanders took it from the goat-men about twenty years ago for trying to cheat them in a horse sale. It was all fair and square, of course, according to the terms of the contract, but this Stone was something like a holy relic to the goat-men. They've been trying to get it back any way they can. Time and again they've tried to buy it back, offering immense sums of money and entire herds of the finest horses, but the Order of Filand has always refused. And it is right to do so. The Stone contains a great power, although only magicians with a diploma in demonology can control it. And also the demons themselves."

"You mean to say that if this Stone falls into the hands of a demon . . ."

"No one knows what would happen then. The demon could release all his brothers from the Darkness or, if he's clever, keep the Horse for himself. And then no spell in the world could do him any harm. He would be stabilized. Magically neutral, if you know what that term means."

"Then why hasn't one of those brutes already grabbed the Horse for himself?" The question was simply begging to be asked.

"I don't know where the Doralissians got the Horse from. Perhaps one of the gods gave it to them on a whim, but the Stone has a special property: No demon can take it in his hands unless a human or a Doralissian gives it to him voluntarily."

Vukhdjaaz is clever. The voice in my head had a superior ring to it now.

"And now I have to find this bauble for you?"

"You get on with the king's Commission," the Master of the Order said dismissively. "We'll search for the Horse ourselves, since you have nothing to do with the business."

"That's not what the Doralissians think," I said, shaking my head.

The goat-men could be a real problem for me in the days ahead.

"I wonder why they decided that Shadow Harold was involved? Either they drew the same conclusions as I did, or someone has set you up, thief."

"I've got plenty of enemies," I admitted as casually as I could, but something clicked in my head. The cogwheels were already creaking and groaning as all the pieces of this dwarves' puzzle gradually slipped into place.

"Be careful. The king needs you. Perhaps I ought to give you an escort of magicians of the Order?"

"No," I retorted hastily. "Thanks for the offer, Your Magicship. It would only be an unnecessary burden for me. I'll deal with the Doralissians myself."

"Very well, very well." Artsivus had recovered his good mood. "It's your choice, and I shan't insist, although I ought to."

"Can I ask a few questions?"

"Yes, of course."

"What can you tell me about the Stain?"

"The Forbidden Territory?" the old man muttered. "The Order knows practically nothing about it. A white patch on the map of the city and a black stain on the reputation of magicians. We can see the streets and buildings from the tower, but you understand that in this case the eyes should not be trusted."

"Well, can you tell me at least something about it?"

"You already know how it appeared. . . . Afterward, a black blizzard came swooping down on Avendoom. And then all sorts of things started appearing out of it. The Order of Magicians created the circle with the help of the only archmagician left alive. Artsis was his name. The circle made it possible to erect the wall, and that served as a boundary. No one can creep out of the Forbidden Territory into the residential quarters of Avendoom anymore, and the city folk don't go poking their noses inside the wall."

"But what's happening in there now?"

"Who knows, Harold? After the Rainbow Horn produced such a

different effect from what the Order had calculated, the archmagician who had managed to save it died on the way out. His apprentice, who later became the Master of the Order, carried the Horn out of the territory while the blizzard was gathering. And another five magicians were left behind forever in the tower. What happened to them, I don't know. Or what happened to the inhabitants of the district. As he was dying the archmagician said they had been mistaken about someone."

"What did those words mean?"

"I don't know. In one day, or rather, night, the Order of Valiostr lost six archmagicians, including the master, Panarik. When everything calmed down and the wall was erected, they decided to get rid of the Horn, put it somewhere out of harm's way. Hrad Spein was the ideal place. By that time it was already abandoned and nobody ever went in there. They carefully added power to the Horn so that it would hold the Nameless One at bay, and took it there."

What a fascinating conversation this was! My head was spinning. How much nicer to be conversing with a pretty woman . . . or with an exotic creature like Miralissa. "But then how did the information about the Horn end up in the tower?"

"After the artifact was buried in Hrad Spein, one of the magicians took the journals recording its hiding place to the old Tower of the Order. At least, I hope he got them there. He never came back from the Forbidden Territory. You see? I know no more than the old women gossiping in the Market Square. I can only give you one piece of advice. Set out at night. I know it seems far more dangerous, all the creatures of darkness are terrified of sunlight, and the night is their natural realm, but . . . The thing is, thief, that those who have gone to the Forbidden Territory during the hours of darkness have sometimes actually come back."

Yes. I'd heard stories about that, too. Many men had decided to take the chance for the sake of the treasure. There used to be a gnomes' bank on the Street of the Sleepy Cat. And there was still a lot of gold in it.

"But those who went during the day have never come back."

"Where in the tower should I look for the information on Hrad Spein?"

"If it's there, it's on the second floor. In the archivist's room."

"Traps, locks, guards?"

"No need to worry about that," the master sniffed. "It all happened too suddenly."

The old man began coughing into his fist and Roderick came in again with a glass, but the archmagician frowned and waved it aside.

"I'm tired, Harold. The long years hang heavy on my bones. Relieve me of your presence, if you would be so kind."

When I was already out in the corridor and the archmagician's apprentice was closing the door, I heard the old man's weary voice again:

"Hey, Harold."

"Yes?"

"When are you planning to set out for the Forbidden Territory?"

"In about three days, when I'm fully prepared."

"Good. Don't forget that the king is expecting you. Now be on your way."

I shrugged in irritation—I'd never had any trouble with my memory—and left Artsivus's apartments without saying another word.

Now I had to see about finding a new place to live, and I knew someone prepared to provide me with one for an unlimited period of time, absolutely free of charge.

"We're here, milord." The coachman decked out in velvet livery politely opened the door of the carriage and bowed.

It was several seconds before I realized that my own humble personage had been referred to as "milord." It felt strange, somehow—no one had ever called me that before.

Well, of course, I could understand the coachman. A man who had been visiting the sick archmagician couldn't be some kind of low thief, could he? He was more likely some rich count in disguise, someone who had decided to take a ride around Avendoom incognito.

I got out of the carriage and set off toward the main gate of the Cathedral of the Gods on Cathedral Square, which was located at the meeting point of three parts of Avendoom: the Outer City, the Inner City, and the City of Artisans and Magicians.

The priests had managed to grab themselves a huge piece of the city, every bit as large as the grounds of the king's palace. In fact, to be perfectly honest, Cathedral Square could quite easily have held two of Stalkon's palaces.

The cathedral was the largest site in all the Northern Lands at which all the twelve gods of Siala were honored. So there was no need to tramp across half the city to find the particular shrine that you were interested in, the temporary residence of some individual god: You could simply come to the square, go in through the main gates that were open by day and night, and then choose the one to whom you wished to address your prayers.

The gods!

I smirked blasphemously.

The gods were not very generous when it came to gracing the world they had created with their own presence. In earlier times, when Siala was young, during the beginning of beginnings, when people had only just appeared, following the elves, the orcs, the ogres, the gnomes, and the dwarves, the gods still walked the roads, working wonders, punishing evildoers, and rewarding the righteous.

But eventually they tired of the vanity of earth, and they left to concern themselves with their own "important" affairs, as the priests called them, affairs incomprehensible to mere humans. I don't know, maybe they are important, but I don't have too much faith in the power of the gods. Nothing but stories for snot-nosed little kids, and the ravings of crazy fanatics. Well, naturally, I believe in Sagot and his power, but I don't really think he was a god. Some say he was just a successful thief in the old times and many stories about his adventures are still preserved to this very day. But the sly priests were quick to promote him to the rank of a god, in order to increase the flow of gold into the coffers of their shrines. Because thieves and swindlers are a superstitious crowd, and they really need to believe in someone.

"Do you struggle with the Darkness within yourself?" one of the two priests standing at the main gates asked me.

"I annihilate the Darkness," I replied, with the standard ritual phrase.

"Enter then, and address Them," the second priest pronounced solemnly.

Naturally, I followed this brilliant recommendation from these two old men who had nothing else to do but roast themselves in the hot sun while greeting and seeing off every visitor.

Interestingly enough, there were no guards at the entrance of the cathedral. I'd heard the priests had forbidden it. And in principle they were right, since the plug-ugly faces of the servants of the law could very easily frighten away half of the city's residents, depriving the cathedral of a substantial element of its income.

But there were guardsmen strolling about inside the grounds—around the flower beds and whispering fountains, the statues of the gods and their shrines—gradually going insane from the heat in their cuirasses and helmets. Of course, they were all as bad-tempered as orcs on the march. And the reason for their bad temper was no great secret, either. The guards sent to the cathedral were those colleagues of Frago Lanten's who had committed some offense or been caught taking bribes and extorting money.

A pair of the poor souls in orange and white went parading past me. Their glances slid searchingly over my figure, probing for something to take objection to, an opportunity to stick the handle of a halberd in my side without a priest noticing. But I simply smiled amiably and couldn't resist giving the dourly furious martyrs a cheery wave.

Ah! How I love teasing a giant in a cage!

The guards frowned darkly, took a firmer grip on their weapons, and started toward me, with the clear intention of battering my sides. But, just as I expected, they didn't get very far.

A priest appeared in their path as if out of thin air and started reciting the divine moral teaching. The soldiers' unshaven faces immediately assumed such a bored and weary expression that I very nearly shed a tear for them. The lads were strictly forbidden to argue back or to show any disrespect to the servants of the cathedral. On pain of losing their pensions. And so all they could do was listen, listen, and listen again for the thousandth time.

I walked along a neat pathway paved with square slabs of stone, rounded a sparkling and foaming fountain in the form of a knight running his lance through a massive ogre at full gallop, and came out into the cathedral yard, where the statues of the gods stood, with supplicants and visitors from the city and the neighboring regions constantly weaving around them.

There weren't many pilgrims from other parts of the kingdom to be seen as yet. They usually came flooding in for the spring festival of the gods, and so right now the yard wasn't very crowded. There were just a few men standing beside the statue of Sagra. From the way they were dressed I recognized them as soldiers.

I cast a casual glance over the eleven male and female statues, the gods and goddesses of Siala standing there before me. And then I looked at the empty pedestal where the twelfth statue ought to have stood, the statue of Sagot.

Somehow it had happened that in all the world there was only one image of the god of thieves. Evidently he didn't really welcome close interest in his own person.

This statue of Sagot was in the Forbidden Territory of the city. When the fiasco with the Rainbow Horn happened, it had wound up on the other side of the wall. And no one had been able to re-create the image of the god of thieves. Even the priests didn't know what Sagot was supposed to look like, and so they had decided not to take any risk of committing sacrilege, and for the time being the pedestal on which the god ought to stand had been left empty.

The patron of thieves and swindlers clearly had no objections to this. In any case, the priests had not seen any signs, except for a few after the fifth jug of wine, but they were so vague and mysterious that no one had taken them seriously. And so now empty marble pedestals stood in all of Sagot's shrines.

Right now, though, there was a vagabond in dirty boots sitting cross-legged on the pedestal in front of me and holding out a coarse clay bowl. Strangely enough, the priests didn't seem to notice the blasphemy of it. Overcome by curiosity, I set off along the row of the other gods toward the beggar in the farthest section of the small green yard. As I walked along I took off my cloak and wrapped my crossbow in it.

"You have a fine seat there," I said in a friendly manner as I halted in front of the stranger.

He cast a rapid glance at me from under the dark hood concealing his face and shook his cup for alms.

"Are you quite comfortable? Haven't your legs turned numb?" I asked, pretending not to notice his gesture.

"I'm a lot more comfortable than you are just at the moment, Shadow Harold," a mocking voice said.

"Do I know you?" I was beginning to feel annoyed that every last rat in Avendoom seemed to know who I was.

"Oh no." The tramp shrugged and rattled his cup again. "But I've heard about you."

"Nothing but the very best, I hope." I had already completely lost interest in the beggar, and was about to set off along a barely visible path, overgrown with tall grass, into the depths of the cathedral grounds, when the beggar's voice stopped me:

"Toss in a coin, Harold, and you'll get a free piece of advice."

"That's strange," I said, turning back toward the seated man. "If the advice is free, why should I give you a coin?"

"Come on, Harold, I have to eat and sleep somewhere, don't I?"

The stranger had intrigued me. I rummaged in my pockets, fished out a piece of small change, and laughed as I flung it into the bowl he was holding out toward me. The copper disk clattered forlornly against the bottom. The beggar raised the bowl to his nose to see what I had given him and heaved a sigh.

"Is that just the way you are, or are all thieves that mean?"

"You ought to thank me for spending time here and at least giving you something!" I exclaimed indignantly.

"Thank you. So shall I give you that advice, then?"

"If you would be so kind."

"Then pay in gold, I don't work for coppers."

I felt like taking him by the scruff of the neck and giving him a good shaking. This weasel could live well for an entire month on a gold piece. But I was already snared in the net that the cunning rogue had spread, and I was even willing to pay a gold piece to hear whatever raving nonsense he had to tell me.

"All right, here you are." I twirled the yellow coin between my fingers. "But first I'd like to see your face."

"Nothing could be simpler," said the beggar, and he threw back his hood.

An entirely unremarkable set of features. Coarse, weatherbeaten, no longer young, covered with gray stubble. A pointed nose, bright eyes. I didn't know him.

"Here's your payment." I tossed the weighty little disk into the cup, and the tramp smiled triumphantly. "But bear in mind that if the advice is bad, I'll shake the money back out of you! Well?"

"This is the advice," said the beggar, pulling his hood back up again.

"Don't stand on Selena. Walk on your own feet, your own feet, Harold, and then you might live to a ripe old age."

"Selena? What's Selena? And why shouldn't I stand on it?" I asked. "What kind of riddles are these?"

But the beggar had shut up as tight as a clam.

"Listen, I'm not joking. Either give me my money back, or tell me where you know me from and what this stupid riddle means."

"Eh-e-eb-b-m-a-a-a," the beggar moaned, making himself out to be a deaf-mute idiot.

But it didn't escape my attention that, as if by magic, the coin had disappeared from the tramp's hands into some secret place under his clothes.

"Stop playing the fool! Give me my money back!" I cried in fury, and took a step toward the swindler.

"Would you be mocking a holy fool?" a coarse, rasping voice asked behind my back.

"May darkness reduce me to dust if he's a holy fool! He's a real swindler!" I just couldn't believe that I had been duped.

"Move on, my dear fellow, move on. People come here to commune with the gods, and you're creating a commotion," said the sergeant of the guard, standing slightly ahead of his morose subordinates. He gave me a menacing smile. "Otherwise we shall have to escort you out of this holy place."

"Moooooo," the "deaf-mute" lowed in support of the guard, and began nodding his head wildly.

There was nothing left to do but shrug and withdraw, seething with righteous fury and indignation. I was surrounded on all sides by thieves and swindlers.

I had been duped with deft skill, like some oafish peasant, caught out by one of the standard tricks practiced by swindlers ever since the dawn of time. Well, Sagot be with him! It won't bankrupt me.

The track wound between green gardens and flower beds. A couple of times I ran into priests going about their business, but they took no notice of me, as if visitors were always walking about in the inner territory of the cathedral.

The path wound to the left and rounded a bed of pale blue flowers reaching all their petals up toward the warm sunshine, then approached a massive building made of huge blocks of gray stone. And there was the dark archway that led to the dwelling of my only friend in this world.

The shadows, afraid of the sunlight, had squeezed themselves tight up against the ancient gray walls, and after the heat of the summer day the coolness that pervaded the narrow tunnel seemed like a blessing from the gods.

My footsteps echoed off the low vaults. I had almost walked right through when my guts suddenly twitched in agony as a familiar grip took hold of me by the sides of my chest and lifted me up off the ground.

The hands were followed out of the wall by shoulders and a head. The rest of the body remained out of view.

"Vukhdjaaz is clever," said the demon.

"Hi there," I said with a joyful smile, greeting him like my own dear mom, and not a demon of the Darkness.

"Vukhdjaaz is clever." The vile beast decided to put me back down on the ground anyway, and then surveyed me suspiciously. "You have the Horse?"

"I was just working on that."

"Quicker!" the demon hissed, and his bright scarlet eyes glinted menacingly in the semidarkness. "I can't hold out for long."

"I need just a little more time."

"Bring the Horse in three days, or I'll suck the marrow out of your bones!"

"But how will I find you?"

"Call me by name when you have the Horse, and I will appear."

Vukhdjaaz shot me another piercing glance and dissolved into the wall.

I leaned back against the rough surface of the stone, catching my breath. Oo-ooph! That sort of thing could give you a heart attack. I never expected the cursed monster to appear again so soon, and during the day, too. Something had to be done about Vukhdjaaz.

I already had a rough idea of where to start looking for the Horse. Whoever it was that set the Doralissians on me had it. No doubt about that. Now I needed to find these persons unknown and filch the Stone before nightfall the day after tomorrow, or I'd have my marrow sucked out. . . .

I walked up a massive stairway with chipped and battered steps, and then along the corridor leading to the quarters of the priests of Sagot. Two priests standing beside a marble tub from which protruded a feeble scruffy bunch of leaves that was supposed to be a palm tree stopped discussing the affairs of the god of thieves and began staring at me. I nodded and formed my fingers into the sign of our guild. They relaxed, lowered their heads to greet me in reply, and went back to their philosophical dispute. I was no longer an outsider to them.

It's no secret that only former thieves and swindlers become priests of Sagot—this is a centuries-old tradition that no one has any intention of abandoning.

When the corridor came to an end, I walked up another stairway to the second floor, where the priests had their quarters. The door I was interested in was the second on the right. It was a rather ordinary-looking door, with its old, dark wooden surface scarred with the deep furrows left by the swords of unfriendly visitors.

But the former thieves were well able to stand up for themselves, and they always carried a knife concealed under their placid gray robes. And so, my friend had told me, those who had invaded the calm sanctuary of this shrine had been buried in the garden, and their swords hung in the prayer hall of the cathedral to discourage anyone else from entering this peaceful and godly place with naked weapons. Sagot might be the least of the gods, less menacing and mighty than his brothers and sisters, but he and his votaries would always defend themselves.

I knocked on the door. On entering without waiting to be invited, I found myself in a large, well-lit room—a hall, in fact. The walls were painted in cheerful colors, a contrast to the dreary, gray corridors that was a delight to the eye. I glanced round this rather wealthy interior, assessing the value of the contents (well, I can't help it, it's a habit). Expensive paintings by well-known masters of the past, illustrating scenes from divine mythology; a yellow Sultanate carpet on the floor; wonderful furniture; a miniature gold pedestal of Sagot. My friend certainly held a high position in the hierarchy of servants of the god of thieves.

"Harold! My boy!" A huge, fat man in the grayish-white cassock of a priest got up from the table and came toward me, throwing his arms wide. "What brings you here? It must be a hundred years since you last came to see this old man!"

"Hello, For. Glad to see you alive, well, and fat!" I laughed as I embraced the old priest.

"Can't be helped, it's the job," he laughed in reply.

"Hey! Hey! Hey! I saw that, you old rogue! Come on, give back my purse!" I exclaimed. "So you haven't lost your touch, you old thief?"

"How can we old men possibly compare with you youngsters?" For replied jokingly, and tossed me the purse he had just removed from my belt. "Come to the table, I was just about to dine."

"You're always dining, whatever time of day I arrive. Serving Sagot has made you three times the size you used to be."

"Sagot's will must be done," For said with a doleful shrug. "You sit here, I'll bring your favorite wine."

He laughed, winked at me, and went through into the next room, puffing and panting. I sat on a massive chair, solid and strong enough to support For, and put my cloak with the crossbow wrapped in it on the table.

Old For—"Sticky Hands For." One of the most famous master thieves of former times, who in years gone by had carried out such daring robberies on the most influential houses that his feats of thievery were still talked about in our professional guild to this very day.

For was the man who had first noticed that skinny, constantly hungry youth, Harold the Flea, taken him under his wing, and started to teach him the art of the Supreme Mastery instead of petty pickpocketing.

For ten years he struggled and strained with me, until finally Shadow Harold emerged, with a skill equal to his teacher's. But it was a long time now since For had retired and entered the service of Sagot.

The good priest, Brother For, "Protector of the Hands."

That title still set me laughing; I simply couldn't believe that the most successful and talented thief of all had actually retired. Of all the living creatures in this insane and dangerous world, the only one I trusted was my teacher and friend.

"Here I am." For's red face beamed a triumphant smile. He was holding a pair of dust-covered bottles in each hand.

"Amber Tears!" I exclaimed.

"Precisely! Old stock, the finest wine of the bright elves from beyond the Mountains of the Dwarves. You'd better appreciate it."

"I already am."

"I was scarcely hoping to see you for the next few years, kid. There are all sorts of rumors creeping round the city."

"Rumors!" I snorted. "What sort of rumors?"

"Well, they say you're at daggers drawn with Markun and sooner or later things will end badly. It's not yet clear exactly for which one of you, but bets are being placed."

"Oh, really?"

"Really."

"I hope you've put your money on the right side?" I chuckled.

"But of course! According to other gossips, Frago Lanten shut you away in the Gray Stones. And then some claimed the Doralissians were searching very hard for a certain Harold. So tell me, kid, are these mere rumors, or have you got yourself into some kind of fix?" For gave me a quizzical look as he gnawed on a pork rib.

"Not exactly rumors," I began cautiously. "The entire world seems to have gone crazy, For."

"May Sagot save your wayward soul," the priest sighed, and set the gnawed bone down to one side. "The world is poised on the brink of a great war, Harold, and you're still wasting time on your idiotic subterfuges. If everything I've heard is right, it's time for you to disappear. To somewhere in the Lowland. Although I don't think everything's calm there, either. The Nameless One is only the beginning, my old bones can feel it. He'll provide the initial impetus, be the fuse, as the gnomes say, that ignites the powder keg. Then it will choose for itself exactly how to blow up our fragile world. The orcs will get a taste of freedom. Miranueh will break out and run wild, Garrak will go for the twin Empires' jugular, then they'll go for each other, the dwarves will go for the gnomes, the gnomes for the dwarves. We'll be drowning in blood, mark my words."

"You think so?"

"Harold, my little one. You're an intelligent man. I knew what I was doing when I spent the best years of my life on you. The learning you received is easily a match for any nobleman's. How many of the books in my library have you read? All of them? But you still think like a five-year-old child. There'll be war, mark my words, there will. It's inevitable. Unless some little miracle happens."

"Sagot's will be done," I muttered gloomily, twirling the glass of wine in my hands.

"His will be done," For repeated mechanically, and took a huge bite out of a crusty bun. "So what was it that brought you to me?" he asked when he finished chewing.

"What, can't I even visit an old friend now?" I asked, genuinely offended, and knitted my brows in a frown.

"Not when it would be wiser to lie low. But then, you always were stubborn and took unnecessary risks," said the priest, gesturing forlornly. "So there's nothing you need from me, then?"

"Yes, there is," I sighed.

"Aha!" For declared triumphantly. "*Quod erat demonstrandum!* I haven't lost my grip on logic yet. So what do you want from a fat old man?"

"Refuge for a couple of nights until I set out on a Commission."

"We have some free cells. Perhaps you might even turn into a priest?" chuckled the former thief, filling the glasses again. "Wait! What Commission? Are your brains completely addled, Harold? You could lose your head here, and yet you're still chasing after money. That's the absolute acme of greed!"

"It's not what I wanted, just the way things have turned out."

For fixed me once again with the gaze of his brown button eyes and sighed as he refilled his empty glass. "Tell me about it."

So I told him. Beginning with that ill-fated night when darkness tempted me into paying a visit to Count Patin. For listened without speaking, biting his plump lips and sometimes scratching the wooden table with a fork, as if he were making notes on it. He only stopped me once, to question me in detail about Paleface, and then shook his head with a frown.

"I don't know any assassin like that in the city. Strange. Where did he come from?"

My story took quite a while, and when I finished my throat was dry. For splashed out some more wine for me and I nodded gratefully.

"You're four times a fool, Harold. You accepted the Commission, although your life would have been in less danger if you'd gone to the Gray Stones. You used a spell nobody knew anything about, and ended up with a hungry demon on your back. You couldn't kill Paleface when you had the chance, and now he'll come back to haunt you again and again. You've been taken for a ride. And some mysterious Master no one's ever heard of before has put in an appearance. Do you admit you're an ass?"

I nodded.

"And you're even more of an ass if you intend to go wandering into the Forbidden Territory."

"It will help me survive in Hrad Spein. Without a map I could be wandering around in there for centuries. Like it or not, I have to, For."

He said nothing, thinking something over.

"Are you sure you really have to make this expedition?"

"Uh-huh."

"You're a fool, oh, what a fool. What was I thinking of when I took you on as an apprentice? All right, listen. Only go there at night. You'll get over the wall without any problems. Better do that in the Port City, beside Stark's old stables. It's a dangerous area, but it won't be your first time in that kind of place. You'll come out straight onto the Street of Men, from there you can get to the Street of the Sleepy Cat, then on to the Street of the Magicians. Don't even stick your nose out onto Grave-yard Street—you know why. The Street of the Sleepy Cat is fairly quiet. If everything goes well, make your way over the roofs—I hope the cladding hasn't rotted through yet and it'll take your weight. Traveling way up there is inconvenient, of course, but it's safe—nobody's heard that dead men have learned to fly yet. On the Street of the Sleepy Cat there's an old statue of Sagot—it's the only quiet spot in the area. You can wait out a spot of bother there, if need be. But you must return from the Forbidden Territory before morning, otherwise you'll stay in there forever."

"How do you know all this?" I asked, amazed.

"How?" For chuckled. "I wandered round the place a bit in my younger days—don't look at me like that, and close your mouth. The gnomes had a bank on the Street of the Sleepy Cat, remember? So I paid it a visit. I couldn't actually get inside, the doors were really solidly made, but I saw all sorts of things. None of your toothy-fanged bug-eyed monsters. No, I won't lie, I didn't see anything like that. In fact, I didn't meet anyone at all. The place was empty. The streets were dead, as if everyone had just disappeared. Nothing but the wind and strange sounds, and all sorts of visions, too, hideous abominations. I won't try to frighten you, maybe you won't see anything of the sort. But you take a piece of meat with you and wrap it as tight as you can in elfin drokr. That material won't let through any moisture or any smell. And if, Sagot forbid, you happen to run into some bloodthirsty beast or some dead men from the cemetery, you'll be able to distract them for a few minutes with the meat. Well, I suppose that's all. Don't trust your eyes and ears, just do the job and get out of there. Harold, get out of there as quick as you can."

"And what about the Street of the Magicians?"

"What I don't know, I don't know. I never got that far, kid. What I saw on the Street of Men and the Street of the Sleepy Cat will last me for the rest of my life. The first was more or less calm, but the second was full of all sorts of er . . . er . . . unpleasant things."

"But why not try to get into the Forbidden Territory from the Street of the Roofers? It's a lot closer, and safer, too, it seems to me."

"Well, you see, Harold, the problem is that no one who has tried entering the Forbidden Zone from the Roofers' side has ever been seen again. So is it really worth taking the risk?"

We both said nothing for a while.

"All right then? Come on, I'll show you where you can sleep. But then again, why don't you stay here with me?"

"Thanks, but I have to get a few things done in town." I got up from the table and picked up my cloak.

"So when have you decided to go?"

"Tonight."

"Tonight? Didn't you say in a couple of days?" the priest asked in surprise.

"Well, I can change my mind, can't I?" I muttered, heading for the door. "Be seeing you, For."

"Good luck, kid. You'll need plenty of it," my old teacher said. "And I'll think about what we can do with that demon of yours."

Evening was coming on, and I hurried to reach the City of Magicians before all the shops closed. Otherwise I would have to fight whoever lived behind the magic wall with my bare hands.

8

CITY OF MAGICIANS

The inner yard of the cathedral was empty; all the faithful had gone home long ago. As I walked toward the exit, I cast a sideways glance at Sagot's pedestal. Just as I expected, the beggar was long gone, and my gold piece with him.

Even in these troubled times the City of Magicians presented a very colorful spectacle.

The wide streets were lined with houses that displayed fanciful architecture, each one like a miniature palace, with a bright-colored tiled roof, lancet windows, and fancy little towers. And every house and every street strove to outdo all of its neighbors, upstaging them with its own prim, tidy beauty.

It was evening, and the lamps on the streets were burning with flames of different colors—pale blue, red, crimson, green, poisonous yellow, and orange. The lamps were magical, and they were always lit every night, no matter what happened in the city. Yet another wonder of Avendoom, spoken of at every crossroads in this world—the lamps lit up on their own, as soon as evening started drawing in, and they went out in the morning with the first rays of sunlight.

On that evening the streets of the City of Magicians were absolutely jam-packed with people. Spontaneous drunken revelry flared up on all sides, like forest fires. The people were celebrating. For a short time at least the citizens of Avendoom had been liberated from the terrors of the night and thoughts of the army of the Nameless One. They were all singing the praises of the Order and Archmagician Artsivus.

At long last the magicians had apparently succeeded in driving the fearsome beasts of the night out of Avendoom.

I merely chuckled. There was no way I was going to take offense at Artsivus for his enterprise in usurping the glorious role of vanquisher of demons. I had no use for that glory myself anyway. I was simply very amused by the move, which was worthier of sly merchants than the master of the high and mighty Order. I wondered how many similar glorious "occasions of victory" the magicians had been able to claim as their own in order to reinforce their own position. Never mind, it was none of my business.

The wide Street of the Sparks was overflowing with magical pictures. Every shop there felt obliged to outdo the one next door by creating more magical illusions to attract as many customers as possible. Above one little shop bright orange letters appeared, and then were transformed into a flock of illusory pigeons. Flapping their wings, the birds soared up into the evening sky, fused together into a small white cloud that sank down to the roof of the shop, and then turned back into letters again.

The people in the street took absolutely no notice of these wonders. There were more impressive things than that to be seen here. For instance, the sight of bolts of illusory lightning slaying an illusory ogre could have kept you enthralled for a year at least.

I walked straight through an illusion of a dragon and found myself in front of a perfectly ordinary-looking house. There weren't any showers of fiery rain or horrific monsters or magicians in brightly glowing silver cloaks on show here. Never mind that—there wasn't even a shop sign. This little trading establishment didn't need to attract simpleminded clients with more money than sense. And the prices here were so high that not many people were willing to buy.

But people in the know came here, to this modest little establishment—they didn't go to the shops bursting at the seams with magical baubles and bright-colored phantoms on the Street of the Sparks.

I pushed the door, and the little bell jangled merrily. Many visitors would have been astonished at the total absence of goods on display. But when someone came here, the owner himself carefully selected the things the customer needed from the storeroom at the back of the shop.

"Who's that the Darkness has dragged in now?" exclaimed a low, none-too-polite voice, sounding like a bumblebee buzzing over a field of clover. "We're closing, clear out!"

A short, stocky figure emerged from the dark inner room. If I stood beside him, the top of the shopkeeper's head would barely have reached up to my chest.

Like all dwarves, he had a massive forehead, small, deep-set black eyes, and a heavy, protruding lower jaw. A powerful, barrel-shaped torso. Strong, muscular arms. And an obnoxious personality.

For some reason, many ignorant philistines from the deep provinces always get dwarves and gnomes confused. In fact, dwarves are fundamentally different from their relatives the gnomes. Gnomes are smaller and look less robust, and they also do something that no dwarf would ever do even under pain of death—they wear beards.

"Good evening, Master Honchel," I said.

"Ah-ah-ah," the dwarf drawled, wiping his huge hands on his leather apron. "Master Harold. Good evening to you. And I was just about to fling you out of the shop. Haven't seen you in a long time. How's your eyesight?"

"No complaints." Honchel was referring to my night vision, which I had improved with the help of an elixir bought in his shop six months earlier.

"And what brings you to me, especially at closing time?"

"Purchases."

"Large ones?" The dwarf screwed up his eyes cunningly, already figuring out how much money he could squeeze out of me.

"That depends how things go: what the goods are like."

"Come now, Master Harold, have you ever had reason to be dissatisfied with the range of goods in my shop?"

"Not so far, but you must admit, dear Master Honchel, that there's always a first time for everything."

"Not in my shop!" The dwarf laughed and led me into the back room. "I get my goods from the very finest magicians in the Order. And there are numerous items that I get from distant lands."

What's true is true. Master Honchel was one of the few dwarves who had stayed in Valiostr and not gone back to his mountains after the king concluded a treaty with the gnomes for the purchases of cannon. I don't know how long it will take before the dwarves overcome their resentment and return to Valiostr, together with all their goods, but in the meantime the ones like Master Honchel will certainly be able to make their fortunes three or four times over.

"What are you interested in, Master Harold? Something standard or something special?"

"Both," I said, stopping behind the dwarf at a large table piled high with crates, large boxes, small boxes, chests, and caskets.

We sat down at the table and, as always, the bargaining began, which I can't stand. Because bargaining with a dwarf is harder than killing a h'san'kor, for instance.

"Be more specific, it's getting late," Honchel said with a frown, pretending to be terribly busy.

Like hell he was; you couldn't have lured him away from me now with all the treasure of the dragons.

"Twenty-five crossbow bolts with spirits of fire, the same number with spirits of ice, a hundred standard, armor-piercing. Part of the order to be delivered. I can't take everything away with me."

"Oho," said the dwarf, whistling and opening his eyes wide. "Are you going to drive the gnomes out of the Steel Mines?"

I didn't answer, and no answer was required in any case. Honchel knew who I was, what trade I was in, and what kind of goods I required for my work.

"Good. Anything else?" the dwarf added with a nod.

"Lights, one bundle. Forty crackers. Traveling companion string, about ten yards."

"What kind?"

"Cobweb."

"Elfin? Where would I get that from?" the dwarf asked in mock surprise. "How can you ever get anything out of that fang-mouthed crowd?"

"Come now, Master Honchel, you're no simple shopkeeper; if you poke about in your boxes and chests, you might just find some."

"I will," Honchel agreed, realizing that this time I had no intention of bargaining. Or almost none. "Is that all?"

"Can you suggest anything else?" I said, answering his question with a question.

The dwarf thought for a moment with his chin propped on his huge fist, then laughed. "I do have a little something here for connoisseurs like yourself, Master Harold."

He disappeared under the table, rattled the lock of a trunk hidden away down there, and grunted as he clambered back out holding a crossbow in his hands. I couldn't help myself, I gave a sigh of sheer delight, immediately raising the price by at least ten gold pieces.

The crossbow had a rather unusual design—it was double. The first bolt was installed in a lower breech and the second bolt in an upper one. The bowstrings on both mechanisms were tensioned by using a short lever. A smooth, polished handle, twin triggers. The weapon was elegant, black in color and a lot smaller than mine. A dream.

"Would you mind, Master Honchel?"

The dwarf smiled and handed me the wonderful thing and two bolts. The little object was incredibly light. I set a bolt in its special slot, then a second one, and pulled on the lever. It was incredibly easy to move. One click, and the heavy bolts were locked in their breeches. Those clever dwarves had come up with a way to make tightening the bowstring simpler.

I looked round for a target, spotted an old helmet covered in dust on a cupboard in a distant corner, glanced at Honchel to ask permission, aimed, and pressed the trigger.

Click! The first bolt struck the helmet, pierced the steel, and stuck in the visor.

Click! And the second bolt was right beside the first one.

The miniature weapon was very easy to use. I fell in love with the baby at first glance.

"Just look at that workmanship, that steel! No one will be able to make anything like it. I made it myself, with these very hands." As if in confirmation of his words, the dwarf thrust his massive paws under my nose. "And it's my own design."

He could have rattled on like that for hours, even if it wasn't a crossbow, but just a dead rat's skin. The most important thing for Honchel was always to sell his goods for as high a price as possible.

"How much?" I asked.

"Three hundred gold pieces."

"How much?" A dozen knights could easily have been kitted out for that sum.

"Three hundred, it's a fair price. I'm not going to haggle, either take it or I'll find another buyer."

"Ah, but will you, my dear Honchel? For a price like that? It's simpler to hire a squad of bowmen. For a hundred and fifty gold pieces."

The dwarf shook his head and bit his lip. Then he scratched the-back of his head.

"You don't need bowmen. But since you're a regular, well-respected client—two hundred and fifty."

"Two hundred. And don't forget that I'm taking your other goods, too."

"Two hundred and five," the dwarf responded, clenching and un-clenching his immense fists.

"The Darkness take you, honorable sir, I'll have it!" There was no point in haggling any more with the tight-fisted shopkeeper.

"Shall we add up the bill?" The dwarf laughed as he took a massive abacus out from behind his back. "Or does the master require something else?"

"How about spells? What I usually take."

"Glass vials? Wouldn't you like some rune magic? I've just got in some very interesting scrolls from Isilia."

"No, no rune magic." After the disastrous scroll that had landed me with Vukhdjaaz, I'd never trust that kind of sorcery again till the end of time.

The dwarf raised his eyebrows. "Then what kind of spells?"

"Well, what kind do you have, Master Honchel?"

"That depends on the kind of glass you want the vials to be made out of."

"Magic glass."

The magic glass for spell vials was made by magicians, and it didn't break unless its owner wanted it to. That is, I could jump up and down in iron boots on the little bottles of magic, and the glass would stand it until I wanted it to break and the spell to work.

Magic glass is an excellent way of protecting yourself against hav-ing a vial with a magical potion break unexpectedly. That's why the price for spells in vials of magic glass is much higher than for ordinary vials.

"Let's see what we've got here," Honchel muttered, setting a pair of spectacles with rock-crystal lenses on his red nose. "Oh, and by the way, pardon my morbid curiosity, but how are you intending to pay?"

"In cash," I hissed through my teeth, and set a heavy bag on the table. "There's a hundred here."

The dwarf didn't even look at the money, and that, it must be said, is a genuinely rare event.

"Master Harold, I've known you for a long time, you're a good client, I won't deny it, but I won't release goods on credit even to you. And the list of things you've ordered already comes to four hundred. Admit it, you don't have the money, do you?"

"You're right."

I wasn't about to argue with a dwarf. Only gnomes and dragons are capable of that.

"You'll be paid, Master Honchel."

"Permit me to inquire exactly who will pay me, Master Harold, if you fail to return from your dangerous trip?"

"He'll pay," I said, casually holding out the royal ring.

Honchel carefully took it with the fingers of his left hand, held it up to his eye, and examined it carefully.

"You'll simply go to the palace and say you've come from me. And you can give the ring back at the same time."

"Hmm. Hmm. Very well. I'll give credit for the first time ever." The dwarf carefully put the ring away in the inside pocket of his waistcoat. "So where were we, my dear fellow? Ah, yes! Spells. Let's see what the poor shopkeeper has to offer the master."

9

STARK'S STABLES

Curses! Over the last two months I'd got used to the silent, empty streets. But this night was special. In a couple of minutes it would strike midnight, and there were still a few rambunctious individuals wandering round the city, bawling out songs at the top of their raucous voices and reeking of cheap wine that you could smell from a league away.

The festivities in honor of the expulsion of the beasts of Darkness from Avendoom were continuing.

Fortunately, there were no revelers close to Stark's old stables in the Port City. Not even drunks befuddled by the vapors of wine were drawn to that dark little street, where the poorest and shabbiest houses in the whole city stood.

I stood there in the dark, in front of the long-abandoned stables. The walls were skewed and twisted with age, and from the outside it looked as if the old building could collapse at any moment, crushing anyone unfortunate enough to be nearby.

This was a place of desolation and silence. In this place people tried to avoid being seen by creatures who would slit your throat for a few coppers or just for the sheer fun of it. Nobody had called *them* people for a long time, and they were far more dangerous than a pack of hungry gkhols.

I glanced straight ahead, to the point where the wall stood, a few dozen yards from the old poplar trees. A patch of blinding white in the nocturnal gloom. To look at, there seemed absolutely nothing magical about it. Walls like that surrounded houses in every district of the city. Only this one was covered with semi illiterate obscenities and indecent graffiti clumsily scratched into its surface. Obviously attempts by the inhabitants of Stark's Stables to express their understanding of literature and art. But to be quite honest, they hadn't been very successful.

The height of the obstacle that I had to overcome was two and a half yards. Not really so very high, if you thought about it. It was not at all difficult to climb over. However, there didn't seem to be anybody around who wanted to take a stroll *on the other side*. I glanced again at the defenses erected by the Order to divide the living and the dead districts of Avendoom. The wall had turned yellow now—a dense wisp of mist had enveloped its white body in a sticky shroud.

The mist seemed to be alive, spectral, mysterious. It glittered in the light of the moon. First at one point, then another, it put out cautious feelers that trembled in the breeze. They gently probed at the air between the mist and the wall, trying to find a crack and overcome this low, but impassable barrier. Glittering and writhing, one of the yellow feelers almost reached right over the obstacle, but the moment it touched the white surface, a tiny spark sprang up between them. The feeler jerked back in fright and pulled away, writhing like a wounded worm.

The magic of the wall had proved itself strong. It hadn't let the mist through, even though it was constantly trying to find a way into the only part of the city that it hadn't conquered yet.

Apart from that solitary string of clouds on the left side, the sky was clear and the different-colored glass beads of the stars glittered and sparkled, set inconceivably high in the dome of the night. The Northern Crown lay across half of the sky like a bright diamond pendant. The Stone—the brightest star in our part of the world—pointed to the north, where the Nameless One was preparing for war in the Desolate Lands.

People who had been there said that up beyond the Lonely Giant it was impossible to look at the Northern Crown—the stars became so bright and large. Not at all like the stars here in the city, although even here the size of the Stone was astounding and its bright blue radiance was truly beautiful.

It was a warm night, you could almost call it hot, but I was trembling slightly and my teeth were beating out a quiet tattoo. I wasn't shivering from cold, but from nervous tension. That happens to me before an important and dangerous job. It's nothing to worry about; as soon as the moment comes to get down to work, the trembling disappears, scattered like fine dust, and its place is taken by intense concentration and precise caution—my much-praised professional qualities.

Hiding there in the darkness, I waited impatiently for midnight to come. According to the rumors, the period between midnight and one in the morning was the safest. So I had decided to set out on my adventure at the most favorable time, especially since I only had a few minutes to wait.

The warm weather had obliged me to abandon my cloak and put on a black jacket with a hood. I could feel in my bones that I'd be doing plenty of running that night, and a cloak hampers your movements too much. You can't go jumping across the roofs when it keeps trying to wind itself round your legs.

The new crossbow was hanging behind my back, together with the thin traveling companion string. I'd only brought some of my purchases from Honchel with me, and asked him to deliver the remainder of the goods directly to the king at his palace.

The trembling passed, simply disappeared like the cold wind from the Desolate Lands. I adjusted my broad belt with the pockets in which the crossbow bolts were drowsing snugly. A little bag containing several of Honchel's glass vials and a knife hanging on my right hip added to my weight, but after doing my job for so many years, I no longer paid any attention to these minor hindrances.

Lying at my feet was an impressive lump of beefsteak. I'd barely got to the butcher's shop in time, just as he was shutting up his shop for the night. I'd wrapped the meat in a piece of elfin drokr.

Boommmm! A single chime of the cathedral's magic bell rang out in the night.

That boom could be heard in every corner of Avendoom, announcing the arrival of midnight.

It was time.

I picked the piece of meat up off the ground, broke cover, and set off at a quick run toward the magic wall. But before I had covered even half the distance, I heard the clatter of feet from behind a crooked little old house with a broken-down porch and a sagging roof. I swore and dashed back into the safe gloom of the abandoned stables.

A lone Doralissian appeared at the beginning of the alley. In his hand he was clutching a club. As it happened, I recognized this particular goat. Doralissians' faces, of course, are all alike, and it's hard for the human eye to tell them apart, but a specimen with only one horn on his head, and a crooked one at that, is not something you come across very often, and that makes him very hard to forget. This bastard had been involved in the memorable run that time when I called Vukhdjaaz down to torment me.

The Doralissian stopped no more than a yard away from me and snorted loudly. My patience finally gave out and I decided to help the stinking beast's mental processes move a bit faster.

"Be-e-e," One-Horn bleated in fright when I set the knife to his throat.

"Drop the club, little billy goat," I whispered politely from behind his back.

Wonder of wonders! Without reacting at all to the words "billy goat," the Doralissian opened his fingers. The club clattered on the surface of the road.

"Good boy!" I tried to breathe through my mouth.

Of course, One-Horn was not Vukhdjaaz, but the smell of musk was still not very pleasant.

"Do you know who I am?"

He was about to bleat something, but wisely remained silent. I had the knife pressed too tightly against his neck. Those beasts are as strong as trolls with a belly full of magic mushrooms; give One-Horn a chance and he'd be perfectly capable of snapping me in two with his bare hands. But I didn't want to give him that chance.

"You'll be able to speak now. But I advise you not to do anything stupid, otherwise I'll start getting nervous, and blood will flow. Do we understand each other, my friend?"

The Doralissian gave a sound like a hiccup, which I decided, by way of exception, to interpret as agreement to behave.

"All right, we'll try the question again. Do you know who I am?"

"No-o-o."

"I'm Harold."

One-Horn tensed up, but I immediately pressed my knife harder against his neck.

"Whoa there! No stupid tricks."

"You-ou've got our Horse! Give it ba-a-ack!" the goat bleated, after which I decided to give him just one more chance.

"Who said that I have the Horse?" I asked quickly.

"A ma-a-a-an."

"Naturally, not a dragon. Who exactly?"

"A ma-a-a-an. Very whi-i-i-ite."

"White?" I asked.

"Er-er-er-er . . ." The Doralissian clicked his fingers, trying to find the word. "Pa-a-a-ale."

I wonder why I'm not surprised? All roads lead to my friend Paleface—wounded, scorched, but still clinging to life. And, consequently, to the guild of thieves of Avendoom, and Markun in particular. They must have lifted the Stone in order to pin the job on me. Not what I'd call an elegant move, but effective.

And then my humble personage conceived a brilliantly insane idea.

"I'll give you back the Horse. In a little while."

"When?"

"In two nights' time."

"Tomo-o-o-rrow night?"

The beast is just too stupid after all. Tell me, if you can, how I can conduct serious diplomatic negotiations with it? It will get everything confused, the halfwit. I rolled my eyes up, imploring Sagot to grant me patience, and said, slowly and deliberately, "This night. Then another one, and then the night when you'll get your relic back. On Wednesday. Do you know what Wednesday is?"

"Yes."

"There, see how simple it all is!" I said delightedly, proud of my talent for explaining everything in a way that even those who have absolutely no brain at all can understand. "Do you happen to know where the Knife and Ax is?"

"Yes."

"Great! You make my heart rejoice, my lad. Right then, in two nights' time. Precisely at midnight. You and your friends come to the inn. You'll get your Horse there. Remember, precisely at midnight, not a minute earlier and not a minute later, or you'll never see the Stone. Got that? Or should I say it one more time?"

"Glok understands."

"Wonderful, my dear fellow. Now, I'm going to take away the knife, and you're going to walk off. If you so much as twitch, you'll get a cross-bow bolt in your back. And you'll never lay eyes on your Horse. Do we understand each other?"

"We do, man. Let me go."

I removed the knife and quickly moved back several steps, at the same time taking the loaded crossbow out from behind my back. The Doralissian didn't move a muscle.

"You're free to go, tell your leader what I told you."

The goat looked round cautiously, saw the weapon, and nodded sourly. His expression really didn't look all that pleased.

"We'll wai-ai-ait, Ha-a-arold. Don't trick us, or you're a dead man."

The Doralissian melted away into the night. I listened to his receding steps, picked up the meat for the third time that night, hurriedly tied it to my belt with its tapes, and ran across to the wall.

The rest was a simple matter of technique. Jump up, grab the edge with my hands, pull myself up, throw a leg over, jump down onto the ground. That was the simple, banal way I found myself in the Forbid-den Territory.

10

A BLIZZARD BLOWS UP

*T*here was a cold wind sweeping down the street and Valder breathed on his hands in their thin gloves in an attempt to warm his fingers.

Immediately after returning to Avendoom after a long journey to the Lakeside Empire, he hadn't even been given time to take his boots off before he was summoned to an urgent session of the Council of the Archmagicians of the Order. And so he had set out for the tower with a perfectly clear conscience, still wearing the clothes in which he had returned to the capital, and disregarding official formality.

Valder was the youngest archmagician in the entire history of the Order of Valiostr. He had received his staff with four rings of rank at the age of only thirty, far outstripping even the present master of the Order, Panarik, who had become an archmagician at the age of forty-five. Both his friends and his enemies predicted that Valder would receive the master's staff in the none-too-distant future. He himself, however, loathed the intrigues that accompanied the struggle for power, preferring work and the special assignments that Panarik gave him. This had earned Valder the nickname of the Sullen Archmagician, since he was absent from most of the Councils of the Order.

The sky was darkening rapidly, and twilight had advanced. It had grown colder. The crust of snow crunched sharply under the soles of his boots. His nose was beginning to tingle unpleasantly.

Winter had come early this year. From the beginning of November, the clouds arriving from the Desolate Lands had brought snow, and the winds arriving from beyond the Needles of Ice had brought cold. But by mid-January Old Man Winter had grown tired of raging and decided to take a break, freeing Avendoom for several days from the heavy icy shackles of unrelenting *frost. And now, in comparison with what it had been like at the beginning of December, the weather in the capital could actually be called warm.*

The magician turned onto the Street of the Magicians, and then someone called his name.

"Master Valder! Master Valder! Wait!"

He looked round unhurriedly toward the sound and saw a teenaged boy hurrying after him. It was Gani, the archmagician's pupil, his face bright red from running.

The magician had found the boy in one of the poor villages of Miranueh, when he was on his way back to Valiostr from the Empire. The orphan had proved to have a gift. He had magic sleeping inside him, glittering faintly, like the spark in a drowsy campfire. But if good kindling was thrown onto that spark, it would turn into a conflagration. And Valder was intending to awaken that flame in Gani in the near future.

The archmagician of the Order had not previously had any pupils, but so far the youth had entirely justified all the hopes placed in him. Bright and diligent, he easily remembered the initial spells for working with Air—the most inconstant, complex, and capricious of the elements. Yes indeed—he began with Air—although all the pupils in the order usually started with the stable element of Earth.

"Master, you forgot this!" said the youth, holding out a long, white bundle.

"What is it?" the archmagician asked with a frown of surprise.

"Your staff, of course. You forgot it. I thought you might need it."

Valder laughed. He had deliberately not taken the symbol of magical power with him, but evidently the gods were against it and had found someone to return it to the hands of the "forgetful" magician.

All right. It would be useful. At least the old fogies wouldn't whine that he didn't respect the traditions of the Order. Besides, the staff was merely a concession to tradition and nothing more. It carried no power within itself. When he was traveling, the "sullen" archmagician usually left it at the very bottom of his luggage.

"But why did you wrap it in a cloth?" Valder asked peevishly as he took the bundle.

"So the guards wouldn't stop me," said Gani, sniffing with his frozen nose. "They're blind, of course, but they probably wouldn't let through a boy with an archmagician's staff."

"Thank you, Gani. That's very helpful."

"Great. But can I go with you, Master Valder? I'd really like to get a look at the tower."

"You'll have plenty of time to look as much as you like. I'm going to the Council, and that's only for archmagicians. Off you go home. It's getting dark already. Will you find the way back?"

"Of course!" the lad said, nodding and casting a regretful glance at the Tower of the Order soaring up above the roofs of the houses.

Valder tucked the bundle under his arm and strode off rapidly along the Street of the Magicians toward the tower. Avendoom was slowly sinking into the sleep of a long winter night. The radiance of the Northern Crown lit up the velvet sky. Its brightest star glowed with a cold, ominous light.

The archmagician could watch the stars for hours at a time. He felt that they made Siala seem a lot more beautiful and pure than it really was.

A minute later the street led the magician out onto the square where the old Tower of the Order soared upward in solitary splendor. The wind seemed to have gone wild and now it was running riot, picking snow up off the roadway and setting it swirling around in a frenzied white dance. And in addition, hordes of clouds had crept across the sky, concealing the stars, and snow had started falling heavily. He could no longer see the houses on the other side of the street; the wall of white was absolutely impenetrable. That sort of thing often happened in Avendoom. In the blink of an eye beautiful weather was transformed into a genuine nightmare.

However Valder, securely protected by his magic shield, took no notice of this snowy insanity. Quite soon he found himself outside the bronze door and it opened of its own accord, confirming his right to enter the Order's holy of holies.

"Valder, my old friend!" said an archmagician descending the staircase. "It's ages since I last saw you."

The man was leaning on a staff exactly like Valder's.

"Hello there, Ilio."

"What have you got in that bundle?"

"Damnation! I completely forgot!" The magician hastily extracted his staff and tossed the piece of cloth on the floor.

Ilio laughed.

"Well, look at you! Zemmel would have a fit if he saw the way you drag the symbol of the Order around. All right, let's go. The Council's waiting."

"What's happened? I was summoned the moment I got back," Valder said, climbing up the staircase after his massive friend.

"Panarik and Zemmel have got an idiotic idea into their heads, and we have to put it into practice tonight."

"An idiotic idea?"

Until that day he had never thought of the two most powerful magicians in the country as idiots.

"Exactly so," Ilio replied morosely. "Precisely the right word for it. Zemmel's been digging through the ogres' old books again—you know yourself that he's the only one who understands any of their gobbledegook. Well, he's found a way to stop the Nameless One forever."

"How?"

"He's decided to destroy the Kronk-a-Mor that protects the wizard. In my opinion the whole idea's a load of nonsense. The magic of the ogres is stronger than steel."

"But—"

"But," interrupted Ilio, continuing his progress along the winding stairway, "Zemmel has managed to pull the wool over Panarik's eyes, and even over Elo's, and that really takes some doing, doesn't it? So today we have the night of the fools. Get ready for it."

Valder bit his lip thoughtfully. Persuading the light elf, who was far from fond of Zemmel, would not have been easy. Almost impossible, in fact. But this time the lover of the ogres' magic had indeed managed the impossible.

"What exactly do you mean?"

"The Order has taken the Horn out of its dusty trunk and decided to work a miracle."

"I see," Valder said, chuckling skeptically. "But what has all this to do with me?"

"Oh, come now!" said Ilio, genuinely surprised. "You and I will act as reservoirs of power. Panarik and Zemmel have to draw their energy from somewhere, don't they? We are the two fools that the Council needed to complete its blissful happiness."

"Are we the only ones who have been summoned?"

"No," said Ilio, stopping beside a door encrusted with bluish ogre bone. "Not the only ones. Elo and O'Kart, too."

"What about Singalus, Artsis, and Didra? Is the performance going to take place without their participation?" Valder asked in amazement.

That would mean that only six out of nine archmagicians of the Order would be involved in this absurd attempt to restrain the Nameless One.

"*Singalus is in Isilia. As for Artsis—well, you know how Zemmel feels about our friend . . .*"

"*The way an orc feels about a goblin,*" *Valder said with a dour nod. "That's a pity; Artsis would have been useful.*"

"*Who are you telling? I know that. But he 'could not be found.' Didra's in Zagraba, with the dark elves.*"

"*So six archmagicians are going to destroy the Nameless One?*" *Valder whispered. "Doubtful, very doubtful. Didn't Panarik think about calling in the higher-order magicians? Or even the entire Order?*"

"*He did, but Zemmel convinced him that the six of us could cope.*"

"*The cretin!*"

"*Worse than that. You've been away for a year and a half, right?*"

"*Two years.*"

"*Well, Zemmel spent all that time poring over the books of the ogres. If you ask me, it would be a better idea to stick your head into a giant's mouth than to read those ancient tomes. He must have completely lost his reason, if he's decided to mess about with the prohibited shamanism of the ogres.*

"*By the way,*" *Ilio said with a smile, "before we go in, would you care to dispose of your shield? That is what I can see glittering, isn't it?*"

Valder had completely forgotten that he was still maintaining the energy of the spell that had protected him against the bad weather.

"*Perhaps you ought to remove it,*" *Ilio suggested good-naturedly. "You know how twitchy O'Kart gets when there are inexplicable energy surges. He's so paranoid.*"

"*He's too suspicious altogether. It's bad for the health.*" *Valder snorted, but he removed his defensive shield. At least, as far as Ilio could see, that was what he did. In actual fact, the magician merely "dimmed" the spell by feeding it with a subtle stream of power that only Panarik would be able to detect, and only if he deliberately searched for it. Some strange, childish caprice prompted him to resist Ilio's friendly suggestion.*

The archmagicians entered a spacious round hall illuminated by ordinary torches, in accordance with the prescriptions of the ancient statutes, reinforced by Panarik's dislike of magical illumination, which made the master's eyes sting and water.

The flames were burning steadily, and the pale shadows stood on the walls as still as sentries. Imperturbable. Self-assured.

Valder did not like this place—it was always too cold and unwelcoming. Emphatically official.

The walls were patterned with a large number of small lancet windows, glazed with the greenish purplish glass of the dwarves. They offered a fine view of Avendoom at night, since the tower was the highest point in the whole city, even higher than the royal palace. The immense flat mirror fused into the floor in the center of this space reflected imaginary stars and a double moon, even during the daytime. There were nine armchairs with tall backs standing around the mirror. Five of them were empty, four were occupied by archmagicians waiting with patient dignity for the late arrivals.

Ilio and Valder bowed their heads reverently as a sign of respect for their colleagues. Their colleagues replied with gracious nods. Equals greeting equals.

The magicians walked to their places, and Valder had a few seconds to examine these men he had not seen for so long.

Seated directly opposite him was Elo, a light elf with ash-gray hair cut short in the human style and protruding fangs.

Next came two empty armchairs, and then the solemn O'Kart—a short, permanently gloomy native of Filand.

O'Kart was excessively suspicious, always anticipating conspiracies against himself, and in conversation he was excessively sharp, rancorous, and intolerant. There were many who did not like him. But nonetheless, Valder had to admit that his antagonist was a talented magician.

Seated alongside Valder's adversary was a gaunt individual with gray eyes, a smiling face, and a snub nose. His rather pleasant appearance was spoiled by the bloodless lips and the slim, dry hands with bony fingers.

Archmagician Zemmel was the oldest member present at the Council. His passion was the ogres' books on shamanism, especially if they dealt with their forbidden battle magic—the Kronk-a-Mor.

Valder did not approve at all of the idea of using the Rainbow Horn to destroy the Nameless One. Hitherto this artifact had only been capable of containing the wizard within the Desolate Lands. What had changed now? How could the Council have agreed to such a risky undertaking without lengthy preparations?

"Glad to see you, my pupil," said Panarik.

The Master of the Order of Valiostr was the most important and influential figure after the king. At seventy years of age he barely looked fifty.

"And I am glad to see you, my master."

"Have you been informed what is happening here?"

"Yes, Ilio has informed me. But I cannot see any point in all this."

"The point is to destroy the Nameless One forever," Zemmel said severely, looking up from his book.

"At this very moment? This very night?"

"And what do you find so unsuitable about this night?" Elo asked, his fangs flashing.

"Well, if nothing else, the fact that there are only six of us instead of nine."

"Don't worry, you won't have to strain yourself," Zemmel said with a smile.

"That's excellent. But I still don't understand what all the haste is about. The Council is not full. Three members are absent."

"Not all of us are required. Six is enough."

"Perhaps so. But why are you so certain that we shall succeed in doing what other magicians of the Order have been unable to do in several centuries?" Valder asked, trying to speak in a calm and friendly manner, although he was very tired after his journey.

"I have been thinking the same thing," said O'Kart, unexpectedly supporting Valder.

"The magicians of the past did not know what I know," Zemmel declared weightily. "They did not make the effort to read several important books. It is all here," he said, slapping the spine of his book with one hand. "The Kronk-a-Mor that protects the Nameless One so securely can be broken by using the Rainbow Horn."

"But let us not forget," Valder objected, "that the Horn, like the Kronk-a-Mor, was created by ogres, and we do not know what to expect from it if we start using the artifact at its full power. We still do not know if it is light or evil!"

"What incredible nonsense!" Zemmel snorted in annoyance. He opened the chest standing beside him and took out the magical relic.

The Horn was encrusted with silver, mother-of-pearl, and bluish ogre bone. The power with which it was filled made it tremble—the same power that so reliably held the Nameless One on the Desolate Lands.

"Do you feel any evil from it, Valder?"

The archmagician shook his head.

No, he couldn't feel anything except primordial power. This magic was not dark. But then, he couldn't have called it light, either. It was simply different. Absolutely alien, incomprehensible, and therefore dangerous. The Horn kept the secret of the ogres secure.

"Surely you don't think the dark elves would have handed over an artifact to men if it contained even an iota of black shamanism?" Zemmel continued.

"If magicians can use the Horn, that doesn't mean it wasn't used by the shamans of the ogres," said Ilio, speaking for the first time and supporting Valder. "I am also opposed to acting hastily. Let us wait for Artsis, Didra, and Singalus."

"I support that," O'Kart put in dourly. "To this day we have no idea what the Horn was created for. And we only guessed that it neutralizes the Kronk-a-Mor by pure chance. There's no point in being hasty. The Nameless One has been sitting up in the north for all these years; nothing's going to happen if he's stuck there for one more week."

"No, we shall do it today!" Zemmel was not smiling any longer. His eyes glinted angrily. "The star charts are favorable for tonight! Today or never. Because there will not be such a night for another forty years."

"I propose an official vote on this insane idea!" Valder snapped curtly.

"Speak on this matter," said Panarik, nodding and looking round at the assembled magicians. "Who is in favor of using the Horn to destroy the Nameless One's defenses?"

"I am opposed," said Valder.

"I am not certain that it will work, but I have complete confidence in the skill and experience of my respected colleague Zemmel," said Elo, drawing out his words slowly. He set the Horn on a plinth that had been made ready in the center of the mirror floor. "I am in favor."

"Naturally, this is exactly what I wish to achieve," said Zemmel, giving Valder a mocking look.

"I am opposed," Ilio said with a frown. "If only because the full Council should decide."

"I am also opposed," said O'Kart. "We ought not to wake a sleeping giant. Afterward, as we know, it is very difficult to get him to go back to sleep again."

Three against two.

Now everything depended on what Panarik would say. If the votes were evenly divided, then the side supported by the master would win, for the simple reason that his vote carried more weight than the votes of the others.

"Zemmel's arguments are entirely convincing," the head of the Order said after a moment's thought. "Let us try it. I am in favor."

Now no one could go against the decision of the Council.

The magicians stood in a circle round the mirror on which the Horn was lying.

Valder saw Ilio's glum face opposite him. The ogrophile was on Ilio's right, with his book in his hands, and Panarik was on his left. The indifferent, abstracted Elo was standing stock-still on Valder's right, and O'Kart was in the position between the Sullen Archmagician and Zemmel.

A feeble circle. Three magicians were missing and the others would have to call on all their skill.

"What is our task?" the elf asked.

"Simply open yourselves up. I need your power. Pass it through the Horn. Stream twelve, profile eight, if you please," Zemmel replied, opening the old book at the right page. "And now . . ."

Valder remembered that phrase very well.

It was the phrase used to teach pupils to concentrate instantly and activate their energy. And now the archmagicians' energy began passing through him and pouring into the Horn in a thin purple stream.

To his right Elo's azure-greenish power, with the scent of fresh leaves, reached out and entwined with O'Kart's fiery red stream. Panarik and Ilio also joined in.

A radiance appeared around the Horn, it pulsated and began changing color. The fiery red flame of a dragon was replaced by an orange sun, which was transformed into a yellow autumn which, in turn, changed to the green leaves of the forests of Siala, then became a bright blue spring sky, the bottomless blue Western Ocean, and then once again, as at the very beginning, became the all-consuming dragon fire. It was this very property—of changing its color under the influence of others' magic—that had earned the Rainbow Horn its name.

The first few minutes passed quietly. The artifact responded well, behaving in a stable fashion and giving no cause for alarm. And Valder did not feel any dizziness from the constant drain of magic.

"Intensify the flow! Ilio, you are working for me now." Zemmel's voice sounded intent, focused.

The magician was about to attempt the most difficult part of the task—arousing the magic of the ogres.

"Elo, realign the flow, you have deviated three degrees toward the sixth coordinate." Panarik's voice rang out sharply in the total silence.

The master was not only directing his own power, he was still able to pay attention to the work of the other archmagicians. Elo started in alarm and directed his azure-green ray to where Panarik had indicated.

Zemmel began a plaintive chant in the ancient language.

For only the second time in the history of the Order the ancient speech of the ogres was heard in its tower—the speech that had once awoken the magic of Kronk-a-Mor.

"Some kind of difficulty in the second field," Ilio murmured. "Valder, why is your power dissipating?"

Valder himself was beginning to feel that he had to make a greater effort and concentrate harder to control the flow. He had the feeling that something was drawing off a small amount of magical energy.

And then he suddenly realized.

Because of the quarrel with Zemmel he had completely forgotten about the magical shield, which he had not bothered to remove. And now it was glowing feebly on the boundary of his awareness, interfering annoyingly with the direction of the flow, consuming power like a leech. But it was impossible for him to remove it—if he was distracted for a second, the circle would be broken, and he could only imagine the catastrophic consequences that the liberated flow of energy would produce.

"It's all right. Nothing that I can't handle," Valder hastily assured his friend.

Panarik cast a dark glance at him. Unlike the others, he could see the obstacle. Which meant that when this was all over, Valder would face a very difficult conversation with him.

Hours seemed to go by in the Council Hall. There was a tenacious, pulsating pain growing stronger in Valder's temples—the price for his magic.

The magic enveloped the group in a warm, glowing cocoon, pulsating gently, spreading out into a multicolored aura and flowing into the Horn in a waterfall of power. The entire hall was filled with energy. It was intoxicating—you wanted to bathe in it, reach out your hands to take possession of it forever. With its help you could create mountains and rivers, heal thousands of sick people, even bring the dead back to life. A single tiny speck of it was enough to destroy all the enemies of Valiostr. It could rid the world of Siala forever of ogres, giants, orcs, and dozens of other creatures hostile to human beings. Valder was overcome by euphoria, a feeling of might that made anything possible.

"Something's wrong!" said O'Kart, alarmed. "Fluctuations!"

"I don't feel anything. Where?" asked Elo, turning his head.

"To the right of the third field, directly above the artifact."

"But where? I can't see it!"

And then Valder noticed it, a little black dot of decay on the rainbow radiance of the Horn. The dot was pulsating to the rhythm of Zemmel's voice, quivering like a candle flame in a gusty wind. And it was growing. . . .

"Stop!" Valder barked, his throat suddenly dry. "We have an unplanned surge of energy!"

"We extinguish the circle now," Panarik commanded. He had also seen the particle of Darkness that had been born.

"Don't dare!" squealed Zemmel. "It will kill you."

"Nonsense!" the master said, and began closing down his flow of power.

"Ghaghaban!" Zemmel suddenly shouted, throwing his hand out toward Panarik with the fingers twisted into a freakish sign.

The master went flying back against the wall and slumped onto the floor with his rib cage ripped open. The magician's death broke the circle and four magicians went flying in different directions. Only Zemmel was left at the Horn.

The rainbow radiance dimmed and became as black as the murderer's heart. No longer under control, the flows of energy seized on their freedom and four blinding shafts of magic struck upward, vaporizing the ceiling and the roof of the tower. A cold wind burst into the tower, driving an army of snowflakes round in a jolly dance.

The fifth flow, the one that had been controlled by the now-dead Panarik, struck horizontally, passing through Elo as he got up off the floor and reducing him to dust, then made a huge hole in the wall of the hall and disappeared.

As Valder, stunned, tried to get to his feet, the energy fell on his shoulders like a hungry bear. The mirror floor onto which he had been thrown reflected his pale, contorted face with blood seeping from the nose. The bitter taste of magic burned his throat, it passed through his body in shafts, gnawing into his bones and causing him appalling pain. An ocean of power controlled only by Zemmel splashed all around him.

"*Murderer!*" *shouted Ilio, who had got to his feet. Forgetting his magical gift, he went rushing at the traitor with his fists held up.*

Zemmel, reveling in the newly awoken Kronk-a-Mor, took no more notice of his opponent than a giant does of a mosquito. A click of the fingers, a an incomprehensible phrase in ogric, and Ilio cried out as he fell into the hole that appeared below his feet as the floor parted. The edges of the mirror came back together with a squelching sound, burying Valder's friend.

"*You!*" *Valder shouted, jerking himself up onto his knees, but he was suddenly swathed in supple black cables of power.*

"*Quiet.*" *Zemmel's voice was quite imperturbable. "I'm busy."*

"*What are you doing, you madman?*" *Valder shouted, trying to break free. "Don't you understand what you've set free?"*

"*I understand. The Master explained it to me. He taught me how to wind you all round my little finger and become immortal. In a few minutes I shall be the equal of the Nameless One, or even more powerful! Why, the Nameless One, that incompetent, will bow his head before me!*"

"*Who is this Master?*" *asked Valder, trying not to pay any attention to O'Karta, who had begun to stir, and to continue distracting Zemmel.*

"*You don't need to know that. Dunces like you are altogether too proud of the might of the Order, you have no idea at all of the might that will soon be mine! Awakening the Kronk-a-Mor proved incredibly easy. All I needed was the Horn and five idiots willing to give me their power. I have studied the language of the ogres, I have pored over their books for decades, mastering the ancient secrets of shamanism. I have achieved my own immortality, and I do not give a damn how many of you are dispatched into the Darkness after Panarik!*"

"*Go there yourself!*" *shouted O'Karta, and struck at Zemmel with the hammer of fire.*

Boooom! the flame roared, and the snowflakes melted in the unbearable heat.

The black bonds loosened, and Valder added his own power to the redheaded archmagician's second blow. But Zemmel merely swayed, and the flames flowed down off his clothes like a waterfall.

The traitor struck a terrible blow in reply. The air trembled and thickened and a semitransparent crimson sphere came hurtling toward the two magicians. Valder could see a densely interwoven Air, Earth, and something else incomprehensible. All he had time to do was to activate his extinguished shield and throw all of his energy into it.

An azure wall sprang up between him and Zemmel and the battle spell crashed into it, shattering it into hundreds of thousands of bright blue sparks that scattered across the ruined Council Hall like grains of millet. The sphere lost speed and changed direction, but it still caught Valder a glancing blow.

A shaft of fire penetrated Valder's chest and exploded, and he collapsed onto the floor. He writhed and twisted, wheezing hoarsely in his pain, and missed the moment when O'Karta struck with fire again, this time not at Zemmel, but at the Horn, from above which the black magic was pouring out into the air.

This blow sent the Rainbow Horn spinning across the mirror floor and, having lost its stable base, the power escaped from Zemmel's control.

"What the . . ." was all that the traitor had time to say before all the power of the Kronk-a-Mor that had already been accumulated struck back at its master like a sledgehammer, then dived into the mirror and retreated deep below the Tower of the Order.

The Council Hall was immediately flooded with silence. There was only the cold wind howling through the holes in the walls and snowflakes falling from the night sky.

"Are you alive?" asked O'Karta, walking across to where Valder was lying.

"Yes, but it's only a matter of time." The magician tried to smile. Blood seeped out onto his lips.

There was a hungry weasel in his chest, devouring his lungs. It was getting harder to breathe. Valder had no illusions about his own condition.

"Excellent," the redheaded archmagician said. "You'll live for another fifteen minutes. Quite long enough."

"Enough for what?" Valder asked, sitting up and keeping his hand against his chest as he spat blood onto the mirror floor.

"To carry the Horn out of the tower." The Filander held out the artifact that had somehow appeared in his hands. "Get a move on. You'll have an eternity for lying down."

"Take it out? Where?" Valder didn't really understand, but he took the Horn.

"As far away as possible. See that?"

Valder looked where O'Karta was pointing. A thin, sinuous crack crept across the surface of the mirror floor.

Then another one. And another.

"When it breaks, the tower will be no more than a memory. And what went down through its floor will flood out into Avendoom. Come on! Get up! You were never a spineless milksop!"

Valder got to his feet, struggling hard not to fall over.

"I'll hold the mirror together for as long as I can!"

"I'm already dead, O'Karta. Let's do it the other way round. You have a chance to save yourself."

"We're all dead already. If you stay, it will be over too soon—you're very weak. I'll try to hold out for as long as possible."

O'Karta turned away from Valder, raised his hands, and began directing streams of energy onto the cracked mirror.

That was the other magician's last memory of him.

Intent and unbowed.

Valder found the winding staircase very difficult. When he reached the ground floor, there was darkness dancing in his eyes and the pain in his chest had expanded to a huge, pulsating sphere. He kept spitting out the blood that constantly appeared in his mouth.

The Tower of the Order was quivering slightly. Inconceivable forces had locked grips with each other in a struggle for liberty, and the archmagician had no doubt that the Kronk-a-Mor, even though Zemmel had not completed it, would be victorious. Valder tried not to think about what would happen after that.

The tower was no longer shaking; it was groaning in a low voice. Massive cracks ran through the walls. The ancient building could feel that its death was near. But the magical door opened gently to let the archmagician out.

The cold air and icy wind stung his face. His hands, firmly clutching the now-dormant Horn, were instantly frozen. Valder staggered away from the tower. Now without a single light burning, it watched him go with a melancholy stare. Every now and then there were flashes of magic at its very top as O'Karta spent his last strength on delaying the mirror's collapse.

The Street of the Magicians was surprisingly empty. No one came out of their houses to see what was going on, as if everybody had been crushed under the weight of heavy sleep. The pain in Valder's chest was growing worse, and he could hardly see anything. He walked blindly, setting his feet down one after the other and moaning softly when the torment became unbearable. Blood filled his mouth, running down over his chin and dripping onto his clothes.

The ground shuddered as it tried to expel the hostile magic of the ogres.

O'Karta held out for much longer than could have been expected. Valder got as far as the Street of the Sleepy Cat.

Even from there he heard the jangling sound of the mirror breaking, and then the triumphant howl of power hurtling up out of the earth. A terrible explosion threw the magician into a snowdrift and his face sank into the gentle coolness. The roaring continued as the magic of the ogres went on a rampage. As he lost consciousness, Valder could sense the threads of people's lives being crumpled and snapped as the dark curse consumed street after street, house after house, inhabitant after inhabitant. . . . They died in terrible torment. This power that was alien to humankind knew no pity or compassion; it took everyone who happened to be in its way.

In only a few minutes the Evil would reach the spot where Valder was lying, and then the Horn would stay there forever.

This thought forced the archmagician to turn over onto his back. He held his snow-covered face up to the falling snowflakes, catching them greedily with his bloody mouth. The wind died down. The world froze in horror at the advancing disaster, anticipating the most terrible blizzard in the city's entire history. With a superhuman effort, in danger of losing consciousness at any moment, Valder got up off the road and looked in the direction of the tower.

Now, instead of solid ground there was a rapidly swirling black whirlwind. Ordinary people would never have seen it, but Valder's magical vision, even though it was weakened by his injury, could clearly distinguish the black vortex reaching up into the night sky.

The magician managed to walk a little farther, and then he collapsed at the foot of the statue of Sagot and could not rise again.

The upper part of the god's face was covered by a layer of fresh snow and Valder could only see the lips. The mentor of thieves was looking at the archmagician with a frank smile of approval.

"I have to save the Horn. Do you hear? I have to. Help me, and I'll do anything you want."

Sagot didn't answer.

Valder felt as if he was engulfed by the delirious visions of fever. He saw dark shadows circling above Avendoom, he imagined he saw a man in a jacket *with a hood, running across ruined roofs and hiding. In his agony he no longer understood where he was or who he was. The archmagician was falling asleep. . . . Life was abandoning his body with every beat of his heart, and his reason was already poised above the abyss from which there is no return.*

"Master Valder! Wake up! Wake up, teacher!" Someone was shaking the magician relentlessly.

He wanted to brush off this annoying fly. He was enjoying dozing, and quietly humming the children's song that his mother used to sing to him. But through the drowsiness of approaching death he could hear someone crying.

"Teacher, it's me. Come back . . ."

With a struggle, Valder parted his leaden eyelids and saw Gani's wet face.

"Wh-what are you doing here?" the archmagician gasped with a great effort.

"I felt worried. And I came running to find you."

"You felt . . ." The magician looked up at the statue of Sagot, listened, and nodded. He was suddenly swamped by a new wave of pain and had to grit his teeth to avoid crying out loud. "Here, take this. It's the Horn. Take it to Artsis. Quickly . . . He can stop this."

"I won't go without you!"

"Take it! This is my last order to you, my pupil. Find Artsis and give him the artifact. Tell him that I ask him to take you as his pupil. T-tell . . . tell him that everything went wrong. Tell him we awoke something that is beyond our understanding. A blizzard . . ." The exhausted magician collapsed back onto the snow. "Go on now. Run. Or it will be too late. Save what can still be saved."

Gani hesitated, then nodded decisively and dashed off, clutching the Horn tightly against himself.

"Run, kid, run," Valder whispered.

The snow circled gently as it fell on the dead archmagician, covering him in a white blanket of warmth and peace. The snow whispered and sang its song, knowing that soon its most frenzied dance of all would begin.

There was a black blizzard gathering over Avendoom.

11

A CITY OF GRAY DREAMS

I pressed myself back against a dirty wall covered with lichen on the Street of Men and groaned. The pain had appeared somewhere in my chest and now it was slowly receding, taking my terrible dream with it.

I still seemed to be there—on the snow-carpeted Street of the Sleepy Cat, beside the statue of Sagot. And I still could not believe that I was not lying dead in the snow on the street in old Avendoooom.

"I am only Harold," I whispered, "who is known in Avendoom as the Shadow, and not the archmagician Valder, who died centuries ago. . . ."

The immersion in the ghastly web of the cloudy nightmare that had snared me had been instantaneous. It happened as I was walking quickly along the Street of Men and suddenly . . .

I remained myself, but in some strange way I was transformed into Valder at the same time. My consciousness was broken and fragmented like the delicate covering of the young November ice on the river. While still himself, Harold the thief slumped helplessly against a wall in the Forbidden Territory and lived a new life, or rather, a section of someone else's life that was incredibly real.

With a trembling hand I wiped away the sweat that had sprung out on my forehead and shook my head in an attempt to force out of it the final leaden grains of my nightmare.

It was an unpleasant feeling, but at least now I knew what had actually happened on that terrible night in the old Tower of the Order and how the legendary curse of Avendoom, the Forbidden Territory, had come to be.

The blame for the appearance of this city of the dead lay with the

Master, who had seduced Zemmel with promises of immortality and power.

Who was he? I had heard that title several times already during the last week. This individual was a mystery and a great riddle not only for me, but also for Artsivus, which meant for the Order, too. Although at least I now knew for certain that this Master and the Nameless One were completely different persons.

But right then I wasn't really concerned with either of them. I had fallen behind schedule again, so I stopped pondering all sorts of unnecessary nonsense and set off on my way.

The Forbidden Territory was certainly strange enough, but nonetheless I must say that I was pleasantly disappointed. There were so many terrible rumors circulating about it in Avendoom, but everything here turned out to be quiet and peaceful. The plans of the old part of the city that had been made by the diligent dwarves and which I obtained in the library had proved to be ideally precise. On clambering over the wall, I had indeed found myself on the broad, twilit Street of Men, beside a low building with its door rotted away. Either a shop or a barber's salon—it was hard to tell from the rusty, faded sign.

I gathered my courage and appealed to Sagot, just to be on the safe side, and set off, constantly checking with the map in my head.

The street was deserted, just as I had dreamed it. Deserted and it felt . . . absolutely unreal somehow.

Yes, in the faceless breaches of the windows there was a spring breeze snuffling gently in its sleep. Sometimes a sign that was almost rusted right through would squeak and sway on one of the half-ruined shops. There was a rotten winter sled standing in front of one of the houses. The streets were cluttered with heaps of rubbish—mostly from buildings and roofs, which had collapsed with the passage of time. But there were no human remains.

Not a soul, not even the scattered bones of the skeleton of a horse or a dog, let alone a human being. The dull gray light of the streets and the pale silver glow of the full moon created a picture of a dead world, abandoned long ago. And another strange thing was the absence of the mist to which I had become accustomed over the last three weeks.

I was unpleasantly surprised to discover that my magical vision completely stopped working as soon as I had walked about twenty yards

along the Street of Men. The colors faded, the world blinked and collapsed into shadows and darkness.

No point in panicking before there was any real need.

I hoped that wouldn't happen to me in Hrad Spein, or I was a dead
man. The most terrible thing that could happen to anyone was to find
himself lost in the impenetrable bleakness of those deep underground
halls, although I wasn't exactly delighted with this place, either.

I occasionally glanced round, turning cold inside as I expected to see
someone or something following in my footsteps, but everything was
calm and quiet. I tried not to make a sound and listened to the summer
night with my hearing heightened to the maximum.

But the only noise was the wind. It would die away, like some little
wild animal, and then, at the most unexpected moment, suddenly start
playing in the black gaps of the dead houses, jumping out of gateways
with a mysterious whistle, swaying shutters that had come off their
hinges so that they banged against the walls of the houses, teasing the
loose sheets of roofing metal and setting them rattling menacingly, then
hiding again.

Only once did an incomprehensible and therefore frightening sound
set icy shivers running up and down my spine.

As I stole past a once-wealthy house with faded green paint, I heard
a faint child's cry that broke off abruptly. Retreating in shock to the
other side of the street, I merged into the shadow and listened in silent
terror. The crying had come from the ground floor. The windows were
boarded up, but that was definitely where the cry was from.

I waited. My heart was pounding rapidly, like some wild bird begging to be released from a cramped cage. Good old Harold was desperately afraid of hearing *that sound* again—the angry, desperate crying of
a hungry infant abandoned by its mother.

But there was not another sound and, after waiting for a few seconds, I went on my way. I walked hurriedly, glancing round all the
time, afraid to believe what I had heard. And the fear gradually released
its grip.

I tried not to show myself in the sections of the street that were illuminated by the moon, but at the same time not to press too closely
against the walls of the dead houses. They made me feel a kind of
instinctive childish horror, with that mournful expression in all their

silent, broken window-eyes. These imaginary glances gave me a really horrible feeling, and my overexcited imagination obligingly kept throwing up all sorts of pictures, for the most part quite unpleasant.

At those moments I really felt like sending the king, Hrad Spein, and the map to hell, and simply disappearing from the city. The only thing that stopped me was the fear of breaking a contract.

The fact that Graveyard Street ran just behind the houses, parallel to the Street of Men, did nothing to inspire me with optimism, either. Finally, I caught sight of the judge's house. I don't know if a judge actually lived there or the name came about for some incidental reason. But the judge's house was what this gray, three-story stone block was called in the plans of the city.

Immediately behind the judge's house, if the plans could be trusted, there was a narrow alley leading to the Street of the Sleepy Cat. Like Graveyard Street, it ran parallel to the Street of Men, but on my left-hand side. In principle I could carry on along the Street of Men and reach the Street of the Sleepy Cat from the broad Oat Avenue, but that was a long, long walk and the Forbidden Territory isn't the kind of place that encourages long, relaxed nocturnal strolls. I swear to that on the Quiet Times! The sooner I could get out of there, the better. The narrow alleyway would cut down my dangerous journey by at least half, which would be most welcome.

"Well, may a h'san'kor devour me!" I swore in a low voice.

The house beside the judge's house had collapsed and one of its walls had fallen into the alley, blocking my way to the Street of the Sleepy Cat. Unfortunately I wasn't a mountain goat, to go scrambling over all that rubble. Even Vukhdjaaz, may his name not be mentioned at night, would break his leg here.

I'd have to go the long way round.

My gaze fell on the point where the walls of the somber houses melted into the night. How far was it to Oat Avenue? I realized that the street was quiet and there was absolutely nobody there, and yet . . . Somehow I wasn't burning with desire to walk along the Street of Men. Slit my throat, but I wouldn't, and that was an end to it. The same intuition that saved me the night I crept into the duke's house had grabbed hold of me by the shoulders and wouldn't let me go on. But then how was I going to get onto the Street of the Sleepy Cat? The only answer was to go through one of the sinister houses standing on my left. Maybe the one closest to me—the judge's house.

Standing there in a shadow as thick as rich cream, I hesitated in torment, trying to decide which was the lesser of two evils—to walk along the Street of Men or to poke my nose into a dead house. I didn't find either option much to my liking, but standing there doing nothing was just as dangerous as continuing my journey.

There was another quiet child's cry from the house opposite the judge's house, and I shuddered. The sound had come from the second floor.

The first time I heard the crying, I had put it down to my overexcited imagination, but this time there was no avoiding the fact that I really had heard it. And this discovery was far from filling my heart with peace and delight. Ghosts? The spirits of the dead? The curse of the Rainbow Horn?

I don't know what it was or what it wanted from me, but I certainly wasn't going to be fooled by a child's cry and go running to save the innocent infant, like some idiotic knight in a fairy tale. There aren't any children here, there haven't been for two hundred years. At least, not any live ones.

I carefully unfastened my crossbow and loaded a fire bolt instead of one of the ordinary ones. It looked just like a battle bolt, except for the red notches on its tip that helped distinguish it from its nonmagical brothers. It was a serious weapon that could easily topple a knight clad in full armor.

A few moments passed, during which my heart sank and became entangled in my guts, then the terrible crying stopped as suddenly as it had started. A second's silence . . . And then I heard quiet chuckling. Malicious laughter. The way a child can laugh when it's torturing a cat and knows that it will never be punished by the grown-ups. The hair on my head began stirring and my back was suddenly streaming with cold sweat. For almost the first time in my life I wanted to yell out at the top of my voice in sheer animal terror. Nothing had ever frightened me so badly before.

It was time to clear out of there, and quickly—that laugh didn't make me feel like having a polite, relaxed conversation with its mysterious owner. I no longer had any doubt that this unknown creature had set out to hunt poor Harold. Otherwise how could it have turned up two blocks away from where I'd first heard it?

When I heard the chuckling coming from the ground floor of the house, I abandoned all doubt and hesitation. I hurtled up the steps onto the porch of the judge's house, pushed open the door, and plunged into the ancient darkness, on the way dragging out of my pocket a disposable magical trinket that gave out a dim light. I could see just well enough to avoid running into the nearest wall or the furniture and to find the old door, warped with age, that led into the inner chambers. There wasn't even enough time to take out one of the bright magical light sources that I had bought from good old Honchel. I could already hear the laughter in the street, beside the porch.

Anyone else in my place would have fired at this unknown mysterious jolly weeper, but I'm more careful than that—it's the way For trained me. What if I didn't kill the weird beast, but only ended up making it even more furious?

I kicked open a door of I'ilya willow, which everyone knows is impervious to the ravages of time, and burst into a dark hall with its walls lost in pitch-darkness. Almost stumbling over the broken furniture lying scattered about in disorder, I dashed on, and the sound of my steps could probably be heard a league away.

Out of the corner of my eye I spotted a skeleton stretched out on the floor in rotted clothes. Another door—and the next hall. And another. And another. I dashed through the abandoned rooms, diluting the darkness with the light radiating from my magic trinket. The blood was pounding in my temples. There were cold icicles of fear stuck in my stomach, refusing to melt. I prayed to Sagot that I wouldn't stumble and break my leg.

Walls flitting past with huge shadows on them, a flickering sequence of light and darkness, a pale circle of trembling light. Another door loomed up ahead. I opened it, pulled the glove off my left hand and flung it into the darkness, then went dashing back in the opposite direction. I turned left, avoiding a table by a miracle, and slipped into a barely visible cubbyhole for servants. I slammed the door and pressed my back against the wall, trying to restrain my frantic breathing, and hid the magical light inside my jacket so that its radiance wouldn't seep under the door and betray my presence. The world was plunged into darkness and I merged completely into the wall, trying to breathe as quietly as possible.

Centuries passed before my ears heard the quiet steps. They sounded most of all like the light steps of a child walking barefoot. As they approached, my finger tightened on the trigger of my crossbow. The steps halted in front of the door. And again I heard the quiet laugh of delight that sent shivers running across my skin. Had I really been found?

It cost me an immense effort not to run for it, but to freeze in the same way as a frightened hare freezes in a moment of danger, hoping that the predator won't notice him in the snow. The door swung open sharply, almost flattening me against the wall, but I didn't move a single muscle, just prayed silently to all the gods of Siala.

The jolly weeper froze in the doorway. I could hear snuffling. The creature seemed to be trying to locate me by smell. Another chuckle sent frosty tremors running through my stomach. The creature didn't go away, realizing that I was somewhere nearby, but it didn't come into the little room, because the other door, through which I had thrown my glove, was open, and it was quite likely that I could be there, waiting for the moment to run.

The grains of sand fell slowly in the hourglass of time. I had time enough to curse my stupid idea of hiding in the house. I ought to have run along the street—perhaps then I might have managed to get away. But now I felt like a goblin locked in the orcs' maze.

Eventually I heard another quiet chuckle and a second later the receding patter of little bare feet. Taking my orientation from the receding sound, I drew the following picture in my mind: the creature had gone through the hall, entered the next room, and stopped . . . Another triumphant chuckle—evidently it had found my glove—and hasty steps moving away until they were swallowed up by the silence.

I slowly slid down the wall onto the floor. There was no way I could stay where I was—the appalling creature could come back at any moment. Should I go back to the Street of Men or take the risk of going on through the darkness and out into the street on the opposite side?

I had been in buildings with similar floor plans a couple of times, so I could easily find my bearings. I had just skipped into the servants' wing, and if I went straight on and then turned left after two doors,

I would come out into the rear half of the ground floor of the house. There ought to be a door into the kitchen there, and getting out of the kitchen into the Street of the Sleepy Cat would be only quick work. I took the magical trinket out again and set off through the dark house, expecting to hear that familiar laugh at any moment.

Stepping over a fallen cupboard with broken panes of glass, I pushed open the door that I needed, went through, and closed it behind me. The dim light picked out a table and a purple vase by Nizin masters, with a bouquet of dried-out flowers: the petals had fallen off long ago and covered the top of the table in a thin brown layer. A chair with a carved back stylized to look like a cobweb—it had to be the work of dwarves, although they don't much like working with wood. A small set of shelves with rows of dusty books.

I must have entered the steward's office. He himself was lying there on the floor, facedown. An old skeleton draped with cobwebs and covered with dust. I cautiously moved closer and leaned down over him. The bones of the legs were crushed or, rather, gnawed apart, as if someone had tried to reach the marrow.

Gkhols?

"It doesn't look like it. The tooth marks are wrong. And there's a slight trace of magic, too."

I shook my head in amazement. What trace? What tooth marks? What was I talking about? It was as if someone else had thought it and pronounced the words out loud. Someone very familiar with the habits of these creatures. Someone who knew about magic. For instance, the person I had recently been in the dream that had engulfed me.

The archmagician Valder.

Sagot, what nonsense is this? My head is my head, and there can't be any dead magician's words inside it!

I hastily moved away from the dead man and looked out of the window.

I swore. There was no end to the strange things that happened in the Forbidden Territory.

Outside it was a winter's night. The roofs of the houses and the road were covered with snow. In some places quite large snowdrifts had built up.

More insane ravings? Ten minutes ago it was summer outside, but now it was genuine winter! Two little boys ran along the street with joyful cries, almost knocking over a fat man in old-fashioned clothes, wrapped up warmly in a fur coat. How many people there were out there! There were lights blazing in the houses opposite, and the buildings themselves looked brand-new.

"The last evening," the familiar voice of Archmagician Valder whispered inside my head. "I died that night."

I jumped in surprise and went flying out of the room, almost breaking down the door on the way.

A table in the middle of the room. A vase with a dried bunch of twigs that had once been flowers, pictures, books, a chair, a skeleton on the floor. A window. Winter. I was back in the room with a view of the winter street.

What kind of nonsense was this?

I walked through the strange door again, and this time I didn't close it behind me.

A table, a vase, flowers, a dead man, a window, winter.

I glanced back into the room where I had just been.

A table, a vase, flowers, books, a skeleton with gnawed, shredded bones, and white snow falling slowly in the street outside. A closed circle.

I was caught.

I tried repeating the passage to and fro through the door about another twenty times, but with unfailing regularity, I found myself back in the very same room. Wouldn't it be amusing if the jolly weeper found its way in here after me? I couldn't hide from it for very long in here.

"Dashing through the same room, reflected a thousand times in reality." Again that quiet, weary voice.

"Who are you?" I whispered in fright, listening closely to what was inside me and already guessing what the answer would be.

"I don't know . . ." I heard after a while. "I am I. And I am alive, thanks to you. But not all of me, only a part of my consciousness."

"You're inside my head!" I shouted.

"Don't be afraid, I'll go as soon as you leave this place cursed by magic. Allow me to live. Just for a little . . . ," the voice implored, and for a moment I hesitated, but then immediately felt scared.

"No! Get out of my head!"

"You know me. You were me when all this happened. You must know that I won't do you any harm. On the contrary, I will help you."

I couldn't give a damn for his help. He had installed himself in my head without my permission! What I wanted was to scrape the voice of that accursed archmagician out of my ears altogether.

"I will help you to get out of here and complete your job." He spoke in a low voice; I had to listen closely to make out the words.

"You were me, and I became you. You knew my life, and now I know yours. All your concerns, all your goals. We are one whole."

"We are not one whole!" I angrily kicked the dead man's skull and it went rolling across to the wall. "This is my body."

"Let it be so." Valder had no intention of arguing. "Simply allow me to fall asleep when all this is over, and I will help you to get out of here."

"Fall asleep? What do you mean, fall asleep? Inside my head?"

"Yes . . . I want peace. I have waited for you too long. To fulfill my promise."

"Waited? A promise? To whom?"

No reply.

"No, a thousand times no, may a h'san'kor devour me! This is my head, only mine. Get out of it!"

"Very well," Valder replied after a long silence. "I'll help you in any case, and then go away. You have wandered into a time mirror. Go out through the window. Just jump and do not think about anything."

Should I do as he said and end up in the winter world? What would I do if I suddenly found myself two hundred years in the past? Would I be able to get back, or would I have to spend the rest of my life in a place that was completely strange to me?

The archmagician said nothing, and basically there was nothing else I could do except follow his advice and climb out of that accursed room through that equally accursed window. Time was passing imperceptibly— another two or three hours and dawn would begin. I had to get out of that lousy place before the first rays of sunlight broke over the line of the horizon.

I walked up to the broken window and looked outside. A light, frosty breeze chilled my face. What was that the archmagician had said? Assuming, of course, that he had said it, and it wasn't my insane imagination.

"Just jump and do not think about anything."

Easily said! Take a run up and leap, like a circus tiger jumping through a hoop of fire. Only here, instead of flames, there were sharp shards of broken glass round the frame. But then it wouldn't be the first time. I had left several rich men's houses in the same way after visiting them.

I put the magical trinket away—there was more than enough moonlight. After a moment's thought I picked up the vase and flung it out into the street. It spun through the air and disappeared, without hitting the ground.

"May the demon of the abyss gnaw on my liver!" I exclaimed, and spat, then took a run and jumped into the unknown.

A glimpse of the room, a white roadway, the moon slowly drifting across the sky, snowflakes falling. I landed on my feet, couldn't keep my balance and started falling sideways, so I rolled over across my right shoulder.

The illusion disappeared. It evaporated, borne away by the wind of time. No snow, no new houses with windows lit in bright invitation, no people hurrying about their business. Just the dead Street of the Sleepy Cat. Dead houses with dead windows. And summer. So I was where I needed to be.

Valder had showed me the right way out after all. Overcome by curiosity, I looked round at the judge's house. I went back and looked in through the window at the room where I had just been. A table, flower stems thrown out of a vase, a skeleton. A door. And beyond it a dark, narrow corridor, leading off somewhere into the gloomy interior of the dark building.

"I'm getting away from here!" I muttered, swinging the crossbow behind my shoulder.

The Street of the Sleepy Cat was no different from the Street of Men. The same desolation, the same thousands of imaginary eyes observing me from the ragged wounds of the windows. Except that here the street was a bit narrower and darker, and the buildings were poorer.

I was making rapid progress, but that didn't prevent me from sticking to the shadows and the semidarkness, as well as listening cautiously to the silence of the night and the dreary song of the wind. Once or twice it brought me the sound of a child's cry, distorted by distance, but it was so far away that I tried not to take any notice.

There was a huge gaping hole in one of the houses on my right, and I hastily crossed over to the other side of the street—there was no point in tempting fate. After all, I knew what kind of ugly creature could be lurking in there on this fine night.

A strange white blob took shape in the air ahead of me. I crept up close and studied it curiously. My way past a well-ruined wooden inn with a fancy sign in the form of a fat cat was blocked by a cloud of semitransparent, silvery white mist.

Round and fluffy, looking like a harmless little sheep, it was hanging right in the middle of the street, with its edges not touching the surrounding houses.

I don't know why, but I got the distinct feeling that some gigantic, fat spider had abandoned a half-finished web. The edges of the substance swayed and trembled, creating an impression of sluggish life. This mist was nothing at all like the June mist of Avendoom, which was yellow and too thick to see through, but this . . .

It was strange, somehow.

I halted about ten yards from this unexpected obstacle, trying to decide what to do next. For had advised me to go across the roofs, but who knew if they would support the weight of a man after all these years? Should I try to slip through? Under the cover of the shadow, pressing close against the wall?

Beyond the silver haze of this strange substance I could see the outline of a human figure. From the height of him, he had to be a giant. His head was level with the roofs of the single-story houses.

As far as I could tell, what I could see up ahead had to be the statue of Sagot.

I had already lifted one foot in order to go over to the wall and slip past the little cloud when I was stopped by that sharp voice ringing out in my head again:

"Stop! Don't move, if you value your life!"

Harold is an obedient lad, and I froze as still as a scarecrow in a village vegetable garden. It was only a few agonized heartbeats later that I realized the archmagician had come back again and it was his voice.

I was about to tell Valder exactly what I thought of him, but before I could, he barked: "Quiet! Not a sound! That rabid beast is blind, but there's nothing wrong with its hearing! Speak in thoughts, I can hear you perfectly well."

"You promised to leave me alone!"

"Then where would you have been? In the jaws of the irilla?"

"I don't understand."

"That's what you're looking at."

I stared hard at the cloud.

"I read about this creature spawned by the Kronk-a-Mor in the ancient tomes when . . ."—the voice hesitated—". . . when I was still alive. Irillas are blind, they like deserted places."

"How do they hunt?" I asked doubtfully. "A blind hunter—that's something new."

"I already told you. They have excellent hearing."

"I think it would have grabbed me ages ago, if everything you say is true," I thought.

"Don't deceive yourself. The irilla heard you two hundred yards away. It's still waiting for you to approach it."

"It'll have a long wait. What kind of fool does it take me for? I'll have to find another way round."

"As soon as you take a step back, it will attack. You have to deceive it."

"I wonder how?" I snorted, keeping my eyes fixed on the calmly quivering clump of mist. "And what do you care if it eats me?"

Valder was silent for a long time. "I have been given life again after a long wait in oblivion. Life, and not a gray nothingness from which it is impossible to move into either the darkness or the light. Although I exist in another's body, where I am regarded as an uninvited guest, that is still better than nothing. Let me fall asleep, I will not hinder you, and perhaps sometimes I will be able to help. Do not drive me out . . ."

"Okay, it's a deal. You can stay for the time being." I had come to the conclusion that the archmagician's help could come in useful after all. "But only until I leave the Forbidden Territory. Agreed?"

"Yes! Thank you."

"So how do I deceive this blind beast with big ears?"

"Try to pick up a stone and throw it as far away from yourself as you can. And then run."

Remarkable, a brilliant plan. And I was foolish enough to think I would get really useful advice. Although I supposed I could try it. If I ran fast, I could end up beside the statue of Sagot, and For told me it was absolutely safe there, no evil beast would dare to touch me.

I picked up a small round stone and threw it into the window closest to the mist. The stone flew into the darkness and bounced off the wall, and then the mousetrap snapped shut. The cloud hurtled toward the sudden sound as fast as an arrow fired from an elfin bow and disappeared into the house, and I darted past the dangerous spot as fast as I could run. Out of the corner of my eye I saw that my trick hadn't been a complete success. The white bundle of mist, looking more like a worm now, was rapidly pouring back out into the street.

And it was clearly intending to play tag with my own humble and frightened personage. I concentrated all my energy into a wild gallop.

"Faster!" Valder advised me, entirely unnecessarily.

I collapsed beside the granite pedestal and watched as the worm that was pursuing me, as crazed with hunger as a starving gkhol, gave out a melodic crystalline note and shattered into a thousand tiny shreds that burned up in the air with a crimson flame.

Well now, my teacher For was right, as always. Sagot's statue really is a safe spot.

I got up off the ground, brushed the dust and small pieces of rubbish off my jacket and trousers, and turned round to see the face of my god at long last.

I gasped in amazement.

The ancient artist had done a really good job in depicting the patron god of thieves. Sagot was sitting on a granite pedestal with his legs crossed, wearing boots on his feet. He looked very slightly tired, like a traveler who has finally completed a long journey. He had elegant hands with slim fingers—they looked too young for a forty-year-old man.

The pointed nose, high forehead, slight stubble on the cheeks, cunning eyes and smile were equally suitable for an old man made wise by experience, or a mischievous boy.

I had seen this man before. And even paid a gold coin for his absurd advice.

Sitting before me was the beggar from the empty pedestal at the cathedral.

I had heard several legends from the brothers of the night about Sagot supposedly liking to wander the earth occasionally and talk to those who appealed to him at difficult moments: to help them, advise them, punish them, or play jokes on them. But I'd never thought that anything like that would ever happen to me.

"You see, I am carrying out the Commission," I said, addressing the statue. "But I still don't understand your advice about Selena. Keep laughing—you bamboozled me out of a whole gold piece."

But the god said nothing and merely continued to look down mockingly. Why should he bother to reply to the cheeky comments of some little insect by the name of Harold? I sighed. Sagot had protected me from the irilla, but it was time to be moving on.

"Good-bye, Sagot." I controlled my insolence and bowed. "I'll try to get that Horn."

I turned round and walked toward the Street of the Sleepy Cat, sunk deep in the darkness of night, and left the statue of the god behind me. After spending just a little while beside it, I had a confident, calm feeling. I was going to complete this Commission.

I felt as if I had just been granted the god's approval, although he hadn't said a single word to me.

The street was as endless as the hatred between elves and orcs. I had already been walking along it for twenty minutes. I wanted to get the job over and done with and get out of this place.

But clearly that was not to be just yet.

First I caught that smell that cannot possibly be confused with anything else. That stench can drive a hungry gkhol insane—the stink of decomposing corpses. I started breathing through my mouth, trying to ignore the unbearable aroma.

A couple of moments later I heard the crackling and chomping—sounds very familiar to those who engage in robbing ancient graves. They were what always gave the vile creatures away.

Dead men, brought back to life by the shamanism left behind by the ogres, which had still not disappeared from the world of Siala after thousands of years. That was who it was.

The magic that brings corpses back to life hinders the process of decay, and the dead men can quite easily exist for several decades before time takes pity on them and kills their flesh. Like many other creatures of the darkness, they cannot bear sunlight. It makes their bodies evaporate, like a lump of sugar in hot tea. And so these zombies mostly live in abandoned caves, mine shafts, earthworks, the basements of old buildings, and, of course, burial chambers. They only come out of their refuges at night, in search of prey.

In principle, a good swordsman can deal with any ordinary returnee from the grave. "Fresh meat" is agile and nimble, while the half-rotten remains can barely move about, owing to the absence of most of the muscles and tendons, or even the bones. The most important thing is not to end up in the grappling-hook embrace of their arms, or things will go badly for you. These guys sink their teeth into their prey as securely as any imperial dogs.

The one thing I couldn't understand was how the zombies happened to be there. It was quite a long way to Graveyard Street. What kind of dead men could hold out for two hundred years? In that time any decent corpse who had come back to life ought to have fallen to pieces, whether he wanted to or not.

I held the meat that I had brought in my left hand and my knife in my right. If necessary, the silver border on the blade would give me temporary protection.

No, silver doesn't kill zombies, it just makes them clumsier and very lazy. Sometimes one of the creatures that has received a silver arrow in the chest won't even take any notice of a person walking by.

I could hear wheezing coming from round the corner of the next brick building. The windows of this building were closed off with massive steel shutters, and the heavy steel door would have withstood a direct hit by a ball from one of the gnomes' cannon. Written in huge letters on the façade was the following:

HIRGZ . . . N & S . . . NS B . . . NK.

Even to a Doralissian it would have been obvious what was meant: "Hirgzan and Sons Bank." A very well-known and rich gnome family.

So this was the gnomes' bank. For had got as far as this point, but had failed to get inside and turned back. I cautiously peeped round the corner, trying not to make any noise. My nose was assailed by the overwhelming stench of rotting flesh and my gaze encountered a dead man peeping round the corner in exactly the same way from the other side.

The dumb scene that followed was worthy of the very finest dramatic production on Market Square. Finding myself nose-to-nose with a living corpse, I behaved like a small, defenseless animal when it runs into a predator in the forest—I froze on the spot.

The creature was not exactly fresh. One arm was completely absent, the ribs on the right were exposed and gleamed a dull white in the misty moonlight. The skin was a dirty gray-green color and one eyeball was missing. The lips had rotted off long ago and the sparse teeth, coated in fresh blood, were exposed in the vacant grin of a village idiot. There was another horrible brute standing there with its back to me.

I had an excellent view of his decayed body and the white spots of his vertebrae protruding through the black flesh. The zombie farther away from me had not yet finished dining and was wheezing loudly as he enthusiastically stuffed lumps of flesh into his mouth after tearing them off the human body stretched out in the alleyway.

There was absolutely no doubt that only that morning this flesh had still been alive.

Brrr! To be eaten alive by creatures like that . . . Not a pleasant way to go!

In any good theatrical production, the silences should not be overdone. The creature that had seen me swung back his half-rotted arm and struck at the spot where I had just been standing. Naturally, I was long gone. I had already skipped out into the middle of the Street of the Sleepy Cat, feverishly unwrapping the drokr to take out the meat.

The corpse moved in my direction quite nimbly, holding out his one arm and hissing menacingly. The other one left his dessert and hurried to his brother's assistance, still stuffing flesh into his jaws as he came.

Dead men aren't jolly weepers—when dealing with them, you need to remain calm, keep a cool head, and use just a little bit of dexterity. And then you have every chance of surviving the encounter.

"We'll think of this as a brief training session for Hrad Spein," I mumbled.

The creatures came closer, and I ran another ten yards away, luring them out of the dark alley. I waited for the right moment and threw the meat into the face of the one-armed zombie. For a while the creature lost all interest in me and started ripping furiously at this prize that had come his way completely out of the blue.

Everybody knows that the risen dead are insatiable, and the fact that the creature had dined just recently did nothing to blunt his appetite. I pulled the magical elfin cobweb-rope out from under my belt. By using that I could overcome almost any obstacle. It didn't require any three-pointed grappling iron on its free end and naturally adhered to any surface so tightly that you couldn't pull it off. And its magical ability to pull its owner up of its own accord only served to make it even more popular among those who were fond of overcoming unexpected obstacles. People like me, for instance.

Of course, this item was expensive. It's no easy thing to get hold of the rope that's used by the dark elves' spies.

I swung the cobweb and the free end went flying off toward the roof of the gnomes' bank, as if there were a heavy weight tied to it. Holding the other end in my hand, I waited for the miracle of elfin magic to attach itself somewhere up above and lift me well away from the ravenous creatures. The first zombie was already finishing the meat, and I regretted that I had taken so little with me. The second had drawn level with the first, but he didn't stop to join in the feast, he continued stubbornly moving in my direction. He walked like a drunk in the Port City—as if he was about to fall over at any moment. But the dead man didn't fall, he kept coming toward me with the persistence of a gnome delving into the body of the earth.

I felt a sharp jerk, and the magic rope began pulling me upward.

Breathing heavily, I threw one leg over the granite cornice that ran the full length of the bank just below the roof and pulled myself up onto it with an abrupt movement. I turned over onto my back to examine the night sky. There were just over two hours left until dawn, and the stars had already paled in anticipation of the morning that had not yet awoken but was very close.

The Archer was already sinking behind the horizon, the Stone had lost its magical brilliance, Svinopas had moved close to the moon. There were still constellations in the night sky, but they were gradually growing dimmer, advising me to make haste.

I stood up and detached the rope, which had taken a grip on the roof like a hungry leech from the Crystal Dream River. Then I rolled the rope into a tight coil and attached it to my belt. I put away the knife, which had not been needed, and looked around.

The moon was flooding the entire world with its magical silvery light. The roofs of the houses lay exposed to my gaze. There was nothing up here to cast any shadows, and a silver glow enveloped everything around me, transforming the roofs into a fairy-tale plain of tiles, rusty chimneys, and broken weather vanes. The houses were set very close to each other; the distance between them was so tiny that even a cripple could probably have jumped from one to another without falling and breaking his bones.

I was about to move on, when I spotted a really large hole in the roof, about twelve yards from the spot where I was standing.

So time had done what all the thieves of Avendoom had been unable to do. It had created a breach in the bank's reliable defenses. And I was immediately tempted to go down into the bank and discover if the Hirgzan clan was as rich as the rumors claimed it was.

But just at that moment money would only have been a hindrance to me, and I didn't really feel like climbing into the black mouth of that hole, especially as the roof beside it was probably no thicker than a moth's wings and could collapse under me at any moment, dispatching unfortunate Harold into dark oblivion.

"Well then, the next brave soul who decides to pay a visit to the bank will be very lucky," I muttered, and continued on my way.

Time was the most precious thing I had now.

I took a run and leapt onto the next building. Took a run and leapt. Took a run and leapt again. After two blocks I was breathing like an excited wild boar.

Once some poorly secured tiles slipped out from under my feet, but by some miracle I managed to grab hold of the cornice and hang there with my hands. Sagot be praised, I managed to scramble up.

Another time the sloping roof of one of the houses began crumbling under my very feet. I put on a burst of speed as I felt everything shifting and heard the rumble of the roof collapsing behind me. I pushed off hard and jumped across onto the next building, my boots knocking out several longish, bright tiles that had not darkened with age.

I made it.

I watched rather gloomily as the ancient dust rose up from the site of the house I had just been standing on. Swirling feebly in the moonlight, it began taking on the form of a gigantic skull, and I decided not to wait to see how all this would end, but hurried on to the Street of the Magicians, which was already close at hand now.

On my travels I caught a few more glimpses of zombies strolling lethargically along the Street of the Sleepy Cat. Fortunately the vile creatures didn't raise their heads to admire the full moon, and so they didn't see me.

I thanked Sagot once again that I had decided to cover the rest of the distance over the roofs and not along the street—if I'd run into that many of the walking dead, I would have been hard put to get away from them.

One final high leap, and I was on the roof of a building with a façade overlooking the Street of the Magicians. The goal of my nocturnal expedition was already close at hand. But the problem now was that there were no more houses anywhere nearby. It was as if some gigantic tongue had licked them clean out of this world. Empty black squares where there ought to have been buildings.

And that was all.

I leaned against an old chimney that had turned dark with age. I had two options for making further progress. The first was to go down and risk my skin by running the rest of the way to the Tower of the Order. The second was to risk my neck by trying to jump to the building standing on the opposite side of the street.

Despite the risk involved, I found the second option more to my liking. I was already certain that it was much safer to stay up high—running through those dark streets was like dancing the djanga on thin ice.

To reassure myself, I tugged on the cobweb rope several times to check its strength. Now all I had to do was commit one of those acts of insanity that were already a habit with me. To be precise, jump off a building, go flying through the air, and end up on the house opposite. I had done something of the kind a couple of times in my life, but that had been when I was a lot more stupid.

A step off into the void . . . The surface of the street came leaping up toward me, and then I was flying above it, holding on tight with both hands to the rope, which suddenly seemed too thin and insecure.

The wall of the building with the dark holes in it was approaching with catastrophic speed, threatening to flatten me into a pancake. I instinctively put my feet out in an attempt to soften the blow, but the cobweb thread stiffened and was suddenly, incomprehensibly transformed from a flexible, pliable rope into something completely opposite.

The straight, stiff rod hung there in the air with me holding on to it, and then began slowly swinging toward the building. But the moment my feet touched the gray wall, the rope's stiffness disappeared; it became its usual self again and pulled me gently upward.

"That's over, then," I said, examining the palms of my hands.

The one without a glove had come off worse—there was a ragged red line running across it. Okay. It's nothing. I'll survive.

The houses on the Street of the Magicians had been built more recently. Or at least the coverings of the roofs didn't groan under my weight in weary old age, threatening to collapse suddenly at any moment. I moved on, making haste—morning was very close now.

Winding and weaving like a drunken snake, the Street of the Magicians was nothing like the ideally straight Street of the Sleepy Cat, Street of Men, and Graveyard Street, which the dwarves might have laid out with a ruler.

And although this wasn't the most prestigious area of town, the little houses looked far richer. There were elegant weather vanes in the form of various magical creatures standing on every second roof. On a couple of façades I even spotted statues decorating the walls. But of course, I didn't look too closely at them; all my attention was focused on not falling off the sloping roof I happened to be on at the time.

Up. Down. Leap. Land. Up. Down. Leap. Land. I moved along like I was controlled by one of the dwarves' mechanisms—precisely, accurately, expending no excess energy. I jumped in the absolute certainty that nothing untoward was going to happen now.

That certainty was my undoing. As I landed one more time, I stopped to catch my breath and look up at the stars. I'm running out of time!

And then there was a mournful creaking sound under my feet. The kind of creak old doors make in abandoned houses. The roof started to shift under me, I flung my arms out, trying to keep my balance and not go tumbling down from the third floor onto the stone surface of the street, and at the same time I tried to jump away from the collapsing section of roof.

But I was too late.

The support fell away from under my feet, and I went flying down after it. There were glimpses of walls, dust rising from the collapsing roof, the starry sky.

And then there was darkness.

12

IN THE DARK

don't think I lay there unconscious for very long. When I opened my eyes and looked up at the sky, the stars had hardly moved at all and the moon was still bright, not yet pale in anticipation of morning.

I groaned and tried to sit up. Surprisingly enough, none of my bones seemed to be broken. Naturally, I was highly delighted. If I'd broken my leg or—Sagot forbid—my back, I'd have been lying there waiting for the dawn to come.

I hadn't fallen very far. The ceiling was very close—if I just stood up, reached out my hand, and jumped, I could reach it with my fingers. I seemed to be in some room on the third floor. The floor was supporting both me and the collapsed section of the roof, on the rubble of which I had made such a successful landing. If I'd gone on down through all the floors to the ground, the king would have been unlikely ever to see me again.

I got to my feet and cautiously moved my arms, still not believing that I wasn't hurt. I had to get out of there; that child's crying was having a bad effect on my nerves.

Stop!

What crying?

It felt like I was suddenly fastened to the floor with a single gigantic nail. I started feverishly trying to understand where the thought about a child's cry had come from.

Yes, there was something there. Something on the very borderline of my consciousness as I was falling into the darkness. Something that had woken me, called me back from oblivion.

Crying. That familiar child's crying.

As if in reply, and in confirmation of all the laws of universal beastliness and my own anxious fears, I heard a quiet sobbing in the dark corner of the room. Feeling rather far from my best, I nervously took out the magical trinket and held it out in front of me at arm's length.

The old room had walls with peeling wallpaper, a scraped and battered wooden floor, and a little girl standing in the far corner, gazing at me with her green eyes.

She was no more than five years old. Golden hair in unruly curls, plump rosy cheeks with the traces of tears, rosebud lips, a dirty, torn little dress, bare feet, and a tattered plush toy—either a dog or a mouse—in her hands. A charming little child who could model for the frescoes in holy shrines.

Except that her still eyes were filled with the anticipation of a snake, the hatred of a wolf, and hunger of an ogre. And lying beside her was my glove, the one I had abandoned in the judge's house.

The little girl sobbed.

Moving very, very slowly, I bent down to pick up my crossbow from where it was lying on the floor. At the precise moment when my fingers closed on the weapon, the little girl sobbed for the last time and then gave a quiet, malevolent laugh.

I froze. So we had met at last. This was the Jolly Weeper in person.

The eyes of the creature—I can't carry on calling it a child—glinted, a wall of rotten air struck me in the face, and I went flying back against the opposite wall. The magical light started blinking and fading rapidly. It was swiftly getting dark in the room, with only those green eyes radiating light, hypnotizing me and suppressing my will, flooding my brain with a sticky mist of calmness.

"Don't sleep! Shoot!" someone's cool, imperious voice ordered, and the mist in my head began dissipating rapidly.

My ears were assaulted by a shriek of protest. The creature could feel that it was losing control over me. I could move again now and, taking my aim at those poisonous green eyes, I pressed both triggers of the crossbow almost simultaneously. The first, ordinary bolt stuck the laughing creature in the shoulder, spinning it halfway round, but it only gave a triumphant little chuckle and continued moving toward me without even pausing.

The magical bolt of fire followed its ordinary brother home and struck the creature in the chest.

A bright flash of fire liberated from its magical captivity, a rumbling sound, and a squeal of protest.

One ... two ... three ... I took my hands away from my face and cautiously opened my eyes. The room was empty. The light from the magical trinket was gradually growing stronger, timidly illuminating the old room and the carnage that had been wrought in it.

The Jolly Weeper had disappeared; there wasn't even any ash left behind. Either the fire had really destroyed it, or the vile creature had cleared off to somewhere a bit less hot. To be quite honest, it was all the same to me, as long as it was nowhere near me any longer.

"Thank you, Valder. You popped up at just the right moment," I mumbled, but there was no reply.

Walking out of the room, I saw a wooden stairway leading downward. I had no more desire to travel across the ancient roofs. I had enough bruises already and I didn't feel like tempting fate yet again.

I slipped out onto the Street of the Magicians. The final drops of time were draining away into the sand. One hour, or even less, and the horizon that was still dark would flare up in the bright flash of an irrepressible summer dawn.

I started moving faster, slipping through the shadows, forward—to where the narrow street broadened out into a small square.

I didn't even notice how I got there. I simply stopped, enveloped in the cloak of shadow cast by an old two-story house with no roof. Opposite me there was another house, the final beacon of human habitation before the empty square.

And there ahead of me the appalling two-story stump of the old Tower of the Order stood in mute, agonizing reproach, alone and dead. The power of the Kronk-a-Mor had not spared it; there was nothing left of the structure's former grandeur and elegance. The black blizzard had made short work of the once-beautiful creation of the magicians of the Order.

"What have you done, Zemmel!" Valder groaned.

Yes, an appalling catastrophe had taken place here, and I certainly didn't envy those who had been nearby when the raging elements had broken free of control. There wasn't a single stone left on the square, it was absolutely bare, surrounded by the skeletons of houses and flooded by the light of the setting moon, like some meadow in a fairy tale.

The tower had once had not just three, but many floors, and when the explosion happened, the debris should have been scattered right across the square. But it wasn't there. The square was clean and empty. As if the rubble had just evaporated.

"How long are we going to go on standing here? Time's wasting." The sudden sound of a voice from the dense darkness of the house across the road startled me out of my mournful thoughts. I stared across the road in amazement.

The words had obviously been spoken by a living man, not some insubstantial phantom.

"Calm down, Shnyg. Or do you want to end up like good old Rostgish?" a repulsive, squeaky voice replied.

"Calm down Shnyg, calm down Shnyg," the first voice grumbled. "It was Rostgish's own fault. He let his guard down and let a dead man get his teeth into him. Let's get those plans then cut and run."

"Just how do you suggest we get into that damned tower? We have to think the whole business through, or we won't get out of this alive."

"You do the thinking, Nightingale," Shnyg said angrily. "Morning's already on the way, it's time to get out of here."

"Shut up, will you! I'm thinking," Nightingale barked, and Shnyg shut up.

Right. I know those names. The two master thieves Shnyg and Nightingale work for the guild, and that means they work for the slimebag Markun.

They're not such bad lads, really, but their work's a bit sloppy.

And I knew Rostgish, too, may he rest in the light. He appeared in Avendoom a couple of years ago and attached himself to this pair. Not a master thief. He drank too much. Those must have been his remains that I came across on the Street of the Sleepy Cat.

I wonder what in the name of Darkness they want in the Forbidden Territory?

"Have you got the plan?" Nightingale hissed.

His shrill, squeaky voice was painful to hear, but the thieves didn't seem to think there was any need to hide, and they made enough noise for the whole street to hear. "The one we got from the Royal Library? Here it is. Light it up."

"What with?" Nightingale muttered. "That damned Rostgish had all the lights."

Aha! So they were the ones that the old man Bolt was talking about. "Gray and untalkative." Shnyg and Rostgish must have gone to the library. The old man would have remembered Nightingale.

They'd stuck some important gent's ring under Bolt's nose, hadn't they? Ah, I never thought to ask the old man about the ring, I thought it was all a senile old fool's imaginings. I'll have to go back and have a proper heart-to-heart talk with him. So who was it that sent them?

"We have to get those cursed maps or whatever else before that skunk gets there ahead of us."

"What are you so nervous about?" asked Nightingale, as calm and rational as ever. "Harold won't try sticking his nose in here any time soon."

"That Harold has really got up everyone's nose. Markun boils over at the very mention of his name, and the client said we should do away with him if it came to it. And the individual our client serves—which means that we do, too—is beginning to express his dissatisfaction."

"Do away with him?" Nightingale said with a nasal snigger. "Have you completely lost your wits, Shnyg? That lad might look feeble and skinny, but I've no intention of tangling with Harold. We do the job, hand over the Commission, take the money, and clear off to warmer parts. For the high life beyond the mountains. No one will ever find us there. We don't want to be hanging about with the Darkness."

"Do you think it's that easy to get away from the Master?" a mocking voice asked, and I shuddered.

I would have known that voice anywhere, out of a thousand. It had changed a lot, lost that lifeless, dead tone, but I still recognized it. It was the voice of the same being that had spoken with the duke and then killed him. That winged creature of the night.

"Don't even think about trying to run. You will only go when he lets you go, little man. You are faithful to the Master, aren't you?"

"I am faithful." Nightingale's voice sounded hoarse and frightened. "We are faithful."

"Yes, yes, Your Grace, we are faithful to the Master," Shnyg confirmed in an ingratiating tone.

There was a quiet laugh of satisfaction in the darkness, and I thought I glimpsed a brief flash of golden eyes.

"Clever little men," the creature drawled. "Get the maps and destroy them, and then you can clear out of here to anywhere you want." There was a note of undisguised contempt in the emissary's voice.

"B-b-but, Your Grace . . . ," said Shnyg, clearly very surprised. "The client said to bring the papers to him. We can't just—"

Shnyg broke off his tirade and started wheezing for some reason, and his partner gasped out loud in fright.

"The Master is not used to hearing 'we can't.' He needs servants who can! Those who are incapable of carrying out an elementary assignment are not worthy to serve him; they are useless!"

Shnyg's wheezing became a charming gurgling.

"May I be allowed to remark that Shnyg did not at all wish to seem to be useless!" Nightingale started keening. "We'll go and get those papers right now!"

I heard the sound of a body hitting the ground and Shnyg wheezing in relief as he tried to force some air back into his lungs.

"You know that your client also serves the Master, and the Master says that the maps of Hrad Spein must be destroyed, otherwise they might fall into the hands of the king and his attendants. Tell that to the fool whom you call your client. He may be rich, but that does not mean he can think he is a link of Borg. Let him remember the deceased Duke Patin."

"We understand everything now, Your Grace," Nightingale confirmed. Shnyg was still coughing. "We'll tell him everything you said."

"Wonderful, and now set about it! Surely you don't think I would need your help if I could enter the tower?"

The emissary didn't bother to wait for an answer to his question. Something even darker moved across the dark gap of the house. There was another glint of gold. The emissary slowly ran his gaze along the dark street and as it slipped over the spot where I was standing, it hesitated for an instant, but moved on before I even had time to feel frightened. With a clap of his black wings, he melted away into the night.

Silence descended on the street, only occasionally interrupted by Shnyg's desperate coughing.

"Damn ... *kha-kha!* Damned bloody beast. *Kha-kha!* He almost ... *kha-kha!* ... choked me!"

"What did you expect?" Nightingale snarled. "Spouting nonsense like that to him? Be grateful you're still alive!"

"The Darkness take that damned creature! And the Darkness take you, too! And the Darkness take me, fool that I am, for listening to Markun, who's bound us hand and foot to this Master of his. The Darkness take this client, and his damned papers!"

Shnyg was overwhelmed by a new fit of coughing. But just at that moment something looking very much like a human figure made its appearance on the stage of this ongoing spectacle. It was approaching slowly from the direction of the Street of the Roofers and its direction made me feel uneasy, because it was moving straight toward us.

Even worse than that, I was almost directly in its path! I had to dash across the street, to the house where the two thieves were: The darkness was thicker there, and so it would be much easier for a scoundrel like me to hide.

But I wasn't able to skip in through the door, since the thieves were coming out of it at that very moment. I managed to dart to one side and press myself back against a wall. But master thieves are masters because they can hear the very slightest rustle.

"There's someone here," Shnyg whispered, and I drew my dagger out of its scabbard with a quiet rustling sound.

Nightingale and Shnyg started listening, but then they noticed the approaching stranger whom I had already seen. "Shhh. Look," Nightingale whispered.

There was certainly something to look at. The figure approaching us was a man. A perfectly normal one. Except that he was semitransparent—the tower and the stones of the roadway were quite clearly visible through him. He was wearing a magician's robes and leaning on a magic staff. ...

"Look at this," the phantom muttered to itself. Its voice sounded twice or even three times, creating a strange echo. "They've all abandoned me. The traitors. Where are they? Where? I wander and wander, searching for them. I'll find them."

The phantom repeated this little jingle over and over, turning its head from side to side and examining the area, evidently hoping to find the aforementioned traitors. It had a blurred spot instead of a face, but I didn't have the slightest doubt that this magician could see everything perfectly well. I was scarcely even breathing. And neither were Shnyg and Nightingale, standing a little farther away.

The phantom halted a few yards away from us and began turning its semitransparent head again.

"I wander and wander. I'll find them. I'll find them." It paused for a moment and then said in a very perplexed voice: "I'll find them. Aha! That's where they are! They're hiding! I know you're there! I'll find you. I'll find you."

He held out his staff and started waving it from side to side, like a blind man, and slowly moving closer. That was when I realized that if I didn't do something quick, the crayfish sleigh would be coming for me. In another ten seconds he would reach me, and that would be the end. I had just one chance, an incredibly stupid one, but I decided to take it, especially since it was time to get rid of my unwanted competition in the shape of Shnyg and Nightingale. I stepped forward out of the darkness onto the moonlit street so that the thieves were behind my back, and I heard one of them swear in amazement.

"Fire!" I yelled, and then dropped onto the surface of the road, putting my hands over my head.

Without even pausing to think, the magician fired a spell at the spot where I had just been standing. Something went screeching through the air above me. A intense impact, screams of terror and pain from the unfortunate thieves. The phantom had hit the target—which was not me. I didn't wait to see what had happened to the servants of the Master, and there was certainly no point in loitering in the street in front of this new danger. I leapt up, darted round the muttering magician, and set off across the square toward the tower, zigzagging and hopping like a hare driven insane by the spring sunshine.

The screaming stopped: I don't know whether the thieves were dead or they had enough sense to stop making noise, but I personally didn't feel the slightest pity for them. It was them or me. Or that damned mumbling phantom would have done for all of us.

Oh yes, about him. The mumbling behind my back stopped, the air howled again, I leapt to one side and saw a sphere of mist go flying across the square, leaving a smoking tail in its wake, hit the surface of the street and bounce like a child's ball, then explode with a boom against a house in the distance, leaving a fair-sized hole in its wall.

I changed tactics: forward, hop, sharp left, forward, hop, sharp right, hop, a sudden stop, sharp right, forward again. Like a flea on a frying pan.

Surprisingly enough, this tactic worked. Another three balls of smoke went hurtling across the square and exploded far away from where I was. Once I had to flop down on my belly again in a most inelegant fashion, when a magical charge struck the Tower of the Order, but didn't explode, and then bounced back on a changed course directly toward me.

I saw the misty charge growing bigger as it flew straight at my face. There was no time to jump aside, so I dropped, and as soon as the sphere flew over my head, I jumped up again, because the tower was already very close.

The damned phantom, may the gkhols gnaw on his bones, was howling over by the Street of the Magicians, while I feverishly searched for the door. I had to run along the wall illuminated by the moonlight, and expose myself in full view to the raging specter. It was closing rather rapidly, muttering malevolently, intent on finishing Harold off.

Yet another charge flew into the building just above my head but, like the previous one, it bounced off and flew back in the opposite direction. Evidently the tower had retained some of its magic even after the cataclysm that had overtaken it, and nobody could knock down its walls simply by flinging spells at them.

Sagot be praised, I finally found the door! I tugged feverishly at the bronze ring. . . . But the door wouldn't budge. There weren't any locks at all, so lock picks were no good here, and that cursed phantom, who was hidden from me behind the wall, would soon appear again and continue his wild bombardment.

I tugged at the door again, then kicked it and swore angrily. Time was running out. On one hand there was the phantom, and on the other, morning was already treading on my heels. I cast a quick glance at the stars. Only the Northern Crown and the Summer Bouquet were still bright in the sky, the other constellations had faded and were barely visible. The moon was growing paler, literally before my eyes, and a few moments later the light illuminating the square became diffuse and pale.

In twenty minutes it would be dawn.

It was the end. Without some kind of miracle, I would never leave the territory, that was certain. I could already consider myself a dead man! If that insane phantom didn't finish me off first. The magician's muttering was very close now.

Could I hide in the tower? Perhaps I would be able to hold out there until the next night! I clutched at a final slim straw of hope and strained every last muscle in a desperate attempt to open that damned door at least a crack.

Hopeless. No, I couldn't get in there; all my efforts had been in vain. I was just about to run for the shelter of the houses when Valder's voice suddenly said: "Open, it is I."

The door swung open smoothly, graciously inviting me into the dark interior of the dead building.

"Soo, that's where you are!" a triumphant voice echoed right in my ear. I jumped forward into the safety of the building and the door slammed shut, leaving me in total darkness.

"Don't worry," Valder replied to my thoughts. "He can't get in, the door won't let him."

"Who is he?" I asked, taking out the magical light.

"I don't know, I've never seen him before."

"Can I wait out the day here? Is it safe in the tower?"

"Alas, my friend. In this part of Avendoom nowhere is safe."

Sagot! So in twenty minutes it will all be over.

Holding the bright trinket out in front of me, I inspected the interior that I already knew from my dream. Nothing had changed, except that the walls were covered with soot, and there was a human skeleton lying on the floor.

"An old friend," Valder whispered sadly.

A friend? Ah, yes! The archmagician. What was his name? Ilai? No . . . Ilio.

I had to go up. To where Artsivus had said the archive was kept. Grab the plans of Hrad Spein and run—and I had just had another one of my crazy little ideas. Valder chuckled inside my head in approval of my plan.

I flew up the black marble staircase that wound round the central column like a gigantic snake. The light of the magical trinket picked images out of the darkness—frescoes that told the history of the Order.

Now the second floor and the door leading to the archive. I happened to raise my head, and saw the broken end of the serpentine stairway pointing up into the predawn sky. This was all that was left of the mighty Tower of the Order.

Bursting in through the door, I found myself in a long, wide corridor. The light picked out decayed Sultanate carpets under my feet, elegant carved furniture, tapestries on the walls, and hundreds of doors.

May the Nameless One take me! Which one is it?

"Go on! The archive hall is farther along!"

I broke into a run. The corridor seemed endless; the magicians of the Order had obviously done something with the space in order to expand the inner premises of the tower a little.

"Stop!"

I had almost rushed past it. The wooden doors were standing slightly open, as if someone had left the archive in a hurry. Perhaps that was what had actually happened, and the magician who had returned from Hrad Spein and carried the maps through the Forbidden Territory had never got as far as the Order. Wouldn't it be funny if he had never got as far as the tower, and there were no maps here?

The magic light began to fade.

"What's happening?"

"The magic of the tower's smothering it. It won't be any more help to you. Hurry!"

I entered the huge room. There was almost no time left now.

Hmm. Not bad. The Royal Library would be green with envy. Even it didn't have this many magic books and ancient tomes. Shelves upon shelves upon shelves. Books upon books upon books. And it was all permeated with magic. A stranger could wander about in here for hours and still not find what he was looking for. May a h'san'kor devour my dear departed granny.

"Straight on!" Valder barked. "Left! Follow these shelves, turn left again at the end! Straight on. Farther, farther, farther . . . Stop! Turn round! There it is!"

Panting hard, I looked down at the elegant crystal table with nothing standing on it except a large black casket, decorated with silver deer. Its lid was raised slightly and I could see a bundle of papers. There it was, my goal!

I grabbed the treasure with trembling hands and stuffed it into my bag. Now it was time to get out of there.

"Vukhdjaaz!" I howled as loud as I could. "Vukhdjaaz, it's me!"

For a few moments nothing happened, and I started getting very nervous, afraid that my plan wouldn't work. And then my old acquaintance appeared straight out of the bookshelves. A real little charmer. And I must confess that if anyone had told me only a few hours earlier that I would be glad to see him, I would have twirled one finger at the side of my head and told the madman where he could go.

"Well? Have you got the Horse?" he asked, his green eyes glittering furiously.

"Take me to the edge of the Forbidden Territory, please, to the start of the Street of the Roofers," I said in a rather polite and cultured manner.

But demons are obviously not taught to be polite and cultured.

"Have you lost your mind, manling?" Vukhdjaaz hissed, grabbing me by the sides of my chest. "Or drunk a drop too much? Do I look like a carriage driver?"

"I have to get out of here!" I had no time for arguing with this creature. "Take me where I ask, and you'll find out where to get the Horse!"

The demon gave me an angry and suspicious look, obviously wondering which way to devour me, then suddenly opened his fingers and let me go.

"All right, I'll take you where you want to go, but if you trick me I'll suck the marrow out of your bones."

"A deal." I took a deep breath.

"Are you ready, manling?"

"Yes." Without even looking, I grabbed a couple of ancient tomes off the nearest shelf.

What can I say, it's a professional habit. I could sell those books to people who appreciated them for huge money—why not earn a bit extra, since I hadn't been able to stick my nose into the gnomes' bank?

"I'll just take ..."

Vukhdjaaz grabbed me by the scruff of the neck and pulled me up against him.

Clack!

In the first instant the wall leapt toward me. In the second something gray flickered in front of my eyes and my ears felt as if they were stuffed with cotton wool. In the third, I was already standing beside the magic wall, blinking in amazement.

". . . a couple of books," I said, completing my interrupted sentence.

"You already took them," the demon snorted. "Well? Where is it?"

"Come to the Knife and Ax tomorrow at exactly one minute after midnight and I'll give you the Horse."

Vukhdjaaz gave a muffled growl and bared his huge teeth. "I can tell you're lying!"

"Why would I?" I asked, shrugging my shoulders and squinting up nervously at the sky. About two minutes to dawn at the most. "You can always find me. Come, but at precisely the time I said, otherwise the Horse might no longer be there."

"Don't try to tell me what to do, you little snake! I'll be there!" the demon growled, and disappeared into the wall of the nearest house. He didn't even remind me about sucking the marrow out of my bones.

I breathed a sigh of relief, carefully set the books on the top of the wall, clambered up onto it myself, and was about to climb down when I remembered a piece of unfinished business.

"Valder, you have to go now."

"Good-bye," the archmagician's voice replied immediately.

"Thank you. Live in the light."

I felt something disappear from inside me. The archmagician was gone.

I jumped down from the wall, then reached up and took the books lying on top of it. Well, that was that. I'd done something no one else had ever done—gone right through the Forbidden Territory. Of course, I'd cheated a bit and obtained help from a demon, but your average philistine didn't have to know anything about that.

I was just about to go when I heard a shout from behind the wall:

"Harold, save me!"

I jumped up, grabbed hold of the top of the wall, pulled myself up, and saw who was calling me.

It was Shnyg, hobbling and stumbling along the Street of the Roofers and repeatedly falling over. So he'd survived, the tenacious son of a bitch! He must have raced the entire length of the street to get here in time.

"Shnyg, old buddy, do you need my help?"

"Harold! Don't leave me!" he shouted.

I'm not exactly overflowing with love for neighbors who would like to stick a knife in my heart, but there was a good reason to help Shnyg . . . if, of course, he was willing to tell me about his client and about the mysterious Master.

"Quick!" I barked. "Speed up! Dawn's almost here."

There was despair written all over the thief's simple face. With all his might, he forced himself to go faster.

"Now," I said, honey dripping from my words. "All you have to do is tell me who your client is, and what you know about the Master. Then, my friend, I'll quick pull you right over the wall."

Shnyg stopped and wailed, "I can't do that, Harold. He'll kill me sure! Please! Help me over and we'll make a deal!"

But then the pink dawn flooded the horizon, dispelling the darkness. I jumped back swiftly, sliding down off the wall onto the ground, and out of the corner of my eye I saw blinding-bright rays of crimson light come bursting out of the unfortunate thief in all directions. There was a muffled howl, and then silence. Oh well, I probably couldn't have trusted anything he said, anyway.

I picked the heavy books up off the ground, hugged them against myself, and set off through the awakening neighborhoods of the Artisans' City.

In this part of the city they got up very early. These hard workers left sleep behind when other people were still dozing. If you want to make money, get up early. Funny, the rich sleep late and they earn more than these poor slobs will ever see.

The baker had lit his stove long ago, and there was a pleasant smell of fresh bread and dough coming from his house. The milkman was hurrying on his rounds, pushing along a huge cart loaded with metal canisters. A tinsmith was on his way to the Port City. An old house painter yawned widely as he wandered along, still not fully awake.

"Go on, get out of it!" said a frail old woman, waving an equally old and tattered broom at a drunk lying on the ground. They don't like idlers in the Artisans' City.

I think that after the announcement that the demons of night had been driven out of Avendoom forever, the number of drunks who didn't get home, but fell asleep on the way, increased sharply. The city went on living its life without paying any attention to what was hidden behind the white wall of the Forbidden Territory. In two hundred years people can get used to even more terrifying neighbors than that.

"Well, there's evil there right beside us, but it stays on the other side of the wall, it doesn't come out here and bother us. So that's all right. Our grandfathers lived here, our fathers lived here, now we live here. And our grandchildren and great-grandchildren will be all right, too!"

That's the way almost every one of them thinks.

Sometimes when I hear these simpletons it makes me feel really angry. It's just like sitting on a powder keg with a lighted fuse out in the open air and hoping for a shower of rain. I understand that there's nothing that can be done with this ulcer on the body of the city, the mysterious Stain. But you can't just close your eyes and hope that the gods will save you! Because . . .

Damn it! I was tired.

The Artisans' City was behind me, there weren't many people out on the streets, and I had no problems as I walked through a part of the city that was still half empty at this early hour of the morning. A few of the locals gave my tattered and dirty clothes a dubious sideways glance, but on this particular occasion, I really couldn't care less about them. My less than joyful expression frightened off the most curious of them and I plodded on quite calmly all the way to Cathedral Square.

Here I was met by the familiar senior priests. It looked as if these old ruins had not even left their posts since the last time I'd seen them. Both of them regarded me with expressions of something less than delight. However, they hadn't been put there to think but to carry out a very important and responsible assignment—to repeat the same phrase over and over again, like parrots from faraway places.

"Do you struggle with the Darkness within you?"

Oh, that's exactly what I was just talking about!

"I exterminate the Darkness," I replied wearily, keen to get the irrepressible cathedral staff's idiotic and pompous nonsense over with as soon as possible.

"Then enter and address Them," the second priest told me, in a voice that sounded rather feeble and uncertain.

Probably my appearance wasn't conducive to long theological discussions.

"I'll address them straightaway," I muttered, heading toward the living quarters of the priests of Sagot. And thinking in particular of someone who took gold pieces for idiotic pieces of advice.

The knight-and-ogre fountain was still gurgling merrily, throwing up jets of sparkling water. There were priests bustling around the statues of the gods. The morning cleanup, before the worshipers arrived. One of them was carefully wiping Sagra's face with a rag, another was laying a bouquet of flowers at the feet of the attractive Silna. They took no notice of me.

I stopped in front of the archway that brought back rather unpleasant memories. After a moment's hesitation, I took a step forward.

Nothing happened.

No over-clever creature of darkness tried to grab hold of me. And no one threatened to suck the marrow out of my bones.

Strange.

Maybe something had happened? I strolled backward and forward, waiting for someone to do me the favor of grabbing me. Nothing. Right, the Darkness take that Vukhdjaaz! I gave up and took myself off to For's chambers.

On the way I came across several priests who were extinguishing the torches that had burned all night. The servants of Sagot took no notice of me; they had apparently been informed of my impending visit. I walked up to the familiar door, pushed it open, and barged into my teacher's dwelling. He had clearly not gone to bed, but sat up at the table all the time I was away. The table, by the way, was empty, with not a single crumb of food, which was another strange thing. For must have been worried about his wayward pupil after all.

"So there you are," he said with a start when he caught sight of me, but gave no sign of being glad. "Did it go well?"

I dumped the bag containing the papers and books on the table in front of him.

"Oho!" he exclaimed. "I didn't expect that. Will you tell me what it was like?"

"Later," I mumbled. "A bit later. Wake me up when it gets dark."

And with those words I pulled off my dirty clothes, flopped onto the bed, and sank into the welcome embrace of sleep.

B

WHAT IT SAID IN THE PAPERS

I was woken by the rustling of pages being turned, but I didn't open my eyes in a hurry, deciding to carry on lying there for a while instead.

"That's enough idling about, it's evening already," For said peevishly when he spotted that I wasn't asleep.

"Is it already dark?" I asked with a yawn.

"It soon will be. Have you got things to do?"

"Unfortunately," I muttered, sitting up on the bed. For had occupied his favorite armchair and was studying one of the old tomes that I had brought back from the Tower of the Order. The other book and the bundle of manuscripts were lying beside him on a small table.

"I took the liberty of throwing away your clothes. Only beggars could wear them now, and even they would probably be too ashamed. There are some new ones on the chair. What do you think, will dark colors suit you?"

I usually leave rhetorical questions unanswered. In any case, For knows perfectly well that it's handier to work in dark clothes at night and—let's be frank about it—far less dangerous. Only a madman would dress up in white to enter the houses of rich men who would probably spot him from a hundred yards away and arrange a warm welcome, followed by a hard poke with something very sharp.

The clothes were a good fit, except that the shirt was a bit tight in the shoulders, but that was only a minor problem. My gaze fell on a table beside the window set with food and my stomach gurgled in craving.

"I see that your nocturnal stroll has not damaged your appetite, so perhaps it's time we sat down at the table and thanked Sagot for another day of life?" said For, putting the book down and getting up out of his chair.

"When did you start reading old books on magic?" I wasn't aware that my old friend had developed a new interest.

"I wasn't really reading it," For said with a shrug as he walked toward the table. "Merely a cursory valuation of the goods. You could get three or four hundred for both books. I can suggest a buyer; I still haven't lost my old contacts."

"I don't need gold just at the moment," I muttered, sitting down at the table.

The warm rays of the setting sun pierced the elegant wooden lattice on the windows like lances and fell on my face. The evening sky was blazing like incandescent steel.

"But you hold on to the books in any case, someday I might have to sell them," I said.

"All right," For agreed with a nod.

He had an interest in the deal as well—twenty percent of the selling price. The money would always come in handy for Sagot's shrine.

"But just what do you think you're doing sitting there? You ought to wash your hands at least, you dirty swine, honestly!"

"I washed my hands, I washed my hands," I growled, but I got up obediently and went to the washstand.

I really was dirty, and I needed a wash. I only grumbled for form's sake, because of the hellish tiredness that I still felt even after sleeping all day long.

"And have a shave while you're at it! You look like a real bandit, kid!" For's voice said behind me.

I mechanically ran one hand over my three-day stubble.

"It'll do as it is. I'm not going to the royal ball, after all!" I snorted, lowering my hands into the water. "There's no time. I still have to deal with a whole gang of horse breeders."

"Well, you know best. Anyway, tell me what it was like in there. We ought to record it for the chronicles and future generations."

"So you've become a chronicler as well now? The things you discover about your old teacher!" I said, going back to the table.

"The old knowledge is slipping out from our world very rapidly. A lot has already been lost." For sighed. "You must agree that your story could help a lot of people, especially as this is primarily for the chronicle of the shrine of Sagot."

"I have no objections," I said with a shrug. "Why not? You don't mind if I talk and eat at the same time, do you?"

"Of course not, kid, of course not. Carry on, and after your story, I'll tell you a bit about the papers you retrieved."

"Is there anything important in them? I just grabbed what was there at hand."

"There is, but we'll get to that later, there's no hurry. Come on then, don't keep me on tenterhooks."

He didn't have to persuade me, especially since I had plenty to talk about and a lot of impressions to share. And I needed to get it all out, otherwise my adventures that night could easily drive me mad.

I started my story from the moment I first arrived at Stark's Stables. For listened without speaking—my teacher had always been a good listener. To judge from his face, what bothered him most were the thieves who had been hired by some unknown individual. He didn't seem particularly impressed by the Jolly Weeper or the long-dead archmagician.

"Someone's following the same road as you are, kid. True, he's always too late, but how long can that go on for? How long can you go on making a fool of the Master by keeping one step ahead of him? I made inquiries, looked through our archives. Not a thing. Not a single mention. As if he didn't even exist and all this was just a fantasy of yours."

"Oh yeah?"

"You just eat that roll. I believe you. But what amazes me is that such secrecy is possible. Something always has to surface somewhere."

"But not this time."

"Right. It's not the Nameless One, but I think you've already realized that. The wizard from the Desolate Lands doesn't have the power to release all the demons. So who is this Master, if he possesses such great might, long life, and extensive knowledge?"

"A god?" I chuckled.

"Don't talk nonsense. Although . . . he is worshiped and served by all different sorts of people. Let's try pulling on that chain. The Duke Patin, no mean figure in Valiostr, served the Master. So does Markun and, consequently, at least half his henchmen in the guild as well. Who else? Magicians? Royal officials? Courtiers? And this . . . emissary of yours. What worries me is that it's not at all clear what this Master wants. And he has as many worshipers as you could wish for. The servants of the

Nameless One are caught pretty regularly, but so far they haven't caught a single one of the Master's minions."

"They've never even heard of them."

"Exactly. And that indicates highly organized contacts, a secret conspiracy, and other such arrangements that make it possible for sects to survive when they're not welcome in this respectable kingdom of ours. Things look bad, kid." For shook his head. "I'll keep on thinking and searching, and maybe I'll dig something up in the archives. And in the meantime I'll give you a piece of good advice."

"For free?" I asked, chuckling mischievously with my mouth full.

"Well, I'm not Sagot, am I, to go taking gold pieces from you! You are my pupil after all."

"Well, thanks for that, at least."

"You're welcome. Especially since you're not the only one who's been left out of pocket for receiving our god's advice," For said with a sudden chuckle.

"I don't believe it," I said, leaning back in my chair and looking hard at him. "Are you really hinting that . . ."

"That I've talked to him, too? Yes, it happened. And I had to pay out a gold piece, too."

"Tell me about it."

"Well . . . ," For began reluctantly, chuckling. "I had a talk with him just before I met you and Bass."

"Oh!" I said, beginning to realize what he was about to say.

"Yes, 'oh' indeed! Sagot advised me to take you both on as pupils! It wasn't even advice. Once he had his gold piece, he told me who he was and simply ordered me to do it. So that was how it happened. Although it seems like he was a bit off target with Bass." He frowned. "Anyway, I shouldn't have brought it up. What were we talking about?"

"Advice."

"Well then, this is my piece of free advice for you: Don't leave matters to the mercy of the gods, go and see this Bolt. If the old man recognized the ring that the thieves showed him we'll find out who this influential figure serving the Master is."

"It's too late now," I said, glancing out of the window at the darkening sky. "The library's closed, I'll have to wait until tomorrow."

"Better not. I doubt if the old man ever leaves. He probably sleeps there. Better call round to Grok Square before you get on with your business. I think he'll open the door for you. No point in putting it off. The Master is playing his own game, and all we know about it is that he wants to kill you, which makes him too dangerous by half. And it seems to me that the last thing he wants is for Harold to go after that Horn."

"You're thinking about him ordering the papers to be destroyed and telling the duke to influence the king?"

"Uh-huh. I think the order to influence Stalkon was to try to persuade him that it's pointless going into Hrad Spein. Or simply to get rid of His Majesty."

The clearer the situation became, the less I liked it. "All right, I'll think about it," I said as I watched For suddenly get up from the table and go into the next room.

Events had woven themselves into a tight tangle of snakes. Now they were winding themselves tight around me and turning my skin cold. I just hoped that none of these snakes would bite!

For came back a few minutes later, carrying two massive bronze candlesticks in his hands, each with five lighted candles in it. The timing was just right; the sun had almost set and twilight had already begun creeping into the room with lazy impudence. The bright light of ten candles forced the gloom to move back, and it huddled into the very darkest corner of the room.

"Well then, I've heard your story. Now let's deal with what you brought back from the Forbidden Territory." For showed me the papers I'd taken from the Tower of the Order. "While you were sleeping, I took a look through these documents. There's a lot that's interesting. . . . But you know, kid, none of it's any good to you. Yes, there's a map of Hrad Spein, and even a plan of how to get to the Horn, but it's . . . it's suicide. It's practically impossible to make it along the route that you have to follow. You study the old maps yourself when you have the time, and you'll realize how unrealistic it is. Hundreds of halls, passages, shafts. And that's only down to the eighth level. These papers don't even show what's lower down. Here, take them."

For pushed the maps toward me.

"Let them stay here for the time being, you hide them somewhere safe, I'll pick them up before I leave," I said to him.

"That's up to you," said For, raking the papers back across the table. "Ah, by the way. I found an amusing little page among these notes, look."

I took the old, yellowed piece of paper.

"What is it?"

"It's ancient orcish. I had to sweat over the dictionary a bit to translate it. There's a lot I still don't understand—the orcs' language is a bit of a tangle—but I managed it, even though it's probably not quite as fluent as it ought to be. It was in verse. Something like a series of clues. A total riddle. Read it."

For handed me a piece of paper with the translation.

> First born of an ogre on the wide snowy plains,
> It dwelt for centuries with elves in the Greenwood,
> And was given to Grok in token of the peace
> Concluded between races during the Long Winter.
>
> It was laid to rest by the might of the Order
> At the time of Avendoom's survival in battle.
> Sharing the grave of one of the glorious dead,
> It lies in the dark caverns upon ancient bones.
>
> As the years pass it lies there in Hrad Spein
> Calling the wind of the tombs to its resting place
> The hour will come when it bares its secrets, consuming
> The magic of the cursed with the fire of truth.
>
> If you are artful and brave, bold and quick,
> If your step is light and your thought is keen.
> You will avoid the tricks we have set there,
> But be wary of earth and water and fire.
>
> And then, carry on! The twin doors stand open
> To the peace of the halls of the Slumbering Whisper,
> Where the brains of man and elf and orc alike
> Dissolve in unreason. . . . And so shall yours.

Through the halls of the Slumbering Echo and Darkness
Past the blind, unseeing Kaiyu guards,
'Neath the gaze of Giants who burn all to ash.
To the graves of the Great Ones who died in battle.

In serried ranks, embracing the shadows,
The long-deceased knights stand in silence,
And only one man will not die 'neath their swords,
He who is the shadows' own twin brother.

The cold frozen body of pallid Selena
Will raise you up to the sacred bed.
No sun has warmed stone here for thousands of years,
For centuries here the cold wind has howled.

Remember, intruder, in the Horn dwells a soul
That will give you strength in the name of men.
But the greed of the thief it will punish severely
And you will rot in the terrible darkness forever.

"Mmm, yes. I can hardly understand a thing."

"Which bits do you think you did understand, my pupil?" For asked
in surprise.

It had turned dark outside, and even the candles could not dispel
the persistent darkness. It would soon be time to go about my business.

I drummed my fingers on the table thoughtfully.

"I think I began to understand the point of Sagot's advice. This poem
mentions some Selena who bears you up, and Sagot warned me I'd
better not just stand on her, but keep my feet moving fast."

"Hmmm . . . ," For muttered, and scratched his chin.

Then he grunted and poured himself some wine from a dusty old
potbellied bottle. He offered me some, but I refused—today my head
had to be crystal clear.

"Yes, well, I noticed the reference to Selena, too. This all requires a
bit of serious thought. And by the way, don't forget to show it to the

elfess; she should know the ancient language of the orcs. She might be able to translate this page better than I have."

"All right."

"There's absolutely no doubt that it's about the Rainbow Horn. Look here: 'First born of an ogre on the wide snowy plains'—that's a reference to the shamans of the ogres creating the Horn, the final artifact of their race, before they all turned into animals. 'It dwelt for centuries with elves in the Greenwood'—I'm sure you remember the old story about the head of the House of the Black Rose trying to invade the Desolate Lands. It was on that campaign that the elves took the Horn from the ogres. What comes next is clear enough, too: 'And was given to Grok in token of the peace concluded between races during the Long Winter.' The dark elves gave the Horn to Grok as an assurance of the peace between elves and men that came into force after the great invasion of the orcs that became known as the Spring War."

"That's clear enough."

"Then there's a bit of standard nonsense. This may be ancient orcish, but it was obviously written by a man. Still, these lines are worth thinking about: 'You will avoid the tricks that we have set there, but be wary of earth and water and fire.' What could that be, Harold, if not a warning that the magicians of the Order laid all sorts of traps? 'And then, carry on! The twin doors stand open to the peace of the halls of the Slumbering Whisper, where the brains of man and elf and orc alike dissolve in unreason. . . . And so shall yours.' The open doors are most likely the entrance to the third level, or the double-doored level as it's called in the maps. They show huge doors that lead into the lower halls of Hrad Spein. It's quite possible that they could be sealed with a spell."

"Is there any way to get round them, For? Is there another entrance?"

"I didn't study the plan for all that long. There are four main entrances to Hrad Spein. One in the north, beside the Border Kingdom. Another in the heart of Zagraba, and two more beside spurs of the Mountains of the Dwarves. But the last two were blocked and walled off by the short folk long ago. Which means there are only two ways in. And they both lead to the doors. So I'm afraid you won't be able to get round them."

"Wonderful," I replied. "And what if I can't get them open?"

"Don't think about that, I'm more worried about the halls of the

Slumbering Whisper and the insanity that's promised. That part wasn't invented just for the sake of the style! And that's only half the problem. Further on, there's a mention of some kind of 'Kaiyus'—that's an orcish word, but from an elfin dialect, it couldn't possibly be anything else. But what does 'Kaiyu' mean? Is it some kind of magic, or creatures, or something even worse?"

"I'll ask Miralissa," I said. All this riddle-me-ree verse was beginning to give me a splitting headache.

"And then the Giants who burn all to ash . . . yet another riddle. Although at least the burial chambers of the Great Ones who died in battle are very well known. There are entire halls of warriors buried on the sixth level over a period of a little more than five centuries. A huge cemetery, where everyone in every grave was a legend when he was alive. And then we have these long-deceased knights with swords, and Selena, who will show you the way to the Horn, and finally a warning that the Horn won't allow itself to be taken all that easily."

"Let's think about all this later!" I implored him. "Otherwise my head will burst! Why couldn't they have just written all this in a normal, straightforward fashion? Here's a beast with big fangs, here's a beast with big claws, and here they'll roast you alive or turn you into a toad! But oh no, they had to practice their poetry-writing skills!"

"What else can you expect?" For asked with a sigh and a shrug. "The Order loves puzzles; magicians' brains are arranged a bit differently from ours. I think I'll do a bit more thinking about this text. And you do what you were going to do. It's already night."

While I was talking with For, the bird of night had indeed furtively spread its black wings over Avendoom. It was time to go to work.

"You're right. It's time I was off."

"Don't forget to question Bolt," For shouted after me.

"I remember, I remember," I replied, already walking out into the corridor.

That night I had to put a final end to the affair of the Horse of Shadows.

14

KNIVES IN THE SHADOWS

Darkness was well advanced in the city, but this time around no one was hiding away at home. There were quite a lot of people on the square and I even spotted five guards parading up and down in front of Grok's statue with an important air, evidently concerned that the good citizens, intoxicated by their new-found freedom, might steal the immensely heavy sculpture.

I glanced in passing at the deceased duke's house. There was no light in the windows, as was only to be expected. I walked round the building of the library into the dark side street and then . . .

I was just about to hammer on the iron door loud enough to wake Bolt and the entire neighborhood with him when I suddenly noticed a thin strip of light seeping out from underneath it. Strange. Very Strange. Bolt must have got drunk and forgotten to close up the library for the night.

And what if it hadn't been an honest and highly respectable person like me who spotted the light and decided to pay him a call, but some light-fingered petty thief? In that case half of the rare books would simply have disappeared off all those shelves as if by magic. I chuckled and pushed the door. It swung back smartly, revealing the dark tunnel of the service corridor.

There was light only beside the door; beyond that was complete darkness. I swore good-naturedly about people who can't be bothered to make proper lighting arrangements, took the torch down off the wall, and set off along the familiar corridor, ignoring the branches to the right and the left.

I'd been here once before already, and that was quite enough to know the way. The journey to the halls with the books only took a couple of minutes. My magical vision had not returned after the Forbidden Territory, and so I had to rely on the source of light in my hand and curses directed at Honchel's head. The light from the lanterns, securely covered with gnome glass to make sure that the flames would not, Sagot forbid, escape from captivity, was quite adequate. It was only way up high, close to the very ceiling that the bookcases and shelves were wreathed in a cloak of darkness.

I went back along the corridor a bit and left the torch on an empty bracket. No point in annoying Bolt; it would give him a stroke if he saw I'd brought a naked flame near his precious books.

"Hey, Bolt! This is Harold!" I shouted, and my voice echoed off the vaulted ceiling, bounced round the walls, and dissolved in the maze of books and bookcases.

Silence. Not a sound. The old man was dozing under a table somewhere. Or it could be that he was simply hard of hearing and couldn't hear my howls of greeting.

"Bolt! Are you here?"

I walked slowly forward, searching for the familiar stooped figure. But as I said before, in this huge building you could wander for thousands of years and not meet a single living soul. I turned sharply to the right and moved in the direction of the tables where I had studied the books the last time. There was a spot there where you could easily drink a bottle of wine without having to worry that anyone might disturb you. If the old man wasn't there, I'd have to turn the whole place upside down. I saw a gleam of light ahead.

"Bolt!" I roared before I even entered the reading hall.

I was right! There was a lantern on the table, and beside it a bottle of wine, a half-eaten crust of bread, and a bunch of spring onions.

The bottle was almost empty, with just a little wine left in the bottom. The old man was stretched out on the floor in a puddle of red wine. Just look at the state of him!

I walked toward the sleeping drunk, muttering something uncomplimentary under my breath about people who like to guzzle wine at the most inappropriate times, feverishly trying to work out the quickest way to bring him back to a state of awareness and question him.

"Bolt! Wake up now! Get up. You look like a pig. It's disgusting!"

I leaned down and shook him by the shoulder. "How long can you go on . . ."

I didn't finish the phrase, because I noticed something rather upsetting—Bolt didn't seem to be breathing. And he wasn't lying in a puddle of wine, as I'd thought at first, but in a puddle of his own blood. I cautiously turned the old man over onto his back.

I was right. Some bastard had slit the poor old man's throat from ear to ear. The body was still warm, and not very much blood had escaped yet. That meant the murderer or murderers had only finished Bolt off very recently. And that meant it was very likely they hadn't got very far yet and I could easily catch up with them on a nearby street.

I almost gave way to this momentary impulse, but the voice of reason cooled my ardor. This time the Master had got here before me, and now I would never learn whose ring Rostgish and Shnyg had shown to Bolt. And it made no sense to go chasing after unknown killers who might well turn out not even to be human. There was no way I could help the poor fellow now.

It was a pity; I'd grown quite attached to the crazy, grouchy old-timer.

There was a trail of blood leading away from the body and winding between the tables into the depths of the hall. I took the lantern off the table to light the way and followed the traces of blood. Before I had even gone twenty paces I came across a second body.

I knew this overgrown lout. He was one of the characters who had gone running out of the alley where Roderick and I were ambushed. This time his luck had run out and he hadn't managed to get away. There was a knife protruding from the stiff's chest. The last time I'd seen it, Bolt had it on his belt. So the old man had managed to sell his life dearly after all—it was true that the Wild Hearts didn't leave this life quietly; one of the killers had paid for his . . .

Three shadows sprang into the circle of light from somewhere behind the dark bookcases, preventing me from completing my thought. I noticed a glint of metal and leapt to one side.

Putrid Darkness! Why had I decided that the killers had already left? I jumped back, pressing up against a bookcase. The three figures were coming closer. As ill luck would have it, my crossbow wasn't loaded, which made it useless. My only hope was my knife. I took the weapon out without speaking, held it out in front of me, and waited for them to attack, somehow certain that we wouldn't part in peace. Lads like these would kill their own grandmother, and the rest of the family into the bargain. I could tell, because I'd seen two of the killers before, and not exactly in the best of circumstances.

The first one, the one who had jumped right at me, was the partner of the stiff that Bolt had killed. This thug was holding a knife in his left hand and smiling.

The second one was none other than the municipal guard Yargi, this time not in his orange and black uniform but wearing civilian clothes, so I hadn't recognized him straightaway. That meant these lads were working for the unknown servant of the Master, if one of the bribed servants of the law was here with them.

I wondered where the rest of them were.

I didn't know the third killer. He looked tough, tanned by the winds, you might say. A wolf between two mongrel dogs. The knife in his hand kept breaking into a dance.

"Just look at the people you can meet in places like this," Thug drawled slowly as he and his partners halted about ten paces away from me. "Now who's this that's taken a fancy to reading books?"

"Enough talk, we finish him and get out of here! The job's already done!" hissed the third man, moving forward again.

"Calm down, Midge," Thug said reassuringly. "We can kill two birds with one stone here. This is Harold."

"That's Harold?" said Yargi, delighted. "His head's worth its weight in gold!"

"Yes, and now we'll cut it off for him," said Thug, moving toward me.

"You're a bit braver than you used to be," I said, curving my lips into an ugly grin. "I recall that only a few days ago you and the stiff over there took off with your heels twinkling."

"Ah, but you don't have the magician with you now," Thug chuckled, tossing his knife from one hand to the other.

"Stop, let me finish him," Yargi said, licking his thin lips and looking at me with a greedy gleam in his eyes. "Let me have a bit of fun."

"Watch out he doesn't finish you," Midge chuckled, but he and Thug moved back, freeing the space for a fight. The lads had obviously decided they would like a bit of light entertainment, and they didn't rate my humble personage's chances at all. "Don't drag it out, now. If anyone else comes, this place will be full of bodies."

"Nobody's interested in this dump. You already topped the old man, Midge. Now relax—"

"But the old man did for that friend of yours first," Midge put in. "A real Wild Heart."

"But you were one of them, too."

"Shut up!" Midge barked.

A Wild Heart? Here? Could he really be a deserter? That meant the lad was even more dangerous than I'd imagined!

"Well then, thief? Shall we let the fun begin?" Yargi smiled with his jagged mouth of teeth and leapt toward me, aiming his knife at my stomach.

I dodged sideways and tried to reach him with my weapon, but failed. I had to jump toward the lantern standing on the floor and wave my knife through the air to drive Yargi well back.

"Where's your crossbow, thief?" Thug asked in a mocking voice, but I ignored him.

Yargi moved into the attack again and we started circling round the lantern, waiting for someone to make the first inexcusable and fatal mistake.

Our knives clashed a couple of times with a repulsive clang, then they started weaving a cobweb pattern of feints and dodges, slowly but surely leading one of us to victory and the other to the grave. Steel sliced through the air and our shadows danced across the walls of bookcases and shelves.

I had to sweat a bit; the damned guard was holding his knife with the Nizin reverse grip. On the one hand that was bad—the skunk could easily shift his blade backward and forward between a cutting or a slashing blow. On the other hand, it was good, because the Nizin technique was intended for soldiers wearing armor that protected the free hand against being cut, but for anyone with just a shirt instead of chain mail and a chain-mail glove, this technique was a double-edged sword.

Whoooosh! My opponent's knife came flying at my face. I parried, but at the last moment his weapon changed direction and I had to twist sharply to avoid being stabbed in the armpit. Yargi was a little bit unlucky, because when his blow missed its target, his inertia spun him round slightly, and I had time to strike at his left arm and jump away before he could realize what had happened. He hissed in pain as he shook his injured wrist.

"You're not too agile, my friend."

"Shut up. I'll kill you!" he hissed. There were heavy drops of blood flowing off his fingers and falling to the floor.

Why strain yourself trying to reach your enemy's stomach or neck, if you can give him deep cuts on his wrists and wait for the wounds to make him weak from loss of blood and admit him into that world that the priests assure us is blessed? Yargi also realized that he didn't have much time left, and he came charging straight at me like a rhinoceros, trying to trick me with rapid feints. I wriggled like an eel, but I still got a slight cut on my chest.

"It's time to stop this fairground performance and leave," I heard someone say. Midge's patience was almost exhausted.

"You'll be carried out of here feetfirst, you skunk!"

When he heard me say that, Yargi hesitated for a moment, and I tore the cloak off my shoulder, flung it in his face, and immediately moved in and struck him with my knife. Thug swore viciously behind me.

Yargi dropped his knife, started to wheeze, and grabbed hold of my wrist. I pulled it free with an effort, leaving the knife behind in his belly. Harold was left without his most important and most persuasive argument.

The other two killers came for me without any more talk. I leapt back in a most inelegant manner, on the way flinging the lantern into Thug's face and sticking my hand into my bag to feel for a magic vial. Thug caught the lantern I'd thrown at him as if it were a ball and clicked his tongue in disappointment.

I fumbled in my bag and tossed a round little bottle of poisonous-yellow liquid at Midge, but he ducked his head and the damned magical bauble smashed against one of the legs of a gigantic set of shelves loaded with books. So instead of the hired killer's head, it was the wooden leg that dissolved into thin air.

A remarkable stroke of luck!

"Come here, Harold! Time to stop running! I'm going to slice you to ribbons!"

Meanwhile the shelves, having lost their support, started tumbling forward, straight onto the unsuspecting killers. Just one moment longer, and they both would have been crushed, but the sound of books slipping off the shelves attracted their attention. Midge dived aside, but Thug, being rather less bright, started turning round, opened his mouth wide in amazement, and was hit by the hail of tumbling tomes. Then the shelves that were missing a leg collapsed, overwhelming the man and flattening him to a pancake. His final howl was drowned out by a loud rumble.

I glanced round. Midge was nowhere to be seen. Without wasting any more time, I reclaimed my knife, wiped it on the dead man's clothes, and put it back in its scabbard. Then I loaded my crossbow: I pulled on the lever to tighten the string and set the bolts in their firing position. Then, for extra reassurance, I put another bolt between my teeth so that if the first two missed the target I wouldn't lose too much time reloading. Having armed myself, I began methodically withdrawing to the exit.

I forced myself not to run, although I wanted to dash through the dark rooms and out into the light as quickly as possible. But to hurry would have been to lose control of the situation and, consequently, to make myself vulnerable.

Eventually the damned bookcases and shelves came to an end and I was left facing the corridor that led to the service door. I stopped, trying to decide how best to sneak along a narrow tunnel where it was hard even to turn round, let alone engage in armed combat with a Wild Heart.

It was his shadow that gave him away. It was pale and weak, almost hidden by shafts of light, but I could still see it. Midge might have been an experienced warrior, but he hadn't done a very good job of hiding. The killer had climbed up a set of shelves and hung there, waiting for me to pass by below him.

We both made our move at the same time—I spun round, raising the crossbow, and he jumped down onto my shoulders with his knife.

The bowstring twanged. The first bolt just missed my enemy as he fell onto me and struck one of the thick volumes standing on the top shelf. I had no time to take a second shot. Or even to jump aside. The killer slumped on top of me with all his weight, and the only reason I wasn't killed was that I managed to strike him across the wrist with the crossbow with all my might. His knife and my weapon went flying off to one side.

I fell onto my back, hitting my head against the stone floor, and showers of bright sparks exploded inside it. The accursed killer landed on me and without a second's hesitation, not disconcerted in the least by having lost his knife, he smashed his fist into my face.

Bang! One of the gnomes' powder kegs exploded on my right temple and I gritted my teeth, almost biting through the bolt I was holding between them. Struggling against the pain, I made a highly inelegant effort to kick him, but this pitiful attempt was unsuccessful. Midge swung his fist back and smashed it into me again. I grabbed the crossbow bolt out of my teeth, swung it, and stuck it into my opponent's shoulder. He roared and slackened his grip a little bit, but then smashed me in the face with his elbow with a furious growl. Unlike his partners, he wasn't given to idle conversation, and simply wanted to finish the job as quickly as possible so that he could be on his way.

The finale of our epic battle, which was worthy of being recorded in the frescoes in the royal palace, was that Midge's sinewy hands grabbed the neck of a certain Harold in a crayfish-claw grip and set about choking him in a rather determined fashion by closing off the flow of air to his lungs.

I punched Midge on the ribs with both hands, but that didn't have any effect, either. He merely tightened his grip like an imperial hound and leaned over me, gritting his teeth. The bolt in his shoulder was no hindrance to him at all.

Someone began wheezing in a most convincing fashion. Then the wheezing began fading away, retreated into the background, and got tangled up in the shadows. When the darkness had completly subdued me, from out of some other world, a beautiful world full of fresh air, I heard the twang of a bowstring, the whistle of an arrow in flight, and a dull thud. Then something very heavy fell on me, finally pinning me to the floor. Amazingly enough it became easier to breathe.

I lay there without opening my eyes, breathing in that priceless gift of the gods—air. Everything inside me was wheezing and whirling and whistling. My neck hurt unbearably, it was even painful to swallow, but I was breathing, and that was the most important thing just at the moment.

"Alive, my lord!" a voice above me said.

"Get him up!" To judge from the angry voice, that was Baron Frago Lanten in person.

Sheer politeness obliged me to part my heavy eyelids and take a look at the new characters in this never-ending comedy. I was right.

The baron, in an unusually dour mood, was standing over me in the company of about two dozen of his faithful dogs. The heavy item that had fallen on me was none other than the dead Midge. They had shot an arrow straight between his shoulder blades, and the hired killer had decided to die right on top of me.

To be quite honest, I must confess that this was the first time in my life I had ever been so glad to see the municipal guard. In my mind I took back all the bad things I'd ever said about their skill and their intellectual capacity, and swore on the health of the leader of the Doralissians that this week I wouldn't think anything nasty about them even once.

A soldier took a firm grip on me under my arms and set me on my feet. For some reason the floor was swaying about rather vigorously and I had to make a serious effort not to fall. After its recent encounter with Midge's fist, my face was burning with an appalling heat, as if someone had briefly held a red-hot poker against it.

"Baron Lanten? You have no idea how glad I am to see you here," I croaked quite sincerely.

My throat was still sore, and I could still feel the other man's remorseless fingers on my neck.

"I should think so," one of the guards snorted.

"Harold, you son of a bitch, what in the name of Darkness are you doing here?" Frago barked. I could see that I'd spoiled his mood for an entire month ahead. "What if we hadn't turned up?"

"Then the story would have ended very sadly for me," I muttered.

I hate it when people yell at me.

"And not only for you!" Frago went on, still howling. "The king would have had my hide!"

"How did you know you should look for me here?"

"We didn't know," snapped the baron, a little calmer now, and sat down on a chair hastily moved up for him by one of his subordinates. Naturally, no one offered me a seat, but I was in no state to be concerned about etiquette and so I took a stool and made myself comfortable facing the baron.

"We didn't know," the baron repeated, and glanced at the guards. "Djig, take a stroll."

"As you say, milord."

"We were looking for this criminal," said the baron, jabbing one finger disdainfully toward Midge's corpse. "A deserter and a traitor. The Wild Hearts were looking for him, too, but we were luckier. A little bird whispered in my ear that this bold lad was in the Royal Library, so we came to catch him while he was available. We weren't planning on meeting you."

It was hardly surprising that Frago himself had decided to take part in the hunt and the arrest. Deserters from the Wild Hearts were regarded as the most dangerous of criminals. And it was very lucky for Midge that he'd caught that arrow in his back. If the Wild Hearts had got their hands on him, they would have talked to him in a rather different tone of voice. He wouldn't have departed this world quite so easily.

"Let me repeat my question. What are you doing here, Harold?"

"I came to look up an old friend. He's the custodian of this library."

"And where is your friend, if you would be so kind as to tell me?"

"He's dead."

"Tell me about it."

So I told him. I had to leave out half of the details, of course. I didn't say a word about the Master and his servants, or the fact that I had seen some of the killers before that night.

"Well, we can say that you have been very lucky, thief," the baron chuckled when he had heard my story. It was clear that he could barely tolerate my presence. It obviously enraged him.

"We can say that I've been very lucky." I had already recovered my wits a little after what had happened, and now I was impatient for an opportunity to slip out of there and get as far away as possible. "Am I free to go?"

There was nothing more for me to do there—I wouldn't learn anything from Bolt's dead body, and the other dead men would be as tight-lipped as ... well, as dead men.

"Why, have you business to attend to at such a late hour?" The baron chuckled. "I hope it doesn't involve entering some innocent rich man's house?"

"Innocent rich men only exist in fairy tales, milord," I harrumphed, and got up off the stool, firmly intending to be on my way.

The baron seemed about to order me to sit down and shut up, but then Djig appeared and distracted him.

"Milord, there's one of our men over there."

"What drivel is this?" Frago asked with a frown.

"If it please milord, there's no doubt. It's Yargi. He was on the night shift with the sixth patrol. The Port City."

"From Justin's unit?"

"They have another commander now. In that business beside Stark's Stables Justin—"

"I know, I know. You don't have to remind me," Frago snapped.

"Well, what a night!" Frago exclaimed, and spat. "Harold, do you at least know that you bumped off one of my men?"

"Of course no, milord. He didn't bother to introduce himself before trying to reduce me to prime cuts."

"I see." Frago sighed. "Well, there's a mangy sheep in every herd."

I could have told the baron that he had more than one mangy sheep in his herd, but I maintained a judicious silence. They say silence is golden, and just recently I'd begun to understand that they're right.

"Come with me; you can identify him," Frago said with an imperious gesture.

Uh-huh. Why, of course! I had nothing better to do than go running after the baron like a lapdog up on its hind legs.

"Pardon me, milord, but I have the king's assignment."

That earned me another dour glance from Lanten. But he decided it was better not to insist. You didn't usually argue with the king's orders, unless you were a goblin jester. It could have a most lamentable effect on your health.

"All right. Get out of here."

I didn't wait for the commander of the guard to change his mind, but disappeared into the corridor in a flash. And I didn't forget to pick up the torch on the way, to make the return journey bright and cheerful. I was in an absolutely foul mood.

15

ANSWERS

Pardon me for the foolish pun, but the Street of the Sleepy Dog was sunk in a deep sleep. It differed strikingly from its sister street— the Street of the Sleepy Cat—in both the arrangement of the houses and their size. The Sleepy Dog was rather short and winding, with an assortment of low-class shops, little old houses, and a couple of inns with reputations that were not exactly the best.

I was standing right in front of one of them. One fine day that huge sign in the form of a knife and an ax promised to forget its public responsibilities and come tumbling down on the head of some unlucky passerby.

As I had expected, the Knife and Ax was empty. For had told me that Gozmo had closed up his little establishment for no apparent reason. Which was rather strange, if you knew how much money he lost by doing that. And not just from the sale of beer, but also from the fees that came his way when contracts for Commissions were concluded inside his inn.

The doors and the shutters were closed, but neither were any real barrier to me. I was in a determined mood and intended to visit Gozmo's inn that night, come what may. A serious conversation between my old friend and myself was long overdue, and night is the most convenient time for catching an innkeeper off guard. Between three and four in the morning he ought to be sleeping like a log and it's not very likely that he would be disposed to resist.

At first I felt like simply breaking in as bold as brass through the main door and walking right through the entire inn as if I owned the place, but I bridled my passion and decided to break into Gozmo's bedroom window. It was a lot simpler, and there would be less fiddling about with locks and bolts.

The window of Gozmo's bedroom was on the second floor. I had the cobweb rope with me, and it only took me a minute to reach my goal. I had to spend a little more time on the catch. Unfastening it without making a racket was no simple job, but I don't earn my bread for nothing.

Gozmo was snoring away, trilling like a nightingale; nothing could have been farther from his mind than uninvited guests. There were several china pots with forget-me-nots in my way and I almost knocked them off the windowsill. I had to twist and turn like one of the circus acrobats on the Market Square in order to avoid breaking anything.

Gozmo carried on sleeping serenely. That's what's it like to have no conscience at all.

I tiptoed up to him, took the rope lying on his bedside table, and then carefully slipped my hand under the pillow. I was right. My fingers came across something cold. My old friend Gozmo wasn't quite as stupid and placid as you might think.

After borrowing his throwing knife, I made my way across to an armchair, brushed a few cheap rags off it, and sat down. I wanted to make Harold's entrance effective. The innkeeper had thoroughly deserved it, so it was worth my while thinking how to arrange everything for maximum effect, so that I could get at least some of my own back on the damned traitor.

When I'd visited Gozmo's room five years earlier (on that occasion I happened to go in through the door), there had been a heavy hunting horn hanging on one of the walls. Quite a valuable item. Now I got up, walked over to the wall, and felt along it until I found the toy trumpet.

I took out my crossbow, sat down in the armchair again, set the weapon on my knees, and imagined Gozmo's face. I felt like laughing, but I restrained myself.

I wasn't afraid of waking anyone else. Gozmo didn't rent out rooms, so there were no guests at the inn, and after their shift the bouncers went home. We were alone in the building, and as for the inhabitants of the houses round about, they had seen far stranger things in their time. Or rather, heard them.

I raised the horn to my lips, filled my lungs with air, and blew.

What a sound that was! Even I hadn't expected such an effect! The sudden roar—which was like the rumble of a mountain avalanche mingled with the braying of an ass crazed with terror—went hurtling round the room, bouncing off the walls and setting my ears ringing.

Gozmo stopped snoring, flew a full yard up into the air, together with his blanket, and when he landed he started shaking his head violently, still too sleepy to understand a thing. I had got my satisfaction and I roared in merry laughter.

"Who's there?" the villain barked. His eyes weren't accustomed to the dark yet and all he could see was the window.

His hand slid under the pillow like a snake and discovered nothing there.

"Harold."

"Harold?"

"Who else could it be, visiting you at this hour? Light a candle."

The innkeeper's hands were trembling and so it took a while for the light to appear, and when it did, it lit up the old swindler more than it did me. He was sitting on the edge of the bed with an absolutely idiotic expression on his face, batting his eyelids crazily. All he could see of me was a shadow in the armchair, a blurred form on the boundary between light and darkness. The light of the candle simply didn't reach me; the darkness devoured it when it was barely halfway there. I had to lean forward to bring my face into the circle of light.

"Well, have you recovered?" I inquired derisively.

"Harold, you're a real bastard!"

"I'm glad that you and I are in agreement on that point. Now let's talk."

"What about?" Gozmo looked angry and dumbfounded at the same time.

"There's a little matter I need to discuss. I've been doing a lot of thinking—"

"That'll do you good," the innkeeper interrupted.

The bowstring twanged, and a bolt went humming across the room and struck the headboard of the bed, very close to Gozmo. He jumped in the air.

"In the name of Darkness! What's wrong with you? Are you crazy?"

He seemed a little jittery.

"Be so kind as not to interrupt me. I've had a hard night and I've been feeling a bit on edge. So shut your trap and be so good as to hear me out."

The innkeeper took my advice and shut up, although his thin lips turned noticeably paler. He couldn't see the crossbow, but he could sense with every pore in his skin that the weapon was trained on him.

"Right then," I went on, "I've been doing a lot of thinking. About that conversation we had, and about a lot of other apparent coincidences. Why would a rogue like you suddenly decide to apologize? I was a bit too hasty at the time; I decided that it was all about the garrinch in the duke's house, the one that you, you shameless villain, apparently forgot to warn me about. You grabbed at that line of explanation because you thought I didn't know anything and so your precious life was in no danger. But it wasn't really a matter of the garrinch. Isn't that right, Gozmo?"

The innkeeper opened his mouth to say something, then changed his mind and merely licked his dry lips. In our little world the usual penalty for selling somebody short, especially in the way that Gozmo had allowed himself to do, was a slit throat. And, of course, the villain knew that perfectly well. That was why he said nothing and put his trust in luck, fate, Sagot, and Harold's kind heart, now that I had so inconveniently found out about everything.

"All right, I can see that I'm not mistaken. And that's encouraging. Let's start from the fact that you knew who gave you the Commission for the figurine from the duke's house and you didn't say a word."

"I didn't know . . ."

"Well, you had a pretty good idea, which is practically the same thing," I said with an indifferent shrug.

The point was that the person to blame for all this trouble I'd got into over the Horn was Gozmo. And so I had no reason to stand on ceremony with the former thief.

"As Sagot is my witness, Harold, I didn't want to set you up!"

"But you didn't hold back. When you saw Frago Lanten visit your dump and then take me away with him, you understood everything. And you evidently decided that I would be sent to the Gray Stones. You must have been very surprised to see Harold out in the street the next day. You thought I must know everything and you decided to cover your rear. I wouldn't be surprised if Markun played quite an important part in all this."

I threw in that last phrase for effect, to check the depth of the water, without really expecting it to produce any great effect. But Gozmo was so frightened he hiccupped so that I could hear him.

"Markun had nothing to do with it, that's not—" He suddenly broke off.

"That's not how it was?" I asked, grasping avidly at this new thread. "I believe you! I do! Especially since I think you weren't really entirely to blame for slipping me that Commission."

Gozmo sighed in relief, realizing that perhaps he wasn't going to have his throat cut after all.

"But I'll change my mind about that, if you don't tell me all about that fat hog's little deals."

"May the Nameless One snatch you," Gozmo whispered wearily. "All right, Harold, I did something stupid. The first time and the second time. But you have no right to complain about the first time—you got your gold pieces for the figurine, and I can see that your misunderstandings with Lanten have been sorted out. That evening, after you went away with the men in orange and black, Markun and his lads turned up. . . . And he let it drop, in passing as it were, that you had decided to join the guild after all and he needed to talk something over with you urgently. I told him that you were already bound for the Gray Stones and you wouldn't be joining any guild, but Markun insisted. You know how he can be."

I did know. Markun's lads had always been well known for their polite way with reluctant talkers, and I doubted that Gozmo had resisted much, even for the sake of effect.

"You let him know where my lair was," I stated rather than asked.

"Yes! But I didn't think that you'd be there!"

"But the Doralissians that Markun set on me thought differently. Because that night they were waiting for me with a warm welcome. Thanks, Gozmo. You're a real friend. You proved it twice."

The innkeeper winced, ready for any kind of beastliness from me. If I had dispatched him into the light then and there, everyone would have supported me and said I'd done exactly the right thing. In our community of thieves nasty little tricks like that come with a stiff price attached, even if they are unintentional.

"My old friend Gozmo!" I began in a joyful voice, and the other man became even more miserable at this sudden and unreasonable amiability. "I am prepared to forget all our misunderstandings and even not to spread the word about the way you have behaved all round the city, but for a couple of favors in return."

"Anything at all!" Gozmo replied hastily, realizing that one pan of the scales held a couple of favors and the other held his reputation and his life. "That's not much to ask!"

"First of all, tell me about the killing of the magician from Filand and the disappearance of a certain item."

Gozmo chewed on his lip thoughtfully, rubbed his chin, and then said, "Markun's men. Shnyg and Nightingale, the word is. They did a perfect job; not even the magicians can figure it all out. They stole some Doralissian trinket or other. It must be something very valuable, if Markun decided to kill a magician."

"And to confuse the trail even further, that scumbag who is unworthy of the name of thief set the Doralissians on to me! Why else would they have been looking for me all these days?"

"He did that, and then he withdrew into the shadows, to wait for a buyer or a client."

"Wonderful! So now for the second favor. You know everyone who wants to buy anything that's a little bit hot?"

"Well, I do a bit . . ."

"Don't be so modest. Tomorrow morning you'll meet the head of the Guild of Thieves and tell him that someone new has turned up who will buy this item from him for, let's say . . . twenty thousand gold pieces."

"But that would be a lie!"

That made me laugh.

"Gozmo, don't try to tell me that you're an honest man and you never lie. I won't believe you."

"But Markun and his lads will feed me to the fish under the piers!"

"Don't worry about it. I swear on Sagot that soon Markun will forget all about you for years and years. Will you tell him?"

"I will," Gozmo muttered.

"All right, say he has to be in the inn at ten minutes to midnight.

Tomorrow. Or, rather, today. Yes! And you can take an advance from him to cover the damage to your inn, in case the deal doesn't go down."

"What damage?"

"Don't get nervous. You'll just have to wipe the blood off the floor and that'll be it. Tell Markun and his lads to be here, and to bring the goods with them. Say this is the only time when the customer can meet them. Markun's too greedy not to show up."

"What about the damage?"

"Forget it. Nothing terrible will happen," I declared in a perfectly honest tone of voice.

"I don't know what you've thought up, Harold, but I don't like it one bit."

"But you have to agree that it's better than losing your life." I got to him there. "All right now, it's time for me to go. It was nice to see you."

"Hey, Harold, I'll do what you ask, but you have to promise you'll forget all the minor inconveniences that I caused you without intending any harm."

"It's a deal, my friend," I lied.

I didn't feel like leaving through the window; the usual way seemed more attractive, although it is true that I had to walk backward all the way to the door, since good old Gozmo was famous for his skill in throwing even the very heaviest of knives. I couldn't be sure that he didn't have some other nasty toys hidden away under the mattress. I didn't trust the old swindler any more than a crayfish duke, and life is far too pleasant a thing to part with it as stupidly as that.

I had no doubt at all that Gozmo would do as I had asked. He really had no choice. Unless he wanted to get out of town or tell Markun all about our nocturnal conversation. But the first choice was impossible—he would have to abandon his beloved inn—and as for the second . . . Would you conclude an alliance with a bloodthirsty snake, knowing perfectly well that he would bite you on the heel just when you weren't expecting it? There, you see. Neither would Gozmo. He would rather put his trust in Harold, and he would try to earn a little bit of money from the guild as well, in the hope that everything would turn out all right.

I pulled back the bolt on the main door and slipped out into the street. I couldn't give a damn whether Gozmo closed the inn after me or left it wide open to the whim of gods and vagabonds.

16

HUNTERS OF THE HORSE

The day that followed turned out pretty topsy-turvy. I went round to a dozen different places in order to put a couple of ideas into action. If everything went well, the night ahead was going to be a pretty dramatic one, although the actors still had no idea of the roles they were destined to play. What I had to do now was put the final touches on the production and warn the last few participants about the imminent performance. And so I paid a visit to Archmagician Artsivus's house.

The archmagician wasn't in, and I asked Roderick to pass on his invitation to the friendly little party. The young lad looked rather astonished, but he promised to relay the message in detail.

And then, having done everything that had to be done, I set off with an easy heart to For's place, to while away the long hours until night.

But my teacher was not in, so I was left to my own devices in his apartment. After spending a couple of hours wandering round the rooms from one corner to another, I finally realized that I was far too nervous altogether and it was not doing my fragile health any good.

I studied For's wine vault and pulled out a bottle of wine. After twirling it thoughtfully in my hands, I regretfully put it back. The last thing I needed now was to arrive at the inn drunk and spoil the party. I would just have to sit here going quietly out of my mind while I waited for night to arrive.

I sat in an armchair for a while, checked my crossbow for the hundredth time, even shaved, since I had more than enough time on my hands. Then I gazed vacantly out of the window, wondering what I could do to keep busy. But unfortunately, not a single decent idea came to mind, and I almost started howling out loud in my anxiety and impatience, until I was suddenly struck by the thought of reading the papers I'd retrieved from the Tower of the Order. Greatly encouraged by this brilliant idea, I was all set to immerse myself completely in the lake of knowledge.

But the papers had disappeared without a trace.

I turned everything upside down, starting with For's writing desk and ending with the mattress on his bed. I even looked under the bed, but apart from a rather impressive layer of dust and a startled spider, there was nothing there.

I had to pause for breath and try a different approach. There was no doubt that the papers were somewhere in these chambers. For wouldn't have taken them anywhere else unless something really terrible had happened. So I started the search all over again, trusting to my own experience and my knowledge of my friend's habits.

I tapped the floor with the handle of a knife until I heard the dull sound that indicates a secret hiding place. And I actually heard it twice. But my discoveries were disappointing. When I pried up a stone slab under the table, I discovered a rather fine casket packed with royal gold pieces. A little nest egg set aside for a rainy day.

I discovered the second hiding place beside an old bookcase, where the floor was covered with a mosaic illustrating the sins of man. Good old For had decided to demonstrate his distinctive sense of humor by concealing his riches under the tile bearing the inscription GREED. There was rather more gold here than in the first hiding place and I assumed I had discovered the secret treasury of the servants of Sagot. To my professional eye, it looked like six or seven thousand gold pieces. A huge amount of money. Enough to build your very own castle, if you wanted. But, as ill luck would have it, the papers I was looking for weren't there. I spent about an hour examining the floor, and then started looking for hiding places in the furniture. In one of the drawers of the writing desk I discovered a double bottom, where my dear teacher kept his correspondence with the priests from Garrak. I don't think it was really secret, otherwise For would have hidden the letters somewhere more secure. These papers had probably been left there to distract the attention of fools from something much more important. Feeling that the solution to the mystery was already close at hand, I returned to the search with renewed zeal and carefully sounded out all the chairs, and even the carved headboard of the bed. Not a thing. Might as well try to find a dwarf who smokes! Now came the most difficult part—checking the walls.

This time lady luck smiled on me, and when I tapped on one of the frescoes with the soft cushions of my fingertips, I heard a faint sound that was very slightly different from the usual one. Now I had to figure out how to get into the hiding place.

Make a hole in the wall? No, that would be vulgar, to say the least. I'm a master thief, after all, not some potbellied petty burglar; I don't like doing things the crude way unless there are good reasons for it. And I wasn't stealing, I was simply taking my own papers, which the solicitous For had hidden. I thought my teacher would be rather upset if I ruined this original set of frescoes and left him a hole in the wall as a memento.

I had to feel every single inch in the hope of activating some secret lock. Of course, if the lock of the hiding place involved magic, I wouldn't be able to do anything about it. I would just have to wait for For. . . . Although I did have something in the stores that I bought from the greedy master Honchel that might do the trick for me.

I got my bag, rummaged about in it for a moment, and eventually fished out a little bottle containing a milky-white elixir. A skeleton key for various kinds of magic locks. I splashed a generous dose of the sharp-smelling liquid on the wall where I assumed the hiding place was concealed. When they landed on the fresco, the drops flared up for a moment like brilliant rubies and melted away into the air, as if they had never been there at all. But the wall became transparent, and then the fresco with the picture of a bull slid smoothly to one side, revealing the entrance to the hiding place, a massive metal door of gnome workmanship.

The lock looked pretty serious. I cleared my throat and moved a table up to the wall, since the safe was set rather high. I climbed up, sat in a comfortable position, took my faithful lock picks out of my bag, and started fiddling about. It was more than twenty minutes before the final spring reluctantly clicked and the door opened slightly, moving a mere hair's breadth away from the wall. I laughed happily and reached out my hand, but then jerked it back again.

I really ought to check the secret safe for traps set for impatient fools.

For was quite capable of installing some horrible device out of old habit. But no—there was no hidden spring or loaded crossbow or any other nasty little trick.

The safe proved to be small. No valuables. Only papers. I didn't start delving into the secrets of the priestly brotherhood—the lads had their own little games and it wouldn't be right for me to go sticking my curious nose into them. I simply took what was mine and closed the door. The moment the lock clicked, the magical fresco reappeared, concealing the ugly opening in the wall. A casual observer would never have guessed that there was a safe hidden there.

I dragged the table back to its former position and sat down to study the documents thoroughly, since I still had four hours left. I glanced quickly through the rhymed riddle and then turned to the map of Hrad Spein.

But the progress I made in all that time was hardly worth a bent penny. Corridors, halls, entryways, rooms, hidey-holes, tunnels, caves, and underground palaces. And it was all woven into some kind of tight tangle of snakes suffering agonizing deaths from their own venom. A labyrinth thousands of years old, the foundations of which were laid by someone unknown at a time when the orcs, the first race of the new age, had not yet appeared in Siala.

When it was almost evening and my eyes were tired and good old For still hadn't put in an appearance, I tore myself away from the maps and put the documents in my bag. I felt too lazy to fiddle with the secret fresco again, and I didn't want to waste any more of the magical liquid either, so I thought my old bag would be a safe enough hiding place.

It was time to be off.

In principle, I didn't really have to go anywhere. But I was tormented by a mixture of doubt and curiosity—would my plan work? And would Artsivus believe what I had asked Roderick to tell him? Because, if the archmagician ignored what I had said, the whole plan would all go to the Darkness, together with the demon who managed to snatch the Horse with his clawed fingers.

Evening was drawing on.

That time of day had arrived when the world is colored in every shade of gray. The sun had not yet sunk behind the horizon, but it was ready to retire, and the moon looked like a snow owl. For just one hour the gigantic, drowsy bird known as twilight had spread its wings over the city.

A suspicious silence had spread along the Street of the Sleepy Dog. This meant that some dark business was in the offing and somebody's blood might be spilled. Therefore the inhabitants of the houses in the area had gone scurrying off on highly important, but imaginary business, with an air of serious haste, and it was hardly surprising that as the lazy twilight's gentle hands felt their way along the stone walls of the houses, they found almost no one in the street.

Ah, but that was just it—*almost* no one.

The street was not actually empty. There were a few lads about with an appearance that was quite easily recognized—the kind of appearance possessed by certain individuals who are at odds with the law and prepared to slip their hands into the pocket of Baron Lanten himself.

Markun had taken the trouble of posting lookouts in order to spot any unusual developments in the form of Frago Lanten and his faithful lads, or even Harold, if it came to that. Well, well.

Thank Sagot, the lads didn't notice me, and I turned onto the next side street, intending to get into Gozmo's inn through the service entrance. Or exit—it all depends on which way you look at it. But there was a stroke of ill luck in store here, too. As if to spite me, there were a large number of angry-looking Doralissians hanging about nearby, keeping an eye out for suspected enemies, and I got out of there in a hurry. The goats were also pretending to be peaceful lambs and acting as if this was their home territory. The local inhabitants were not objecting.

I'd have to do it the old-fashioned way, over the roof. Using the cobweb, I was soon standing on the roof next to the roof of Gozmo's inn, and with a hop and a skip I was on the other building. I dived into a little attic window . . . and almost ended up in a lovingly positioned mantrap.

These hunters, may the dark elves roast me alive! You could catch an adult obur in a trap like that! Nothing could possibly be more dangerous than the hospitality of my best friend Gozmo!

As I expected, the attic was dusty and dirty, and so it cost me quite an effort to find the hatch in the floor; I had to scrape away a heap of old rags, and the dust almost made me sneeze. The trapdoor was locked from the other side, and I cursed the lock, and Gozmo, and Markun's lads, and the stupid Doralissians a dozen times before I finally managed to get it open.

There were no steps, so I simply jumped down onto the floor of the second story, almost colliding with Gozmo as he strolled along the corridor. The innkeeper squealed in surprise and jumped back against the wall.

"Harold! You'll be the death of me!" he exclaimed and spat when he recognized me. "Couldn't you choose a less eccentric way of visiting?"

"Did you do as I said?" I asked, ignoring his question.

Somehow I didn't enjoy visiting Gozmo as much as I used to.

"Yes, may you be cursed three times over! Markun and his lads have been here for more than an hour already."

"My sympathies." The head of the Guild of Thieves was as impatient as ever. He had decided to turn up well in advance of the set time. "What sort of mood is he in? Bad, as usual?"

"Bad?" Gozmo wrung his hands despairingly. "I'm done for! The moment he learns that there isn't going to be any deal, those lads of his will have our guts!"

"Stop whining," I said good-naturedly. "You've got nowhere to fall back to now."

What's true is true. Even if Gozmo betrayed me, he was a dead man. The fat slug who through some mistake of the gods had become the leader of the Avendoom Guild of Thieves never forgave anyone who tricked him. The hospitable water below the piers was waiting for Gozmo.

"Curses on that night when I listened to you," Gozmo muttered.

He had probably been visited by thoughts about the water under the piers as well.

"Don't panic. It's bad for the job. Better think about something pleasant. Have you already received your share of the gold?"

"No," Gozmo said with a frown. "That cursed fat man promised to pay after he closes the deal."

"You'll get a deal. At exactly midnight. Meanwhile, pour the lads some beer, so they don't get too bored. Or they might get upset and start trashing the place."

"Who's going to pay for it?" There was no more warmth in the old thief's eyes than in an icicle on the S'u-dar Pass.

"You are, of course, or did you think I'd pay a brass farthing to help fill Markun's belly?"

Gozmo didn't think so, and he spat on the floor again.

"Go and keep them busy, give them some beer. I'm going into the office."

"The Darkness take you," Gozmo muttered, and set off toward the staircase leading down to the first floor.

I was under no illusion about Gozmo's feelings for me, but it really wasn't in his interest to sell me out. It was better for him to count on Harold coming up with something to make everything turn out all right.

The office was a little room directly above the main hall of the inn. Something like a closet with a magical floor that was transparent from one side, so that you could see what was going on underneath your feet.

As far as I'm aware, Gozmo acquired the inn without the magical floor. But one day a magician who had been expelled from the Order locked himself in the closet with a young maiden, and this was the result. I won't even try to imagine what they got up to in there, but the outcome was a very convenient observation point. I found out about it completely by accident. That day good old Gozmo had taken a drop too much, and his tongue was flapping faster than the sails of a windmill. The next day the innkeeper denied everything, of course, but I cornered him, and he had to admit I was right. So today I was going to watch the show with every comfort and, most important, in absolute safety.

Just as I had anticipated, no customers were expected that day. No man in his right mind—or even out of it—would go barging straight into a hornet's nest, especially when the chief hornet was Markun himself. Better to spend the day at home and go without drink. Or visit the inn on the next street along.

Gozmo, of course, did not share the opinion of those regulars who were too timid to visit his establishment today but, to do him justice, he suffered in silence.

The role of customers had been usurped by Markun's faithful jackals. There were about two dozen of these items spread around the tables. I call them items rather than men because these lads were no more than the living appendages of their swords; they were a brute force that simply carried out the instructions of the head of the Guild of Thieves. And they were even more hard up for brains than the Doralissians.

The lads were downing the free beer provided by the generous Gozmo, who flitted from table to table filling the orders of the insolent bandits. The entire gang was very heavily armed; they looked as if they had just dropped in for a minute before going off to make war on the Nameless One.

It looked like I was in for a genuine fireworks show.

His Majesty, Milord Fat Ass, the head of the Gang of Corpse-Eaters that was unworthy to bear the title of the Avendoom Guild of Thieves, was sitting at a separate table straight below me. If there had been no barrier between us in the form of the floor, I would have been absolutely delighted to spit on his bald, shiny head—something that he deserved a thousand times over.

The fat leader of the guild was decked out more richly than the peacocks in a sultan's courtyard. The dark brown suit of fine velvet was fit for a king, not the owner of three chins and a pair of little rat's eyes drowning in fat. I found Markun repulsive. He was a slug who had managed to crush the once beautiful and all-powerful Guild of Thieves under his own vast carcass through crude deception.

There was a time when we could still pass each other by on the narrow path of our personal interests and Commissions, but now the day had arrived when the path was too narrow for both of us.

There was a man in black sitting opposite Markun, with his back to me. It was Paleface, of course. They were talking about something and the killer began waving his hands about in nervous irritation, but Markun took no more notice of him than a gkhol would take of a well-gnawed shinbone.

"What are you so nervous about, Rolio?" asked Markun.

"I'm not nervous!" Paleface hissed. "I'm just saying that I don't like all this."

"What don't you like about it?" The argument seemed to have been going on for some time already, and Markun was beginning to get irritated.

"The buyer. How did he find out that you had the Horse? And where would he get so much money from?"

"What difference does that make to you? I don't think Gozmo would dare try to trick me. And as for the buyer—that's not our concern," Markun laughed.

"You're right about that," Paleface muttered, getting up off his chair.

At last I was able to get a look at his face. Several burns and a mass of scratches made Paleface look like a visitor from the next world. It was not so easy to look handsome after suffering the effects of Roderick's fireball. And his arm was still in a sling—it would be a long time before he forgot that shot from Bolt, may he rest in the light.

"It's not our concern! It's your concern! Our common acquaintance gave you the Commission for the Horse. And you'll be the one to pay with your stupid head for deciding to sell the Horse to someone else and bypass the client!"

"And I seem to recall that our common acquaintance ordered you to kill Harold, but the thief is still alive, while you look like something that's come back from the dead. And I also remember very well that my best men never came back from your adventures. Two of them never got out of that nameless alley and another three were finished off by the guards in the library. And I'd like to ask what in the name of Darkness those guards were doing there in the first place. And then another three of my most experienced men disappeared somewhere in the Forbidden Territory. And they were all sent by you! Under cover of my name!"

"I didn't send your jackals into the Forbidden Territory," said Paleface, interrupting Markun. "The Master's servant did that."

"Oh, don't give me that, Rolio!" Markun said with a dismissive gesture. The expression on the face of the fat master of the guild was one of frank disdain for the world in general and for Paleface in particular. "You were the one who dragged me into your business with the Master. If only I'd known, I'd never have got involved."

"Come on, Markun, you were serving the Master long before I ever came to Avendoom. So don't go hanging all your dead men round my neck! All I did was remind you that you can't just go on taking money for nothing; it's time to repay our lord with some real service. And you have no right to complain." Paleface snorted as he sat back down at the table. "You've had more than enough gold."

"Gold won't save my head," Markun muttered.

"Nothing will save your head if you sell the Horse!" Paleface growled, beginning to lose patience.

Several of Markun's minions looked round from their mugs of beer to see what was going on at their chief's table.

"I've no intention of selling the Horse!" Markun snapped, slamming his plump hand down on the table. "We'll just take the money and leave the buyer floating under the piers! Do you really think I'm stupid enough to give that Stone to anyone except the servant of the Master? You'd do better to handle your own assignment and put an end to our common problem at long last."

"I'll put an end to him," Paleface growled in a more conciliatory tone. "Harold won't be in this world for much longer."

"That's what you said five days ago," Markun said with a repulsive giggle. "I'm beginning to have doubts about your professional skill."

"You'd do better to think about how to keep the Horse safe and sound until the client comes to collect it."

"What's so hard about keeping it safe?" Markun asked with sincere surprise. "I keep it with me all the time."

The head of the guild snapped his fingers casually and one of his bandits immediately placed the Horse of Shadows on the table.

I've always said that the Doralissians are rather strange creatures. Only they could have called something that looks like the phallus of some ancient pagan god the Horse of Shadows. If that's a Horse, then I'm the emperor of the Lakeside Empire.

"Hey, Gozmo!" Markun shouted across the entire room. "Where's this buyer of . . ."

Unfortunately, he never finished what he wanted to say. Several things happened at once.

Bleating repulsively with that remarkable skill that they have, Doralissians started running in through both of the doors. I could see that their leader was my old acquaintance Glok. The goat-men were in a really foul mood and looked as if they intended to make serious use of the clubs, hand axes, and grappling irons that they were clutching. There were only a couple of dozen men in the place, but about fifty goats came piling in. The inn was immediately crowded and the atmosphere was explosive.

This time the Doralissians almost managed to surprise me. Ten of the goats had been bright enough to bring crossbows, but they were still too stupid to make use of their advantage. They should have fired first and then got involved in the fighting. But as the goats always do, they got everything backward. The ones without crossbows went charging forward stupidly, leaving their archer brothers behind them. And the ones with crossbows turned out not to be blessed with the gift of patience either: They decided that the sooner they fired, the better.

So they fired. Of ten bolts, three hit the wall, six hit the backs of the charging goat-men, and only one—clearly by complete accident—pierced the shoulder of one of Markun's men.

The Doralissians just don't know how to play their trump cards. Having killed six of their own kind, the goats stopped in amazement, wondering how they had managed to hit their brothers-in-arms. Markun's lads, who hadn't been expecting to find themselves in the middle of a goat farm, jumped up from the tables—knocking over their chairs—and grabbed hold of their weapons. They had more than enough time while the Doralissians were dithering like genuine ... er ... Doralissians.

At the very beginning of the scuffle, Gozmo dived down under his counter. To be quite honest, I wasn't at all concerned about his health. I would have bet my own liver that the innkeeper had some kind of hatch hidden under a beer barrel down there and in a couple of minutes he would be far away.

"The Horse! Our Horse!" Glok started yelling when he spotted the Stone standing all alone on a table.

"Thieves!" the Doralissians suddenly started bleating, waking from their stupor.

And then the fun really began!

Howls, yelling, a genuine ruckus with weapons clashing. Dead and wounded, blood flowing everywhere. The goat-men were really wound up and intent on annihilating the new owners of their precious relic. They lacked the brains to realize that they might get killed themselves.

The bandits fought back desperately against their advancing enemies, swinging swords, knives, and stools, but the sides were still unevenly matched, and the ranks of the guild were thinned significantly. As, indeed, were those of the Doralissians.

Markun was squealing something in a cowardly voice from behind the backs of his cutthroats, while they howled and swore, trying to keep the furious avengers away. Paleface was spinning like a top, with the knife in his good hand flashing to and fro, and there were already five goat-men lying around him as dead as could be. But the men were doomed. In a couple of minutes they would be overwhelmed by sheer force of numbers.

One of the Doralissians managed to reach the Horse. With a jubilant bleat, he tossed his ax aside and lifted the sacred relic high above his head, like some triumphant knight who has been awarded the cup at a tournament. One of Markun's lads immediately took his chance and used his knife, grabbing the Horse out of the dying goat's hands.

And at that moment new actors appeared on the stage.

Vukhdjaaz came leaping out of the wall, frightening the besieged men to death, but the goats didn't realize what was happening, or they simply didn't care who they battered with their clubs—those creatures had absolutely no instinct of self-preservation.

"Vukhdjaaz is clever," the demon announced to everyone there, and ripped off Markun's head with a single blow of his hand—through some miracle the Horse of Shadows had found its way into the hands of the head of the guild.

The demon roared in triumph and reached out for the treasure. But the boldest of the Doralissians, despising the danger and the likely consequences, dashed at the demon who had dared to lay claim to their holy of holies. Vukhdjaaz was seriously upset and he began a genuine goat slaughter. The demon was obviously a bit on the blind side, too, because a couple of times he missed and his hands hit the walls, gouging out large holes. So large, in fact, that two of the bandits who realized that guarding Markun's corpse was not very interesting and actually rather dangerous for their health, slipped out through these newly created doorways into the street.

Vukhdjaaz was engrossed in the sporting exercise of reducing the number of Doralissians in Siala. I saw the clever demon grab Glok by the back of the neck and bite off the one-horned goat's head, then start flailing left and right with his hands.

Surprisingly enough, I even spotted Paleface in the melee of those still left alive. The bright lad was sneaking along the wall toward one of the holes that Vukhdjaaz had made. I swear on Sagot himself, he was about to slip away yet again!

I started wondering where Artsivus and the cavalry had disappeared to, and thinking that perhaps I ought to clear out while I still could—make a run for it while the going was good.

There was a deafening boom, and the magicians of the Order stared appearing out of thin air. Five, seven, ten, twelve of them! The entire Council of the Order was there, with Artsivus at its head, and the demonologists into the bargain.

The demonologists—magicians in black robes with gold trim on the sleeves—waved their hands, and a magic net woven of out pale gray rays began glimmering around the demon. Vukhdjaaz began howling even more furiously and tried to break through the magical restraints, but there was a flash and he was obviously burned. He flopped down and went quiet.

"Tighten the flows." Artsivus coughed and gave a chilly shiver. The old man clearly felt a little uncomfortable away from a warm hearth. "The job is done."

The net around the motionless Vukhdjaaz began drawing tighter. I was amazed to see the monster start to shrink. The gray mesh glowed brighter and brighter. And soon all that was left on the spot where a minute earlier a huge monster had been battling was a small, faintly glowing sphere, about the size of a fist. I hoped my demon friend wasn't feeling too cramped and uncomfortable. The magicians had really bundled him up good and tight.

"Take him, Master Rodgan," Artsivus said with a nod. "Put the beast in a secure cage and start studying him. The Council will help to the extent of its modest abilities."

Positively glowing with delight, one of the demonologists quickly picked the little sphere up off the bloodstained floor and put it into a small bag. Well, now at last the magicians would have a chance to study a real live demon and not just descriptions of them in dusty old tomes.

Artsivus paid no attention to the dead, striding between the corpses as if they were rocks, not dead men and Doralissians, until he reached Markun's headless body and picked up the Horse of Shadows.

"Don't move! In the name of the king!" a voice cried, distracting my attention from Artsivus, and I saw a group of guardsmen led by Baron Lanten come bursting in at the door and start rounding up the bandits and goat-men who were still alive and trying to slip away from the scene.

"Ah, Baron," Artsivus coughed. "Right on time, as always."

"What shall we do with them, Your Magicship?" Frago asked, appar-

ently not at all concerned about the ironic tone of the archmagician's
words.

"How should I know?" Artsivus said with a casual shrug. He couldn't
care less about what happened now to the participants in the brawl.
"That's your business, Baron. Interrogate them, and then act as you
think best."

The baron nodded and ordered his guards to take away everyone for-
tunate enough to have survived this night in the Knife and Axe. In this
former inn . . . It was hard to call what was left of the building, especially
on the ground floor, a venue for relaxation and entertainment. Devasta-
tion, blood, and dead bodies. It would take a lot of serious work and a
fair amount of money to make this establishment look decent again.

Artsivus handed the Horse to one of the archmagicians, then looked
up at the ceiling and asked irritably: "Harold, do you intend to sit up
there, or will you condescend to come down?"

So much for the ceiling! For the master of the Order it was just as
transparent as it was for me. I had to go down. On the way I got the
idea of slipping out over the roof. But I didn't think it was a good idea.
Artsivus was in a grumpy mood, as always, and I had no desire to spend
the rest of my life as a frog.

As I said once before, His Magicship's glance boded no good to my
own humble personage. But this time the archmagician didn't seem inclined to skin me on the spot.

"There you are," the old man harrumphed. "Come with me, I have a
couple of questions for you."

Good old Gozmo still hadn't emerged from under the bar, and I became even more convinced that he was long gone and his tracks were
already cold. Artsivus left the inn in the care of two archmagicians and
walked out. I followed.

Outside it was dreadfully dark. No one had bothered to light the
street lamps, and not a single window was lit up. But somehow I was
certain that no one was sleeping on the Street of the Sleepy Dog. Deaf
trolls couldn't have fallen asleep with all the noise that had been coming
from the inn for the last half hour. People would be talking about it
right across the Port City tomorrow. And what wild stories they would
tell! Especially the ones who claimed to have been at the scene and observed it all with their own eyes.

"Shall I get into the carriage?" I asked, just to be sure.

"You can run alongside if you like." Artsivus harrumphed and groaned as he climbed up onto the step. Two coachmen supported the archmagician and helped him climb inside. I couldn't withstand the magician's gaze, and started looking out of the window, since it wasn't boarded up this time.

"I'm cold," the magician muttered, picking up the woolen blanket lying beside him.

I personally didn't feel at all cold; it was a warm summer night.

"All right, tell me everything."

"What is there to tell?" I was about to ask, but I changed my mind. A dead goblin could have guessed what he wanted to know from me.

"Allow me to assist you," the old man sneered. "Let's start with how you discovered who had the Horse and how the demon, who you said had disappeared for all eternity, happened to reappear in Avendoom."

I heaved a sigh, gathered my strength, and started telling my story. The truth and nothing but the truth. Artsivus had already heard the first part of my story, so I simply made a few corrections, adding in the conversations with the demons. After that I had to tell him about the Forbidden Territory, but I claimed that it would take too long to tell him everything, and limited myself to saying that I went there, got the papers, and came back. I left all the details for the next time, hoping that it would never come.

The spiteful magician simply cleared his throat and assured me that the king was not as kind as he was, and I would have to tell him absolutely everything. I heaved another sigh to let him know that when the king required it, I would do as he wished.

As I understood it, the carriage was simply driving us aimlessly through the city. The coachmen had been ordered to drive us around Avendoom until Artsivus had said everything he wanted to say and satisfied his curiosity. By my calculation, we had already been riding about for an hour, and the damned old man still wouldn't calm down and leave poor, tired Harold in peace. From the demon the conversation moved on to the Horse, from the Horse to the Master, from the Master to Hrad Spein, from there back to the Horse again. . . . It just went on forever! But eventually the archmagician got fed up, too, or he simply got too cold and wanted to hurry to get back to his warm fireplace, but in any case the questions finally dried up.

"All right, thief," the old man said, and looked out of the window. "It will be morning soon. I should have been asleep long ago, not riding round the city like this. I'll drop you off—"

"Where, Your Magicship?" I interrupted.

"At the king's palace, naturally! You need to be watched very carefully. Or you'll create the kind of mess that not even the Beaver Caps can get you out of."

"But the week I was given isn't over yet," I protested.

"I know," Artsivus snapped. "But we don't have that week anymore. You have to start out. Immediately. Soon we shall no longer be in control of events. So to wait until the end of the week would be suicide."

"All right, but in any case I need to collect the papers I got from the Forbidden Territory. I'll come to the palace tomorrow, or rather, this morning."

"What, don't you have the maps with you?" Artsivus asked in surprise.

"No, I'm not so stupid as to carry them about with me everywhere I go," I lied, feeling the documents burning me through the side of my bag.

"And where did you hide them?" Artsivus harrumphed, making it clear that he didn't regard the intellectual capacity of the man sitting opposite him too highly.

"In a safe place," I replied evasively.

"In a safe place," the archmagician muttered discontentedly. "In our times there are almost no safe places left, Harold. And I'm a little surprised that you, of all people, don't seem to know that. Hmm, hmm . . . All right, have it your own way. But remember that if you don't turn up at the palace in the morning, I shall deal with you in person."

"Please have no doubt, Your Magicship, I'll be there," I hastily assured Artsivus with an air of crystal-clear honesty.

I don't think that the old magician believed me at all, but nonetheless he shouted for the carriage to stop. So now I would have to walk to For's place.

"All the best, Harold," said Artsivus, letting me know that I was free to go.

"Goodnight, Your Magicship," I said, maintaining the high tone of the conversation. When I have to, I can be extremely polite. I got out of the carriage and closed the door behind me.

So, it looked like I was on the boundary of the Inner and Outer Cities, no more than one block away from Cathedral Square. I could manage that all right.

The coachmen whooped at the horses, and they set off at a brisk trot. But the carriage only went a few yards before it stopped again.

"Hey, you!" one of the servants called to me.

What kind of people were they? No manners, no kindness for an unfortunate man out walking in the night!

"Come here."

I had to trudge all the way back and open the door for another look at the archmagician swaddled in his blanket.

"Harold, I completely forgot." Artsivus coughed. "Thank you for your help. The Order will not forget this."

Long after the carriage had dived into darkness and been swallowed up by it, I was still standing there in the middle of the street with my mouth hanging open. I couldn't remember anything like it ever happening before. The Order had acknowledged someone's help and even said thank you. Now I was absolutely certain that the world was poised on the edge of a precipice and at any moment the sky would come tumbling down.

17

NEW ACQUAINTANCES

Do you struggle with the Darkness within you?"

I gave a sigh of relief.

So, after all, there were some things in our sinful and long-suffering world that remained unchanged. The old fogey, so advanced in age that all the stuffing had spilled out of him ages ago, was still at his post in front of the gates of the cathedral. His partner was at the other side of the entrance, dozing on his feet and in danger of keeling over and collapsing on the ground at any moment.

"I annihilate the Darkness," I replied.

"Then enter and address Them," said the dozy old man, suddenly coming to life.

It's amazing what the force of habit can do!

"I think I'll probably do that in the morning. Why bother the gods with pretty trifles?" I said with a chuckle.

"Quite right," the first priest responded. "The gods get tired of our stupid requests and prayers."

"Well, be seeing you." I waved to the old-timers and went on my way.

"Are you a worshiper of Sagot, too?" the first old man called to me.

"Yes," I shouted without looking back, but then I suddenly froze and swung round sharply to face him. "What do you mean by 'too'?"

"Why, some lads came in no more than five minutes ago. They asked where they could find the refuge of the Protector of the Hands, the priest For. Are you with them, too?"

I didn't answer. Instead I set off at full tilt for the sanctuary. I don't like it when people come looking for my old teacher in the middle of the night.

All the grounds of the cathedral were brightly illuminated with oil lamps. The warm July night was quiet and serene. There was only a solitary cricket chirping merrily under a bush, playing his little concert for all those who refused to sleep. Even as I ran, I knew that I could be too late. Whoever it was that had been looking for For, they had already done what they wanted to do. But I was propelled by the insane hope that everything might turn out all right, even though I realized that was simply impossible.

The statue of the knight locked in eternal combat with the ogre flashed by like a ghost; the statues of the gods flitted past in a blur of faces and figures. The path curved to the left, but I ran straight on across a flowerbed, crushing the sleepy, pale blue flowers with the mournfully drooping petals.

Forward, forward!

The gloom of the archway sucked me in and instantly spat me out at the other end. I went flying into the dwelling of Sagot, on the way snatching the crossbow out from behind my back. The accursed sweat was flooding into my eyes so that I couldn't see properly or—even worse—aim properly. The door into For's chambers . . .

I was too late. The door wasn't there anymore. It had been chopped into several pieces and was no more than a heap of rough boards lying on the floor. I burst straight into the room—a stupid thing to do, I won't argue, but just at that moment I wasn't in any state to think straight.

I was greeted with weapons. About a dozen naked swords and a couple of lances very nearly made holes in Harold from every direction. The only thing that saved me was the sudden way I came to a halt. And, of course, that thunderous howl from For:

"Nobody move! He's one of ours!"

Everybody there froze on the spot, and only then was I able to see that the men threatening me were the good priests of Sagot. Their expressions were determined and not exactly friendly, but I had to assume they had serious reasons for that in the form of the five dead bodies lying on the floor. The dead men's clothes were anything but priestlike. Only those who considered themselves members of the Guild of Assassins dressed like that.

"For, are you all right?" I asked, trying to make out my teacher behind the wall of priests.

"What could possibly happen to me?" my teacher boomed, pushing his way through his volunteer bodyguards.

And indeed, if you discounted the bruise on his face, very much like the one on my own, only brighter and fresher, and his torn priestly robe (the ceremonial one, I think), For was certainly alive and perfectly well.

"Brother Oligo, remove these . . ."

"Of course, Master For," a bearded priest said with a nod. "There are still plenty of places left under the apple trees . . ."

It was interesting to wonder just how many dead men who had threatened the health of the glorious brothers were buried in that garden under the old apple trees. Quite a lot, I imagined.

"I suppose you won't be informing the guards?" I asked, just to be on the safe side.

One of the brothers, who was wiping the blood off the floor, gave a loud guffaw, a simple sound that perfectly expressed his attitude to that error of the gods that bore the title of the municipal guard.

"I need to have a talk with you," said For. He seemed a bit depressed.

"What happened here?"

"Nothing too serious. I come back here from the Chapel of the Hands, ready to eat a hearty supper and at the same time ask you about what's going on in this vain world of ours, and suddenly . . . Well, I see that the door into my chambers has been chopped into pieces in a most brazen fashion and the dead men you've already seen are walking around in my rooms. I might have forgiven the poor sinners for just walking around! But they were also rummaging through the drawers of my desk and sticking their noses where they had no right to look. Well, I got really angry . . . and then these lads took out their weapons and tried to finish me off for good measure. Fortunately, I'd brought this thing back with me from the chapel and I was able to hold them off until my colleagues arrived."

For nodded casually in the direction of a heavy ceremonial mace lying on the table. Oho! From the look of it, someone's head must have taken a real battering.

Meanwhile the priest had finally finished cleaning up. He grabbed his bucket in one hand, his rag in the other, and left For and me on our own. The servants of Sagot are not like other priests. These lads in gray cassocks can do more than just pray to the gods, they can wash the floor, mend a hole in the roof, or fight off professional killers.

"Sagot!" For exclaimed, raising his hands toward the ceiling. "They can only put in a new door in the morning, meanwhile we'll have to pass the time without it. Has he gone?"

"Uh-huh." I glanced out of the room and then sank down onto a chair with a weary sigh. That day, like every other day that week, had been a hard one, and very eventful. "So what did you want to say to me?"

"Harold, kid," For began, "the papers have disappeared . . ."

"Which papers?" I asked, not realizing what he was talking about.

"*Those* papers," said For. "When I got here, one of those men was rummaging in the safe, but they weren't there anymore."

"Don't worry, I took the papers," I said to reassure my teacher, and slapped the bag with the valuables from the old Tower of the Order inside it. "Yesterday evening, while I was waiting for you."

"Thanks be to Sagot." For sighed in genuine relief, and then he peered at me and asked: "How did you manage to open the safe?"

"Very easily, but apparently not as easily as your uninvited guests. I think they found it and opened it far more quickly, only they didn't find what they were looking for."

For shook his head.

"And since when have members of the Guild of Murderers gone in for theft? And where did they get the courage to attack priests in the sanctuary of their god?"

"For, I'm not sure that these men were from the guild. The murderers don't usually work like that. And you've always been on good terms with the guild; Urgez wouldn't be likely to send his lads here. No, this is someone else."

"The Master again?" For quipped acidly, taking out a bottle of wine. We both definitely needed a drink.

"Anything's possible."

"How did it all go?"

"You mean my little problem with the Horse?"

"Well, yes," said For, taking a swig of wine from a beer glass.

All his wineglasses had been broken in the battle with the unknown

killers, and he was obliged to pour the beverage of the gods into vessels
not intended for that purpose.

I told him.

"Hm, you managed to break Borg's link by the most elementary
method of setting all the sides against each other. Clever, but not new
by any means. Well, that's just an old man's grousing. Pay no attention,
kid. The only thing that really bothers me is that Markun and his gang
and that Paleface of yours . . . what's his name?"

"Rolio."

"Rolio, Rolio . . . ," For repeated, as if he were savoring the taste of
the word. "I've never heard the name before. He's definitely not from
Avendoom. Now what was I saying. Aha! Yes, they also serve this
Master. Whichever way you turn, everybody's his servant."

"Well, Markun won't be serving anybody anymore," I laughed.

I didn't feel at all sorry for the fat thief who had been killed by
Vukhdjaaz.

"No, Markun won't. And I hope that now his place in the guild will
be taken by someone more worthy and it will become what it used to
be in the days of my youth. But this Rolio's never going to let you be.
Markun is dead, but he wasn't the one who gave the murderer his
Commission, it was some influential servant of the Master, and that
means you'd better watch out for your head."

"I will," I agreed. "But anyway, I came to say good-bye. I have to go to
see the king, and then set out."

"Only don't go at this time in the morning! Everyone at court is
asleep, and there's certainly no one expecting you there. Better take a
rest, Harold, you look to me as if you've been used as a plow horse for
every field in Siala."

It was hard to disagree with that. I felt more than ready to get my
head down for as long as possible. A hundred years or so would probably do, and while I was asleep this spot of bother with the Nameless
One would sort itself out naturally. . . .

But of course, next morning nothing had changed for the better. The
Nameless One was still up there beyond the Needles of Ice, nursing his

grudge against Valiostr, and I had to travel more than a hundred leagues to collect that magical penny whistle.

For and I parted with few words.

"Take care of yourself, kid." That was all that he said before I gathered up my things and left his hospitable dwelling, hoping I'd be able to come back to see the old priest after my visit to Hrad Spein.

I walked to the palace without any adventures. There had been a light shower of rain in Avendoom while I was sleeping, and the air still had an elusive scent of coolness that was threatening to disperse in the hot rays of the sun. The rain had fallen and disappeared without trace. The sky was a clear azure blue that could compete with the eyes of a goblin, and there was not a single cloud in sight. It was just past midday, and the sun was really scorching. There was a wind, too, but it was so hot that it brought no relief. Something very strange was going on with the weather that year.

In the Inner City the rich men were carrying on with their calm, unhurried lives, ignoring the heat and other minor difficulties of life. The houses here were white and packed with the best life had to offer. But the first thing that strikes you when you walk into the Inner City is how clean everything is. Not a single speck of the dust and dirt that you get so used to in the Port City.

And the people here are respectable, too. These lads don't steal purses. The gents in the Inner City handle such huge sums of money and steal on such a grand scale that I could never earn that much in ten lifetimes of nonstop thieving.

I was stopped once by the Inner City Guard. My appearance was none too respectable, on account of my clothes. But it was okay. They just asked where I was going, and when they got the answer, they left me alone. It turned out they had already been warned about my visit.

The huge bulk of the royal palace, surrounded by walls that were anything but decorative, occupied a substantial part of the Inner City. A small fortress within the fortress city. Every new king in the Stalkon dynasty regarded it as his duty to finish building something, build something new, or improve something. The result was that the palace had grown to an immense size, while remaining what it had always been since it was first founded—a fortress.

First of all I planned to go in through the gates for servants and those delivering food to the royal kitchen, but then I thought: Why should I go in through the little back gate like some rustic peasant? The king has personally invited me to come and see him, I didn't ask him to do it, so they can open the central gates for me.

I crossed the Parade Square at an angle, walking confidently straight toward the gates. When the guards on duty spotted me, they livened up noticeably.

"What can we do for you?" one of them inquired, clutching a spear with a long narrow tip.

Ever since the Stalkon dynasty ascended the throne, the palace had been protected by the king's personal guard, which was now commanded by the eternally gloomy Milord Rat. Only nobles could serve as guardsmen, and guarding the king was regarded as an exceptional honor, especially for youngest sons who could expect no pickings from their fathers' estates, while here they could actually distinguish themselves and acquire estates of their own.

These lads didn't like to put on airs and graces. All those fancy ceremonial halberds or poleaxes carried by the guards of the emperors of the Two Empires were no use for the normal defense of a head of state in unforeseen circumstances. A spear—now that's a weapon of war. Ever since the father of the present Stalkon was attacked by rebels from the western provinces, no one had tried to persuade the guards to change their weapons for anything else. It was the warriors' spears that had saved the king and the kingdom.

"I wish to see His Majesty," I said.

The young noblemen are well educated, of course, but everyone enjoys a joke at the expense of an idiot. The entire platoon of ten guards burst into delighted peals of laughter.

"Would you like to go straight to him?" asked the guardsman who had begun the conversation. "To join him for a small glass of wine, no doubt?" he said, winking merrily at his comrades. "Well, well! We're very pleased to have a jester from the Market Square come visiting!"

"And how shall we introduce you, milord?" another guard asked with a bow that was elegant, despite being humorous. "You're probably a marquis, like me? Or a duke? Your business with the king must be very urgent, I'm sure!"

The guardsmen started laughing again.

"You're a jolly lad. But now be on your way. The king's not seeing just anyone today, as usual."

"Wonderful!" I said with an indifferent shrug. Just let Artsivus say that I hadn't even tried. "Good-bye, milords."

But before I could leave, a soldier with the badges of a lieutenant of the guard appeared out of nowhere and demanded that I name myself.

"Harold," I replied.

The guards' faces immediately dropped and the marquis even spat on the ground at his feet.

"So what was that comedy all about?" he asked me. "Why couldn't you have said straightaway?"

"Follow me, I'll show you through," the lieutenant told me. "And next time, gentlemen, I'll have your hides if you disobey an order from milord Alistan."

The young noble lords had enough wits to keep quiet and not argue with the lieutenant. But their mood had definitely been spoiled. Too bad.

The road led from the gates directly toward a huge gray building with tall arched windows. There were plenty of people on the grounds, both servants and those who lived here thanks to Stalkon's gracious generosity. I took a sly look around, just in case I should ever happen to come back here on my own account.

However, we didn't go into the building. The lieutenant turned aside and led me along a path paved with yellow sandstone.

"So tell me, Harold, what is this business you have with milord Markauz, if he's dashing off somewhere and dumping all the guards on me?" the lieutenant suddenly asked.

"I don't know, milord." I wasn't going to give away state secrets to the very first person I met.

I thought I heard the lieutenant sigh.

"He's going away at a bad time. A very bad time. The guards and the king need him here."

I didn't say anything.

"This is your spot. Sit somewhere and wait. Someone will come for you."

The lieutenant walked away, with the silver buttons on his blue and gray uniform glittering in the sun.

I looked around.

A small garden with a round open space at the center, spread with sand. It was probably used for something like a fencing ground. Or whatever it is they call that place where guardsmen are trained to wave their shafts of metal about. I could see through to the palace; it was almost directly behind it, in fact. I adjusted my bag on my shoulder and started waiting, carefully observing the people around me.

Oh yes, I was not the only one there. There were ten quite serious-looking lads hanging about nearby. I remembered their faces, because I'd seen them that night when I visited the duke's house. They were the soldiers who had escorted Miralissa through the dark city.

Wild Hearts.

I drew a few mildly curious glances from them. But that was all. What in the name of a h'san'kor did they care about some stranger who had turned up out of the blue? Especially since all the Wild Hearts had urgent business to attend to. Some were playing dice, one was sleeping in the shade of the little fountain, some were checking their weapons, and one had decided to practice with his swords. And so Harold was ignored in a quite shameless manner.

In one corner of the garden there were four gnomes puffing and panting beside a bed of red roses. These short lads with narrow shoulders, so unlike their massive, smooth-faced cousins the dwarves, were circling round a massive cannon. They seemed to be trying to load it, but they couldn't manage it somehow, and they were arguing irritably and waving their fists at each others' red faces. This wasn't really helping matters along, and the furious swearing only fueled the fire of argument.

The gnomes ran out of breath and started seeking a compromise. They tipped some powder into the cannon from a small, bright-red barrel. The ball was lying nearby, on the sand. One of the little folk, probably the youngest, to judge by his beard, tried to light his pipe, but received a smart cuff round the back of the head from one of his partners and put it back in his pocket with an offended sniff.

And I should think so, too! All we needed right now was to be blasted up into the air because of some bearded idiot's carelessness.

I heard light, stealthy footsteps behind my back and said with a smile: "How's life, Kli-Kli?"

"Ooh!" the goblin said in a disappointed voice. "How did you guess that it was me?"

"You were snuffling."

"Oh no I wasn't!" the jester protested, and sat down beside me on a step.

"Oh yes you were."

"Oh no I wasn't! And anyway, what do you mean by arguing with the king's jester?" Kli-Kli asked resentfully, and to confirm what he had just said he put on the green jester's cap with little bells that he had been holding in his hand.

"I'm not arguing," I said with a shrug.

"Would you like a carrot?" the goblin asked amicably, producing one from behind his back.

The carrot was almost half as big as Kli-Kli himself. A queen of carrots. A massive great carrot.

"No, thank you."

"You don't want any? All right then. I can only ask, and there'll be more left for me, anyway!"

The jester didn't try to insist, he just bit a good-sized piece off the orange vegetable and started crunching on it, squinting contentedly at the sun.

"Vegetables are good for you, Harold," the jester declared with his mouth full. "You can't live on just meat."

"Are you and I about to have a gastronomical debate?" I asked, arching one eyebrow.

We just sat there like that, me saying nothing and watching the gnomes at work, Kli-Kli dining and sometimes twitching his little feet, evidently trying to perform some dance that only he knew. I must say that it looked very amusing.

"I have two pieces of news, good and bad. Which one shall I start with?" Kli-Kli asked when there was exactly half of the oversized carrot left.

"The good news, I suppose," I muttered lazily.

It was hot, but the weather was marvelous, and I was enjoying basking in the sun.

"The good news is this," said the goblin, shaking the tip of his cap so that the bells jingled joyfully. "You're going tomorrow morning." *Jingle-jingle.*

"Now let's have the bad news."

"The bad news is this." The jester sighed sadly and the bells tinkled mournfully. "Unfortunately, I'm staying in the palace and not going with you."

"Hmm . . . Your sense of values is all topsy-turvy, jester," I hemmed. "It's the other way round for me. The good news is bad and the bad news is good."

"Hah," Kli-Kli sniffed resentfully. "You'll be sorry yet that I didn't go with you!"

"Why's that?"

"Who's going to protect you on the way?" he asked with a perfectly serious expression on his face.

"I think I'll get by all right," I replied in the same tone of voice. "What are the Wild Hearts and the Rat for?"

"By the way, about the Wild Hearts," Kli-Kli said, and sank his sharp teeth into the unfortunate carrot again. "Have you had a chance to get to know them yet?"

"No. Why, have you?"

"I should say so! They've been here for about a week," the jester answered indignantly.

But of course. How dare I cast doubt on his ability to make new acquaintances.

"I'll introduce them to you, only from here, at a distance, if you have no objection."

"Have you managed to offend them already?" The only possible reason for Kli-Kli's reluctance to approach the soldiers was that the little parasite had played some kind of nasty trick on the Wild Hearts.

"Why do you assume I've offended them?" the jester asked sulkily, looking at me with his bright blue eyes full of reproach. "All I did was pour a bucket of water into each of their beds, and they got upset about it."

"I expect they did!" I chuckled.

"Well then. You see those ones playing dice? The big one with the yellow hair is Honeycomb. The one beside him with the beard is Uncle.

The skinny, bald one. He's the leader of this glum group. And that one over there, the plump one, is called Tomcat. *Miaow!*" said Kli-Kli as loud as he could, and stuck out his tongue.

"I see," I said, examining the threesome playing dice.

Honeycomb was a broad-shouldered hulk two yards tall with powerful, sinewy hands, a head that appeared to have no neck but grew straight out of his shoulders, and hair the color of lime-blossom honey. His rather simple features identified him as a country boy. You can tell them from the city types straightaway.

"Huppah!" laughed Uncle as he tossed the dice once again and leaned down over them with his comrades.

Uncle was more than fifty years old, with a few sparse gray hairs that had somehow survived on his bald head, and a thick gray beard. Compared with Honeycomb he didn't look very tall, but he and the giant Honeycomb and the other Wild Hearts all had one thing in common: the experience of men who serve on the walls of the Lonely Giant on the edge of the Desolate Lands.

"I swear on a h'san'kor," Tomcat growled, "but your luck's in today, Uncle! I pass."

The fat, round-faced Wild Heart's behavior and harsh voice were nothing at all like a cat's. The only thing that did lend him any resemblance to the animal was his mustache, which looked a bit like a cat's whiskers.

"Don't play if you don't want to," his leader laughed.

Tomcat waved his hand at his partners and lay down on the grass in front of the fountain, beside the sleeping soldier.

"I suppose that one must be called Sleepy or Snorer?" I asked ironically.

"The one beside Tomcat?" the jester asked. "No, they call him Loudmouth."

"Why?"

"How should I know?" asked Kli-Kli, pursing his lips. "They won't talk to me. And all I did was leave a dead rat in their room!"

"Don't I recall that just recently you mentioned water in their beds? You didn't say anything about rats."

"Well, the rat was a little bit earlier . . . ," said the jester, embarrassed.

"Never mind, let's forget it," I said. "Why don't you tell me about that pair over there?" I nodded, drawing the goblin's attention to two soldiers sitting apart from the others and sipping wine from a bottle.

"The rotten swine," Kli-Kli muttered, ignoring my question. "That's my wine!"

"Then why have they got it?"

"A trophy of war," the goblin muttered.

"What?" I asked, surprised by his answer.

"I stuck a nail in that swine's boot for a joke. But they got angry about it—"

"Naturally, I would have got angry, too, and torn your green head off."

"They tried to do that, too." The goblin bit off another piece of carrot. "But all they could get was the bottle. Eh, Harold! If you only know how much effort it cost me to steal it from the king's wine cellar!"

"You're the king's jester. Couldn't you have just taken it?"

"Pah! How boring you are!" Kli-Kli shook his head in disappointment, setting his little bells jingling in lively fashion. "I can take it, but it's much more interesting to steal it."

I didn't try to argue with him.

"An amusing pair, don't you think?" he asked, and showed his tongue to the soldier who was holding the bottle.

Amusing? That was putting it mildly! They were amazing! I never thought I would ever see a gnome peacefully sipping a bottle of highly expensive wine with his eternal enemy—a dwarf. The powerfully built dwarf, who could bend horseshoes with his bare hands, and his smaller, narrow-shouldered cousin with a beard, obviously had no intention of going for each other's throats.

It looked to me as if the lads had already taken a drop too much. Which was strange—one bottle wasn't usually enough for that with these races.

"Kli-Kli, are you sure that the trophy of war is only one bottle?" I asked the miserable goblin slyly.

"Of course it's only one," the jester said, and spat. "They swiped a whole crate from me, but that's the last bottle."

That certainly seemed closer to the truth. Even a gnome and a dwarf could easily get tipsy on a crate of wine.

"The ginger one's called Deler," Kli-Kli said with another sigh.

"In the language of the dwarves that means 'fire.' And his friend who stepped on the nail goes by the name of Hallas. In their language that means 'lucky.' That one there," said Kli-Kli, pointing to a man beside a bed of roses, who was practicing with two swords, "is called Eel. Never says a word, and he simply takes no notice of my jokes. It's impossible to get him stirred up."

Kli-Kli simply couldn't bear that kind of insult to his profession. My attention was entirely absorbed by the Wild Heart's practiced, precise movements. They were entrancing: in the hands of the Garrakan—he was definitely a native of Garrak, you can always tell them by their swarthy skin and blue-black hair—the "brother" and the "sister" swords.

Eel flowed from one position into another, his stance changing every second, the blades slicing through the air with terrifying speed, the sister stabbing so rapidly that my gaze could only catch a blurred gleam of silver lightning. A stroke, another stroke, a jab, a sharp move to the left, the brother descends onto the head of an invisible opponent, a swing around his axis and Eel's arm stretches out to an unnatural length, extended by the sister, to reach a new enemy's stomach. The Wild Heart takes a step backward, covering himself with the brother against an imaginary slashing blow from the right and then, out of defense, he suddenly strikes with both blades at once. The sister pierces the head of an imaginary opponent in a predatory thrust and the brother strikes a terrible blow lower down, below the shield.

"Beautiful!" the jester said with an admiring whistle.

I entirely agreed with him. Despite the heat of the scorching sun, Eel continued with his training and performed it astonishingly well. He was well muscled and agile, with a red, aristocratic face and a slim beard.

"Harold, take a look at that individual over there, the funny one."

I couldn't see anything funny about the soldier the jester pointed to. He looked a bit like Tomcat, but he wasn't so well fed. An entirely unremarkable face with thin lips and arched eyebrows, pale blue eyes, and a lazy glance that loitered for a moment on me and Kli-Kli.

"So what do you find funny about him?" I asked the jester.

"Not the man, you blockhead!" the jester exclaimed. "By the way, his name's Marmot. I meant the animal on his shoulder."

It was only then I looked closer at what I had taken for a tasteless decoration of gray fur on the soldier's shoulder. It was a small, furry animal, dozing quietly.

"What is it?" I asked, giving the jester a curious glance.

"A ling. From the Desolate Lands. It's tame. I tried to feed it some carrot a couple of times. It actually scratched me," the goblin said.

"You were unlucky," I sympathized.

"I was really lucky," Kli-Kli disagreed. "If Marmot had caught me when I was feeding his little animal rotten carrots, he wouldn't have given me a pat on the head. I swear he would have flattened me!"

At this point I couldn't restrain myself any longer and burst into laughter.

"Now I understand why you've decided not to go with me, Kli-Kli! Almost everyone who's traveling has a grudge against you. They'd throw you into the first ditch at the edge of the road!"

"Nothing of the sort," the goblin protested with a sniff. "It's Artsivus and Alistan. They don't want to let me go."

Kli-Kli shook his fist at the sky in annoyance.

"Hey, Marmot, don't happen to feel like going to the kitchen, do you?" the Wild Heart who hadn't spoken so far asked his friend stretched out on the grass.

Judging from the chain mail and the lack of hair on his head, the soldier was a native of the Border Kingdom. Only they would be prepared to burden themselves with metal even in this blazing sun. The man from the Borderland had just stopped sharpening his sword, and now he was looking for something to do.

"What for? What is there I haven't seen in the kitchen?" Marmot asked in a lazy voice.

"You can feed Invincible; he'll die from hunger soon. He doesn't do anything but sleep and sleep."

"He sleeps because it's hot, but let's go to the kitchen anyway, I know what you're after."

"We all know that," Tomcat put in, getting up off the grass. "The cooks are really tasty!"

Honeycomb and Uncle started laughing merrily and the Wild Heart who had suggested the walk joined in the laughter.

"Well, are we going then?" asked the Borderman.

"That's Arnkh," said Kli-Kli, introducing the man to me. "It means 'scar' in orcish."

"He doesn't look like an orc."

"He's a man, blockhead! It's just a nickname."

There was the thin white line of a scar running across Arnkh's forehead.

"Listen, Kli-Kli," I said impatiently. "The lieutenant brought me here and told me to wait until someone came to get me. How long do I have to wait? I'm about ready to melt in this heat."

"I came to get you," the jester giggled.

"Then what are we waiting for?"

"Hang on, Harold, what's the hurry? The king's lecturing his subjects, giving them what for, and they're all silent, pale, and sweaty. Why would you want to be there? Look over that way; I still haven't told you about the last Wild Heart."

The last of the ten Wild Hearts was sitting under a spreading apple tree, clutching a massive bidenhander with both hands. It looked to me as if the two-handed sword was too heavy for this short and apparently not very strong man. There was a golden oak leaf on the hefty black handle of the sword.

"Is he a master of the long sword?" I asked the goblin in disbelief.

"You can see the handle, can't you? Of course he's a master, unless he stole that lump of metal from someone."

"But that thing weighs more than he does!"

"No it doesn't," the goblin objected. "But it is heavy, that's true. I checked that myself."

"Don't tell me you tried to pinch the lad's sword!"

"Naah, I just wanted to know how much it weighs. There was a real crash when I couldn't hold it any longer and dropped it on the dwarf's foot."

I didn't answer; I was busy studying the man. He wore a funny hat that looked like one of the cathedral bells.

"He's called Mumr. But everyone calls him Lamplighter. Oh no!"

Kli-Kli's final phrase was not addressed to me. Lamplighter had taken out a little reed pipe, set down the bidenhander, and was about to play.

"Anything but that!" the goblin wailed.

Mumr blew, and the pipe gave out an excruciating, hoarse screech. The jester howled and pressed his hands to his ears. If there had been any dogs nearby, they would certainly have started howling, or died in torment.

"I'm going to throw this at him!" Kli-Kli said, grinding his teeth and shaking the stub of the carrot in his hand.

"Hey, Uncle!" Deler called to the leader of the Wild Hearts. "Tell Mumr to shut up!"

"That's right!" Hallas agreed, raising the bottle to his mouth.

"Let me get some sleep, will you?" Loudmouth muttered sleepily, turning over onto his other side.

Without interrupting his game of dice, Uncle found a small stone beside him and flung it at Lamplighter. In order to dodge the flying missile, Lamplighter had to break off tormenting his poor whistle.

"You ignoramuses," he said, annoyed. "You don't know a thing about music!"

"And that's what it's been like all week, Harold," Kli-Kli said, taking a deep breath.

"And, of course, you know about Miralissa," he said. "It doesn't take a wizard to see that your interest has been awakened. La-la, she *is* something, isn't she?"

"Jester, you must be hallucinating. I think these Wild Hearts have bopped you one time too many."

I hadn't noticed Kli-Kli reaching into my unguarded bag. Now he was holding one of the little magical bottles in his hand, one that contained a dark cherry colored liquid with gold sparks floating in it.

"Put it back," I roared at the goblin, but it was too late.

Kli-Kli nimbly dodged my outstretched arms, dashed across to the gnomes, who had finally loaded the cannon, and flung my magical purchase. The bottle tinkled as it broke against the barrel of the cannon. There was a bright crimson flash, and the weapon disappeared.

What in the name of the Nameless One had possessed me to buy a transport spell from Honchel? (Does carrying a mountain of things seem too much like hard work? Nothing could be simpler! Break one little bottle against your load, and it simply disappears. Break another, and it appears again.) I'd been keeping that magic for Hrad Spein. Just in case I stumbled across any old heaps of diamonds or emeralds. Farewell, treasures of the dead! I've inherited the gnomes' cannon instead.

A shocked silence hung over the garden. Even Eel stopped twirling his swords. But the silence didn't last for long. It was shattered by the insane howling of the furious gnomes. Kli-Kli didn't bother to wait for their retribution; he came dashing back to me at full tilt, bells jingling.

"Harold, stop dawdling!" Kli-Kli exclaimed. "Follow me, I'll take you to the king."

And so saying, the goblin disappeared through a door. I was seething with fury, but there was nothing I could do except follow the little blackguard.

18

THE COUNCIL

I could glimpse the jester's figure up ahead of me, so I wasn't going to get lost in the immense labyrinth of corridors and stairways. But I had to hurry to keep up with Kli-Kli in his gray and blue leotard. Well-trained servants in livery opened the doors for the goblin to admit him, and therefore me, into the inner sanctum of the royal palace.

My desire to tear the little green mischief-maker's head off was gradually fading, but my new friend decided not to tempt fate and he kept his distance from me. And basically he was right. The joker certainly deserved a good thump.

I swerved round a corner, trying to catch up with the goblin, and came nose-to-nose with a bevy of court matrons taking their aging little daughters for a stroll. Without even stopping, the jester bowed with an irreproachable technique worthy to be included in all the textbooks on etiquette, and skipped straight through this unexpected barrier of wide skirts.

I smiled politely at the ladies, but failed to make an impression. Or rather, I made precisely the opposite impression to what I had intended. The ladies wrinkled up their high-society, aristocratic little noses as if I reeked of the cesspit.

In actual fact, they were the ones who stank. Their aromas were so pungent that I almost fainted. The scum! They think their made-up titles and phony airs make them stink less than those of us who have to struggle.

"Your Excellency!" the jester called to me from the far end of the corridor. "How long do I have to wait for you, duke?"

When they heard that I was a duke, the ladies suddenly changed their opinion about my own humble person. The wrinkles on the little noses disappeared, and coquettish smiles appeared on the little faces. They weren't at all disconcerted either by my less than elegant garb or the bruise on my face. I was a duke, and an aristocrat can get away with anything.

I scowled and dashed on by. Who needed them anyway? Life is complicated enough without adding a woman to the chaos.

The goblin was shifting impatiently from one foot to the other as he waited for me in front of a pair of massive white doors with gold inserts showing an obur hunt. There were six guardsmen standing rigidly to attention beside the doors. While I was walking toward them, the jester managed to pinch one of the men in gray and blue on the leg, stick his tongue out at another, and then try to grab yet another man's sword from him. The goblin was basically making as much mischief as he could. The soldiers in the guard of honor didn't turn a hair, but I could quite clearly read in their eyes the desire to flatten the little snake just as soon as the watch was changed.

As soon as he saw me getting close, Kli-Kli stopped his comic antics and pushed open the doors. "Harold, keep your wits about you, now," he squeaked in a merry voice.

Easily said. It was the first time I'd been in the throne room. It was huge—so huge that it could accommodate all the nobles in the kingdom if they were packed in good and tight. And wouldn't I love to see that. But seriously, the space was quite big enough for rehearsing military parades. At least there would be more than enough space for the cavalry.

The windows were huge, too. They ran from the square black-and-white tiles of the floor all the way up to the ceiling. Somewhere far, far away in front of me was the king's throne with two guardsmen frozen beside it in a guard of honor. Apart from them there was nobody in the hall.

"Didn't you tell me the king was hauling his courtiers over the coals?" I asked Kli-Kli, and then immediately shut up.

My voice, amplified tens of times, echoed all the way round the hall. There must have been some magic involved. Even if you spoke in a whisper, anybody anywhere in the throne room would hear you.

"Well, what if I did? You never know what sort of things a jester might say." The goblin giggled. He listened to the resounding echo and then began doing something which, in his own goblin opinion, was extremely important: He lifted up his left foot and started skipping on his right one from one white square on the floor to another, trying not to step in the black ones.

We walked the entire length of the throne room like that: the goblin hopping on one leg, and me walking at a moderate pace, trying to resist the powerful temptation to break into a run and strangle the light-hearted villain. The jester hopped as far as the throne, which, I must say, didn't look at all special against the general background. There were no gold castings, no rubies the size of a tiger's head. None of those rich and extravagant whimsies for which both of the Empires were so famous. The emperors there try to outdo each other in their display of luxury. Our own glorious Stalkon, may he sit on this throne for another hundred years, preferred to put his gold into the army, not into gorgeous playthings of dubious value.

Paying no attention to the mute guards, the jester climbed up onto the throne, picked up the royal scepter (which looked more like a heavy staff, the kind you could easily use to beat off attackers) off its velvet cushion, and jumped back down onto the floor.

"Don't hurt yourself now," I jibed, which earned me a contemptuous glance.

Kli-Kli did put his new toy back on the cushion though, only he added the stump of the carrot to it. He stepped back, holding his head on one side, like an artist admiring the work he has created, and then, pleased with the result, he beckoned me onward. At the very end of the hall there was another pair of doors exactly like the ones through which we had entered so recently. The jester kicked them as if he were the master of the house.

"After you!" he said, gesturing for me to go through.

I found myself in the room to which Frago Lanten had brought me the time before. I already knew everyone there, so no introduction was necessary. I bowed politely. When I looked up, I was looking straight into sparkling golden eyes. We acknowledged each other and looked away.

"Enough of that, Master Harold," said the king. "Let's leave your dubious etiquette to my courtiers. Have a seat. What took you so long, Kli-Kli?"

"Why ask me?" the jester asked, pulling a sour face. "It's so hard to get Master Harold to move. . . . It took me at least fifteen minutes to persuade him to come."

I choked on my indignation at this barefaced lie, but controlled myself and decided to ignore the king's jester.

"Thank you, Your Majesty," I muttered.

This time Stalkon didn't look anything at all like a genial innkeeper in a sweater and soldier's trousers. I thought the expensive clothes and the narrow ring of the crown on his head suited this man far better.

"Master Artsivus has informed me that your endeavors have been crowned with success," said the king.

Artsivus frowned. He was obviously out of sorts. One of my friends used to have an expression like that when he was tormented by constipation. I just hoped that the archmagician had a different reason for his bad mood. He gave me a look that wasn't exactly the friendliest, but he didn't say anything.

"Yes, Your Majesty, I have completed all the preparations for our . . . er . . . little undertaking."

"I have many questions. Would you be so kind as to tell us once again what has happened to you?"

The king's wish is the law. I sighed and for the umpteenth time that week started telling the story of my adventures, only on this occasion I kept nothing back. Well, almost nothing. I didn't say a word about Valder this time, either.

Halfway through my narrative, my throat finally dried up and I began talking more and more quietly. Noticing this, Stalkon clicked his fingers casually, and the attentive jester poured me some wine. I kept my eyes on him to make sure there was no laxative in the glass. Then I went on with my story.

Artsivus merely raised an eyebrow every now and then, usually when he heard something for the first time. Something I had kept secret from him during our ride in the carriage. The most interesting thing was that no one interrupted me and my listeners were not bored by my interminable story. But everything comes to an end sometime, and eventually I was able to sigh in relief and wet my throat once again with the remarkable wine from the king's cellars.

"A fine kettle of fish," said Kli-Kli, the first to break the silence.

"You put it too mildly, fool," Alistan Markauz blurted out. This time he was dressed in an ordinary guards' uniform. The famous armor that had become a legend among the warriors of Valiostr must have been taking a rest that day. "The kettle is boiling over, my dear jester, and we can only hope that we won't get scalded. Forgive me, Your Majesty, but despite all our secrecy the forthcoming expedition has become known to our enemy."

"Not only to our enemy," Miralissa purred. "You are forgetting about the Master." For a moment I wondered how such a sinister sentence could sound so pleasant. The race of elves were known to have good voices. Where had I heard that bit of wisdom?

"Have you heard of him before?" the king asked the elfess.

"No."

"The archives will not be of any help to us, either," the Rat added morosely. "The royal sandmen have searched for days and found nothing."

"Not exactly nothing," Stalkon objected. "They have found *something*."

"Ah," the captain of the royal guard said with a dismissive wave of his hand. "That's nonsense."

"What are you talking about?" asked Artsivus.

"You see, Your Magicship, as we were plowing through the old chronicles, we came across the interrogation of a certain Djok Imargo. The man whom everyone knows under the name of Djok the Winter-Bringer. He claimed that he had been deliberately framed for the murder of the Prince of the Black Rose, which was committed by the Master's henchmen. Of course, no one could find any Master, nobody had ever even heard of him, and Djok was handed over to the elves."

"Did he tell you anything about this, Lady Miralissa?" the archmagician inquired.

"I'm sorry, milords, but I don't know that piece of history very well," Miralissa said with a shake of her head. "And in addition, it was an internal matter of the House of the Black Rose, so the House of the Black Moon did not intervene. I will ask Ell. He is one of the elves accompanying me, from the House of the Black Rose."

"Very well. Let us consider the Master to be perfectly real and just as dangerous as the Nameless One—if not more dangerous. After all, we still don't understand what it is he wants," said the king.

"A retarded ogre could understand what he wants," Kli-Kli objected. "He doesn't want the Horn to fall into our hands."

"There are many who do not wish to see the Horn return to the world. Even the Order is among those who regard it as too dangerous, but unfortunately it is essential. Do you have the papers with you, Harold?" Artsivus asked.

I nodded reluctantly. It had cost me much effort to obtain them, and now I didn't really feel like handing the plans of Hrad Spein over to the Order. Not even on a temporary basis.

"Would you please let me have a look at them?"

There was nothing I could do but reach into the bag and hand the papers to the archmagician. He began studying the maps, moving his lips occasionally when he came across lines that he found interesting.

The others began waiting patiently for the archmagician to condescend to share his observations. But just then the doors of the room swung open and the lieutenant of the palace guard whom I already knew came in.

"I beg your pardon, Your Majesty, but the gnomes are outside. . . ." The lieutenant looked a little crestfallen.

"And what is it that they want, Izmi?"

"They say that a goblin remarkably similar to your jester stole their, or rather, *your* cannon, as soon as they managed to repair it."

"How can that be?" Like everyone else, the king could not really understand how little Kli-Kli could have made off with the huge, heavy cannon.

"The gnomes say he used a spell and the cannon simply disappeared."

"Kli-Kli, is this true?"

"Well, not exactly," the jester muttered, studying the toes of his boots.

"What does 'not exactly' mean?" the king roared.

"Well then, it's true," the jester muttered, acknowledging Lieutenant Izmi's accusation. "I only wanted to try out one of the spells from Harold's bag."

"You tried it, and now I'll have to pay for it! Who's going to settle matters with the gnomes?"

The jester maintained a polite silence, pretending to be very, very ashamed. No one believed in Kli-Kli's repentance, of course.

"Try to smooth this matter over."

Having received this impracticable order, the poor lieutenant did not hesitate for an instant, but found the inner strength to nod and set out to do battle with the gnomes. The assignment he had been given was dangerous and difficult. Not to mention impossible.

"Listen here," Artsivus said, clearing his throat. The archmagician had not taken the slightest notice of the unpleasant incident that had just taken place. All of his attention had been focused on the old papers. "There's something very interesting here. . . ."

The master of the Order read out the riddle in rhyme that had interested For so much. But unlike my teacher, the archmagician had no need to reach for a dictionary; he had complete command of the original language of the orcs and elves—ancient orcish.

"I can say straightaway that one quatrain is the most absolute and blatant piece of plagiary that I have ever seen in my life," the jester put in as soon Artsivus finished reading.

"And which one is it you don't like?" the archmagician asked in surprise.

The jester declaimed in a singsong voice:

> In serried ranks, embracing the shadows,
> The long-deceased knights stand in silence,
> And only one man will not die 'neath their swords,
> He who is the shadows' own twin brother.

"That's from the *Bruk-Gruk*."

"From the goblins' *Book of Prophecies*?" Miralissa inquired. "Are you certain?"

"I've never been more certain in my life. It's definitely from the *Bruk-Gruk*. Only, some learned scribes have altered the rhythm." The goblin seemed about to burst in his indignation that someone had dared to corrupt a great goblin prophecy.

"What book are you talking about?" Alistan asked. Like me, he had never heard of any Bruk-whatever book.

"My dear count," said Kli-Kli, his voice oozing venomous disdain. "You really ought to set your sword aside and take up reading. The *Bruk-Gruk*, or *Book of Prophecies*, was written by the insane shaman Tre-Tre three and a half thousand years ago. It is an account in verse of the most important and crucial events that will take place in the world of Siala for the next ten thousand years. For instance, it foretold the appearance of the Nameless One. And there are lines about the Forbidden Territory, too, although the Order took no notice of them in times gone by."

Artsivus frowned even more darkly at these words from the goblin, but apparently decided it was below his dignity to argue with a jester.

"My grandfather was a shaman," Kli-Kli went on. "And he trained me, too. However I was not born to be a magician. But I do remember the *Book of Prophecies* by heart, and so I recognized the quatrain immediately."

The jester's voice positively rang with pride. I think his shaman grandfather would have been no less proud of his grandson. Memorizing an entire book written by some crazy madman—that definitely requires persistence and talent.

"And what was the quatrain in the original?"

> Tormented by thirst and cursed by darkness,
> The undead sinners bear their punishment.
> And only one will not die in their fangs,
> He who dances with the shadows like a brother.

"That's not so smooth. I liked the first version a lot better," I said, letting him know my opinion of the poetry of the goblins.

"Oh, just look at you! The great connoisseur of literature and art! That was written by the great insane shaman Tre-Tre!" said Kli-Kli, trying to put me in my place.

"That's pretty obvious." This time I didn't intend to let the jester have the last word.

"But then we don't steal other people's prophecies and transform them into neat little verses," the goblin snorted, and turned his back on me.

My ignorance of the literary masterpiece by a goblin shaman who gorged himself on magic mushrooms had finally convinced the little jester that I was basically illiterate.

"By the way, Kli-Kli, what is that prophecy about?" Stalkon asked.

"It's called 'The Dancer in the Shadows.' I could recite it for you in full, but that would require a couple of hours."

Oho! It seemed like the old shaman didn't know when to stop! Whenever he wrote a poem, it was at least two hours long!

"And in brief?"

"Er-er-er . . . ," said the jester, wrinkling up his forehead. "Let's put it this way. It's a prophecy about a man who makes his living from an iniquitous trade, but who has decided to serve the good of his homeland. There are all sorts of things in it, but in the end he will attain salvation for the peoples of Siala and halt the advance of the enemy. Salvation comes from the Mysterious Stone Palaces of the Bones. That means Hrad Spein, in case anyone didn't understand," said Kli-Kli, casting an expressive glance at me. "It's a prophecy about you, Harold. Well, I never thought I'd meet a real live hero out of the *Bruk-Gruk*."

"Stop telling fibs," I said dismissively. I didn't like the idea of becoming the hero of some goblin prophecy made up by an insane old shaman. "I don't believe in stupid fairy tales. That Tre-Tre of yours got something confused, or he ate something that disagreed with him. And why does it have to be me? As if there weren't plenty of people plying iniquitous trades!"

Well, let them try to guess the meaning of some useless fairy tale if they want to! What's important is that I don't believe in the insane ramblings of shamans driven crazy by charm-weed, but you can't expect too much from a goblin, especially if he happens to be the king's fool.

"All right then, 'The Dancer in the Shadows' . . . Interesting . . . I tell you what, Kli-Kli, you write out this prophecy on paper for me, and I'll familiarize myself with it when I have the time," said Artsivus.

"A toy-oy-oy," a deep voice said behind my back, and a man jumped forward into the center of the room.

His respectable shirt was dirty and stained, his trousers were crumpled, and the hair on his head was a genuine disgrace, a bird's nest.

"I want a toy," the man said, then he flopped down on the floor and banged one foot on it.

The eldest son and former heir.

No one really knew what it was—a punishment from the gods or something that just happened—but King Stalkon the Ninth's eldest son, a man the same age as myself, had the mind of a four-year-old boy. Naturally, he would never be able to claim the throne, which would have to pass to the younger prince, who also bore the name Stalkon, like all the men in this dynasty.

The older son had been given several nannies to care for him, and he lived in his own childish, fairy-tale little world, which was probably very happy, without any of the pain, dirt, and blood of the real world.

"Shouldn't you be asleep? Where are your nannies?" the king asked his son. I sensed an unusual tenderness in his voice.

"Rotten beasts!" That was all the prince had to say about his governesses.

"I'll take him," Kli-Kli intervened. "You come with me, Stalkosha, come on. I'll give you a toy."

"A toy?" The king's eldest son bounced up onto his feet and stomped after the jester, who had already slipped out through the door.

There was an awkward silence in the room.

"Please accept my apologies."

"Come now, Your Majesty." The elfess's yellow eyes flashed in understanding. "You are not to blame."

"Then who is, if not me? The gods?" There was a clear note of bitterness in the king's voice.

No one answered him.

I could understand the man. When, for no particular reason, a healthy twenty-year-old heir is suddenly transformed into an idiot with the reason of a four-year-old child and all your hopes are dashed, it must be appalling. And frightening. As appalling and frightening as being an orphan alone in the streets. Stalkosha, at least, had people who cared for him. Some of us weren't so lucky. But our king had always had the reputation of a strong man. After all, he had survived even that. And if he hadn't completely recovered, at least he never showed his grief. There were rumors that the young prince had been damaged by magic. But what kind of dark wizardry it was and who had worked it, the rumormongers never got a chance to say. The king's sandmen shut the talkative lads' mouths by dispatching them forever to the Gray Stones—or perhaps to even more distant places.

"So, it's a prophecy about you, Harold," said Stalkon, finally breaking the heavy silence.

"I very much doubt that, Your Majesty." I really didn't believe in the goblin's tall stories. "An unfortunate coincidence and nothing more."

"It can hardly be about our dearest thief," said milord Alistan, supporting me. "Thieves don't end up in prophecies. The best a thief can hope for is to end up in the Gray Stones."

Artsivus also paid little attention to the goblin's fairy tale. The Order is very old-fashioned in this regard, and it pays no attention to any prophecies at all unless they were created by magicians from the tower.

"Lady Miralissa, can you tell us what this Selena mentioned in the poem is?"

"Selena? That's ancient orcish, the first language of this world, unless you count ogric. But a very strange dialect. If one uses a bit of imagination, it could simply be a play on words. In the old language 'sellarzhyn' is 'moon' and 'ena' is 'purple.' A purple moon? It's the first time I've come across the word. It is not mentioned in our *Annals of the Crown*."

"So there's a purple moon in Hrad Spein," Kli-Kli giggled as he returned to the room. Somehow he seemed to find this fact extremely amusing.

"That is only my provisional translation," Miralissa said with a barely noticeable frown. "We need to do some work on the documents before we can understand exactly what is what."

"And the work will be done, do not doubt it. Harold!" said Artsivus, turning to me. "You don't object if I take this document, do you?"

I shrugged indifferently. Why not? I remember verse pretty well, so he could take it; maybe the Order would dig something up.

"That's excellent," Artsivus said delightedly, handing the rest of the papers to the goblin so that he could pass them on to me.

Kli-Kli gave a humorus curtsey in the finest tradition of the ladies at court, crossed his legs, and sat down, holding up the papers. I put them away in my bag, paying no attention to the fool, which didn't seem to upset him very much. In any case, he pulled a face that only I could see and went back to the carpet.

"I have another two questions. What are the halls of the Slumbering Whisper and the Slumbering Echo?"

"I don't know, Harold. In Zagraba we have legends about many terrible things to be found in the Palaces of Bones, but I have never paid any attention to them. And I have never heard anything about such halls in Hrad Spein."

"And what are the Kaiyu?"

"More precisely the blind servants of Kaiyu," the elfess corrected me. "That is yet another tale that has lived on for over a thousand years. It came into being at the time when we began fighting the orcs in the Palaces of Bone. In order to protect the graves of the elfin lords against defilement, our shamans summoned creatures from distant worlds, so that they would guard the peace of our dead forever. This is a very, very old legend. No one has been down to those levels for hundreds of years, and our records about Kaiyu contradict each other."

"You are setting out tomorrow morning," said the king. "Lady Miralissa and her companions will lead the expedition through the Forests of Zagraba. Alistan, you are in command. Try not to be detained anywhere and to get back as quickly as possible. As soon as spring comes and the snow in the pass melts, the Nameless One will set out from the Desolate Lands."

"My king, perhaps we ought to send several thousand troops to the Lonely Giant as reinforcements?"

"Pointless. The Wild Hearts will not be able to hold out in any case. And the regular army will only get in their way. The Lonely Giant is merely a small dam, and it will burst under the combined pressure of the Desolate Lands. The border has always held only because of the bravery of the Wild Hearts and the aggressors' inability to unite. Sending the army there, Alistan, would mean risking the very life of the kingdom. You understand that yourself. We'll send a hundred Beaver Caps and the Jolly Gallows-Birds from two ships. They will help the Wild Hearts to hold out for as long as possible. A week, two at the most, so that I'll have time to prepare the counterattack. Closer to winter we'll have to send another thousand soldiers."

"My father and the other heads of houses intend to send about three hundred archers to help you," said Miralissa.

"Yes?" The king was not the only one delighted by this news. "Please convey my gratitude to your father, milady."

I chuckled. It might seem to many that three hundred archers are a mere drop in the ocean. . . . Well now, that's true, just as long as they're not elves. But three hundred elfin archers can reap the enemy in a deadly harvest. It was more than eight hundred years since Filand fell out over something or other with the light elves of I'alyala, but everyone still remembered how less than thirty elves had routed the heavy cavalry of the Filanders. Hitting the joints in the armor and the eye slots in the helmets, firing twenty arrows a minute, the handful of elves forced four select legions of cavalry, four hundred men, to retreat. Or rather, only two hundred men actually managed to retreat. The same number were left lying on the ground.

"We shall pass through Valiostr, cut across the Iselina, and enter the forests from the side of the Border Kingdom," Miralissa said.

"Those are dangerous parts," Markauz said with a frown of disapproval. "That's orc territory."

"But that is where our nearest entrance to the Palaces of Bone lies; we would have to travel through the Forests of Zagraba for another three weeks to reach the other entrance," said Miralissa, adjusting a strand of ash-gray hair that had come loose from her tall hairstyle. "So we shall have to take the risk, just as the previous expeditions did."

Alistan Markauz said nothing, but it would have been obvious to a hedgehog that he was not very pleased at the prospect of making his way to Hrad Spein through the forest of the orcs. Neither was I. My preference would have been to stay at home and drink wine.

"I think that you will reach the goal of your journey in a month. That is, you should arrive during the first days of August," Artsivus declared.

"That is if there are no unforeseen circumstances," Stalkon objected.

Everybody understood what kind of unforeseen circumstances he was talking about—the kind that had prevented the first two groups from completing the expedition.

"I hope that everything will go well. And while we are on our expedition, the army will have to be made ready. Not too much hope can be placed in our undertaking."

Count Alistan was not really all that keen on setting out on the journey. And his reluctance was quite understandable. Not only would he have to pass the time in the company of a thief, he had to leave the king without his protection, too.

"You know that I am already doing everything I can," Stalkon retorted irritably. "But there are still too few of us anyway. Catastrophically few. What are a few tens of thousands against the countless hordes from the Desolate Lands? King Shargaz has sent us his apologies, but he will not send us a single soldier. All the forces of the Borderland are now beside the Forests of Zagraba; the orcs are running wild. The Border Kingdom is expecting an invasion and they will need every soldier. By the way, Harold, I have heard everything that I wanted to hear from you. You are free to go. I don't suppose matters of state are of any great interest to you. Kli-Kli, take our guest and show him his room, his things, and all the rest of it."

Realizing that the conversation was at an end, I got up, bowed, and followed the jester out of the room.

"Follow me, Dancer in the Shadows." The depth of seriousness in the jester's voice was ominous.

"Don't call me that."

"Why?" asked the goblin, peering at me innocently.

"Because I don't want you to!"

"Oh," the jester said considerately. "Then I won't."

We walked back through the massive throne room and out into the corridors of the palace.

"What would you like to see first? Your temporary quarters or a new friend?"

"What new friend?"

"Come on, I'll show you."

I had to walk for quite a long time. First we went out of the building and past the garden, which was now almost empty—the only Wild Heart still there was Loudmouth, already on his fourth dream, if not his fifth.

"Kli-Kli," I said as we walked along, "these Wild Hearts, where are they from?"

"The Lonely Giant, of course," the goblin snorted.

"No, I don't mean that," I snorted back. "What unit of the Wild Hearts?"

"Oh! Apart from Arnkh, they're all from the Thorns. Arnkh's from the Steel Foreheads."

The Thorns . . . Now I really felt that my skin was safe. And there were any number of stories about the skill of the Thickheads, as the other soldiers called the Steel Foreheads.

Eventually the jester led me to a outbuilding standing quite a long way from the palace. Or to be absolutely precise, the goblin led me straight to the stables. There was a smell of fresh hay and dung (also fresh, as a matter of fact). The horses in the stalls peered out curiously at the uninvited visitors. Every now and then one of them would reach its face out toward us in the hope of getting a treat.

There were about fifty horses here. Elegant Doralissian steeds, imperturbable draft horses, the powerful war horses of Nizina that seemed so terrifying to the ignorant . . .

"Here, let me introduce you," said the jester, putting his hand on the muzzle of a large ash-colored mare. "This is Little Bee. She's yours now."

"Oh, yes?" I asked uncertainly.

"What's wrong, Harold?" Kli-Kli asked with a frown. "Don't you like the king's gift?"

"What makes you think I don't like it?" I asked, stroking the Nizin breed horse behind the ear when it reached its head out toward me. "I like it very much. It's just that I'm not very good at riding them."

"Mmm, all right, I'll teach you today."

I gave the jester the same look I would have done if he'd asked me to kiss a poisonous snake.

"Calm down, Harold. I really can help you. It's fairly simple. Little Bee's clever, she's been trained. And what's more, she's a war horse, or a war mare, or a steedess. . . . Well, you know what I mean. . . . Here! Give her a treat."

Kli-Kli took out a huge red apple from somewhere and handed it to me.

Little Bee happily crunched the treat and her amicable expression became even more kindly. I found it hard to believe that she was a war mare. . . . Damn it! Now I was doing it, too!

"Come on, I'll show you your room," said Kli-Kli, tugging at my sleeve. "Your things are there, by the way. A dwarf brought them, together with the ring."

So Honchel had already brought the things I hadn't been able to collect on the evening when I bought them from him. I meekly followed the king's jester, realizing that he wouldn't leave me alone today and I'd have to put up with him until tomorrow morning, when I would happily wave good-bye to the little green goblin.

"By the way, we need to go to the armorer and pick out a decent sword and some chain mail for you." Kli-Kli was simply bursting with the desire to do something.

"Now that's one gift I don't need," I said, shaking my head.

"So what's wrong this time?"

"I need a sword like a drowned man needs a noose. I don't know how to use it anyway. These are all I need, my dear jester," I said, slapping my hand against the short blade at my hip and sticking my crossbow under the nose of the king's fool.

"Well, you know best," he said, too lazy to argue with me. "Then we'll choose you some armor."

"I'm not Alistan Markauz, Kli-Kli! I don't intend to carry the work of an entire mineful of gnomes around with me."

"Don't get nervous. We'll find you some light, safe armor." The goblin was not about to give up this time.

"I don't need it. It's awkward moving about in chain mail."

"Harold!" The jester pointed one finger at me and pronounced his verdict. "You're a boring, tedious fellow."

19

A NIGHT IN THE PALACE

Groaning in disappointment and cursing the entire world, I turned over onto my back and stared up at the ceiling. Cowardly sleep had fled from me like a healthy man fleeing from a leper. At first I thought I'd been woken by another one of the goblin's tricks. But I couldn't see the little jester anywhere around. I hoped very much that he was sleeping like a log somewhere as far away from me as possible, after exhausting himself during the day. After all, it must have taken a serious effort for him to give Harold a lesson in how to control a horse and then go on to wear me down with all his whining about the chain mail I hadn't chosen, so that eventually I had to give way and go with him to select an iron shirt from the king's armory. The delighted jester had taken himself off to his bed with a smile of triumph.

But if Kli-Kli wasn't to blame, then what was it that had woken me up? There it was again! That was it, definitely. Those shouts. They had woken me up. And that clash of weapons.

It sounded as if there was a full-scale battle taking place in the corridors of the palace. But then who was fighting whom, and what about?

I tried to think on my feet as I searched for my trousers in the darkness and at the same time groped for the crossbow and the bag with my bolts that I had left on a chair. Outside, bugles sounded to rouse the guard. First one, then another, and after a short while the alarm signal was ringing throughout the palace grounds.

I grabbed my crossbow and dashed to the window. There was no question of lighting a candle. It would have taken too long to find one. I would have to load the crossbow by the light of the stars. Yes, I can load it in complete darkness, but it would have been annoying to confuse an ordinary bolt with one of the magical ones, then roast myself as well as my target when I fired.

"Alarm! Alarm!" The bugles rang out, echoing each other.

Outside, people were dashing about with lighted torches—for some reason, not one of the magical lanterns the Order had installed in the grounds of the palace was lit. Several guardsmen ran past right below my window, two of them carrying a wounded man. A little farther off there was a unit of soldiers heading in the opposite direction with the points of their spears glinting menacingly in the flickering light.

Two human shadows darted out of the palace and ran off into the depths of the garden. One of the guards in the first detachment spotted the fugitives and most of the soldiers ran off in pursuit, leaving their two comrades with the wounded man.

One of the men they were chasing stopped and threw his arms up. Then he started spinning round and swaying from side to side. The guards slowed from a run to a walk, approaching the strangers cautiously, not really sure what this madman was doing. They realized the answer to the riddle too late. The man stopped his crazy spinning and flung one hand out toward the soldiers, and the guards were simply tossed in all directions like children's straw toys.

Darkness! He was a genuine shaman!

In immediate response to the shaman's magic, a silver streak of lightning struck from somewhere in the upper stories of the palace. I ducked down in surprise, trying to get rid of the multicolored carousel that was spinning in front of my eyes, and when I could see normally again, the fugitives no longer existed. On the spot where they had been standing there was a huge round circle of scorched earth, with the grass still burning around its edge. Some magician of the Order had really put everything into his blow against the enemy. There was nothing left of the intruders.

The bugles began calling again, sounding the alarm and calling men to arms. The din outside my door was unbelievable. There was already fighting at the end of the corridor where my bedroom was. Which meant there must be a lot more of the attackers, otherwise why couldn't I hear cries of victory from all those guardsmen?

"The king! Stalkon! Valiostr!" The royal guard roared out their battle cry.

"The Nameless One! Vengeance!" was the reply.

So it was the supporters of the Nameless One who had resolved on this bold move!

Those rotten skunks were everywhere now. Sometimes it seemed like it would be wise to suspect your own frail old granddad of sympathy for the Nameless One, even if he wouldn't normally harm a fly. And the stronger the rebel magician became, the more supporters he acquired among humankind.

Someone pounded hard on my door and I trained the crossbow on it just in case.

"Harold, it's Kli-Kli! Open up, quick!"

The voice certainly sounded like the one that belonged to the king's jester.

The battle was moving quite rapidly in my direction and if the little goblin really was outside my door, he could be in big trouble pretty soon.

I hastily opened the lock.

"I'm not alone, don't shoot!" shouted Kli-Kli, darting past me into the bedroom like a little green mouse, with two shadows following straight behind him. They were a little bit bigger than the goblin, but a lot smaller than me.

"Close the door," said the goblin. It was a good idea. "Deler, let's have some light."

I did as I had been told and turned the key, wondering if we ought to barricade the door with furniture.

A small flame flared up, and then a torch, illuminating the faces of my visitors. The jester was without his cap with the bells and his expression was unusually serious and intent. There was a dark, shallow scratch on Kli-Kli's cheek and he was clutching an ax in both hands. Standing beside the jester was Deler, holding the torch in one hand and a double-edged poleax in the other. It had a vicious-looking half-moon blade. Unlike the goblin, the dwarf didn't look disheveled. Even the hat with the narrow brim sat on the short fellow's head as if it were a part of him.

The third visitor was Hallas. The gnome paid no attention to me, as if he were simply visiting his home in the Steel Mines, and ran across to the window and looked outside. He casually leaned his battle-mattock against the wall.

"This is Master Harold," said Kli-Kli, introducing me to the warriors.

Deler politely doffed his hat; the gnome simply nodded.

"What's happened, Kli-Kli?"

"An attack! They were trying to get through to the king, but the guards suspected something was wrong and the sparks started flying!"

"And the rotten skunks have really got cheeky!" Deler boomed. "They're dressed up in guards' uniforms."

"But who are they?"

"Crayfish," the gnome said, and spat, without turning away from the window. "Creatures of the Crayfish Dukedom. And probably other supporters of the Nameless One from among your townsfolk!"

He pulled a face that suggested he cared no more for the townsfolk of Avendoom than he did for gkhols.

"Anyway, listen, Harold," the jester started gabbling. "One of those units is moving down the corridor toward us. Alistan's lads are holding it up, but still falling back, the numbers are too uneven. We have to help them."

A din as loud as the one in the corridor suddenly broke out below the window.

"Those lads are done fighting." Hallas chuckled and slammed his fist down on the windowsill in an excess of enthusiasm. "The guards have threaded the lot of them on their spears."

"Come away from the window, you bearded fool!" the dwarf shouted excitedly. "We have to give the others a hand now!"

"Fool yourself!" the gnome retorted to his partner, but he came over to us, picking up his mattock on the way.

"How can we help them, Kli-Kli?" I asked, pulling on my shirt and ignoring the argument between the two Wild Hearts.

Four of us against that number of men? And not forgetting that two of us didn't even know how to hold a weapon properly. Or were the dwarf and the gnome so good that they didn't need me and the goblin?

"The guards are falling back and those skunks are following them. As soon as the killers are past our door, their backs will be exposed. And that's when we'll strike."

"They're getting close already," said the gnome, listening to the battle with his ear pressed against the door.

My face must have betrayed too skeptical an opinion of the goblin's crazy plan, because Kli-Kli added: "Harold, use your brains! You've got bolts loaded with fire magic and ice! If we blast them from the rear, it will really make a difference!"

"How do you know what I've got?" I asked, already unloading the crossbow, removing the ordinary bolts.

After a moment's hesitation, I flung the bag with the rest of the charges over my shoulder.

"I had a rummage in the things your dwarf tradesman brought with Stalkon's ring," Kli-Kli replied, not embarrassed in the least.

"Just a little farther!" Deler had joined Hallas and was frozen beside the door, holding up the torch and his poleax at the ready.

"Gentlemen, don't get in the way," I warned the Wild Hearts. "Or you'll catch it from my bolts, too."

"Magic!" said the gnome, pulling a disdainful face.

"Don't you be so clever," Deler told him. "Whatever you say, Master Harold. And if this wiseacre tries anything, I'll rip his beard off."

Just then, the gnome roared: "Now!"

He swung open the door and went tumbling out into the corridor, together with the dwarf. Kli-Kli and I followed right behind them. I prayed hard that I wouldn't end up on the edge of someone's sword.

The guards were fighting desperately, but retreating. They were being forced back by about twenty-five men in exactly the same gray and blue uniforms as themselves, but with white armbands. Fortunately the corridor was rather narrow, so the king's men could more or less hold off their attackers, who were unable to take advantage of their superior numbers. And the spears that the small group of His Majesty's men were holding also gave them a certain advantage over the enemy. The attackers were advancing in two ranks. The ones at the back had not yet joined in the battle and were simply walking along behind. Their backs were unprotected. . . .

I had to take advantage of that as quickly as possible. The guardsmen had almost exhausted themselves holding back the enemy.

The bolt struck the crowd of conspirators, releasing the elemental fire. There was a rumble and a flash, and someone screamed in horror and pain. At least five of the killers were dispatched into the darkness. All that was left of the man I had hit was a smoking firebrand. But

I must give our enemies due credit—they were quick to figure out what was going on. Seven men separated off and came in our direction, leaving the rest of the unit to continue the battle.

The gnome roared and went dashing toward the fighters who were running in our direction, but Deler tossed aside his torch to free his hand and managed to catch Hallas by the beard and yank it downward, hard. Hallas howled in surprise and indignation and fell to the floor. Deler and Kli-Kli did the same, knowing what was about to happen.

I shot for the second time, aiming at the massive brute who was bearing down on me with the fluent stride of a delirious wild boar. This time there was a shrill ringing sound as the elemental snow was released from its magical trap, and my face was pricked by hundreds of chilly little needles. The impact was quite close, and it was a miracle that my own skin didn't suffer any unpleasant consequences. As was only to be expected, the brute fell apart into two solidly frozen halves and the two men who were running immediately behind him had all the protruding parts of their bodies frozen solid, too. The others were stunned—they shook their heads, and put their hands over their eyes as they slid about on a sheet of ice and they all howled. Especially the lad who now had icicles instead of fingers and whose clothes were covered with a crust of snow.

Hallas started beating the enemies who had still not recovered from my latest shot. Deler decided that he wanted a bit of amusement, too, and his poleax started singing in unison with the gnome's battle-mattock. One of the enemies tried to strike at him from above with his sword, but the ginger-headed dwarf dived under the blade as it descended, and sliced off both of the bold warrior's legs. The man fell, choking on his scream, and the gnome ruthlessly finished him off by bringing his mattock down on his head. In literally half a minute there was no one left of the bold group of seven, or rather the group of four who had survived my shot. The dwarf and the gnome made an inspired team.

"Stalkon and the Lonely Giant!" Hallas roared, waving his mattock as he ran toward the rest of our enemies, who were now battling with guardsmen revitalized by the unexpected help that had come their way.

Deler went after him.

The advantage of numbers was on our side now, and the guards all roared together as they crushed the final resistance.

"We showed them!" Kli-Kli said spiritedly.

The goblin jester was standing there with his short little legs set wide apart, and the blade of the ax, which looked huge in his hands, touching the marble floor. He noticed my skeptical look.

"All right, all right, Harold! You showed them," he agreed amicably. "But if I hadn't been defending you . . ."

"*You* were defending *me*?" I asked indignantly, reloading the crossbow as I spoke, but this time with ordinary bolts.

"Yes, I was!" It was not easy to embarrass this jester. "But even if you don't agree that I saved you, my contribution is still worthy of all the treasures of Siala. After all, I was the one who invented the brilliant plan of attacking the unsuspecting enemy."

"Be careful you don't brag yourself to death," I told Kli-Kli as I watched the final villain being run through by a guardsman's sword.

"Behind you, Harold!" the goblin squealed, and I swung round sharply.

An entire detachment of warriors was coming toward us from the other end of the corridor, but it was hard to tell who they were—guardsmen or enemies dressed in guards' uniforms.

When they saw me point the crossbow at them, the new arrivals shouted: "Stalkon and the Spring Jasmine!"

"Harold, they're ours!" the jester shouted, concerned that I might shoot the king's younger son by mistake. He was given the name Spring Jasmine for that time when . . . But that's another story altogether. I hope someday there'll be a time and a place for it, and grateful listeners.

The large detachment of guardsmen under the command of Stalkon the Spring Jasmine drew level with us. Miralissa strode alongside them, bow in hand, a long dagger at her side dripping with gore. Her eyes sparkled, as always, but this time it was an icy, focused gleam, fearsome to behold. I gave thanks to every god I could name that she was on our side.

"I see that you're in the battle, too, Kli-Kli," the prince chuckled.

The lad was only sixteen years old, but he held a sword with confidence, and the gentlemen guards would have followed their future king onto red-hot coals if necessary. The young Stalkon's breeding was obvious. Like all his kind, he had been given every advantage—some of us had to learn the hard way, but not him. He seemed competent and well liked by his men, though. I'll give him that. He didn't look a lot like his father and his older brother, Stalkon Divested of the Crown. The slim, agile prince was more like his mother, Stalkon the Ninth's second wife.

"Our glorious jester will defeat them all," laughed the baron, whom I already knew from our encounter at the gate.

"We gave them a good hiding!" said Hallas, coming up to us with his mattock bloodied right up to the handle.

Other guards from the unit that we had helped to hold out started joining us.

"My prince!" Lieutenant Izmi's shirt was soaked in blood, but he was standing firmly on his feet, ignoring the slight wound on his forearm. "I am happy that you came to our assistance!"

"It wasn't him," I said, determined not to be cheated of my share of glory and gratitude. "If the jester hadn't come up with a brilliant plan, I wouldn't have fired my magical bolts and the glorious gentlemen Deler and Hallas wouldn't have put their weapons to work, and you, lieutenant, would be in the next world by now."

The bugles started sounding again, but this time there was a note of victory in their voices, and immediately a messenger came running up to the prince and started gabbling rapidly:

"The north and west wings of the palace have been completely cleared. There are still isolated skirmishes in the east wing, but Milord Alistan and the guard will deal with the curs themselves. On the third floor of the south wing the battle is in full swing. The enemy is well entrenched in the small ballroom and we can't smoke him out."

"What about my father?" the prince asked curtly.

"The king is safe. He is on his way with three units to join Milord Markauz. He asks you to enter the south wing from the Pearl Stairway, and Alistan will proceed from the Hall of Flowers."

"Let's go and crush these woodlice!" the prince growled.

The guardsmen went dashing after their future king. The gnome and the dwarf went with them, running in the front row and almost overtaking young Stalkon himself. Those two races really would give anything for a good battle.

"Let's go, Harold," said Kli-Kli, tugging on the edge of my unbuttoned shirt. "Your crossbow will be needed again."

"I'm a thief, not a soldier," I protested. "And anyway, there are plenty of men here with crossbows."

I really had counted at least eight men among the guards carrying heavy army crossbows, which fire bolts that can go right through a soldier in heavy armor. But I tagged along with everyone else anyway, not really knowing what made me do something so insane.

The signs of battle were everywhere. Weapons lying around, broken urns, tapestries torn off the walls, blood, and bodies. There were guardsmen and impostors lying on the floor. Before the morning came someone would lose his head. It was more than just fifty or a hundred warriors who had managed to get into the palace. The count ran to hundreds, and there was no way that many could have slipped in here without help. So there were traitors among the servants of the court and also, I feared, in the ranks of the guards. The king's sandmen had a big job ahead of them trying to uncover the villains.

As our unit moved through the corridors, stairways, and halls of the palace, more guardsmen joined us. Sometimes just one man, sometimes twenty at a time. The battle was already over; the critical point that decided whose side Sagra, the goddess of war, would take today, had been passed. We had held out.

The enemy had thought that the men in gray and blue could be taken by surprise, and he had paid for that. Whatever goal the supporters of the Nameless One had set themselves, this time they had failed completely, and I didn't think there was going to be a next time. At least, not another daring attack like this one. Milord Rat would do absolutely everything possible to prevent even a mouse from slipping in, let alone several hundred killers.

"Izmi, take four platoons and enter the south wing from the garden," the prince commanded. "We'll spring this mousetrap shut!"

"Marquis Vartek, are your men ready?" Stalkon asked the white-haired guardsman.

"Yes!" Yet another of my acquaintances from the gate was in a determined mood.

"Along the north corridor, pin them to the wall. Everybody else follow me!"

"Harold, we're with the marquis!" said Kli-Kli. He had completely taken command of my actions now.

The rest of the guards were following the prince into another corridor.

"An extra crossbow won't come amiss," Vartek said with a nod, accepting our company into his little unit.

We turned into a wide, dark corridor where there were no torches or lanterns burning. They had either been put out or quite simply never been lit. The only light was about a hundred paces ahead of us, so we almost had to feel our way along. Fortunately, no one attacked us, only Deler started groaning and hissing when someone stood on his foot in the darkness. In this part of the palace four corridors came together all leading into an immense hall with mirror walls. Of course, it wasn't as gigantic as the throne room, but it was quite big enough for the remaining supporters of the Nameless One to assemble in. They were crowded together in the center, waiting with their weapons drawn. About forty men in a circle. There was something large and dark behind them, covered with a black cloth. I couldn't really see what it was—the defenders' backs screened the unknown object very securely.

We had cut off all four corridors: the prince and his guards were approaching from one side, Izmi's unit from a second, Alistan Markauz, in his beloved armor, was creeping up with his spearmen from a third, closing the ring. And we were on the fourth side, with five guards and the Wild Hearts. Now there was simply nowhere for the intruders to go.

"So there you are," grumbled Uncle, giving the gnome and the dwarf a look of disapproval. "Where did you get to?"

"We've been having some fun," said Deler, casually wiping the blade of his poleax on the rag hanging at his belt.

"All right, Vartek!" Izmi shouted from the far end of the hall.

The eight crossbowmen moved forward and the army sklots froze in predatory anticipation, ready to spew bolts at the target at the first word of command.

"Hey you!" barked Markauz. His voice sounded muffled, coming from under his helmet, which was so much like a rat's head. "Surrender, and the king promises you a fair trial."

The reply that followed from the ranks of the Nameless One's supporters advised the king what he could do with his extremely fair trial and where he could stick it. These lads had committed at least three crimes against the crown, and so they had absolutely no grounds to hope for the king's mercy. You could say they were as good as dead already.

Markauz gave a barely perceptible nod, and the sklots all clicked in unison. Eight bolts flew straight through eight enemies. The captain of the guards had no intention of throwing his warriors into a bloody battle: he thought it easier to shoot the traitors from a distance.

"Reload!" Vartek commanded loudly.

Resting their crossbows on the ground, the guardsmen set their feet in the stirrups of their weapons and furiously set about winding the mechanism that drew the bowstrings taut.

While the soldiers were making their crossbows ready for action, a man emerged from the ranks of the enemy. Without speaking, he lifted up his arms and slowly turned round his own axis, at the same time swaying from side to side, like a tree battling against a gusty autumn wind. I'd already seen this happen once that night, and it looked to me like we were about to have serious problems. If someone didn't do something during these few seconds, the power of this ogric shamanism would come crashing down on our heads like a massive club.

"Alistan!" I roared. "They have a shaman!"

The crossbowmen had only just finished tightening their strings and now they were putting in the bolts, but they were too late. Far too late.

I fired. First one bolt, then the other. And I missed. Either my hands were shaking too much, or death had decided to spare the shaman just at that moment, but the bolts went flying wide, with the second one just nicking the sorcerer's gray and blue guards uniform.

We were all saved by some soldier from Izmi's unit who threw his spear. The shaman was either half-witted or lacking in skill, but in any case he was too slow to put up a barrier. The heavy weapon flew the length of the hall like a swallow and struck the sorcerer in the stomach, throwing him backward into the crowd of the Nameless One's supporters.

And that was when it happened.

I don't know why it became active just then—perhaps it was angered by the death of the shaman, or perhaps it had been under the sorcerer's control—but the hall suddenly echoed with a furious roar, and the creature that had been hiding under the black drapery torn down from some wall in the palace pushed aside the last remaining intruders and stood there before us.

"An ogre!" the guardsmen shouted.

Their voices were full of genuine terror.

I stared hard at this creature that I had only ever seen before in pictures. These villains had managed to bring a genuine, live ogre into the palace! A member of a race that had not set foot on the land of Valiostr for thousands of years.

It is hard for the uninformed to believe that an ogre is a distant relative of the orcs and the elves. It is three and a half yards tall, with glassy, blue-black agate skin and a face in which the only similarity to the elves and orcs lies in the black lips, the huge fangs, and the ash-gray mane of hair.

The little black pupils of the ogre's eyes almost fused into the irises against the background of the light-blue whites. The muzzle, like a wild boar's, and the immense pointed ears, each the size of a large burdock leaf, were repulsive. The ogre had no neck at all, and its head seemed to grow straight out of its shoulders. Its muscles rippled like steel-hard cables across a powerful, square-set body that was clad in the skin of a polar bear. And to add to the list of our problems, the monster was holding a massive ax in its hand. With a bit of effort, that notched blade could easily have chopped through the column supporting the façade of the Royal Library.

"Everybody back!" Honeycomb growled. "Against the walls! You crossbowmen, look lively now!"

The guardsmen all darted aside and started withdrawing into the corridors. The crossbowmen fired another salvo. And as malevolent fate would have it, only one of them hit the target. The bolt slammed into the upper right section of the ogre's chest, forcing it to take a step back and . . .

And that was all, actually. The entire effect. According to rumors, these creatures had two hearts, and in order to kill an ogre, you had to destroy both. So what could you expect if the bolt had not even nicked any vital organs? I took a magical bolt out of my bag. It looked as if I was going to use up all my emergency supplies before I even got to Hrad Spein.

"Marmot, from the right! Loudmouth, move in from behind! Now we'll carve up this tough little nut!" Honeycomb was already advancing on the ogre, whirling his terrible ogre-club above his head. The chain connecting the handle and the striking head of the weapon hummed angrily.

Marmot and Loudmouth had already circled round the ogre, clutching their hand-and-a-half swords with both hands. The monster growled, swung round sharply, and struck downward with its ax, aiming for Loudmouth's head. He jumped aside and the ax hurtled down, smashing the elegant tiles on the floor. Fragments of stone flew in all directions.

Marmot took advantage of the ogre's miss to dart up to it from behind and run his sword across its leg in an apparently casual stroke that severed the tendons below the knee. The ogre immediately thrust the handle of its ax backward and hit the shield held out by the warrior. The blow was so powerful that Marmot was sent flying and then slid about eight yards across the floor on his back.

"Stikhs!" Hallas swore, clutching his mattock tight in his hands, but he didn't go dashing into the battle, in order not to get in his own men's way.

"Tomcat, lend a hand," Uncle ordered curtly, and the fat man went bounding forward like a round ball, coming between the stunned Marmot and danger.

Just then the enemies who were still left alive realized that this was their chance, while everybody was busy with the ogre, and they tried to break through to the corridor where Izmi's men were standing. If Alistan's men hadn't dashed to cut them off, ignoring the danger of running into the monster's ax, then the curs would have got away.

A fight broke out in the hall. Only the jester and I were left in the corridor.

"Harold, don't get involved, they'll manage without you," Kli-Kli suggested.

It was an excellent idea, so I did just that and observed the skirmish from a distance. Meanwhile, the ogre had become really furious. He had only one target—that cursed man with yellow hair who was spinning the heavy ogre-club above his head. Limping on its right leg, the monster flailed the ax about in front of itself like the sails of a windmill, hoping to catch the Wild Heart. The giant Honeycomb, who looked tiny compared to the ogre, waited, drawing all of the ogre's attention to himself.

Then the right moment came. Loudmouth ran in from behind with a crooked grin and slashed his sword across the ogre's other leg, then darted back out of range of the ax. The monstrous beast fell to its knees with a dull groan and Honeycomb's ogre-club slammed into its head, crushing the bones of its skull.

Loudmouth walked up to the ogre's body and kicked it.

"Yu-uck," Honeycomb drawled, wiping his sweaty forehead with his sleeve. "Bringing down one of them takes years off your life!"

"And I hear that from someone who once did away with six of them in a single day?" Loudmouth chuckled. "Strong, mature ogres, too, not young and green like this one."

It was all over. Our enemies had been crushed. Tired after their night battle, guardsmen started sitting down on the floor. Not a single supporter of the Nameless One had survived; they had all preferred to die fighting.

"Harold, come on!" the jester cried, wriggling his way between the soldiers like a little fish. He climbed up on the ogre's body. "Hey, how about this!"

"I'll give you hey!" Lamplighter said, and spat. This time Mumr didn't have his huge bidenhander with him and he had had to fight with an ordinary sword. "Just what am I doing fighting ogres so far away from the Desolate Lands?"

"Hey there!" Arnkh protested. "I thought whining was Loudmouth's favorite pastime, not yours. . . ."

"We must check all the corridors and every room. Some of the villains might have survived," the prince said.

"I'll give instructions immediately," Alistan said with a nod.

I tried not to push myself forward, so that I could slip away as inconspicuously as possible, but I was afraid of going back to my room on my own. What if I ran into someone? It didn't really matter who it was—enemies who had survived or zealous guardsmen, ready to thread anyone on their spears just to rack up the numbers. Then they could figure out later who I was—friend or foe.

"Come on, Harold, we're not appreciated here," Kli-Kli said, walking over to me.

"And where are we going?"

"We can have a drink at least!"

"Oh, no! I have to be on the road this morning, and I intend to get a bit of sleep first."

"Ah, you're always such a bore!" the goblin complained, but even so he tagged along to see me to the door.

Deler and Hallas joined us. The dwarf was intending to look for his favorite hat that had been lost in the heat of battle, and the gnome wanted to have a friendly drink with Kli-Kli.

"How's Marmot?" the jester asked the dwarf a little while later.

"The shield saved him. He sprained his arm, but his ribs are all right. And his head, too. What else do you need?" Deler scratched the back of his own head. "Our Marmot's always collecting things. He managed to grab a shield from somewhere."

"But if the ogre had belted Tomcat with that handle . . . ," the gnome said slowly.

Yes indeed, Tomcat had been fighting in nothing but his drawers.

"Deler, will you join us?" Kli-Kli asked, jumping over the sprawling body of a guardsman in a gray and blue uniform, but with a white arm-band.

"I should think I will!" The dwarf didn't need to be invited twice to wet his whistle.

"See, Harold," the jester taunted me. "Not everyone's a spoilsport like you."

I gave the goblin a sour glance, and he shut up, realizing that my patience was exhausted for the day. The gnome muttered something to himself, stuck his mattock under his arm, and started sticking out the fingers on both hands. He was counting how many enemies he had felled. The count came to forty-five. When he heard this figure, Deler stumbled over his own feet and said that some gnomes' conceit was even longer than their beards.

"What are you haggling for?" Hallas asked, annoyed. "How many do *you* think I finished off?"

"Nine of them," said the dwarf, picking his battered hat up off the floor.

"How many?" the gnome asked indignantly. "Why, the gnomes are fighters like—"

"You're lousy fighters," Deler interrupted. "You wore yourselves out on the Field of Sorna. We know, we know."

"Who wore themselves out?" The bearded gnome was ready to start an all-out fight. "We kicked your backsides!"

"Our backsides!" The dwarf stopped and clenched his fists. "You kicked our backsides? How come you didn't have a single magician left after that battle?"

"Never mind that, we'll have magicians again."

"Oho! Sure you will!" said the dwarf, setting his thumb between two fingers and sticking it under his friend's nose. "We've got all your magic books! Come and take them back, you damned mattockmen!"

"We will! We will take them!" Hallas cried, spraying saliva. "Give us time and we'll flatten the Mountains of the Dwarves to the ground! We'll bring in the cannons . . ."

I didn't listen to any more, just went straight into my room and closed the door firmly behind me. No slanging match between a dwarf and a gnome was going to distract me from the most important business of all—sleep.

It seemed like my head had barely even touched the pillow before the ubiquitous Kli-Kli's annoying little hand was shaking me by the shoulder.

"Harold, get up! Wake up!"

Growling quietly, with my eyes still closed, I started groping around for something heavy to splat the little pest with.

"Kli-Kli," I groaned. "Show some respect for the gods! Let me sleep until morning! Go and drink with your new friends!"

"It's already morning," the goblin objected. "You're setting out in half an hour."

At this far from joyful news I leapt up off the bed, shook my head drowsily, and gazed out of the window. In the east the night sky was gradually turning paler in anticipation of the sun's new birth. Four o'clock in the morning at the most.

"Has Alistan completely lost his mind, deciding to go this early?" I asked the goblin, who was sitting on a chair.

"Did you want them to see you off with music and fanfares?" The jester giggled. "There are too many eyes in the city during the day. Rumors would start."

"Everyone who's interested already knows about our little excursion," I objected reasonably.

The jester merely chuckled in agreement.

"And by the way!" I exclaimed in sudden realization. "How did you get into a locked room?"

"You're not the only one who can open locks, Harold," the goblin said, and his blue eyes flashed merrily. "There's a secret passage here. . . . Are you ready?"

"Just a moment, let me get my things together," I muttered.

"Everything was collected and packed into Little Bee's saddlebags ages ago. I took the liberty of making sure my best friend was all right."

"And just who is this best friend of yours?"

As ever, the jester left my ironical question unanswered, and handed me a plate with a breakfast that was still warm.

On the way we met that inseparable pair, Hallas and Deler, also walking in the direction of the stables, arguing animatedly. Those leopards would never change their spots. I was surprised to see them both alive and well, which meant that the battle between them had not taken place after all. The Wild Hearts joined us and we walked the rest of the way together.

"Why don't you tell me where you went last night?" Deler growled resentfully.

"To visit relatives in town," Hallas replied imperturbably.

"Aha, of course," the dwarf chortled. "They'd be really glad to see you at two in the morning. They'd be expecting you. You were chasing the women again, I suppose?"

"And what if I was?" Hallas retorted furiously. "What business is that of yours?"

"And you brought back some kind of sack," said Deler, still growling.

The gnome had a plain canvas sack hanging over his shoulder. The kind that miners use for carrying precious stones in the Steel Mines.

"And what of it?" Hallas asked, and started lighting his pipe. Deler wrinkled up his nose contemptuously.

"What are you carrying in that sack?" the dwarf asked curiously.

"I don't ask you what you've got in your keg," said the gnome, trying everything he could to change the subject.

"Who needs to ask?" said Deler, rather surprised, and he shook the large keg that he was carrying with both arms, puffing and panting. I ought to say that the keg was half the size of the dwarf, and there was something splashing about happily inside it. "It's got wine in it."

"And where did you manage to get hold of such valuable treasure?" Hallas chortled, blowing rings of tobacco smoke.

"Kli-Kli gave me a hand," the dwarf said with a joyful smile. "It's from Stalkon's cellars."

"And what are you going to do with it?"

"Drink it! You stupid mattockhead!" the dwarf roared. "What else can you do with wine? I'll hang it on my horse and gradually drain it dry." Deler pronounced these last words with a dreamy expression on his face.

We reached the stables, where the first things to catch my eye were saddled horses and armed men. All the familiar Wild Hearts were here, too, only now it would have been hard for the inexpert eye to tell that they were Wild Hearts and not just ordinary soldiers from some border garrison.

The famed badges in the form of hearts with teeth had been ruthlessly torn off the worn leather jackets. And I noticed that the handle of Lamplighter's huge sword had been wrapped in a strip of black cloth that concealed the golden oak leaf of a master swordsman. Just one more precaution or attempt to avoid attracting any unnecessary attention. In some miraculous way, Mumr had actually managed to attach his favorite toy, the bidenhander, beside his saddlebags, evidently frightening his unfortunate dappled mare half to death in the process.

"Time to go, Harold," the jester reminded me.

So there weren't going to be any farewell speeches from the king and Artsivus. They weren't even there. But then, why should they bother seeing off men who were already as good as dead, and anyway they must have been up to their eyes sorting out the consequences of last night's attack. What time could they spare for thinking about our little expedition?

I walked up to Little Bee and greeted her with a pat on the neck. She replied with a joyful whinny, and I climbed into the saddle.

The jester looked up and said: "There are the last of your companions." He pointed to the two elves beside Miralissa. "Ell from the House of the Black Rose and Egrassa from the House of the Black Moon."

I cast a curious glance at the elves. Ell, with a thick head of ash-gray hair and a fringe that almost covered his amber eyes, was just putting on a helmet that completely covered his face. He had a rather broad nose and a heavy lower jaw.

Egrassa had a thin silvery diadem on his head—evidently a mark of distinction of some kind—and he and Miralissa were talking in low voices. I looked closely at the thoroughbred face with high cheekbones, the slanting eyes, and the solidly built figure of a true warrior.

"Are the two of them related?" I asked Kli-Kli, leaning down as far toward him as I could.

"Mm, yes, I think he's her cousin. But he's definitely a relative of some kind and definitely from the royal line—that's a fact! Even you can tell that from the idiotic *ssa* in his name. Right. I'll go and say good-bye to the dwarf and the gnome," the goblin muttered, and disappeared.

Miralissa sensed my glance and looked round. The luxurious Miranueh dress was gone, replaced by ordinary male elfin clothes. The tall hairstyle was gone, too, transformed into an ash-gray braid that reached all the way down to her waist. And the elfess, like her companions, had an elfin sword, or s'kash, hanging behind her back and, nestling beside it, a formidable bow and a quiver full of heavy arrows fletched with black feathers.

Unlike human soldiers, the elves have a conservative attitude to weapons, and they normally use only crooked swords or longbows. Other weapons are employed only on an occasional basis.

Uncle's platoon, however, had all sorts of death-dealing devices with them, from the ordinary swords and crossbows hanging beside their saddlebags to ogre-clubs, battle-mattocks, poleaxes, and bidenhanders. And then every second man had a round shield, too. An impressive little arsenal for an impressive team.

I was greatly surprised by Milord Alistan's appearance as he gave final instructions to Lieutenant Izmi, who was taking over his command of the guards. He wasn't wearing his famous armor. It had been replaced by a jacket just like the ones the Wild Hearts were wearing, with metal badges sewn onto it. Of course, I wouldn't be surprised if he had chain mail or something even heavier on a pack horse, like all the Wild Hearts, but the very fact that the Rat was setting out without the armor that had become like a second skin to him . . .

Meanwhile Alistan finished briefing Izmi and leapt up into the saddle of his huge black steed.

No, really, what was I so worried about? In company like this? With the protection of their swords I was in for a pleasant outing, perhaps with a little miraculous adventure.

"Forward!" shouted Count Markauz, slapping his heels against his horse's flanks.

"Good luck, Dancer in the Shadows!" The jester whispered his farewell to me in an absolutely normal voice.

May a h'san'kor tear me to pieces. At long last we're on our way, may all the gods of Siala help us.

20

ON THE WAY

Avendoom had been left behind. The majestic, forbidding walls built of gray stone from the Quarries of Ol had dissolved in the morning mist that the waking sun had startled from the earth and then left to tremble in the air for a few minutes like a frightened white moth. And after that the morning had simply flitted past, like some elusive, phantom bird, and disappeared beyond the horizon to make way for a scorching hot noon.

All the Wild Hearts had taken off their jackets and were wearing just their shirts. The only exception was Arnkh, in the eternal chain mail that he never removed even for a second. Perhaps if I'd been born beside the Forests of Zagraba and was used to expecting an attack by orcs at any minute, I would have put on Markauz's armor, let alone chain mail, even in this heat.

I had also unfastened the collar of my shirt and rolled up the sleeves—something that I greatly regretted when the evening came and my skin had turned a magnificent shade of crimson, so that for the next few days it became a serious obstacle to my enjoyment of life.

Markauz and the elves led the way along the road, followed by the Wild Hearts, in twos and threes. At first Marmot kept me company—and he proved to be a rather talkative and interesting companion—then we were joined by Hallas and Deler.

The sure-handed dwarf had managed to make a long tube out of the materials at hand and stick it into his cask of wine. Now, when Uncle wasn't watching them, the dwarf and the gnome took sly sips of the nectar of the gods, occasionally exclaiming in delight at this heavenly bliss vouchsafed to them. They were both gradually getting merrier and merrier, and I began to feel worried that one of them would overdo it, slip out of his saddle, and smash his head on the ground. But no, they simply got a bit red in the face and started singing a bold soldier's song about some campaign or other. Uncle, who was talking to Eel, kept casting suspicious glances at these new singers and his face gradually turned darker and darker. The platoon leader clearly sensed that there was something shady going on, but he simply couldn't figure out how his soldiers could suddenly be drunk.

The dwarf discoursed with the air of a connoisseur on Miralissa's good points as a woman. Apparently, I wasn't the only one who looked upon her forthright but very feminine grace with pleasure and interest. He and Hallas agreed that she had quite a few good points, only the fangs spoiled the general impression. After a moment's thought, the gnome said that you could always put a cloth over her face and then proceed as Mother Nature prompted, to which Marmot, who had kept silent all this time, suggested that the two learned theoreticians should shut up, or at least lower their voices half a tone, otherwise Miralissa would draw her s'kash from its scabbard and slice the beard off one of them and something a bit lower off the other. I couldn't have agreed more. There was silence for a moment, and then the dwarf said, "I didn't mean any offense. I only decided to talk about the elfess for a bit of relaxation."

"You can relax in the Forests of Zagraba, when the elves hang you upside down from a tree for insulting a princess of their house," Marmot retorted, and stroked his pet ling.

That finally soured the discussion of the elfess, and the gnome and the dwarf launched into a two-hour philosophical debate about the advantages and disadvantages of weapons with long handles. As always, Hallas and Deler contradicted each other furiously, constantly clenching their fists and trading lavish insults.

As was only to be expected, the argument between the gnome and the dwarf ended in a tie. And after another hour or so, Deler made a truly difficult decision and declared that enough wine had been tasted for one day, otherwise they'd soon have to start looking for another cask, and the likelihood of finding one on the road was illusory to say the least, not to say equal to zero. For some reason Lamplighter, who was riding last in our unit, found this last phrase highly amusing. He was tootling some simple little tune on his reed pipe, and I must admit that this music was better than the first time I had heard Mumr play— this time it only made me want to howl mournfully at the moon.

I jabbed my heels into Little Bee's sides, hurried forward, and quietly fell in behind the horses of Miralissa and Markauz.

"According to my calculations, if we keep moving at this pace, we'll reach Ranneng in less than two weeks. From there to the Iselina is no distance at all, and then it's another two weeks to the Border Kingdom. And another week to the Forests of Zagraba," the elfess said to Markauz, who was listening carefully.

"That means a month and a half, then?" asked Milord Alistan, chewing thoughtfully on his mustache, before he noticed that I had joined their group.

"That's not allowing for any unplanned events," said Egrassa, who seemed inclined to look on the dark side.

Well, well, so there were pessimists among the elves, too. And I thought only human beings were capable of doubting and expecting the worst.

"And in addition, we can't stay in the saddle round the clock. I think we'll need at least a couple of days' rest in Ranneng."

"I don't think we ought to go into Ranneng," I put in.

"Thanks for your advice, Harold," Alistan replied rather impolitely.

I could see he didn't feel he needed advice from anyone, especially not from a thief.

"I beg your pardon, Milord Alistan, but you don't understand," I continued insistently. "We're already attracting unwanted attention by traveling along one of the busiest high roads in the kingdom, and we're attracting it because elves, a gnome, a dwarf, and ten men armed to the teeth make rather unusual company. Believe me, milord, the peasants and ordinary travelers will find plenty to chatter about. Such a strange party. And rumors spread like wildfire. Anyone who finds those rumors interesting could easily draw certain conclusions and arrange a welcome for us. And yet, as I understand it, you wish to enter the second largest city in the kingdom! I think that certain rather unpleasant gentlemen are already looking for us. Whoever let the enemy into the royal palace has had more than enough time to report that our expedition has set out. We should not be seen in Ranneng."

"What the thief says makes sense," Ell said with a gleam of his fangs. "We need to avoid places where there are too many people."

"Then what do you suggest?" asked Miralissa. She spoke to the elf but was looking at me thoughtfully. "Should we leave the central highway and head farther to the southeast?"

Ell gave an almost imperceptible shrug, indicating that the decision was up to Alistan.

"Farther to the southeast?" Alistan didn't much like the suggestion. "Turn off a good road, which is busy, I admit, and head across open fields and forests with fallen trees? We'll lose so much time, we won't even reach Zagraba in September!"

"The highway is heading due south at the moment," Egrassa replied. "After Ranneng it turns to the west. And farther south there are no more cities, only barons' castles and small towns or, rather, villages with garrisons. No humans wish to live near Zagraba. And so, in order not to lose time, we shall have to take a risk and keep following the same road. It's a little more than a week to get to Ranneng. If we travel along the highway, that is. From the city we can turn to the southeast, toward the Iselina. There's a ferry there that will take us across. And then it's not very far to the Border Kingdom and the Forests of Zagraba."

"We can't avoid the cities. We'll have to renew our supplies," said Alistan, making it clear that the conversation was at an end.

Miralissa nodded at me. I nodded back and smiled but she just turned and walked off with the others.

From the very beginning of the journey Count Markauz set the pace for the horses, and they moved at a brisk trot. Let's say that we weren't exactly hurrying, but we weren't creeping along like blind snails, either. And every few leagues the horses were given a rest.

The areas we passed through were quite populous, with messengers darting this way and that way along the highway, carts carrying goods to and from Avendoom. There were peasants, artisans, and members of guilds going about their business. Once we encountered a unit of soldiers riding toward us—Beaver Caps on their way to the Lonely Giant.

Little Bee proved to be an amazingly sturdy horse. I didn't really notice her getting tired at all. Her stride was the same as it had been in the morning—smooth and light. In fact I was more tired than my horse was.

By the evening my entire body ached and I knew just how criminals in the Sultanate felt when they were set on stakes. Not a very pleasant sensation, I must say.

When it was already twilight, Alistan decided to halt at a neat, clean village by the name of Sunflowers, located not far from the highway. Tidy little white houses, clean roads, and friendly locals. It was clear that the people round here lived well. And the sight of so many sunflowers growing everywhere, with their heads already bowed under the weight of ripe seeds, was dazzling.

The local tavern had a huge inn, and rooms were found for every member of our expedition. It was called the Golden Chicken, and its name was well deserved, for two reasons. First, it earned its owner a very decent profit and, second, there were about fifty chickens wandering around in the yard. I climbed down off Little Bee with an effort and allowed one of the inn's servants to take the horse to the stables. May I never hold gold pieces in my hand again if horse riding is not a very dubious pleasure for the unaccustomed. My backside was scraped raw all over. But that wasn't all. The sun had also done its work, roasting me gently from all sides, and I felt old, battered, and sick.

"Hey, Harold!" Honeycomb separated off from the group of Wild Hearts and came toward me with a cunning smile on his face. He showed me his fist.

The other soldiers observed me with interest. I carefully inspected the . . . er . . . object that he had stuck almost right under my nose. There were several straws sticking out of it.

"What's this?" I asked Honeycomb with cautious curiosity, in no hurry to touch the straws just yet.

"Lots!" The tall Wild Heart chuckled merrily. "The lads and I consulted and we decided you should join in, too."

"Join in what? And, by the way, why are the elves and our glorious count already in the inn, while we're standing out here drawing lots?"

"The elves and Alistan are high society," Uncle answered for Honeycomb. "But our little draw's very simple. Whoever draws the short straw shares a room with Lamplighter."

"Until the end of the journey," Arnkh added quickly.

Mumr followed all these preparations with poorly concealed hostility.

I didn't really care who else I had in my room and so I took the nearest straw out of Honeycomb's fist with the most casual air I could muster. It was short.

There were loud sighs of relief on all sides. Someone gave me an encouraging pat on the back; someone else winked at me merrily. I had no idea why no one wanted to spend the night in the same room as Lamplighter, and I didn't get a chance to ask—the tables in the tavern were already set for supper and the hospitable host was filling the glasses with his finest wine. There weren't many guests at the inn, and most of the people in the hall were from the village.

And the only food they served was chicken. In all its forms. Roasted chickens, chickens baked with apples, steamed chickens, chicken wings with pepper. The sheer abundance of chicken was enough to make you jump up and start crowing like a rooster. So if you take into account the fact that I don't like chicken very much, it should be easy enough to understand why I wasn't exactly in the best of moods. By contrast, the Wild Hearts were in fine fettle, as if they hadn't spent the entire day in the saddle, so I said I was tired, went off to my room, and lay down on one of the beds, regretting yet again that I had allowed myself to be drawn into such an insane venture.

In the middle of the night I found out just what a dirty trick cruel fate had played on me. Lamplighter showed up very late, when I was already asleep, and I was so exhausted after a day in the saddle that I didn't even hear him arrive.

But I did hear Mumr very clearly when he started snoring with enthusiastic gusto. Never mind good old Gozmo, with his gentle nocturnal trilling and tweeting—by comparison with this warrior's snoring, Gozmo's was like the buzzing of a little mosquito compared with the roar of a hungry obur.

Naturally, I woke up and, of course, I tried to drown out the terrible sounds. I tried whistling. I tried singing a song. I even threw a boot at him.

It was hopeless. He had absolutely no intention of waking up, or even turning over onto his other side.

After an hour of torment, when I was beginning to get used to the snoring and was just about ready to sink back into sleep, Lamplighter changed the order of the sounds he was making and everything started all over again. Eventually I stuck my head under the pillow and at long last managed to get to sleep, after swearing to myself that next time I would find a more comfortable spot to take my rest.

Mumr woke me up in the morning. I gave him a surly glance, quite certain that no one had come between him and his dreams.

Amazing enough, I felt better after the night. No doubt thanks to Ell, who had noticed the state I was in the evening before and splashed something out of his own flask into my glass of wine. Whatever it was, it had certainly helped.

"We're up a bit late this morning," I said to Mumr. "Aren't we in a hurry?"

"Lady Miralissa is waiting for a messenger," Lamplighter replied, groping around under his bed. He pulled out the bidenhander, set it across his shoulder, and walked toward the door of the room.

"Let's go and get breakfast, Harold."

"I'm coming."

I reached out one hand for my crossbow and knife. Hmm . . . Strange . . . Very strange . . . The knife was there all right, but my little junior with the double sting had completely disappeared. And at that very moment I heard the twang of a crossbow shot outside in the yard, followed by the frightened clucking of chickens. I glanced out of the window and swore, then dashed out of the room and started down the stairs to the ground floor.

Some of the Wild Hearts were already having breakfast in the large hall of the tavern. They said good morning and asked politely how I had slept. I replied politely that I had slept well, but I didn't really fool either myself or them.

"Harold, where are you going? It'll all get cold!" Hallas exclaimed in surprise, clutching a lump of fatty bacon in one hand and piece of smoked sausage in the other. The gnome seemed to be having some difficulty in deciding what to start his meal with.

"I'll just be a moment," I told him, and dashed outside.

Arnkh, Tomcat, and Loudmouth were absorbed in watching an

original competition between Eel and a certain little individual whom I knew only too well. And to the innkeeper's considerable dismay, this competition consisted of trying to shoot as many as possible of the chickens running around the yard in the shortest possible time. There were already about fifteen motionless bundles of feathers, little chicken corpses, lying here and there on the sand.

Eel was shooting with a sklot taken from Markauz. Kli-Kli—yes, it was him all right, I would have known that face with my eyes closed now—was felling the chickens with my crossbow.

"Having fun?" I asked the goblin.

"Good morning, Harold," Kli-Kli replied, and brought down another unfortunate bird with a well-aimed shot. "Ten-six. I win!"

That was addressed to Eel, who nodded in agreement without even trying to argue.

"Thanks for letting me use your crossbow," said the jester, handing the weapon back to me.

"I don't recall giving you permission."

"Oh, don't be so finicky," the goblin said with a frown. "I galloped all night and scraped my backside raw before I caught up with you! I have to relax a bit somehow."

"And why, if I may ask, have you come?"

"Am I imagining it, or did I hear a note of irritation in your voice?" the jester asked, looking me straight in the eye. "I came to pass on a certain item to Miralissa, something the king didn't have yet when you left."

"So it's due to your good services that we're in no hurry to go anywhere?" the taciturn Garrakan asked gruffly.

"And basically," said the goblin, brushing aside all possible objections, "I'm going to join you for the rest of the journey."

"As our jester? Well, how about that!" snorted Loudmouth.

He and Tomcat had come across to us while Arnkh was pulling the bolts out of the birds' little corpses and sorting things out with the aggrieved owner of the Golden Chicken.

"Do you see any cap?" Kli-Kli asked, jabbing a finger at his own head.

The goblin was not wearing a jester's cap with little bells, or a leotard. He was dressed in ordinary traveling clothes with a cloak on his shoulders.

"I'm going with you as a guide, not a jester. The place we're going to is my homeland. And I'm just as much at home there as the elves are. I also happen to be the king's authorized representative."

"If I were in the king's place, I wouldn't authorize you to guard my chamber pot!" said Loudmouth.

"Why, you've never had a chamber pot in your life," Tomcat said, laughing at Loudmouth.

"Whether I have or I haven't makes no difference!" Loudmouth retorted to his colleague with the mustache, and then scratched his long nose. "I'm sorry, goblin, but guarding one more civilian in these difficult conditions is just too much. Especially since we know the kind of dirty tricks you like to play on us."

"My name's Kli-Kli, not goblin, Mr. Griper-and-Grouser," the jester snapped. "And I don't need protection from anyone. I'm quite capable of looking after myself."

And with that he flung aside the flaps of his cloak to allow us to see a belt with four heavy throwing knives hanging on it—two on the right and two on the left.

Nothing important happened for the next few days. We carried on heading south, stopping for the night in the fields round about.

The nights were warm and nobody suffered at all from the vagaries of the weather. If it had been the usual kind, that is, the same as it had always been in July for the last ten thousand years, we would all have felt a bit chilly at night. But as it was, you could quite happily sleep on the grass, or lie there looking up at the starry sky. If not for the mosquitoes, who had gone absolutely crazy in this unexpected warmth, life would have been splendid.

The reason we had spent the night in the fields was simple. For two days now the highway had avoided all the villages as it looped elegantly round to the southeast. We would only reach the next village on the road in the evening of the next day. Amazingly enough, out in the open air Mumr didn't snore. Marmot told me that Lamplighter only performed his raucous concerts when he had a roof over his head. So by now I had completely caught up on my sleep.

Little Bee and I had gradually grown accustomed to each other and, to my great delight, I discovered I didn't feel any fatigue even after an entire day's riding. No, that's a lie. I did feel some fatigue, but it was by no means fatal. Not the sort of fatigue that makes you want to collapse on the ground and lie there for four years and not get up again for all the jewels in the kingdom.

At first Markauz didn't want to take the jester with him, but the goblin, with a perfectly innocent expression on his roguish face, handed the count a paper with the king's seal on it, and then there was nothing the stern warrior could do but allow Kli-Kli to travel on with us.

The jester's horse was every bit as large as Alistan's mount, and while the undersized Hallas and Deler looked—how shall I say it?—rather amusing on horses, the goblin looked simply comical on the huge black monster that had been dubbed Featherlight. Kli-Kli's feet didn't even reach the stirrups. But I must say that Kli-Kli felt perfectly confident in the saddle, and Featherlight responded to all his master's commands at the first asking.

The jester was incredibly quiet. By "quiet" I mean that when you woke up in the morning, there was no need to be afraid of a snake in your boot or a briar in your horse's tail. But the little goblin creep spent all day long dashing from the head of our unit, stretched out along the road, to its tail, and then back again from its tail to its head. Kli-Kli had time to get everywhere. In the course of the day he could be seen singing songs with Deler and Hallas, telling one of his stories to Tomcat and Eel, conducting an abstruse discussion with the elves, or arguing with the unyielding Alistan Markauz until his throat turned hoarse.

On the third day after Kli-Kli's arrival we came into a town. And that's when disaster struck.

The tavern in this little village was a lot worse than in Sunflowers. But there was no choice. And after the nights under the open sky I was glad to accept any bed.

The villagers cast curious glances at us—it wasn't every day that they saw so many new people and nonpeople. The elves and the goblin provoked the most oohs and aahs, but the other races were only rare visitors to the lands of Valiostr, so the locals felt that they had to drop everything else and come running to gape at these freaks from the world outside. When would they ever get another chance?

The master of the nameless inn was simply overwhelmed by this great influx of guests and stood there on the porch with his mouth hanging open. Fortunately for us, the innkeeper's burly wife jabbed her husband under the ribs with her elbow and set him and his two drowsy daughters, who had already attracted an extremely interested glance from Arnkh, about their work. Naturally, despite their mother's prods and pokes, the drowsy daughters were still moving slowly and lackadaisically, until the ling suddenly took matters into its own hands by leaping from Marmot's shoulder onto one girl's head, and there was Kli-Kli, who had arranged the whole scene, to shout:

"A rabid rat!"

In the tumult that followed, Invincible was almost trampled underfoot, while Kli-Kli was honored with a cuff round the back of his head from Marmot. After that the goblin sulked and he wouldn't talk to anyone. At the end of supper the jester expressed a desire to sleep in the same room as Harold and Lamplighter, and he was very surprised when nobody raised any objections.

"Harold." Egrassa had approached unnoticed and was leaning down over my ear. "Her Tresh Miralissa would like to have a word with you. Come on. I'll show you the way."

I got up from the table and followed the tall elf.

A word? What about? And why now, not earlier? Lucky Harold, going to see elf royalty, but, really, I was intrigued by her invitation.

There in the room with Miralissa were Markauz, who was gazing thoughtfully out of the window, and Ell, who was peeling an apple with his knife.

"Good evening, Harold." The elfess's slanting golden eyes sparkled in the candlelight. "Do you know what this is?" she asked, holding out some object to me.

As I took it, I barely managed to stop myself exclaiming out loud in admiration.

"Is it not beautiful?"

I could just manage a nod as I examined the precious item that was lying in my hands.

It was a key, the size of my palm and very heavy. But more than a key, it was a genuine work of art. The blasphemous thought flashed through my mind that people who knew about such things, the kind who collect old artifacts, would be willing to pay me several mountains of gold for the right to possess this key.

The ancient item looked as if it were made of crystals of ice, so frail that I was afraid to breathe on it, in case it might melt. But I knew that even if I took Deler's poleax and battered the trinket nonstop all day long, nothing would happen to it, but I would have to buy a new poleax.

"Dragon's tears? Is it dwarves' work?"

"Yes, you're right," Egrassa said with a nod. "This is the handiwork of dwarves; only they can work this mineral like that. Do you see how delicate the work is?"

Delicate was not the word for it! It was ideal, elegant, perfect, and ancient. In our time no one would be able to create anything like it. Working that most rare of minerals, dragon's tears, which possesses the enduring strength of the very mountains that created it, requires magic in addition to the usual tools. And unfortunately the magicianship of the dwarves was in a state of decline and not even the masters would be capable of such creations. Far too much had been forgotten during the Purple Years.

"What is this the key to?" I asked as I reluctantly handed the precious thing back to Miralissa.

"Have you ever head of the double-doored level?"

"The third level of the Palaces of Bone?" I asked, remembering my recent conversation with For and the ancient maps of Hrad Spein. "And then, carry on! The twin doors stand open. . . ."

"Absolutely right. The double-doored or third level of Hrad Spein, with its magic doors. The doors are sealed with very powerful spells, but this key, created by dwarves two and a half thousand years ago at the request of the Lord of the Dark Houses, will open the way down." She was all business. I could almost see her thinking, comparing possibilities, planning the moves in this deadly game. Somehow, I found this comforting: You want to know that your leaders are working hard, thinking ahead. All the best thieves—like Harold—know that preparation, hard work, imagination, and adaptability make for a successful job . . . and vastly increase the odds that you would be alive to enjoy it.

"This object was brought to us by Kli-Kli," said Alistan, turning away from the window. "When the jester left, he was . . . But that doesn't matter now. The most important thing is that we now have the key, and if the doors that Lady Miralissa mentioned to you are locked, we shan't have to waste time looking for the way round them."

"If the way round exists, that is."

"It does, Harold. Or it did. The magicians of the Order who took the Horn to Hrad Spein managed to reach Grok's grave somehow. The magicians didn't have the key then, it was in Zagraba," said Miralissa.

"The artifact has already been in Hrad Spein this spring," said Alistan, folding his arms across his chest. "Before setting out for the Desolate Lands, Lady Miralissa gave it to the king, and Stalkon gave it to the magicians of the second expedition. We must thank the gods that the only unfortunate to return from the burial chambers managed to bring the key out, even though he lost his mind."

"It was thanks to the key that the magician survived," said Egrassa, lighting another candle and setting the candlestick on the table beside the first two. "Whatever it is that dwells there, it didn't touch the man with the key."

"It's no great joy to be alive, but insane," I muttered. "So, you have this thing now, and that's wonderful. But why tell me about it?"

"The key is not a toy." Ell finally stopped peeling his apple and came across to me. "Before it will open the doors, it has to be harmonized with its owner. Made to comply with his will."

"Marvelous," I responded with no great enthusiasm.

Stay well away from those who work magic—that's always been one of my many mottoes.

"We have to harmonize it with you. Everything is ready. Here, hold it." Miralissa handed the artifact to me again, ignoring my sour grimace.

With or without my consent the elves intended to indulge in a little shamanism, and there was no point in getting uppity, or they might get some word confused and I'd be left wearing horns on my head for the rest of my life, or something even worse.

"Sit down on the bed." Egrassa lit another candle, but he stood it in the headboard of the bed instead of on the table. "Milord Alistan, if you would be so kind, please leave us while the ritual is taking place."

The count left the room without the slightest objection, closing the door firmly behind him.

"What are you waiting for, Harold? Sit on the bed!" said the elfess, taking some bundles of dried herbs out of her traveling bag. I was on the bed, sitting before I could think. There was real iron in that voice.

A sweetish scent of bog flowers and late autumn drifted through the room. I sat down and Miralissa came up to me with a cup in her hand. She dipped one finger in it and then drew some signs on my forehead and cheeks. At her touch, a light current went through my body starting at my face and quickly sparking down to my toes. It was a madly pleasant sensation. Ell was already standing over one of the candles, whispering and tossing dust up into the air. It looked to me like some kind of powdered herb.

Somehow the dust seemed to fall very slowly, touching the flame of the candle, giving off a thin streamer of white smoke and disappearing. So this was the shamanism of the dark elves. Long whisperings, dances, signs, and all sorts of rubbish like dried bat dung. Yes, sometimes this art could do things that wizardry could never manage. The ancient magic, correctly performed, is far more powerful, but its cost . . .

A single mistake, a single mispronounced word, the absence of the most unnecessary-seeming ingredient—and nothing will happen. And the most important thing is the time required for working the shamanic magic. Time is invaluable, and the need for it puts the magic of the dark elves at a disadvantage compared with human wizardry.

Some elves understood this and became the light elves, but others, like the orcs, goblins, and ogres, do not wish to abandon their ancient knowledge and stubbornly continue to use this ineffective anachronism, as the magicians of the Order call it. But then, I'm certain that wizardry also has another, weak side to it, which the Order of Magicians, in its polite fashion, simply forgets to mention.

Meanwhile, Miralissa began singing. Her low, resonant voice began twining itself into the air, swirling through it in a taut spiral of words. Her singing was spellbinding. For all its native coarseness, the orcish language, or rather its elfish dialect (the elves thought of themselves as too proud to use the language of the orcs) was like a mountain stream. Its gurgling was very pleasant to listen to.

The elfess sang as she approached me, and I felt as if she and I were alone in the room with her voice. Egrassa and Ell had moved back and away, become just one of the many shadows hemming me in on all sides.

The voice, the shadows ... And the eyes. Miralissa's golden eyes, with tongues of amber flame flickering in them. They drew me in, leading me away to distant places and times. They filled the entire room. The signs she drew on my face began burning, and the key clenched in my fist was also getting warmer and warmer.

The walls of the room flared up in bright fire, trembled, collapsed outward, then began falling in blazing banners into endless darkness. I cried out, my feet searching hopelessly for support that was not there; I flung my arms out in a futile attempt to fly. The darkness burst into flame and the furious flames born in the darkness came rushing toward me from all sides, scorching my neck, my back, my shoulders. The unbearable heat licking at my body set my hair ablaze. The pain ran through me like a blunt knife. I don't remember, I think I screamed, but then an ink-black shadow that had appeared out of nowhere in this hell of amber fire touched my back and pushed me forward. Into the yellow eyes, into that roaring heat.

A single instant.

Flight. Blindness. Silence.

Night.

21

THE KEY

I swear on the peak of Zam-da-Mort, may its snows never melt! Are you sure that on the way here, honorable sir, you didn't fall into the old quarries? It's dangerous around there now; the gnomes' wits have completely deserted them and they throw the exhausted rock straight down on your head. You have to be careful not to get hit."

The dark elf whom the old dwarf was addressing restrained himself with an effort. Probably only those well acquainted with this race could understand just how much of an effort this restraint required. Neither the dark nor the light elves, may a dragon's flame devour them, were known for the mildness of their tempers, and they responded to any insult, real or imagined, by reaching for their weapons. But this representative of the forest folk remained calm. Who better to persuade a dwarf master craftsman to carry out a special commission than the eldest son of the House of the Black Flame?

Elodssa was not only a fine warrior (even his enemies, the orcs, accepted that he was), but also an excellent diplomat. And in addition, his knowledge of shamanism improved his chances of getting what the elves wanted from the dwarves, and the short people would never even suspect that they had been given a gentle nudge. But Elodssa was in no hurry to employ his secret knowledge. That was his last resort. For the time being he could restrict himself to normal negotiations.

"No, honorable Frahel, nothing fell on my head."

"Oh really?" The old master craftsman seemed rather perturbed by this circumstance. "But then your race is a bit touched in the head without any help from stones."

"Every race has its shortcomings." The elf bared his fangs in an attempt to smile, although he really wanted to do something quite different: take the

obstinate dwarf by the scruff of the neck and smack his head against the wall several times.

But he must not! He must not lose his self-control. For after all, among craftsmen, Frahel, may the forest flame tear out his liver, was one of the small number of Masters with a capital M. *Only this dwarf was capable of creating what the race of elves required.*

"Well, there's no doubt about that. Every race has its shortcomings," the dwarf continued. "For instance, take our cousins, the gnomes, curse them, every one. They don't know how to do anything except mine ore and drill corridors in the rock. They've never created a single thing, the rotten idlers!"

"Let us not discuss your relatives," Elodssa said hurriedly.

"That's right, we won't talk about relatives," the dwarf grunted, getting up from his workbench. "You and the orcs have been slitting each other's throats since time out of mind, and you still can't simmer down."

At this point Elodssa was obliged to grit his teeth. Frahel was openly mocking him, in the realization that if the elf had endured the preceding insults, he would endure this one, too, and many others as well.

"Very well, very well, my worthy sir elf," the master craftsman said, raising his hands in a gesture of conciliation. "I know I have touched on a sore spot, and I apologize for it. But as for your little proposal . . . It is very tempting but, alas, impossible."

"Why?"

"I do not have that much talent."

"Oh, come now," the elf said with an irritable frown. "My dear Master Frahel, modesty becomes you as the absence of a beard becomes a gnome."

The dwarf imagined the gnomes without their beards and appreciated the joke.

"Master Frahel's fame resounds throughout the northern lands of Siala. Was it not you who created the magic bell and the suit of arms for the emperor? Who else should the elfin houses turn to? Vrahmel? He is too greedy, so he will damage the material. Smerhel? His fame as a craftsman is somewhat greater than he deserves. Or perhaps we should pester Irhel? But he has not a shred of talent. Dear master, for our commission we need the very best. You!"

When the elf said that the finest master craftsmen of the dwarves were not capable of doing anything, he was lying in the desire to flatter this obstinate dwarf. Frahel found the flattery to his liking, and he thawed somewhat.

"Well then," he said, scratching his chin thoughtfully, "perhaps I will take

on this little commission of yours when I have some free time. You can see for yourself . . ."

He gestured casually at the tables crammed with jobs and feigned an expression of regret.

The elf was not at all disconcerted by this little performance. Frahel was simply trying to push his price up.

"We cannot afford to wait. The doors have already been made and now we need a key. At least one."

"They need a key," the dwarf grumbled, casting a quick glance at the elf. "You're masters when it comes to hammering together the doors for your underground palaces. But as soon as you need a little key made, you come running to the dwarves. I'm not even sure that it will work. Our types of magic are too different."

"Of course, that is so," Elodssa said with a polite smile. "But that is why the elves have come to you and no one else. Only you are capable of creating an artifact fitting for the Twin-Door level."

"All right!" the dwarf agreed in a slightly irritable tone. "I can do it. But the key has to be special. I think you know what I mean. The material must be worthy of the doors. I don't have anything suitable, and I don't know how long it will take to obtain it."

"I think I can help you there." The elf took a long, elegant case out of his bag and handed it to the dwarf.

"Hmm! Red Zagraban cherry?" said the master craftsman, turning the wooden case over in his immense hands, and then he slowly opened it.

Inside there was a small black velvet bag tied with a golden thread. The dwarf snorted in annoyance. These elves loved all sorts of frills and flourishes. They couldn't just give you something, they had to bundle it up in a hundred wrappings, and then you had to unwrap them!

But Frahel's annoyance evaporated without a trace when he saw what he had been given.

A large, long, dirty-white stone of irregular form. At first glance it was nothing special—there were plenty of cobbles like that to be found on the bank of any river. But that was only at first glance. If it was worked with skill, this stone would become a genuine treasure: a bright gem that would glitter in the light, sparkling with all the colors in creation. This was the magical child of the mountains, the rarest of stones, which the earth only surrendered to alien hands with the greatest reluctance.

"A dragon's tear! And such a huge one!" The old dwarf's face glowed with rapturous delight. "But where did you get it from? The last time we found this mineral was more than two hundred years ago!"

"This stone has belonged to my house for more than a thousand years," the elf replied. "In those days dragon's tears were found far more often than now. The House of the Black Flame bought it in your mountains."

"The dwarves would never have sold such a treasure!" Frahel protested indignantly.

"The gnomes sold it to us," the elf admitted.

"Those bearded midgets!" Coming from a dwarf who was only slightly taller than a gnome, these words were, to say the least, amusing.

"It will take a great deal of time," the dwarf said, tapping his fingers on his workbench. "You know what I mean, working the material. Magic. It will take me two months to make the first designs."

"The key must be ready in a week," Elodssa replied sternly.

"Do you want me to work day and night?" Frahel asked indignantly.

"Why not, if we pay you well for it?"

"How well?" the dwarf asked, screwing up his eyes.

"Name your price."

Frahel thought for a moment and named it.

"I agree to a quarter of the sum named."

"This is a serious conversation," the dwarf snapped.

"Plus you can have all the material that remains after working."

"You offer me leftovers?" Frahel exclaimed furiously.

But this was only for form's sake. The cunning craftsman knew perfectly well that even the small scraps of the mineral which were certain to be left over would be beyond price.

"All right," he said, chewing on his lips with a discontented air. "Have it your way, Tresh Elf. I'll start work immediately."

"Then I will not dare to distract you any longer," the elf said with a bow.

The dwarf waved casually in farewell to Elodssa. In his mind he was already at work.

The elf hated these cursed underground halls and corridors with all his heart. The stubborn bearded gnomes who built these rocky tunnels had not been concerned about the fact that elves were a lot taller than their own stunted race.

And so, for most of the way to the chambers that the dwarves had allocated to the prince of the House of the Black Flame, Elodssa had to walk hunched over, almost doubled over in fact, to avoid hitting his head on the low ceiling. The entire maze was enough to depress and dismay anyone who had been born under the green crowns of oaks and not in the bowels of the earth.

One wrong turn at a crossroads, one heedless moment, and you could say farewell to life. You would find yourself in some old workings long-ago forgotten even by the gnomes who had created them, and you would never see the blue sky and your native forests again. Perhaps your remains might be found a year or two later, when some drunken gnome or dwarf stuck his nose into the wrong corridor. And the worst thing was that the populated parts were right there beside you: Take just one step, turn the right corner— and you would be saved.

The elf shuddered. To him a death like that, seasoned with a large dose of despair, seemed the most terrible death possible.

Elodssa and his guide walked on for an interminably long time. The elf had long ago lost his bearings in the capricious bends of the corridors that must have been carved out by gnomes whose brains were befuddled with charm-weed. Only once did they meet a group of bearded miners. With glow-worm lamps attached to their helmets, clutching work-mattocks and other tools in their hands, the gnomes were bawling out a simple song at the tops of their voices as they walked down toward the very heart of the earth.

"Why are there so few people here?" Elodssa asked his guide.

"Who would agree to live here?" the dwarf asked, surprised at the question. "This is the fifty-second gallery. It's an eight-hour walk up to the surface! Everyone lives higher up. Only our master craftsmen, like the venerable Frahel, require seclusion for their work. To avoid being disturbed by anyone, or accidentally affecting them with their magic. And then sometimes the gnomes walk through on the way to their workings. But in general this area is deserted. If you get lost, you're really in trouble. We're here, my lord elf."

They stopped in front of a lift. There was night below it and night above it. The travelers had to go up more than nine hundred yards through the round tunnel. Of course, they could make the ascent on the steep stone staircase that threaded through the body of the mountains in a dizzying spiral, but that would have required too much time and effort. So they would have to trust their lives to the precarious swaying platform.

There was a drum on the lift, and the dwarf struck it three times. The sound went soaring upward, and after a while Elodssa made out a quiet reply, muffled by distance.

"Off we go!" the dwarf said with a smile, taking hold of the railing.

For just a moment the lift lurched downward, taking his heart with it. But almost immediately it began slowly, but surely, creeping upward.

"Here we are, then," his guide said good-naturedly, getting off the platform. "The twenty-eighth gallery, if you count all the way from the top. Will you find the way on your own, sir elf?"

"I don't think so."

"It's all very simple. From here you go straight along the main corridor, through the hall with the emerald stalactites, and then count the branch corridors. The sixth on the right is yours. Then after every second crossing turn left three times, and you'll find yourself in the sector where we accommodate our guests. Don't be afraid, it's almost impossible to get lost here. If anything happens, ask one of our people the way. But not the gnomes—just recently those bearded clowns have completely forgotten how to use their heads. All they can do is cut new galleries!"

After that the dwarf climbed back onto the lift, struck the drum, and set off downward.

The elf went in search of his room, not intending for a moment to actually stay in this accursed catacombs. He wanted to collect his things and go up to the first gallery, closer to the sky and the sun. If he loitered down here for a whole week while Frahel was making the key, he could go insane. It would be better to come back at precisely the right time, collect the artifact, and never, ever again come anywhere near the mountains.

As Elodssa walked along he looked around. Unlike the lower galleries, there were plenty of sights worth looking at here. The handiwork of the gnomes and dwarves could only be rivaled by the works of the elves and the orcs in Hrad Spein. Although, in the Palaces of Bone Elodssa did not feel like a rat buried alive deep below the ground. But still, he had to give the underground builders their due—everything, absolutely everything, from the finest details to the octagonal columns soaring up toward the ceiling, was beautiful.

When he entered the amazingly large hall with the emerald stalactites, he froze in admiration. From a small window somewhere up in the ceiling a ray of sunlight that had somehow made its way down to this depth sliced through the deliberately created twilight to fall on the green stalactites. Its gentle caress set the green stones glittering as if they were sprinkled with fine diamond *dust. And in the center of this display there was an image of a dwarf and a gnome.*

"They are the great Grahel and Chigzan—the first dwarf and the first gnome. Brothers," said a voice behind Elodssa's back.

The elf looked round and saw the elfess who had spoken to him standing beside one of the green columns.

"They say that the gnomes were the first to discover this image, when someone decided to provide light for the stalactites. So you can tell your people that you have seen one of the great relics of the underground kingdom."

"Midla," said Elodssa, bowing ceremonially and trying to conceal his amazement.

"Tresh Elodssa," she said, bowing no less ceremonially, holding the bow without moving for several seconds, as etiquette required when an elf met a member of the royal family of a house.

"I am most surprised to see you here," said Elodssa.

"Pleasantly so, I trust?" the elfess asked with a smile.

Her hair was not cut in the manner of the dark elves, who normally preferred tall hairstyles or thick braids. It fell onto her forehead in an ash-gray fringe, and was cropped short on the back of her head and the temples. She was dressed in the dark green costume of a scout, and hanging at her back, instead of a s'kash, she had two short, curved swords with jade handles like the one on Elodssa's sword. He himself had given her the pair of swords at a time when life had seemed simpler. How young they had been then!

"That depends on what you are doing here," Elodssa replied as distantly as possible.

"What could a scout from the House of the Black Flame possibly be doing here but protecting the crown prince?" she asked with a crooked smile. The crown prince. Those cursed words had come between them two years earlier, shattering their happiness forever. "The head of the house has ordered me to be your shadow."

"That cannot be! My father would never have sent you."

"Have I ever lied to you? Unlike you, I have no right to do so." She, too, could not forget what had happened.

"I did not deceive you," Elodssa blurted out. "What happened between us was not a lie!"

"Of course not." Another bitter smile. "It was all the fault of your father and stupid prejudice."

"I cannot contravene the law, and you know it! It is not my fault that we cannot be together. The son of the head of a house cannot commit his life to . . ."

"Carry on, Elodssa," she said in a gentle voice when the prince broke off. "To whom? To one who brandishes swords? To one who wanders round Zagraba in search of units of orcs who have invaded the territory of our house? To one who teaches young elves to hold the s'kash or fire a bow? Or simply to one who has no noble blood flowing in her veins?"

"This conversation will come to nothing, like all those that have preceded it."

"You are right," Midla agreed sadly.

"You may go back to my father and tell him that all is well with me."

"Do I look like a messenger?" There was a glint of poorly concealed fury in the yellow, almond-shaped eyes.

He knew that expression well. When they were still seeing each other, he had seen similar rage in her eyes a few times. But now, for the first time, it was directed at him.

"I have enough guards," Elodssa snapped.

"Your guards are up there," said Midla, jabbing one finger toward the ceiling. "A league above us. Long before they could get down here, the heir of the House of the Black Flame would be lying dead and still."

"Who is going to attack me here? The dwarves and the gnomes?"

"I am carrying out the orders of the head of the house," she said with an indifferent shrug.

"And I order you to go back to Zagraba!" Elodssa declared furiously.

"You do not yet have your father's authority," she said with a triumphant smile.

The elf gritted his teeth and clenched his fists, then turned and walked away, cursing Midla's obstinacy.

The young elfess watched Elodssa go, trying to hold back her tears. Her eyes were clouded with pain.

That week dragged on forever.

Elodssa changed his mind about going higher up. Midla would only follow him, and the elf did not want anyone talking about him behind his back. Everyone still remembered how close they had been and how Elodssa's father had forbidden the marriage. And so the heir of the House of the Black Flame *spent most of the time sitting in the accommodation allocated to him by the dwarves, only occasionally strolling through the nearby halls, admiring the beauty and magnificence of these subterranean places. At such moments he was accompanied by the silent Midla. Somehow or other she always knew that he had left his room, and immediately appeared beside him.*

They both behaved with emphatically cool politeness. And they both felt awkward. Every stroll concluded with Elodssa losing his temper, mostly with himself, and returning to his quarters alone. And so the elf was relieved when the deadline he had set for the dwarf craftsman finally arrived.

This time he was lucky and managed to get away without disturbing Midla, although her room was opposite his own. But that was most probably because the elf had deliberately not warned his dwarf guide that he was planning to visit Frahel: Elodssa suspected that Midla knew about his strolls from this little informer.

He found his way to the lift with no difficulty, and there he came across several gnomes in armor, holding battle-mattocks. The bearded little folk were arguing heatedly about something.

"Good day, respected sirs," Elodssa greeted them.

"What's so good about it," grumbled one of the gnomes. "You've heard what's going on, I suppose?"

"Unfortunately not."

"All the sentries at the hundred and fifteenth gate near Zagorie have been killed. Eight dwarves and the same number of gnomes have lost their lives."

"Do you know who has done this?"

"No." The gnomes' faces were all darker than a storm cloud. "But there is a chance that the killers could have made their way into the kingdom."

"Maybe that's so, of course, but what in the name of a soused turnip are we hanging about here for?" a mattock-man in heavy armor asked angrily. "That's a hundred and fifteen leagues away from here. No mortal being who doesn't happen to be a gnome or a dwarf will ever get that far on his own! He'll lose his way in the galleries!"

"Never mind, we've been posted here, so this is where we'll stand," the first gnome said calmly. "Where do you want to go?"

The question was addressed to Elodssa.

"To see Master Frahel."

"The fifty-second gallery, isn't it? Right, get onto the lift. Do you know the way?"

"Not very well."

"Turn left at every second crossing and do that five times. Then straight on for six crossings and take the third corridor to the left. Will you find it?"

"Yes, thank you."

"Hey!" the gnome shouted upward. "Take the honorable gentleman to the fifty-second!"

"Right!" a voice called back down.

The lift shuddered and started downward.

Frahel heaved a sigh of relief and sat back in his chair. He had managed to do the impossible. This work was the finest thing he had ever created in all his long life.

The effort had completely absorbed the master craftsman, the challenge to his skill had required his absolute commitment—and now there was the key made out of the dragon's tear, lying on the black velvet. The slim, elegant object already contained immense power, and after the dark elves endowed it with their magic, it would become a truly mighty artifact.

Frahel grinned. The orcs were in for a big surprise when the doors stopped opening for them. The elves were cunning and sly; they had decided to deprive the orcs of the memory of their ancestors by slamming the door in their face!

Now for the final, quickest, and most complicated stage—endowing his creation with life and memory. The master craftsman stood up, opened an old book, and raised his hand above the slumbering key.

And at that moment someone knocked on the door of his workshop. The dwarf swore furiously. That elf must be here already. Too early! Well, prince or not, he would have to wait until Frahel had done everything that was needed.

"Wait, honored sir!" Frahel shouted. "I haven't finished yet!"

Another knock.

"Ah, damn you! It's open!" Frahel called, preparing a couple of choice endearments for his client.

A man came into the workshop. "Master Frahel?" the man asked, looking carefully round the room.

"And who's asking?" the craftsman replied rather impolitely.

"Oh! Allow me to introduce myself, my name is Suovik."

"Suovik?" The dwarf was quite certain that this Suovik had a title. If only because there was a gold nightingale embroidered on his tunic. He thought that someone in Valiostr wore that crest.

"Don't trouble yourself, Master Frahel. Simply Suovik will do."

"Simply Suovik" was about fifty years old. He was tall and as thin as a rake, with gray temples and streaks of gray in his tidy little beard. His brown eyes regarded the dwarf with friendly mockery.

"What can I do for you?" Frahel asked, attempting to conceal his irritation.

"Oh! I would like to buy a certain item. Or rather, not I, but the person who sent me. My Master . . ."

"But, by your leave," said Frahel, interrupting his visitor with a shrug, "I am no shopkeeper. I do not have anything for sale. I carry out private and very well paid commissions. If you wish to buy something, talk to Master Smerhel, two levels higher, gallery three hundred and twenty-two."

Frahel turned his back to Suovik to indicate that the conversation was at an end.

"Oh! You have misunderstood me, respected master." The man showed no signs of wishing to leave the workshop.

He walked up rather presumptuously to the table and sat down, crossing his legs.

"My Master wishes to acquire an item created by your own hands."

"And what exactly does he intend to buy from me?" the dwarf asked with unconcealed mockery, setting his hands on his hips.

Politeness was all well and good, but he would take great pleasure in throwing this man out of his workshop.

"That amusing little trinket," said Suovik, half rising off his chair and pointing one finger at the sparkling key.

For a moment the master craftsman was struck dumb.

"Have you lost your mind, dear sir? The elfin key? I have a client for it! And what do you want it for?"

"Mmmm . . . My Master is a man"—for some reason Suovik hesitated slightly over the word "man"—"a man of very special tastes. Let us leave it at that. He is a collector, and this remarkable key would suit his collection very well."

"No!" the dwarf snapped. "You wouldn't have enough money to buy the work, and I will not break my word."

"Oh! You need not be concerned about money, Master Frahel!"

Suovik got up off his chair, went across to the table on which the artifact was waiting for the final touch from its maker, and began taking stones out of his bag and setting them on the table. Frahel's teeth began chattering and his eyes turned as big and round as saucers. The man put a dragon's tear on the table—a stone in no way inferior to the one that the elf had brought. Then another one. And another. And another.

"My Master is very generous, you will have no cause for regret," Suovik said with a smile.

The dwarf said nothing: he gazed wide-eyed at the stones, expecting them to disappear at any moment. This simply could not be! The dragon's tears lying there were equal to the amount found by the dwarves and the gnomes in the last thousand years! Without waiting for an answer, Suovik placed another two specimens of the mineral on the table. The last one was simply enormous.

"You must agree, dear Master Frahel, that this price is enough to make you think. Let your client wait for one more week, and you can make him another key; you have more than enough material here."

"But the key is not ready yet, it has not been endowed with life," said the dwarf, trying to convince himself.

"No need for you to be concerned; I can manage that on my own."

"Human wizardry is of no use here," the dwarf said, shaking his head.

"There is other magic besides human wizardry," the man said with a smile.

"Other magic?" Frahel screwed up his eyes suspiciously. "There is also the stone magic of my people, and shamanism. The magic of the gnomes and dwarves is not suitable for men, and your tribe can only study ogric shamanism . . ."

"And what if this is so?" Suovik asked with a shrug.

"Who are you?" the dwarf blurted out, looking round the workshop in search of his poleax.

"Is that really so important? Well then, have we a deal?" Suovik reached his hand out for the key.

"No," the dwarf forced himself to say. "Take your junk and get out of here."

"Is that your last word?"

"Yes!"

"What a shame," the man sighed. "I wanted to do things in a friendly way."

The door opened and five shadows slipped into the room. Frahel turned pale.

Despite everything, Elodssa still somehow managed to lose his way and turn off into the wrong corridor. For a moment the elf's dark skin was covered in sweat at the sudden thought that he was lost. But after walking back and turning twice to the right, the elf found himself in a familiar corridor with a low ceiling.

Eventually he found himself outside Frahel's workshop and pushed the door open.

The dwarf was lying on the floor as dead as dead could be. A man was frozen absolutely still over a key—his key—singing a song in the ogric language, and the artifact was responding with a poisonous purple glow, pulsating like a living heart in time to the words.

The singer cast a single swift glance at the elf and snapped: "Kill him!"

Five orcs with drawn yataghans came dashing at Elodssa.

Elodssa's s'kash slid from its scabbard with a quiet rustle as his other hand grabbed the dagger from his belt and flung it at the shaman. The blade sank into the stranger's neck below the Adam's apple and he slumped over onto his side, wheezing and bleeding heavily. Now he could not say another word and he would not use any magic. The purple glow that had been spreading around the key began gradually fading. But the elf could not take the artifact yet—the first orc had drawn back his yataghan to strike. The s'kash and the yataghan clashed, parted, and clashed again. The orc jumped back, waiting for his fellows to move up.

"You're finished, you scum!"

Elodssa did not bother to answer. Of course, five against one was very bad odds, but the elf was saved by the fact that he was standing in the doorway and only two of them could attack him at once.

"Duck!" a familiar sharp voice said behind him.

He did as he was told and the bow that appeared above his shoulder fired an arrow that buried itself in an orc's eye. Another shot, and a second orc fell, shot through the heart. Midla fired her third arrow point-blank into the face of the enemy running at her. Elodssa joined in the fight, giving the elfess time to put her bow away and draw her two swords.

Dodging a blow from the right, he raised his s'kash over his head, offering the flat side of the blade to his opponent's yataghan. The orc was caught out, *his yataghan slid along the downward slope of Elodssa's s'kash, and the force of his own blow carried him forward an extra step, exposing his flank. The elf's curving blade sliced through his opponent's left arm and deep into his side. The elf then raised his weapon, stepped to the side—and the s'kash severed his enemy's neck, sending the head tumbling across the floor until it stopped somewhere under the table.*

Elodssa hurried to assist Midla, but she had already dealt with the final orc herself. There were two curved blades protruding from the enemy's dead body. Midla slumped back against the wall, hissing in pain as she squeezed shut the gaping yataghan wound in her leg.

"Are you all right?"

"No, by a thousand demons! How could you be so stupid as to come here alone? What if I hadn't got here in time?"

"I'd have had to manage on my own," he said, tearing up a cloth he had found in the dwarf's workshop.

"On your own," Midla muttered, tightening the knot. "That wolf's spawn even managed to wound me."

"Can you walk?"

"I don't think I'll be able to walk for the next few months."

"We have to get out of here. Who knows how many enemies entered the galleries."

"Are these the ones who killed the guards on that distant gate?"

"Probably. I'll carry you."

Midla simply nodded. "Pull the swords out of the body—they mean too much to me."

"Of course." Elodssa pulled the twin blades out of the dead body, handed them to Midla, and set off toward the body of the man, intending to pull his own dagger out of it.

In defiance of all the laws of nature, the shaman was still alive, although there was bloody foam on his lips and it had dribbled down onto his chin and beard. Elodssa indifferently tugged the dagger out of the wound and listened to the man wheezing, gurgling, and whistling.

"You . . . ," the man began, trying to say something. "The Ma . . . ster will po . . . ssess the key . . . any . . . way."

"I don't know who your master is, but elves don't part with their property that easily."

Elodssa finished off the wounded man, watching with satisfaction as the

brown eyes turned glassy. Then he took the key off the table, thought for a mo-
ment, and raked all the dragon's tears into the bag lying on the floor, reason-
ing quite soberly that the dead had no more need of them, while the gnomes
and dwarves would be able to get along without them.

"Is he dead?" Midla asked when he came across and lifted her up in his
arms.

"Yes, he was working a spell when I got here. Doing something with the
key."

"That's none of our business, let the shamans sort that out. Was he work-
ing for the orcs?"

"More likely the other way round," Elodssa panted as he carried Midla out
into the corridor. "They were working for him."

"How is that possible? The orcs never obey anyone they consider inferior to
themselves."

"I didn't have time to ask them. By the way, did you notice that they
weren't wearing clan badges?"

"Yes. That's very strange."

"That's exactly what I mean."

"What are you going to do now?"

"Report everything to the gnomes or the dwarves and get out into the open
air."

"And then?"

"Then?" Elodssa thought for a moment. "Then I'm going to give the key to
my father and change a few old laws, regardless of the opinion of the head of
the house."

"What laws?" Midla asked in surprise.

"Those that forbid the son of a royal dynasty and a scout to be together.
Have you any objections?"

Midla's smile was enough to let Elodssa know that there would be no ob-
jections from her side. Neither of them had noticed that in the depths of the
key lying in the elf's bag a faint purple spark was still glowing.

22

CONVERSATIONS IN THE FIRE

There are many who think there is no life in the darkness.

That is a great error. Perhaps, in the pitch-black emptiness of Nothing, life is not so obvious as in our own colorful world, but there can be no doubt that it exists. On this side and on that, doors opened for a brief fraction of a second with a despairing creak—columns of light in the boundless darkness, leading into goodness only knew where. I was suspended in emptiness and I saw many dreams, both beautiful and terrible at the same time. Dreams in which I was merely an observer; dreams in which I lived a thousand lives; dreams that were the truth and dreams that were simply dreams.

How long did this go on for? I don't think that it was longer than eternity; anyway even eternity has to end sometime. And like dreams, eternity has the disagreeable habit of coming to an end at the most inappropriate time.

After several ages that seemed like mere minutes to me, the first crimson sparks were born in the darkness, the children of a gigantic bonfire that I could not yet see.

The number of sparks increased, they started flying faster, and now they were flying horizontally as well as upward, as if they were driven by some mischievous wind. Sometimes, when there was too much of the fiery snow, the snowflakes swirled together into an orange whirlwind. And at those moments, pictures of the past appeared before my eyes.

Another eternity passed and at one spot the darkness swelled up and turned yellow—the way paper turns yellow if you bring it near the flame of a candle—and then burst. Tongues of crimson flame appeared. Then more and more of them, and a moment later the flames consumed the darkness and filled the entire space of my infinite dream.

I can remember that those eyes looking at me are the slanting, golden amber eyes of an elfess whose name, I think, is Miralissa.

"Dance with us, Dancer!" The sound of jolly laughter made me look round.

There were three shadows whirling in a furious dance on the tongues of flame. They were not frightened at all by the presence of light; they remained as black and impervious to it as if there was no fire there at all.

"Come on, Dancer, do not be afraid!" One of them laughed, and made a circle round me.

"I don't dance, ladies," I said. My throat was dry, either from the cold fire or from my dreams.

"Look, he doesn't want to dance." Another shadow laughed merrily, flying right up to me.

For an instant I glimpsed the outline of a woman's face.

"Why do you refuse to dance, Dancer? Why do you not wish to grant us the gift of at least one dance?"

"I have to go." The flame behind my back was howling ceaselessly, and I thought it was beginning to grow warmer.

"Go?" The third shadow was there beside the first two. "But in order to go, you have to make us a gift of a dance. Come on, Dancer! Choose! Which of us is most to your liking?"

"I do not know how to dance," I said, shaking my head and turning away.

The amber eyes had still not disappeared, but they were slowly moving away, disappearing behind the wall of flame. I dashed toward them, but instantly I was scorched by the searing cold. I covered my face with my hands in fear.

"You see, Dancer," the second shadow said with a nod. "You can only dance your way through the fire. Dance, or you will remain here forever!"

I could already distinguish each of them by their voices. They were so similar and at the same time so different.

"Which of us do you choose?" the third one asked again. The heat behind my back was becoming unbearable.

"All three," I said sullenly.

One piece of foolishness more or less. What difference did it really make?

A momentary bewilderment.

"You are truly a Dancer," the first shadow said in surprise. "You take everything from life."

"Well then, we shall lead you through the barrier. Hold on!"

The shadows embraced me, shielding me with their dark bodies against the fire advancing from all sides. And they led me. An eddying swirl, a darting, sliding lightness, a black flash of lightning piercing the wall of flame and pushing me toward the amber eyes.

I am falling . . .

"We will dance the djanga with you yet!" I heard a voice say behind me.

A final, angry spurt of crimson flame enraged at its own impotence. Night . . .

"What's wrong with him?"

The voice pierced through the dense cobweb of unconsciousness, severing its threads like the blade of a dagger. It snatched me from the bottom of my sleep, slowly lifting me up to the surface so that I could take a gulp of the fresh air of life.

"He's coming round! Egrassa, give me the flowers! Quickly!" Miralissa's voice was tense and . . .

Perplexed? Frightened?

"What, may the Darkness devour me, is going on here?" asked the first voice.

I thought I knew it, too . . . Alistan Markauz.

"Calm down, count, explanations later! Egrassa, why are you taking so long?"

"Here." The elf sounded calm.

I smelled the sour scent of some herb and winced involuntarily.

"All right, Harold, time to stop this comedy! Open your eyes!" The imperturbable Ell's voice was sharp and tense.

I tried. I really did try. But my eyelids were terrible heavy; they were filled with lead and refused to obey me.

"Come, Dancer, open your eyes! I know you can hear me!"

Miralissa calls me that, too—Dancer! It's all Kli-Kli's fault. The goblin was the first one to claim that I'm supposedly in some prophecy or other. I ought to strangle him, but I feel sorry for the little green creature.

One more effort. This time everything was much easier. The elfess had a will of iron. The first thing I saw was her face. Miralissa was leaning down over me and, despite her swarthy complexion, she was exceptionally pale. "Thank the gods," she said when I looked up at her and smiled. Standing a little farther away were the two elves, as tense as two taut bowstrings or the strings of some musical instrument. Markauz was standing beside them. He looked gloomy. But then, that was his constant mood; we had all grown used to that long ago.

"How are you feeling?" asked Miralissa, putting her hand on my forehead again.

How am I feeling? My arms and legs are all there. I don't think I have a tail. Everything's all right. Just what are they all in such a flurry about?

"I feel fine. Why?"

I attempted to get up off the bed, but Miralissa gently pushed me back down.

"Lie down for a while."

"Will someone explain to me what is going on?" asked Milord Alistan, unable to restrain himself any longer.

"I wish someone would explain to me," Miralissa snapped irritably, and shivered, as if there was a chilly draft in the room. Quickly, she recovered her composure and was all business again. "Everything was going as usual. The standard procedure for attuning the key—it can be carried out by any third-year apprentice who knows almost nothing about shamanism. Everything was normal, and then the key suddenly flared up with a purple light and I lost contact with Harold. His consciousness was transported to such distant realms that we had great difficulty in bringing him back here. Or rather, somehow he made his own way back—all our attempts were unsuccessful. I don't understand a thing!"

The artifact flared up with a purple light? That happened in one of the dreams. Some man ... Sunik? Suonik? I can't remember. He did something to that key. Something not exactly good. Another of the Master's minions, that was who he was.

"Harold, can you remember anything?"

"Well, something," I said slowly.

"Stop muttering! What do you remember, thief?" Alistan was still furious.

"Dreams. Thousands of dreams."

"What dreams?"

"It's all your key's fault, you should have made it yourself, instead of sending a prince to the dwarves!" I said in a reproachful voice.

"How do you know that a prince commissioned the key?" Miralissa's eyes widened in surprise.

"From a dream, I suppose . . . ," I said after a moment's thought. "I even remember the elf's name—Elodssa."

"Elodssa the Destroyer of Laws," Ell said, nodding to confirm that I wasn't lying. "There was a head of the House of the Black Flame with that name. Long ago, more than a thousand years. But I did not know that he commissioned the key."

"He didn't commission it," I said, defying Miralissa's prohibition and sitting up on the bed. "His father did. Not even his father, all the elves. Dark and the light. And Elodssa went to the dwarves. That was how it all happened."

"What happened?"

"Pay no attention. It was only one of many dreams."

"Dreams have the quality of showing the past. Or the future. It is quite possible that without even knowing it, you saw a page from that book."

So I had to explain.

"If we can rely on my dream," I concluded, "then something bad was done to the key and now it doesn't work the way it should."

"But before it worked just fine!" Alistan objected.

"We didn't know anything about the Master before," Ell retorted. "Something in the key could have awoken, and it almost drew Harold in."

"Enough!" said Miralissa, clicking her fingers in annoyance. "We shall carry on with what we have been doing. In any case, the artifact has remembered Harold."

"And I think I'll be going. If none of you have any objections, that is."
I got up off the bed and walked toward the door.

"Don't forget the key," Alistan said.

"No, let it stay with me for a while," said Miralissa, unexpectedly
supporting me. "I shall check it again. We have to be sure that it is absolutely safe."

Marvelous! I left the thoughtful elves and the disgruntled Count
Rat.

On the way to my room Tomcat called me. He looked somber.

"Have you seen Alistan?" he asked without stopping.

"He's with Miralissa."

Tomcat nodded and set off toward the elfess's room.

"Where have you been gadding about?" That was how the jester greeted
me when I appeared in the doorway.

Lamplighter wasn't there yet, and Kli-Kli was making up a bed for
himself on the floor, between the two beds with cracked wooden frames.

"Are you fond of sleeping on a hard surface?" I asked, ignoring the
goblin's question.

"I'd advise you to do the same, it's good for the health," said Kli-Kli,
plumping up his cushion.

"Thank you, I think I'll pass on that." I took a plug of cotton wool
out of my pocket—one of several that I had taken care to request from
the innkeeper's helpful wife—and put it in my ear.

"What's that for?" my green friend asked, screwing up his eyes suspiciously.

"I can't get to sleep without them," I said with a crooked grin, and the
goblin let it go at that.

After several nights spent under the open stars, the bed seemed like
a gift from the gods, and I slept like a baby. . . .

As was only to be expected, the next morning Kli-Kli was morose
and taciturn. He was out of sorts with the entire world, especially with
Lamplighter, and also, for some reason or other, with me.

Neither Miralissa nor Alistan said a word about the key that morning. They merely hurried us along, eager to set out as soon as possible.

We left early, before the dawn arrived. While Milord Rat was pushing the entire group along, I finished sleeping on Little Bee's back, since the horse was not dashing along at a gallop. Marmot, riding beside me, merely sniffed, understanding the state I was in, and began keeping an unobtrusive eye on Little Bee to make sure that I didn't tumble out of the saddle.

An hour later the horses moved up into a fast trot and there I was, wide awake, sitting upright in my saddle in dashing style. That's what regular practice can do for you. And only then did I notice that certain changes had taken place in our small expeditionary force.

"Where are Tomcat and Egrassa?" I asked Kli-Kli as he rode past me on Featherlight.

"They've been given an important assignment," said the goblin, opening his mouth to speak for the first time that morning. "That's it, Harold. All the fun and games are behind us now. Now difficult and perhaps even dangerous days lie ahead. Something has to happen, I can smell it!"

And Kli-Kli sniffed loudly to support his own words.

"What's happened, Marmot?" I persisted.

The Wild Heart merely shrugged, but he looked concerned. "The Nameless One only knows. Tomcat was out of sorts all day yesterday. He kept muttering something to himself, and by evening he'd begun glancing round over his shoulder. And this morning he took the elf with him and disappeared. You heard what Kli-Kli said, didn't you? Something's going on. I hate being surrounded by riddles."

"Who doesn't?" Loudmouth asked with a yawn. "Just look at the way Alistan's driving us along. At this pace we'll be in the Sultanate before evening comes."

We turned off the highway onto an old, deserted road that continued to lead us to the southeast, although Honeycomb said that later it would turn back toward the south and merge with the highway before Ranneng. This route was a lot shorter, but less busy. This was not a populous area and there were no villages, so once again we would have to spend the night under the open sky.

The morning passed, the hot afternoon arrived and dissolved into the approaching evening, but Alistan kept driving us on, sparing neither horses nor riders. The worm of alarm began stirring somewhere in my soul. Something must have happened, otherwise why all this hurry?

Neither the elfess, nor the count, nor Uncle replied to the jester's questions; they merely drove the horses on even harder. There were brief halts, simply in order to allow the exhausted horses some rest, and then the dusty road was flitting past again below our feet, as the disk of the coppery red sun slipped down behind the horizon on our right hand.

Our group did not stop for the night until the sky was a fiery crimson that was gradually turning dark purple, and there was nothing of the sun left above the horizon apart from a narrow rim. We didn't go far from the road and were so exposed to view that we might as well have been sitting on Sagot's palm. There were unplowed fields stretching out to the right and the left of the road and the light of a campfire would be seen a league away.

The pale, horned crescent that had replaced the full moon while we were traveling appeared in the sky and began conversing with the first stars. But there was no time for admiring the beauty of nature—we still had to collect firewood.

Within the group duties were precisely distributed. Two men gathered wood and kept the fire going, one cooked, a fourth watched the horses, and the rest prepared the site for the night's rest. Everybody had a job to do; no one was allowed to shirk. Even Markauz, our very own count, checked the horses every evening to make sure that—Sagot forbid!—none of them had gone lame.

Nobody asked me to do anything, but I didn't want to seem like a useless idler (after all, I would have to share my final crust of bread with these people), so I also did whatever I could. Mostly I helped Marmot gather firewood or feed Invincible. The ling had turned out to be a most amusing animal and pretty damned smart, too. We got on perfectly well together: I allowed him to climb onto my shoulder and he allowed me to stroke him. Marmot found this idyllic love affair very surprising. He told me that Invincible wasn't usually very keen on anyone touching him. Apart, of course, from his beloved master.

That night Alistan posted sentries for the first time. The first to go on watch were Arnkh and Eel. In three hours' time, they were due to be relieved by Uncle and Honeycomb, and during the early morning the next four would take their shifts.

I couldn't sleep. Sleep had abandoned me and I simply lay there with my hands under my head, looking up at the starry sky that was like a bottomless lake. The warm night breeze ran its soft hand across the tall wild grass and the sleeping flowers, gently bowing the plants down toward Mother Earth. The grass pretended to be angry and rustled, but as soon as the wind was distracted, it playfully raised its head again, calling the wind back.

The skinny old crescent moon floated above the world and its light fell into the grass like silvery dust, making it look like precious jewelry that had escaped the control of some talented master craftsman's hand. There was the smell of damp earth, wildflowers, summer freshness, and boundless space. After the constant stony stench of the overheated city, the scents of nature were intoxicating.

Somewhere far off in the fields there was the melancholy call of a solitary bird. I was not the only one who did not feel like sleeping that night.

For an instant a black silhouette blotted out the stars as it flitted over my head and silently dissolved into the night, only to return an instant later. The shadow turned in a circle above the camp and, realizing that it would not find any interesting prey beside the campfire, lazily flapped its wings and moved away, with its body almost touching the grass, disappearing into the silvery moonlit fields.

An eagle owl out hunting. Watch out, all you mice. Just as long as it doesn't take our Invincible. Although it's not so very simple to eat a ling. Just try grabbing a creature with teeth like that, and you'll soon find yourself with no beak or feathers! I could still hear the little beast rustling in the cooking pot, finishing off the remains of supper.

The campfire was dying down and the coals it had created were quietly twinkling back at their distant sisters, the stars, to see who could glow brightest. I felt I ought to throw on a few sticks of firewood, but I was too lazy to get up—the soldiers were sleeping lightly and I was certain to wake someone up. Loudmouth was lying beside me, stretched out on his back with his mouth open. If Kli-Kli had not been asleep at the time, he would have been sure to exploit the soldier's incautious pose and slip a dandelion or some small bug into his open mouth as a jolly joke—you could expect any kind of rotten trick from the green goblin at absolutely any moment.

I still hadn't managed to understand the goblin's character: Either he was simply playing the part of the royal buffoon, acting crazily all over the place, or this really was the normal condition of his little green soul. Before I met Kli-Kli, I hadn't really had any serious contact with his race—there were so few of them—and so my general impression of goblins had only begun to take shape quite recently.

But this time Loudmouth was in no danger—the jester was too tired and he was snuffling softly with one hand under his cheek, as sound asleep as everyone else. Close by, Lamplighter was sleeping with his arms round his beloved bidenhander. Deler was over closer to the fire. Hallas was stretched with his precious sack on the boundary of light and darkness.

The others were lying on the other side of the fading fire. They merged into the darkness, transformed into mere dark silhouettes, and it was impossible to make out who was sleeping where. Eel walked by several times, keeping watch. But then, convinced that all was quiet, he sat down not far away.

Eel was probably the only one of my human companions about whom I had not yet formed a definite opinion. Always taciturn and as erect as a pikestaff, the dark-complexioned Garrakan rarely got involved in conversation. Sometimes he threw in a few sparse words, but only in cases when he thought it was worth sharing his opinion with the others.

He was well respected in the unit, that was clear straightaway, but I couldn't see that Eel had any friends among the Wild Hearts. To him we were all campaign comrades, the companions who would fight beside him, if necessary, against the common enemy, but not at all the kind of friends with whom he could enjoy drinking a glass of beer on some fine spring day. He kept his distance; he didn't poke his nose into the others' business and didn't let them into his confidence. None of the soldiers took offense and they accepted the Garrakan's character at face value. Once I asked Lamplighter how a man like that had come to be with them.

"I don't know, he's not much inclined to talk about his past life," Mumr said with a shrug. "And we don't try to force him. The past is every man's personal business. Take Ash, now—he's the commander of the Thorns at the Giant—he used to be a petty thief. He wound up in the Wild Hearts when he was still a boy. And now we'd follow him to the Needles of Ice and beyond if need be. And I couldn't give a damn what he used to do before—thieving, killing, or kidnapping old women. It's the same thing with Eel. He doesn't want to talk about anything before he joined up—and that's his right. I've known him for almost ten years, and none of our lads have ever had any reason to doubt his courage. I heard a rumor once that he came from some noble family in Garrak. And I don't think myself that he's any kind of simple lad. Just look at the way he handles those swords, like he was born with them. In a word, a nobleman."

The night bird called again. The brief sound lingered and rippled across the fields, making Eel turn his head sharply in that direction. But the very creature that had made those howls seemed to have taken fright at its own voice.

Sleep still would not come. I was too worried by the fact that Tomcat and Egrassa had been away for so long. The goblin was right when he said something nasty was on the way. What could detain two warriors on a seemingly safe and peaceful road?

Hmm . . .

Was it really that safe? Really that peaceful? It might be only just over a week to Avendoom on horseback, but that didn't mean everything was peaceful and quiet on the highway. Anything at all could happen. What had Tomcat been so dour and upset about? A whole day before I was introduced to the key, he was already quite obviously concerned, frequently glancing round behind him without any need, staring down the empty road, stroking his cat's whiskers far too nervously, and muttering strangely to himself under his breath.

What had he seen? What had he sensed? All the others, including Miralissa and Egrassa, who were skilled shamans, had been quite unperturbed.

But then, who could understand a tracker? In their profession, those lads were obliged to see what others failed to notice.

The stars gradually blurred and the world sank into a deep sleep.

I opened my eyes without knowing what had woken me. The crescent moon had sauntered quite a distance across the sky while I was asleep and now it was clutched in the embraces of the Arrow of the Sun, an immense constellation spread out at the very line of the horizon.

Eel was dozing beside Loudmouth, whose mouth was still wide open. More than three hours had passed since I fell asleep and now Uncle and Honeycomb were on watch, having taken over from the Garrakan and Arnkh, who had gone to their beds.

Someone had taken care to prolong the life of the campfire and its small scarlet flower was slowly consuming the sticks of firewood. Miralissa was sitting beside the fire, occasionally dipping a stick into the flames. The fire hissed in annoyance and shot out sparks that went streaking up into the night sky.

I stood up and went toward the elfess, trying not to wake anyone, but I almost stepped on Deler on the way. I sat down cautiously beside her and started watching the fire lick the bark off the stick.

"You cannot sleep either?" she asked after a long silence.

"No."

I looked at her imperturbable face, at her hair gleaming with scarlet highlights in the light of the campfire.

"It is a good night." She sighed.

"Bearing in mind that I haven't spent the night in the fields very often in my life, yes it is. A good night."

"You have no idea what a lucky man you are," the elfess said suddenly, her fangs glinting.

I still hadn't managed to get used to those protruding teeth the elves had. No doubt men are subconsciously afraid of anything different from themselves, especially if the unknown has fangs like that in its mouth.

"Yes, if finding yourself in a situation that leaves you no option but to take a trip to Hrad Spein is good luck," I replied rather gloomily.

"I won't try to console you there. You chose a rather risky profession and you knew what you were doing. It's dangerous to be a thief. But that wasn't what I meant. How often have you been outside the walls of Avendoom?"

"Three times," I said after a moment's thought. "And not farther than five leagues."

"There, you see. A lucky man. Always close to home."

"It doesn't feel all that much like home."

I had no sentimental yearnings at all for the walls of Avendoom.

"But it still is your home. Do you know what my most cherished wish is?" she suddenly asked.

I looked into the yellow eyes and shook my head very slightly.

"I want finally to go home. To see my native forest, my family, my palace, my daughter. Why do you smile? Do you think this is too much like a woman?"

"No, milady. I don't think that. Everybody wants to go home at some time. Especially if their child is there."

"I have not been in Zagraba for two years. I have traveled all over Siala with my unit. The last time we went as far as S'u-dar. Ell, Egrassa, and I were the only ones who returned. The rest remained behind in the snow."

"My condolences—"

"Don't," she interrupted me gently. "We have a different attitude to death. We are not people, after all. Elves regard it more lightly and accept it more easily. All depart this life at some time. Sooner or later it happens. Running away from it is foolish—and closing your eyes to it is even more so."

Silence fell again, with only an occasional hiss from something between the coals and the wind fluttering the hairs that had come loose from the elfess's braid.

"I've been wanting to ask," I began. "Why did you get involved in this adventure? After all, this is our misfortune. This is a human problem."

"The dark elves concluded an alliance with Valiostr."

I said nothing. Alliances are made and they are broken. That is a matter of high politics, and an alliance, even if it has held for several hundred years, is no reason for sticking your head into a hungry ogre's mouth.

Miralissa understood my unspoken thought.

"Harold, are you always in such a gloomy mood?"

"It all depends on the circumstances."

"You must understand that if we do not help you now, then we shall pay for it later. The orcs have nominally acknowledged the authority of the Nameless One, even though he is a man. But they have only acknowledged him because it is in their interest to do so. Since the Spring War they have not managed to make any progress across the continent, not even once. They were finally driven back into Zagraba."

"I understand."

"If the Nameless One crushes Valiostr, then the Border Kingdom, the ancient land of the orcs, will be left without protection. The Bordermen will not be able to hold out against the full forces of the Firstborn. If the Nameless One is satisfied with vengeance and his armies halt in Valiostr, that will not be the end. The orcs will gather strength and take Isilia and in time they will undermine Miranueh, and then they will think of some reason to turn against the Nameless One. They are proud and inclined to think that they can defeat a man with their yataghans, even if he has the power of a thousand magicians. Or perhaps they will leave Valiostr in peace; there are plenty of other lands to the south."

"The south is strong. It is Garrakh, the Empires, the Lowlands, Filand, and the light elves if it comes to that."

"When a landslide gathers speed, the lower it gets, the more danger-ous it becomes. They will be hard to stop. In their obsession with the greatness of their race, they will exterminate all. The orcs are the gods' Firstborn, after all. Siala was granted to them, the ogres retreated into the shadows, and all the other worms—other races—appeared here through some misunderstanding. Only the orcs are worthy to live, the others should be dispatched into the darkness. Sooner or later the elves' turn will come. And without the support of men, the war will be hope-less. We will drown in blood, Harold. That is why the elves are helping Valiostr. We want you to hold fast in the present, or we shall perish in the future. We shall fall. We shall lose everything. The Nameless One is only the beginning. Merely the snowball that will set in motion the avalanche of a new division of the world. We will all have to work as a team . . . you and I must work together."

I nodded, flattered. The orcs really had been building up their forces for a long time, and the only reason they weren't already testing the sharpness of their yataghans was that the combined forces of Valiostr, the Border Kingdom, and the dark elves were still just about able to restrain them. But if just one of those three were to disappear, the Firstborn would have a lot more breathing space. There would be a little gap in the dam, and a little trickle would flow through it. And everyone knows that water wears away stone. After a while the dam would burst.

"I shall lead the group tomorrow," Miralissa suddenly announced.

"Milord Alistan and Eel will go back. We have to know what has happened to Tomcat and Egrassa."

"Won't they disappear, too?"

Markauz and Eel were excellent warriors, and in case of need their assistance would be far from superfluous.

"Let us hope that my cousin and Tomcat have forestalled any unforeseen circumstances."

"What happened, anyway? Why did they leave the party so suddenly?"

"Tomcat saw something."

"Tomcat saw something?" I echoed in amazement. "But you don't send men off somewhere or other just because someone has seen something. Anyone could imagine that he saw something."

"Tomcat sees things that others do not," Miralissa said in a quiet voice, and put her charred stick down on the ground. "Do you know that before he joined the Wild Hearts he was an apprentice with the Order?"

"I don't believe it." Somehow I couldn't imagine this short fat man with a mustache as a magician's apprentice.

"But nonetheless, it is true. I don't know why he left the magicians, but he still has his knowledge. Tomcat notices interesting things, although sometimes he himself cannot explain his instinctive feelings. Wake up any of the Wild Hearts and ask them what they would trust most, what they would choose in a moment of danger—reason and facts, or Tomcat's shadowy feelings? I am quite sure, Harold, that they would all choose the latter. This ordinary-looking man has proved right and guided their unit away from danger too often."

I made the effort to put a few more branches in the flames.

"That evening when you saw the key, Tomcat came to me. He said that he sensed danger. Not even danger, but its phantom. Something was being prepared behind our backs, and something else was following right behind us, about a hundred yards away. He could sense someone watching us, but no matter how hard he looked, he couldn't find anything."

"Did you believe him?"

"Why not? What sense would it make for him to lie? Since we judged it impossible to turn the expedition back and go dashing off with no particular destination in mind, Alistan and I decided to carry on, but to turn off the busy highway onto this road. We are not so easy to spot here, and if anything happens, others will not suffer. Tomcat and Egrassa, the junior prince of the house and a knowledgeable shaman, were to go back and see what was happening."

"And stop it . . ."

"If possible, but that was not the main goal. Tomcat said that it was not far, only three leagues away at the most. By any calculations, they should already have caught up with us."

"There's a hostile shaman somewhere nearby?" I guessed.

"Yes, you're right. But even I didn't sense anything." She reached up and gently picked a small leaf from my shoulder. "If not for Tomcat's caution, we would already have been attacked from behind."

"And how long are we going to run like this?"

"Certainly as far as Ranneng. You must agree that joining battle with someone unknown is too dangerous; we might lose the advantage that we have at present. And there are magicians of the Order in the city, so our enemies will not venture into it."

"Pardon me, milady. But I do not agree with you there," I said, and shook my head. "If they could get into the king's palace, they will certainly get into Ranneng."

"Do you suggest that we should not enter Ranneng at all?"

"It could be that they are trying to lure us there."

"Why?" she asked, looking at me curiously.

"Let's just call it a premonition."

"Like Tomcat's?"

"No—unlike Tomcat, I am sometimes wrong."

Miralissa's black lips smiled sadly.

"Perhaps you are right. But we cannot do without the city. There is no way we can avoid it. Otherwise, once past the Iselina, it will be too hard without fresh horses and supplies. In any case, attacking us there is not the same as attacking us here when there is not a soul around. We shall be in Ranneng in three days. There are still two hours left until dawn, go and sleep."

"I won't fall asleep now."

"I have to compile a few spells. Just in case. I sense there may be trouble ahead."

"Then I will not disturb you. Good night."

A slight bow of the head and she had already picked up her stick from the ground and was drawing signs in the ashes.

I went back to my place and straightened out my crumpled blanket. As morning approached it had turned cooler and the first, topaz-like drops of dew had appeared on the stalks of the grass.

"Why aren't you asleep?" Uncle asked me peevishly as he made his round of the camp. "Even the horses are sleeping like logs, and here you are making a racket. Ah, you're as green as they come. In your place I'd be glad of every free minute I could get."

He walked away, muttering quietly.

Well, what the Wild Heart had said made sense. I lay down on my improvised bed, and immediately leapt back up, trying not to shout out. Some swine had put a briar in my blanket! I cast an angry glance at the jester, but he was sleeping calmly. Or at least pretending with consummate skill.

No point expecting a leopard to change his spots. I stopped worrying, threw the briar as far away as possible, and lay down. And at that very moment I almost choked on my own laughter. Someone had come off even worse than me, only he didn't realize it yet. Loudmouth was still sleeping with his mouth wide open, and there was a dandelion stalk sticking out of it.

The last thing I saw before I fell asleep again was Miralissa, a solitary figure sitting beside the fire, drawing incomprehensible signs on the ground. I wanted to go to her, but knew I could never follow this road where it might lead . . . even if she let me. She is what she is—an elfess and a royal one, no less, and a magic user. Harold is what he is—wolf-single, thank you, and planning to stay in that happy state. We were comrades, no more. That was fine with me.

23

VISHKI

Guess who was to blame for the general tumult and commotion the next morning? Why, Kli-Kli, of course. Miralissa caught the goblin just as he was writing "eensy weensy spider" in the ashes beside the elfess's magical signs. Naturally, she almost tore his hands off for his artistic efforts. And so all morning the goblin tried to keep as far away from her as possible.

"Harold!" he whined guiltily, not having found any more willing listener in our little party. "I really didn't mean anything by it! I thought they were just scrawly scribbles and that was all! Please talk to her for me. She's very mad at me."

"I think you should talk to her yourself. I don't have any influence with her."

"You do. You have the most influence on her royal elfess majesty."

"Oh, really? The elf princess listens to the thief? The madhouse is just down the road, they're expecting you."

"Harold, she doesn't think of you as a thief, she thinks of you as a Dancer."

I looked at him blankly for a moment, then shook my head. A Dancer.

Eel was already in the saddle, waiting for the count.

"We're setting off now. Follow this road and do not turn off anywhere. We'll try to catch up with you by evening."

"If we do not meet along the way, look for us in Ranneng, at the inn called the Learned Owl," Miralissa told them in farewell.

Alistan nodded, then he and Eel dug their heels into the sides of their steeds and went galloping back to the place where Egrassa and Tomcat ought to be.

"Come on, men," Uncle said with a clap of his hands. "Mount up."

That day was the hottest of our journey so far. The sun was so pitilessly fierce that even the stalwart and obstinate Arnkh removed his chain mail. Honeycomb stripped completely down to the waist, exposing his bulging muscles, with their abundant display of scars and tattoos. Many others followed his example. Kli-Kli borrowed some rag from Marmot and tied it round his head, after first moistening it with water from a flask.

The road set our backs to the hot sun and wound between open fields and thickets of low, scrubby bushes. There were no clouds and the azure blue of the sky was so painfully bright in our eyes that we had to squint all the time. Apart from the imperturbable elves, the entire party looked like a herd of cockeyed, delirious Doralissians.

The syrupy, incandescent air flowed into my lungs in a clammy, scorching wave. I would have given half my life if only it would rain.

After about two hours of uninterrupted galloping under the unblinking eye of the intense sun, the broad fields fell away behind us and fused into the horizon, giving way to a hilly area with a generous scattering of low pine trees. Instead of the smell of wild grasses and flowers, the constant buzzing of insects and chirping of crickets, we caught the sharp scent of pine resin and heard the serene, impassive silence of the forest.

The road wound between the low hills, sometimes climbing up onto one of them and then immediately, without pausing, diving downward again. Smooth ascents alternated with equally smooth descents, and the journey continued like that for quite a long time.

The forest along the sides of the road grew thicker and the trunks of the trees crowded closer together, hiding almost all the sky behind their leaves. The low, crooked pines gave up their place in the sun to aspens and birches. All the ground in the forest along the road and on the surrounding hills was covered with bushy undergrowth. Now at last, thanks to the dense wall of trees, we had some blessed coolness— the weakened rays of the sun no longer lashed our shoulders like redhot whips; everybody heaved a sigh of relief and Arnkh hurried to put his beloved chain mail back on, now that he had the opportunity.

For the next hour we rode in the relative coolness of the welcoming forest.

But our good mood didn't last for long. How could it? As yet, we still knew nothing about the missing Tomcat and Egrassa, or about Alistan and Eel. What reason did we have for feeling jolly?

And so everyone was tense and taciturn. Lamplighter completely forgot about his beloved reed pipe. Kli-Kli didn't crack any of his eternal dim-witted jokes, and even Deler and Hallas stopped arguing, which was something absolutely unheard of since the very beginning of our journey. The dwarf glowered and stroked the blade of his enormous poleax; the gnome puffed away on his pipe, exhausting his final reserves of tobacco. Uncle growled and tugged on his beard. Loudmouth snarled good-naturedly.

As soon as the road climbed the next low hill and the wall of the forest no longer blocked the view, one of my companions was certain to look back. But the road was still empty, and we rode on, gradually becoming ever more sullen.

Miralissa and Ell talked about something in low voices and she occasionally chewed on her lips, either in frustration or fury. Waiting is the worst thing of all. I know that from my own experience.

At a place where a stream crossed the road, Miralissa said, "We'll stop on that hill." She glanced back over her shoulder at the empty road for perhaps the hundredth time that day. "We'll make a halt there."

"Alrighty," said Uncle, supporting the elfess's proposal. "We need a rest. It'll be evening soon, and we're still riding hard."

Uncle was right. My back was aching outrageously after galloping for so long. What I really wanted to do was get down off Little Bee, lie on the grass, and have a good stretch.

"Harold," said Lamplighter, riding up and distracting me from my daydreams, "do you think Milord Alistan will manage to catch up with us?"

"I don't know, Mumr," I replied wearily. "It's not evening yet."

"I hope Miralissa won't be foolish enough to send anyone else on these dubious reconnaissance missions."

I was also hoping very much that the dark elfess's sense of reason was in good working order. If anyone else left the party, our numbers would be reduced to a laughable level. Our group needed to stay together for as long as possible.

The road started running up a hill, and the forest reluctantly slipped downward—the hill was too tall for it, and the time had not yet come for the trees to climb to its summit.

"A halt," said Loudmouth, jumping down smartly from his horse to the ground.

"I don't think so," said Miralissa, shaking her head. "Get back in the saddle."

I followed her gaze. Up ahead of us, a little more than a league away, there were several columns of thick smoke rising up out of the forest.

"What is it?" asked Uncle, screwing up his eyes.

"As far as I recall, it's Vishki, a small village, maybe forty or forty-five households," Honeycomb replied.

"And what's there that could burn like that?" asked Deler, reaching for his poleax again without even realizing it.

"Well, it's definitely not the houses, the smoke's too black, as if they're burning coal," said Hallas, puffing stubbornly on his pipe.

"Get ready, lads! Put your armor on, and we'll find out what the fire's eating down there!" Uncle instructed.

"And I'd like to know what swine lit it!" said Lamplighter.

The moment there was something to do apart from the hard riding that the soldiers had grown so sick of during the last few days, they all livened up. Any goal was better than being left in a state of total uncertainty for days on end, not knowing where the enemy was and which foul creature you could feed a yard of steel to in order to improve your own foul mood. I could understand the men perfectly; for soldiers, inactivity is the worst possible torment.

"Harold, do you need a special invitation?" asked the goblin, riding up to me on Featherlight. "Where's your chain mail?"

"What chain mail?"

"The chain mail we chose for you," Kli-Kli responded irritably.

"I'm not going to cover myself in metal," I said rudely.

"You really ought to," said Marmot, who had already taken his chain mail off the packhorse and was putting it on over his shirt. "Armor, you know, can be quite wonderful for saving your life."

"Ordinary chain mail won't save you from a crossbow anyway. A sklot will shoot straight through it."

"Not everybody has sklots, and the enemy doesn't just use crossbows. It'll stop you getting scratched, if nothing else."

Rip me into a hundred pieces, but I have a prejudice against wearing metal on my body. I've been used to managing without armor all my life, and I feel no better in chain mail than some people do in the grave. Cramped and uncomfortable.

"Just look at all the others," Kli-Kli persisted.

The warriors of the platoon were already dressed up in the armor that had so far been left on the packhorses because of the rather hot weather. But in my view an ordinary fire, even if it was rather big, didn't merit such precautions.

The elves were sporting dark blue chain mail and steel breastplates with the emblems of their houses engraved on them. Miralissa had the Black Moon and Ell had the Black Rose. He put on the helmet that hid his face and Miralissa threw a chain-mail hood over her head, concealing her thick braid and fringe. Hallas, dressed up in something that looked more like fish scales, was helping Deler button up his steel leg plates. The dwarf set his hat aside and put a flat helmet on his head. It had protruding sections at the front to cover his cheeks and nose.

To avoid being the odd Doralissian out, I had to take my "packaging" out, too. It weighed down uncomfortably on my shoulders and I winced in annoyance. Because I wasn't used to it, it felt cramped and uncomfortable.

"Ah, stop going on like that. You'll soon get used to it," Lamplighter consoled me.

He was wearing armor that consisted of strips of steel fitted closely together. Catching my curious glance, he smiled: "A magnificent thing for anyone who likes swinging a bindenhander from side to side. It doesn't cramp your movements and your grips."

Instead of a helmet, Mumr tied a thin strip of cloth round his forehead to prevent his hair from getting into his eyes.

"Are we off?" asked Uncle, looking at the elfess.

"Yes," she commanded tersely, but then she thought for a moment and added: "You take over command."

Uncle accepted the suggestion as only natural. Unlike the platoon sergeant, Miralissa didn't know what his men were capable of.

"Hallas, Deler—to the front! You have the strongest armor, in case . . ."

Uncle didn't say any more. Everybody understood in case of what. If disaster struck, the soldiers in the strongest armor might survive a hit from a heavy crossbow bolt and distract the crossbowmen's attention from their less well-protected comrades.

"Have you forgotten about me, sergeant?" I heard a muffled voice say behind me. "I'm with them."

I turned round to see who it was. Instead of his old chain mail, Arnkh had put on heavy armor. Plus a helmet that looked like an acorn and completely covered his face, with narrow slits for the eyes. Then there were the leg pieces, shoulder pieces, chain-mail gloves, and the round shield. A real wall of steel.

In fact, almost everybody had a shield, including Lamplighter, Honeycomb, and the elves. My companions were all set for a good fight, and they would be very disappointed if it turned out that the fire in the village was just another ordinary blaze caused by the negligence of some drunken peasant.

This time we didn't hurry, but moved along slowly, gazing attentively into the undergrowth, anticipating a possible trap. There was already a smell of smoke and soot in the air, and we still had a long way to ride to Vishki. Kli-Kli was pulling faces as if he had a toothache—the smoke was tickling his throat and stinging his eyes. And, by the way, the goblin himself was not wearing any chain mail. Since when has a traveling cloak been considered any kind of protection?

"Kli-Kli, why did you pester me like that and not put anything on yourself?" I hissed, jabbing a finger at the chain mail covering my chest.

"Oh, they don't have a size to fit me anyway," the goblin answered casually. "And apart from that, I'm very hard to hit. I'm too small."

"Quiet there!" Loudmouth hissed in annoyance.

We crossed a wooden bridge over a wide stream, or a little river, whichever you prefer. The water was flowing under it at the speed of an obese snail, and the streambed was overgrown with some kind of swamp grass. A bend and a sudden halt.

"Mother of mine!" Uncle explained with a quiet whistle.

The road was blocked with tree trunks. The straight, neat young pine trees with their branches trimmed off had been placed on top of each other and there were banners waving in the air behind them. The first was gray and blue—the banner of the kingdom—but the sight of the second set the hair on the back of my neck stirring. A yellow field with the black silhouette of an hourglass.

The flag of death. The banner of the most terrible illness that existed in the world of Siala—the copper plague. I also saw thirty soldiers dressed in white jackets and crimson trousers. The Heartless Chasseurs in person. The nose and mouth of every soldier was covered with a bandage.

As soon as they spotted us, the men behind the barricade raised their bows at the ready. And behind our backs pikemen crept out of the trap that we had not even noticed and lined up quickly and busily, like ants, cutting off the road.

"Halt!" a harsh voice shouted. "Keep your hands in sight! Who are you?"

"We come in the name of the king!" Miralissa shouted, and to confirm her words, she waved a paper with the gray-and-blue seal of the royal house of Stalkon.

Even at the distance of thirty yards that separated us from the blockage, the seal was clearly visible. The bows in the soldiers' hands relaxed a little.

My first fright at the unexpected encounter passed. These were not bandits, and they would listen to us before they sent arrows whistling past our ears. And as for the banner . . . Who could tell what was going on here? Perhaps the peasants were in revolt. Perhaps they hadn't been able to find any other banner, so they'd taken this one out, and there wasn't any plague in the village at all.

"How do I know that royal seal isn't false?" the same voice called out.

"I'll draw you a dozen as good as that one!" one of the pikemen standing behind us shouted.

No one was in any hurry to come out to us.

"Then take a look at this!" Uncle barked. "Or do you want me to ride closer?"

Despite his chain mail, the platoon leader had managed to bare his arm up to the elbow. The tattoo on it was clearly visible.

"Or will any of you white-and-crimson lads dare to say that the Wild Hearts don't serve the Stalkons?"

No one said so. How could they? If the Wild Hearts were traitors, then who could you trust? Nobody even doubted that the tattoo was genuine. As I said earlier, impostors usually had their tattoos removed together with their arm. Or even with their head.

The bows and pikes were lowered, no longer threatening us. But the chasseurs were in no hurry to put their weapons away. They kept hold of them, just in case they might come in handy.

A soldier with a corporal's badge on his sleeve came out to us.

"You're a long way from the Lonely Giant," he said. "Who are you and what are you doing here?"

Like the rest of them, the corporal had his face hidden behind a bandage.

"Is there plague in the village?" Miralissa asked unhurriedly.

"Yes."

How could some ordinary piece of rag save you when not even the much-vaunted magic of the Order was any help? There was only one thing that anyone who caught the copper plague could do—try to dig his own grave in the time he had left. In ancient times entire cities had died of this terrible illness. Not just cities—entire countries! It's enough to recall one of the most terrible epidemics, when the still unified Empire was hit by the plague. Nine out of ten people died. And then half of the survivors died. And the next year half of those who were left followed them.

Nothing had been heard of this curse for a very long time. No one had thought about the plague for more than a hundred and fifty years. And now the old disease had reappeared all of a sudden, out of the blue, in the very heart of Valiostr? There was something fishy going on here.

The plague usually appears on the borders of the kingdom, brought in by refugees from another state, and then spreads like wildfire into the central areas of the country. But on the other hand, it has to appear somewhere first. For instance, if some clever dick digs up the old burial sites. . . .

"Everything is written here," said Miralissa, holding up the royal charter.

The corporal didn't even reach out to take the document.

"There is pestilence in the village, milady. We have been forbidden to touch other people's things in order not to spread the infection through the district. We have also been forbidden to allow anyone either in or out, no matter who they might be. Anyone who disobeys will be executed immediately as a traitor to the king and a propagator of pestilence. I ask you once again: Who are you and what are you doing here?"

"None of your business, you damn chasseur," Hallas muttered to himself, but fortunately the corporal didn't hear him.

"We are on a mission for the king," said Miralissa, with a hint of anger in her voice. "We are on our way to Ranneng. That is all you need to know, corporal. And any hindrance caused to us is regarded as a crime against the crown."

"There is nothing I can do," the corporal muttered, caught on the horns of a dilemma.

The problem was clear enough: on one side an order not to allow anyone through and on the other the royal seal. So try to figure out what to do: Let them through and you'll lose your head; don't let them through, and you're in for big trouble anyway.

"I have my commander's orders," said the corporal, clutching at his last straw.

"What can supersede a command from the king?" Miralissa insisted, sensing that her opponent's defenses were cracking.

"A threat to the life and prosperity of the kingdom," said a voice behind the barrier.

The ranks of soldiers parted and two figures came out to join the corporal. Their faces were concealed by bandages, but they were still easily recognizable as members of the Order. A magician and an enchantress.

"The plague sets all of us on the same level. If the disease escapes from this localized pocket, the country will face catastrophe, Tresh Miralissa."

"I don't believe I have had the pleasure," the elfess said coldly.

"Magicians of the Order of Valiostr, Balshin and Klena," said the man. "Of course, you did not recognize me in this protective mask, but we have met, Tresh Miralissa, at one of the receptions in his majesty's palace."

"Anything is possible," Miralissa said with an indifferent nod. "What has happened here? Can you tell me, magicians?"

"Do you mind if I take a look?" the enchantress asked, holding out her hand.

As Miralissa coolly handed the document to the woman, I saw her nostrils flaring in fury. The elfin princess was not accustomed to having obstacles put in her way.

"You are free to go, corporal," Balshin said in a low voice. The chasseur gave a sigh of relief and withdrew to join his men, leaving the magicians of the Order to deal with us.

"Genuine," said the woman, after making a few passes over the paper.

For a split second the royal document flared up with a pink glow.

"That ought to eliminate any possible infection," said the enchantress, handing the paper back to Miralissa.

"What is going on here is as follows," said the magician, not disconcerted in the least by having to throw his head back to look up at the riders on their horses. "Enchantress Klena and I were riding past the village when the first case of infection appeared. That was three days ago—"

"How did the illness come to be here?" Ell interrupted.

Ah, so I wasn't the only one who was confused about the strange way the pestilence had appeared so dangerously close to Ranneng. Just a few days' journey from the second-largest city in Valiostr.

"We do not know. That still has to be investigated," said Klena. "But the symptoms are authentic. We were able to summon a regiment of Heartless Chasseurs quartered in the city. They closed off all the roads and paths to make sure that not a single inhabitant was able to leave the center of infection and spread the plague across the country."

"And have there been any attempts?" Arnkh boomed from under his helmet.

"There have," the magician said with a perfunctory nod.

A very perfunctory nod. Nobody asked any more questions, although it was clear to all of us what must have happened to the desperate people who found themselves caught in the trap with the victims of the infection. They had been shot with arrows from a distance, that was what. And it made no damn difference who was trying to break through the chasseurs' blockade—healthy peasants with pitchforks or women with children. No one blamed the Heartless Chasseurs, though—it was a matter of kill a few dozen now or expose thousands more to danger.

"And what of the chasseurs themselves?" Miralissa asked.

"Securely protected by magic."

"And since when has magic protected against the Copper Killer?"

"Magic is constantly developing," Klena declared pompously. "The Order has learned how to prevent the illness from infecting people, but there is no way to help those who have been infected before we can protect them."

The longer this conversation went on, the less I liked it. There were just too many things in the story the magicians had told us that didn't fit. And apart from that, they weren't even telling us half the story. If that kind of protective magic did exist, it was clear enough why the chasseurs were still here, and not running as hard as they could away from the plague spot. But then why had the magicians used their wizardry to protect an entire regiment of soldiers, but not done the same for the villagers at the very start of the epidemic when, according to the magicians, only one person was infected?

"How many people in the village are not yet infected?" Miralissa inquired.

"Not a single one," the magician said dispassionately, turning away from her.

Not one? How could that be? Everyone knew that people died on the seventh day, and it had only started three or four days ago.

"Some new form of the disease?" asked Ell. He still had his helmet on.

"Precisely," Balshin replied in the same dispassionate tone.

Miralissa didn't say anything. She was thinking and twirling a small charred stick between the fingers of her left hand. The stick she had used to draw spells in the ash.

Oh no!

What was she thinking? To start a fight with the magicians was madness! I was quite sure she only had to break that stick, spit on it, lick it, or do something else very simple, and the slumbering shamanic magic would awaken. I glanced back, as if casually, at the road. The pikemen were still there, but they were already standing nonchalantly along the sides, talking to each other. Our group wasn't any danger to them, especially since both magicians were dealing with us, so why not have a little chat and leave your cumbersome three-yard pike leaning up against a tree?

"You are on your way to Ranneng?" Klena asked.

"Yes," Miralissa replied curtly.

"For what purpose?"

"On the king's business."

"And why did you travel along a deserted side road, and not the main highway?" the magician asked scathingly.

Now what were they after, may snow vampires tear me apart? Wasn't it clear that our document was genuine and by hindering us this magician was letting himself in for big trouble, not only from an angry king, but also from the Order, which would never condone such headstrong behavior by its members?

"Nobody warned us that it was closed," Hallas growled impatiently.

"All the worse for you," Balshin said, and shrugged.

"And so we cannot pass here?" Miralissa asked, to make absolutely certain.

"Neither pass nor leave. Unfortunately," said the magician, spreading his hands in a gesture of feigned regret. "You will have to stay here until we have defeated the disease. We cannot put the welfare of the kingdom at risk. Naturally, you will be afforded every possible comfort."

"But we are healthy!" Lamplighter exclaimed indignantly, speaking for the first time.

"Perhaps so," the enchantress agreed. "But you have already been told that we cannot take any risks. We shall have to detain you."

"And how long will it take you to defeat the disease?" Ell spat out venomously.

"Three or four months. Then, if there are no new cases, we will lift the quarantine."

"Three months!" Hallas exclaimed, choking on the words.

That left our plans in tatters. If we complied, it would be well into autumn before we reached Hrad Spein, and that meant we wouldn't get back in time. What could we do? Break out the way we had come? But how many men would we lose in breaking out? How many would be felled by arrows, pikes, and the magicians' spells? Almost all of us.

Our last remaining hope was the shamanic spell that Miralissa had prepared. I kept my eyes fixed on that small charred stick twirling between her fingers.

"Quiet, Hallas," she said sharply. "Do you intend to detain us, regardless of the king's order?"

"Yes."

"You may find yourselves in trouble with the Council of the Order. I shall certainly inform Master Artsivus of this," said the elfess, making one final attempt to avoid a fight.

"As you wish," Balshin said with a polite smile. "Inform him, but only after the quarantine has been lifted, not before. You have nothing to fear. Our magic will protect you."

It seemed to me that the magician's advice wasn't worth a spit from the top of the cathedral dome. And the enchantress's cheek had twitched nervously when Miralissa mentioned the Order.

"What will happen if we refuse to obey you?" Ell asked calmly.

"We shall be obliged to use force," Balshin said regretfully.

"Calm down, k'lissang," Miralissa said to Ell. "We shall not spill blood and we shall comply."

"I knew that you would heed the voice of reason," the magician said with a polite bow.

"Where will you accommodate us?" asked Miralissa. She snapped the small stick in half with a casual gesture and threw it away.

The magicians took no notice of the elfess's gesture. What did it matter what she might have broken and thrown away? Balshin and Klena were far too delighted that the haughty elfess had not pulled out her s'kash to pay any attention to such trifles.

"Oh, you need have no concern, Tresh Miralissa! You will be in the chasseurs' camp, it is very—"

Balshin never finished telling us about the camp, because there were sudden howls of horror from the area of the banners. And—why deny it?—I was terrified at first, too. Until that day I'd never seen a human hand strolling down the road all on its own.

Oh yes, at first glance it was a straightforward human hand, only a bit larger. About a hundred times larger. Three riders and their horses could have fitted on its palm.

The monster shuffled its fingers in lively style as it rambled along from the direction of the village straight toward the howling bowmen. As it approached it panted sadly, and the red eyes, set on the joints of each finger, peered disapprovingly at the bellowing men.

Everyone was howling and yelling, the voices of the bowmen supported by a ragged chorus of pikemen. The shouts were growing louder, more and more panic-stricken.

The monster stopped, supported itself on its thumb and little finger, and raised its other three fingers skyward to reveal its palm, a large area of which was occupied by an immense mouth with sparse, needle-sharp teeth. The hand clearly felt it had done enough panting already, so, for the sake of a little variety, it roared.

And that was when everyone started to run. A couple of the very bravest bowmen fired their arrows at the monster, but they got stuck in its finger-legs without hurting the hand at all.

"Get out of here! Run for it! Save us! Into the forest!" Kli-Kli's piercing shouts were taken up by the chasseurs dashing along the road.

"Into the forest! Into the forest! Run for it! Run for it!"

The soldiers in white and crimson disappeared as if the wind had swept them away, leaving behind only the most stupid and those who hadn't found a place to hide yet.

The magicians joined in the fray, shooting fiery beams of light at the hand.

"Come on! Our group has already taken off!" Kli-Kli dug his heels into Featherlight's sides and dashed off after the rapidly receding Wild Hearts.

I followed him, leaving behind the elves and the battle between the magicians, the bravest of the chasseurs, and the monstrous hand.

There was a sudden shrill gust of wind, and I looked back. Miralissa and Ell were galloping right behind me, leaning down low over the necks of their horses.

The monster hand went flying sideways, crushing a few birch trees. The magicians were weaving their hands about constantly, and it was clear that they had the advantage. Little Bee's hooves drummed on the wooden bridge and I caught a brief glimpse of the stream before it flew back and away at tremendous speed. We had broken out. Nobody had even tried to stop us. They were all too busy trying to save their own lives.

"We have to keep moving," Loudmouth gasped. "If they come after us . . ."

Our group had stopped on the summit of the hill from which we had first seen the village of Vishki burning. Nothing had changed—the black smoke was still staining the sky, showing no sign of abating.

"Calm down," said Arnkh, taking off his helmet and running one hand over his sweating bald patch. "Didn't you hear them say that the village is under . . . what's it called?"

"Quarantine," Kli-Kli prompted.

"That's it! Quarantine! They won't stick their noses out for another three months! You've no need to worry about any pursuit."

"Well, then they'll report to Ranneng so that we can be intercepted," Loudmouth persisted.

"Damn it, you stupid man! I said quarantine! They won't send out a messenger or even a lousy pigeon! Isn't that right, Lady Miralissa?" asked Arnkh, turning to the elfess to confirm that he was right.

"If there really was copper plague in the village," she said thoughtfully, keeping her eyes fixed on the sooty smoke rising over the forest.

"But what was it, if not the plague?" asked Marmot, genuinely surprised.

"It could be anything!" Hallas declared. "You can expect anything at all from that Order of theirs. You human beings look the other way and meanwhile the magicians get up to all sorts of dirty business behind your backs. Well, who says I'm wrong?"

The gnome gazed round the group sternly, searching for someone to disagree with his opinion. There were no fools who wanted to get into a fight.

Hallas was right. The Order was always playing with fire. I immediately recalled my dream about the blizzard that had raged in Avendoom after the unsuccessful attempt to destroy the Nameless One with the help of the Horn. That had earned us the Forbidden Territory. And no one knew about the part played in all of that by the Order that everyone loved so much. If we didn't know about one of the magicians' little slips, there might be another one we didn't know about. And the other one might be far more serious. Even if there was plague there, they probably started it themselves. The learned have cast their spell, for their own profit, and too bad for everybody else.

Hallas bent his arm in a gesture known to the whole world since ancient times. The gnome was simply bursting with hate for the Order. I wondered why.

"Forgive me, Lady Miralissa, but this is a sore point with me! The magicians themselves set up the whole thing. I don't know what happened there, but there was some kind of mess-up, and then they sent a dozen bolts of lightning and a hundred fireballs shooting down from the sky to cover their tracks. Flattened the entire village!"

"How do you know they flattened it? Did you see?" Honeycomb boomed.

"A gnome doesn't need to see. We work with fire from when we're kids, and you only get smoke like that if you burn a heap of earth's bones in the furnaces. That's magical fire! I can smell it. That's why they brought the chasseurs here, so they could detain everybody until the magicians finish what they're doing!"

"All right," said Loudmouth, interrupting Hallas's accusations. "Whether there was plague there or something else, we'll never know now, but in any case, we have to get as far away as possible. We can't be too careful."

"But did you see that beast they'd lured in?" Deler asked thoughtfully. "Maybe there are as many hands like that in the village as there are gnomes in the mountain caves!"

"That beast wasn't theirs; Tresh Miralissa created it!" said Kli-Kli. "By the way, milady, how did you know that we'd need a hand like that?"

"I did not know, inestimable Kli-Kli." The elfess's black lips stretched into a venomous smile. "I actually prepared a sleeping spell. They should all have fallen asleep."

"But then where did that beast come from, Tresh Miralissa?" asked Ell, genuinely surprised.

"Ask our green companion that, my faithful k'lissang. He was the one who drew beside my spell! The credit for the appearance of such a creature must go entirely to Kli-Kli."

"How was I to know?" the goblin said with a guilty sniff. "I didn't think you'd written anything special there."

"You ought to be isolated from society, Kli-Kli." Deler chuckled good-naturedly.

"Why, you ought to thank me!" the goblin declared indignantly.

"If not for that hand, who knows how the whole business would have turned out? I told you my grandfather was a shaman. It's hereditary!"

"Playing rotten tricks?" asked Marmot. "If you're a shaman, I'm the leader of the Doralissians!"

"I tell you, I have the blood of the finest goblin shamans running in my veins, including the great Tre-Tre! He's an ancestor of mine through my mother's grandmother."

"That's enough. Loudmouth is right. We need to get as far away as possible," said Miralissa, interrupting Kli-Kli.

"Shall we try the forest?" Honeycomb suggested.

"Go round the village? I don't think that's a very good idea," Uncle said. "The chasseurs could have traps under every tree, and if we run into them again, they won't let us go so easily."

"Do you suggest going back?" asked the elfess, clearly not pleased with this idea. "The ride to the highway is a lot farther than to Ranneng. We would lose a huge amount of time."

"There is another road," said Honeycomb. Like me, he had already removed his chain mail, and now he started drawing a simple map in the sand. "This is the highway." A straight line ran across the sand, looping in its middle like a horseshoe and then straightening out again. "This is Ranneng."

The line ran straight into the blob that represented the city. From the point at which the highway looped, another line ran down and to the right. It crept farther and farther away from the highway until at one point it started running parallel with it, and then converged with the highway again, meeting it right beside the city.

"There's an abandoned track here. Or at least, there used to be."

"You suggest that we ought to take it?"

"Yes, Lady Miralissa. At least it offers us a way out of our situation. The road through Vishki is closed and it is too far to go back."

"It is decided then," the elfess agreed. "We will go back to the place where the track starts and await the return of Milord Alistan, otherwise he will ride on and fall into the hands of the magicians."

"Won't we lose more time, making our way over the hills?" Lamplighter asked doubtfully.

"No," said Honeycomb with a shake of his head. "We'll leave the hills on our left. The area is known as Hargan's Wasteland. Thin forest, ravines, clumps of heather, and not a single person for twenty leagues in all directions. A desolate area. If our enemies are trying to find us, they'll have to look very hard."

"Then what are we waiting for?" Loudmouth growled, putting one foot in a stirrup.

It was already late evening; the July sky was gradually turning paler and the sun had almost set. We set out along the road back with the twilight treading on our heels. All of us were in a subdued mood. The men didn't speak. Hallas puffed on his pipe and swore quietly to himself and Kli-Kli tied knots in a piece of string, threatening to show us all the famous shamanism of the goblins.

24

It took us a long time to find that almost invisible track in the total darkness. Several times Honeycomb stopped the group, dismounted, and walked along the wall of bushes, thoughtfully scratching the back of his head. Then he climbed back into the saddle and we galloped on, moving farther and farther away from the hills and the unfortunate village of Vishki. The point came when we had to light torches—the moonlight was simply not enough—and Loudmouth immediately started grumbling that now even a blind man could see us.

When Honeycomb dismounted for the tenth time, even the imperturbable Marmot started groaning:

"So where is this track of yours? How long can we carry on prowling about in the dark? Let's put it off until tomorrow! We're all tired, and the ling needs to be fed."

"Just wait a bit with that mouse of yours," the huge man retorted. "It's somewhere near here. I think we need to turn round and ride back a bit."

"You said that half an hour ago," muttered Hallas.

"Let's look for it in the morning," said Kli-Kli, supporting Marmot.

The goblin had been tying knots in his string almost without a break. Now he had hundreds of them, and he claimed that very soon they would produce some terrible goblin magic.

No one took any notice of his blather, except for Deler, who asked to be warned when everything was ready so that he could hide as far away as possible from the place where the failed shaman planned to demonstrate his abilities.

"Are you sure this track is here? Have you walked along it yourself?" Eel asked.

"No. I was still a little kid then. My grandfather showed me it. The shepherds used it to take their sheep out to graze all summer in the wasteland. The grass there was really something."

"That's hardly surprising," Kli-Kli commented dryly.

"Do you know something about this place?" Miralissa asked.

"I'll tell you all an interesting story at the halt, if you don't fall asleep."

"I remember!" Honeycomb suddenly howled and slapped himself on the forehead. "I remember! It began beside two trees that leaned toward each other like a pair of drunks!"

"There was something like that," said Ell, brushing aside a lock of hair that had fallen over his eyes. "About fifty yards back."

Everyone heaved a sigh of relief, realizing that the halt they had been anticipating for so long would soon arrive. I myself was barely able to stay in the saddle and my dearest wish was to get down from Little Bee.

"That's it! There they are, the darlings!" Honeycomb exclaimed when the silhouettes of two aspens emerged from the darkness, looming up in isolation above the bushes. "The track starts right between them."

"Right then, a halt." Hallas climbed gratefully out of his saddle and I followed his example. "Uncle! Are we going to eat anything today or do we bed down on an empty stomach?"

"You never think of anything but filling your belly, longbeard." Deler laughed.

Do I need to tell you what the gnome said to that? Everything had come full circle.

"Someone promised to tell us a story," said Arnkh some time later, when we were all sitting round the campfire with hare stew in our bellies.

"If you wish," said Kli-Kli, setting aside his bundle of knotted strings. "What would you like to hear?"

"You mean you know a lot of stories?"

"I am the king's jester, after all," the goblin said, offended. "I have to know them for my job."

"You promised to tell us about Hargan's Wasteland, if I'm not mistaken."

"Ah-ah . . . ," Kli-Kli drawled. "Have none of you ever heard about Hargan's Brigade?"

Some shook their heads, some shrugged indifferently. The name didn't mean anything to anyone.

"You people have such short memories." The goblin sighed. "You know, it all happened only a little less than five hundred years ago."

"Come off it," Loudmouth laughed. "That's time enough to forget anything at all."

"But not the Dog Swallows Brigade to which Avendoom probably owes its very survival to this day."

"Dog Swallows?" Uncle echoed with a frown. "I don't recall any such unit. At least, it doesn't exist in Valiostr . . ."

"It doesn't now, and it never will again," Kli-Kli said in a sad voice. "It all happened during the Spring War. The orcs came pouring out of the Forests of Zagraba in an endless flood, taking everyone by surprise. Tens of thousands of them descended on the Border Kingdom, but the main thrust of the blow was directed at Valiostr—"

"You don't need to tell us that," said Arnkh, interrupting the goblin.

"Who's telling this story, you or me?" Kli-Kli asked furiously. "If you're so smart, you do the talking, and I'll go to bed! But if you can't, keep quiet!"

Arnkh raised both hands in a gesture of submission.

"Grok set his army on the march and gave battle on the banks of the Iselina. For six days the Firstborn tried to force the river, but the men held firm. On the seventh day, at the cost of enormous losses, the orcs broke through Grok's defenses in four places and threw back the army of men, forcing it to retreat to the north. The whole of south Valiostr was lost. There was no news from Shamar, and Grok thought that the Borderland had already been annihilated."

"Ha! The Borderland doesn't surrender that easily! We withstood that siege!" said Arnkh, but fell silent when he caught Kli-Kli's eye.

"Isilia, as usual, did not get involved in the war, hoping that the cup of woe would pass it by. It was pointless to ask for help from Miranueh— your state had never lived at peace with that country. It made absolutely no sense to say anything to the dark elves after the Long Winter came, following the grotesque death of their prince; none of them had even been seen in Valiostr for many years. . . . The kingdom was left to face the enemy alone. Only destiny and the army, gentlemen, could halt the flood of orcs."

"The Firstborn had never attacked in such numbers before. That was a terrible time," Uncle said with a nod.

"The humans despised the other races too much. How could they accept half animals as their allies? And then this happened. No one had anticipated the coming of the orcs, and they paid a heavy price for their lack of vigilance. After a long retreat, the weary army engaged the Firstborn under the walls of Ranneng and lost the battle. The capital was taken and then destroyed. The army and the king retreated to the north. The exhausted men, constantly harassed by the advance units of the enemy, fell back toward Avendoom in order to fight its final battle there—they had nowhere else to retreat to. Except to the Cold Sea, or past the Lonely Giant into the Desolate Lands.

"Either of those would have been suicide. All they could do was to die with dignity. Grok needed time to prepare for the final battle—time which, unfortunately, he didn't have. The army had to rest, if only for one day.

"This area used to be covered with thick forest. There weren't any villages yet . . . that is, there were some, of course, but pitifully few. In those times, no one thought about building a road or a main highway, there was only a fairly large track from Ranneng to Avendoom. And it happened to pass straight through the area that is now known as Hargan's Wasteland. In our times the old road has been forgotten and abandoned, but then it was the vital thread that connected the central cities of Valiostr. The army retreated along it. A council that included both soldiers and members of the recently founded Order of Magicians decided that part of the army had to be sacrificed so that it could hold up the invaders for at least a few days. The area was advantageous—full of forests and marshes, with just one road, which was the only way the enemy could advance. At one point the road crossed a deep ravine with impassable swamps on its left and its right. It was decided to hold the enemy back here for as long as possible. To allow the main human forces to get as far away as possible."

The goblin broke off, wrapped himself in his cloak, and continued.

"They put out the call and looked for volunteers. People who would decide to stay and give battle. You men are amazing creatures. Sometimes you'll tear each other's throats out for a copper or some piece of rubbish, and sometimes you decide to cover your comrades' backs, knowing that you'll never get out alive. Just over three thousand soldiers volunteered. Three thousand men willing to condemn themselves to death, to dig their nails into the slopes of that ravine, but not let the orcs pass. Four hundred of them were chosen; it would simply have been stupid to sacrifice the rest."

"Well, I would have argued with that," Hallas, who was sitting beside me, muttered to himself—but quietly, so that the goblin wouldn't hear.

"The men who were chosen to stay behind were named the Dog Swallows. I don't know why. The main army left. The new unit was commanded by an old soldier who had commanded a regiment with Grok. He was called Hargan, and a grateful posterity later named this place after him. The defenders' primary goal was to hold back the enemy for at least one day, no more than that. But they managed to halt the orc army's advance for a full four. In that time not a single orc got through. Hargan's soldiers gave Grok's army precious breathing space, and time to prepare for the encounter at Avendoom. If not for the Swallows, there's no knowing how the history of the kingdom would have gone.

"The subsequent events are well known to you. Grok gave battle and the orcs broke into Avendoom, but then the dark elves arrived on the scene. No one had been expecting them. Neither the men nor, in particular, the orcs. The elves forgot their quarrel with men and came to their aid at the very last moment. The dark ones could not ignore such a good opportunity to settle scores with their cousins. The Spring War was won. And that, I think, is all."

"And this wasteland?"

"The wasteland?" the jester echoed. "The wasteland remained a wasteland. A new road appeared somewhere else, of its own accord. No one wanted to disturb the bones of the fallen warriors. But then, to be quite honest, most of them were not actually buried. People had too many other things to deal with, setting the country to rights after the

war. The years passed and Hargan's Brigade gradually began to be forgotten. The road gradually fell into disuse. Only the shepherds used it
to move their sheep. The land round here is really rich, and so the grass
is high. Only the name was left—Hargan's Wasteland—and with time
people even forgot where that had come from. Now not even the old
men remember those soldiers' feat of heroism."

An oppressive silence fell round the campfire. Each of us was thinking about those men who stood firm against the crooked yataghans of
the orcs and did not retreat.

"Gnomes would never have forgotten something like that."

"Or dwarves!"

I felt shame for my race. Probably for the first time in my life I felt
ashamed of people for forgetting such a sacrifice. . . .

"Come on, Loudmouth," grunted Lamplighter, getting up off the
ground. "We're on the first watch tonight."

No one spoke to anyone else. One by one we all went to bed, leaving
only the solitary figure of the jester still sitting beside the small campfire, gazing at the dance of the flames. . . .

*The slanting downpour from the sky was like whips lashing at their clothes,
it soaked them with its soft hands, it was cold, warm, angry, prickly, stinging, caressing, biting.*

*The soldiers were tired, cold, and soaked through. The bowmen squinted
furiously up at the sky—moisture spoiled the bows, and no elves' tricks for
preserving the condition of the string did any good.*

*"Wencher!" Hargan called in a low voice, wiping his wet face with his
hand.*

"Yes?" responded the commander of the swordsmen, running up to him.

*"Take your lads. Grab every ax you can find in the brigade and cut down
the trees on that side of the ravine."*

"Very well," said the soldier, without batting an eyelid.

*"Drag the trunks over to this side, and then we'll dismantle the bridge.
We'll arrange a pleasant welcome for the Firstborn."*

*The other man gave a gap-toothed smile, clenched his fist in the military
salute, and ran off to rouse his men.*

Hargan sighed.

It was hard. Ye gods! It was so hard to look at them! He was an old man, almost sixty years old—he wasn't afraid of dying. But the men fate had decided that he should command . . . boys. Twenty-year-old, thirty-year-old boys. He regarded them all as too young to die in front of this bridge thrown across the abyss of a nameless ravine.

The orcs had attacked suddenly. No one had been expecting this war, and during the first days of the catastrophe that overwhelmed the land of Valiostr, the army had been defeated in battle after battle. And now there was only one hope left. Hargan and his men had only one goal—to detain the enemy for as long as possible, until the main human forces could dig in at the new capital of Valiostr. The retreating army was already far behind them, and in front of them, beyond the curtain of mist, the army of the enemy was waiting.

The orcs were in no great hurry. What difference did it make if they spilled the humans' blood an hour earlier or an hour later? They were the Firstborn, they would conquer all the lands, and men . . . Men would be dispatched to feed the worms. First the Valiostrans, then the men of Miranueh, then it would be the turn of the gnomes and dwarves, and finally of their detested relatives, the elves.

The rain eased off somewhat until it was no more than a gentle drizzle. The air was filled with fine drops of water. It was early morning and mist was rising from the ground in thick white streamers. Three hundred yards away, on the opposite side of the ravine, the road was concealed in a dense white shroud and they could only guess how far away the enemy was. Yesterday the scouts had reported that the advance units of the orcs were at a distance of one day's march. But that was yesterday. . . .

The bottom of the ravine was hidden from sight. Its walls were not actually sheer, but they could certainly not be called shallow. If you were careless going down, you could easily break your neck. Somewhere far below there was a stream tinkling; sometimes you could hear it above the rain. So after they dismantled the bridge, the orcs would first have to climb down one slippery clay slope and then climb up another. That was the only way they could reach the fortifications.

The brigade had only been named that morning, when the final soldiers of Grok's army retreated, leaving the volunteers alone to face the foe. Nobody at

protecting themselves and covering their comrades. Blidkhard's men came off worse—not all of them were quick enough to put down their bows and pick up the wooden arrow shields lying at their feet.

Hargan felt one arrow strike the board, then another. Another buried itself in the ground beside his foot. The soldier beside him, trying to take cover behind a small round shield, cried out when one of the arrows hit him in the thigh, uncovered himself for an instant, and took a second arrow in the neck. He wheezed hoarsely and tumbled to the ground.

The bombardment finally ended, and Hargan cast aside the board bristling with arrows. The enemy's arrows were everywhere—in the ground, in shields, in the wall of the fortifications, and in men.

"Crush those bastards!" Blidkhard yelled hoarsely. "Come on then, you sons of whores!"

The bowmen took up their bows again.

"Fire at will!"

"Wencher!" Hargan roared. "What are our casualties?"

"Eighteen killed!" the answer came back after a while. "Mostly Blidkhard's lads! I haven't counted the wounded yet!"

"Fire!"

Slap! Slap! Slap! *The bowstrings thwacked against the mittens and the arrows whistled through the air, drowning out even the howls of the dying.*

The fifth wave of attackers had taken advantage of the pause in the bombardment by Blidkhard's bowmen and fused with the fourth. They were running toward the ravine, with the sixth wave already following them. The enemy's bowmen were no longer firing; they didn't want to become a target for the Dog Swallows. The Wind Jugglers began choosing their targets. One of the enemy fell every second, but time had been lost and a large body of men disappeared into the ravine, bolstering their courage by shouting.

"Wake up, you whores! Keep your eyes open! As soon as the enemy appears, move back behind the swords! Target the sixth line! Together, fire!"

"Stop them shooting!" shouted Siena, bounding up to Hargan. Her chainmail hood had slipped back off her head, her light brown hair was tousled, her face was pale and determined. "Let them get down into the ravine! And as soon as that happens, move back from the wall!"

"Cease fire!" Hargan roared. "Withdraw behind the swordsmen!"

"Cease fire! Withdraw! Withdraw!" The order ran along the line.

"Are you sure you know what you're doing, Lady Siena?" Hargan *would be taking a risk by trusting in the young enchantress's talent.*

"Yes! Now just don't interfere!"

The only ones left by the wall were the enchantress, the two shield-bearers from her bodyguard, and the centurions.

The sixth wave slithered down into the ravine, shouting triumphantly. The seventh and eighth waves were on their way.

"We won't be able to hold them," the commander of Siena's bodyguard *hissed through his teeth. "By Sagra, I swear we won't be able to hold them!"*

Hargan didn't answer, hearing only Siena's whisper, which seemed to drown out even the shouts of the enemy.

All of a sudden the fog burst into flames and was transformed into a mass of liquid fire, making the ravine look like the inside of one of the gnomes' furnaces. The blast of heat struck Hargan in the face and he felt as if his eyebrows and hair had burst into flame. The men staggered back from the heaving fiery abyss, and the enchantress was left alone, staring unflinchingly into the scorching flames. Everybody down below in the ravine must have been burnt to a cinder.

Siena had incinerated about four hundred men at a single stroke!

The enchantress began slowly sinking down onto the ground, but her shield-bearers dashed over to her and caught her before she could fall.

"Are you alive, milady?" asked the sergeant from the Borderland.

"Y-yes," she said uncertainly, and spat blood. *Her hand was clutching the amulet and there were glowing strings of sparks running across the silvery droplet.*

"Quick! Get her to the healer!" Hargan barked.

After seeing what had happened to their comrades, the seventh and eighth waves were beating a hasty retreat. Blidkhard's men managed to fire several times more before the enemy moved out of the range of their arrows.

Silence fell in the ranks of the defenders.

The opposite side of the ravine and the road were littered with bodies. The black, charred walls of the ravine gave out a smell of soot and burnt meat. Thick smoke from this hellish scene rose high into the air above the soldiers' heads.

"Ah, we gave them a good battering," Wencher *said delightedly as he came up to* Hargan. *"It's just a shame that the swords had no work to do."*

"You'll get your turn! We haven't killed all of them."

"Yes, there are about three hundred left. But they're not likely to attack. They'll wait for the orcs."

Morning came and merged imperceptibly into day. But the road remained deserted. The enemy had pulled back and concealed himself behind the dark wood, and the only sound from that side of the ravine was the cawing of the crows feasting on the corpses. By noon the sky was clouded over even more thickly, the rain had become a downpour, and the road was almost invisible behind the wall of falling water.

From somewhere beyond the shroud of rain there came the faint rumbling of drums.

"Everyone to his station!" yelled Hargan, emerging from under the lean-to and putting on his helmet.

The rumbling of the drums was moving closer; the orcs had moved onto the offensive.

"Can't see a thing!" said a bowman with straw-blond hair and no helmet, gazing into the white shroud.

"Listen, then!" barked Bildkhard, who was walking along the line of bowmen. "Listen to what your commander tells you!"

Hargan could not stand giving impassioned speeches. He was not Grok, nor was he some pompous, self-important colonel, to go ranting on about duty, honor, and devotion, but right now he really ought to offer his lads some kind of moral support.

"Soldiers! Our time has come! Let's show these Firstborn what we're made of! Let them break their teeth on our shields! The more of the brutes we kill, the fewer our lads will have to stick and bleed at Avendoom! Let's make Grok's job easier! Slash, stab, and cut! Kill them the same way they kill us! Show no mercy!"

And, like the last time, the cry echoed down the ranks of men:

"NO MERCY!"

The volley of arrows struck at the orcs but, unlike the men of the First Human Assault Force, they made rational use of their shields. The huge rectangular sheets of metal covering the heads of the Firstborn allowed them to weather the attack of Blidkhard's bowmen with practically no casualties. The shields parted, and another swarm of arrows flew out at the humans through the gaps. Now Hargan's soldiers had to hide behind their shields and wait out *the bombardment. The orcs seized their chance, losing no time in moving forward to the very edge of the ravine.*

Another volley from the brigade's bowmen. The impenetrable barrier of the orcish shields. And an immediate volley in reply.

Hargan had no time to hide, and an arrow bounced off his breastplate. He swore vilely as he saw the orcs flood over into the ravine.

"Come on, you whores! Shoot! Or they'll roast your heels for you!"

While the orcs were climbing down and then climbing up again, the bowmen managed to loose off six salvos. During the storming of the ravine the shields of the Firstborn were less effective, the formation fell apart, and the arrows finally began to inflict significant losses.

On the orders of their commander, the Wind Jugglers once again divided into two sections. The first lashed at the advancing wave of the enemy, while the second sought out the archers constantly firing at the men from among the mass of the orcs.

Another arrow whistled past Hargan's head and yet another hit the light-haired archer in the stomach. His light chain mail didn't save him and he dropped his bow and fell.

"Swordsmen!" Hargan commanded. "Another twenty paces back! Maintain your spacing!"

The order to leave the wall might have seemed stupid to many. After all, this was a spot where you could take a stand and repel attack after attack, while withdrawing meant giving the enemy the chance to maneuver, gather his wits after the climb, and go on the attack. But a simple defensive trick like that wouldn't work against the orcs. The only thing that would save you here was to close formation and strike like a battering ram, and for that you had to move back. The line of men began slowly withdrawing, protected by shields and bristling with spears, swords, and axes. The orcs had already reached the stakes set in the ground and the bowmen's final arrows were striking them, piercing straight through their armor.

The bowmen were already running toward the waiting swordsmen, slipping between them and forming a new second line of defense. Hargan withdrew with them, leaving only Fox's crossbowmen behind.

"Come on, Fox!"

But the old war dog knew well enough what to do.

Forty crossbows suddenly appeared before the eyes of the startled orcs who had already begun climbing over the wall.

Thwack!

A massive, invisible chain crashed into the ranks of the Firstborn, sending them flying backward so that they knocked their own comrades off their feet and dragged them back down to the bottom of the ravine.

The soldiers slung their crossbows behind their backs and dashed toward that secure wall of shields and swords. The first orc climbed over the fortifications and immediately collapsed with an arrow in his neck. He was quickly followed by another two, then another four . . . and then there were dozens of the Firstborn jumping down onto the ground.

"Swordsmen! On one knee!" Hargan barked.

The sergeants repeated their commander's order and the front line went down on their right knees.

"Fire, you whores!"

The bowmen standing in the second row didn't need to be reminded of the basic rules of war—if the front line gives you the chance, then lash away at the enemy until your arm is exhausted or he manages to reach you! The arrows whizzed over the heads of the swordsmen and halted the running orcs.

"Will you look at that!" someone beside Hargan said with a whistle. "Stubborn, aren't they, the mangy dogs!"

The orcs weren't bothered at all by the death of their comrades. There were at least a hundred of the enemy facing the ranks of humans now. And more and more of them kept climbing over the wall of the fortifications. Then the orcs' bowmen appeared on the fortifications constructed with such care by Hargan's soldiers.

Before the two forces clashed, Blidkhard's men fired for a second time. And while the bowmen mostly tried to pick off the orcs' archers, Fox's lads, who had already reloaded their crossbows, aimed them at the advancing mass of Firstborn.

"Stand firm! Lock shields! Lower spears! Maintain formation! Stand fiiirm . . ."

Impact. Shield struck against shield with a deafening, indescribable clatter. Uproar, shouts, the clash of weapons. For an instant the spears halted the avalanche of orcs, then they sank down under the weight of the bodies, and the surviving Firstborn came within striking distance for a yataghan.

The men withheld the pressure of the enemy for just a few seconds, and then their line snapped under the ferocity of the attack like a flawed string.

Now there were only scattered groups of soldiers fighting to hold back the pressure: in the best case ten or fifteen soldiers opposing the enemy, and in the worst case only isolated individuals. Somehow they beat the orcs back, somehow the men had successfully weathered the first, most dangerous rush, and they were slowly but surely forcing the orcs back toward the wall.

An arrow glinted in the air, then another. Hargan swore, assuming that the orcs had managed to send in more archers, but when he looked, he spotted thirty bowmen led by Blidkhard right at the back of his brigade. The bowmen had created space for themselves by moving back to a safe distance, and now they were firing at the attackers, choosing their targets. Several of the Firstborn tried to reach the bowmen, but their way was blocked by Wencher's swordsmen, who shielded the Wind Jugglers.

Bolts of lightning began raining down from the dark clouds with a dry crackling sound, striking down the orcs one after another. Armor was no protection against Siena's magic. Before Hargan's very eyes a bolt of lightning appeared from somewhere up in the sky, divided into branches, and felled seven orcs at once, leaving behind nothing but black earth and charred armor.

The Firstborn flinched and faltered, unable to withstand the rain of lightning and hail of arrows. From somewhere behind the enemy, the war drums sounded, calling the retreat. The orcs withdrew tidily, in good order, leaving behind a small detachment to cover the main forces. But the men had taken fresh heart and they struck a crushing blow against the wall of shields, beating down the enemy to right and left, while those bowmen who had not changed their bows for swords in the course of the battle ran up, ignoring the battle raging around them, and began showering arrows on the Firstborn who were crossing the ravine.

Not one of the detachment of orcs covering the retreat was left alive.

Blidkhard spat, then he looked his commander in the eye and said: "Don't you go thinking that we've beaten them off. This is only the advance force of the orcs' army. The main forces haven't arrived yet; this lot just tried to take us in a rush. It didn't work. They didn't even have a single shaman with them, otherwise our enchantress wouldn't have got away with much magic. But when the Bloody Axes or the Gruun Ear-Gougers get here, they'll brush us aside like a feather. We won't even last an hour against those clans."

"By the way, how is our enchantress?"

"I'm alive," Siena replied.

"I'm glad your health is in good order, and thank you for the help."

"It wasn't me," the girl said, embarrassed.

"How's that?" asked Hargan, raising one eyebrow. "Then who was it?"

"I mean, it wasn't just me." The enchantress became even more embarrassed. "The amulet helped."

Hargan glanced at the magical drop of silvery metal.

"My teacher said it would protect me against the shamanism of the orcs. The amulet neutralizes that magic, if it is directed at me. And it turned out that it also restores my strength. This time I tried to use it in a slightly different way, and it gave me so much power I was almost crushed."

The rumble of war drums drifted above a world soaked in blood. During the night the orcs had attacked the humans' fortifications eight times. They had managed to force their way past the wall three times, despite the hail of arrows from the bowmen and the determination of soldiers who stood to the death. Every time the orcs were thrown back the losses had been greater. The Firstborn simply went on and on testing the mettle of the Dog Swallows. The ravine was half full of bodies. There were almost no arrows left and the bowmen had to pick up what the orcs had sent them in order to manage to return the fire from the wave of attackers.

Hargan's brigade had done the impossible—it had held out against the enemy for almost four days, giving Grok's army a huge start. The commander glanced round at the few survivors. Thirty-nine men. Thirty-nine tired, bandaged, bloodstained men. The only ones who had survived this far, who had endured.

Blidkhard was gone. The young Borderman protecting the enchantress was gone. And the girl herself had been killed. After Siena destroyed one of the enemy's shamans, the orcs had set out specifically to hunt her down, and during the last sally they had eventually succeeded, managing to surround her and her bodyguards.

But meanwhile, at the cost of catastrophic losses, the men had forced the orcs to show them respect. They had forced a race that despised everyone else living in Siala to act with caution and not simply come dashing headlong across that cursed ravine.

The soldiers would not survive the ninth attack. Everyone who was still alive knew that.

"We'll show the Firstborn how soldiers ought to die!" said Fox, picking up his beloved flails and listening to the rumble of the approaching drums.

"Yes, we'll show them," said Hargan, getting up off the ground. "Look, Fox, it's stopped raining!"

"That's a good sign."

"Raise the banner! Bugler, sound the alert. Bowmen to the battle line! Kill the enemy, show no mercy!"

And the orcs advancing on those cursed fortifications that would not sur-render heard the cry that others before them had heard and feared each time they retreated from the walls of the ravine.

"NO MERCY!"

25

THE DANCER IN THE SHADOWS

Harold!" said someone, cautiously touching my shoulder. "Harold, get up."

I opened my eyes and looked at the jester, who was leaning down over me.

"Kli-Kli!" I groaned in desperation. "Now why aren't you asleep?"

He looked at me reproachfully and made himself comfortable on a saddlebag.

"You were shouting last night," said Kli-Kli. "What was it, nightmares?"

"It was all your fault," I muttered.

"Eh?"

"You tell us all those stories, and then they give me no peace all night long."

"What stories? You mean Hargan's Brigade?"

"Yes, I was dreaming all night about them fighting the orcs."

"Oho!" Kli-Kli exclaimed admiringly.

"By the way, Alistan and the lads arrived during the night," the goblin threw out casually.

"Why didn't you say so straightaway?" I asked, jumping to my feet.

"Shhh!" the joker hissed, opening his eyes wide. "Don't yell like that. Can't you see everyone's asleep?"

It was true. Even though it was already light, everyone was still lying wrapped up in their traveling blankets. Only Deler and Hallas were walking round the border of the camp, keeping watch over our rest.

The jester had not lied about our comrades' return. I spotted Markauz's huge steed and the horses of the Wild Hearts who had arrived with him.

"Then why did you wake me up?"

"I told you, you were shouting. And I wanted to tell you before the others what it was that our Tomcat sniffed out."

"Then tell me."

"He was right all along. There was something going on behind our backs. He and Egrassa got there just in time. The tracker's instincts led him to a small forest glade quite a long way off the highway. And there were three fellows there, every one of them exactly like the sorcerers who sneaked into Stalkon's palace. Tomcat says they all had rings like the attackers that night."

"What rings do you mean?"

"Ooooooh . . . ," the goblin gasped disappointedly. "I can see you just slept through the whole thing. All the men who attacked the palace had rings made like ivy. That's one of the Nameless One's emblems. So that they could recognize each other. Anyway, these lads in the glade had got a fire going and put a pot over it. I don't know what they were planning to cook up, but it certainly wasn't a fancy cake. As soon as the purple smoke started rising out of the pot—"

"Purple?" I asked.

I hated that color ever since Miralissa had sent me off to that incredible vision when I was being introduced to the key. Besides, it's a color for the rich and privileged.

"I was surprised, too, but that's exactly the way Tomcat tells it. And don't you interrupt! Well, then . . . You've put me off now, Harold!" Kli-Kli whispered furiously.

"Purple smoke," I prompted him.

"Ah, right! Well then, as soon as the purple smoke started rising out of the pot, Egrassa took his bow and killed the two shamans so fast, they never even knew what was happening. Tomcat overturned the pot and stamped out the fire, and then the creature that had been following all the way appeared out of thin air. Tomcat sensed it a long time ago, only it was invisible. It was some kind of tracker dog. Anyway, they killed it and set off to catch up with us—"

"And it took them all this time to do it," I said acidly, completing the goblin's story.

"Just wait, will you!" Kli-Kli said exasperatedly, jumping to his feet.

"Now look, you've put me off again. I'm not going to tell you anything."

"They set off back to catch us up," I said hastily.

"Only they didn't get very far," said the goblin, sitting back down beside me again. "Either Tomcat and Egrassa missed one of those skunks, or the elf didn't shoot fast enough, but one of the shamans must have managed to raise the alarm. Anyway, the road was blocked off in front of them and behind them by several squads of men who appeared out of nowhere. And Tomcat sensed that they'd started working their sorcery again somewhere close to the place where he'd just been. There must have been another group of sorcerers in the forest, but so far they'd been keeping quiet, and that was why Tomcat hadn't sensed them. The Nameless One's followers had our lads caught in a trap, so Tomcat and Egrassa had to turn off into the forest to get away from them, and that's why it took them so long to get here. Their pursuers dropped back, there was no point in hunting the two of them through the undergrowth and fallen trees—the elf's too good at confusing his tracks. And a day later, when Tomcat and Egrassa came out onto the road, they ran into Alistan and Eel. And that basically is the whole story."

"Brrrr! I don't understand a thing."

"You're not the only one." The jester sighed. "The count and the elves were talking all night. It seems there are more shamans in Valiostr than Doralissians in the Steppes of Ungava. And the Nameless One's supporters are absolutely countless. And then there's your Master and his henchmen, and the strange magicians in the plague village. All hunting us, and all using magic to do it. It's quite likely that if Tomcat and Egrassa hadn't interfered in time with the spell those shamans were working, our group wouldn't exist any longer."

"But someone has worked the magic. You told me that someone else could have replaced the dead sorcerers."

"So what?" The jester shrugged. "You have to understand that shamanism isn't the wizardry of the Order, its laws are quite different. It only has to be knocked slightly off course and it turns out quite different from how the person working it intended. Remember the hand monster! Well, it's the same thing here. There's no knowing what it eventually turned into. We're still alive, anyway."

"Where did you get all your brains from, Kli-Kli?"

"From my grandfather, he was a shaman."

"Yes, so you've told me a hundred times. So you think that whoever was plotting against us will simmer down now?"

"Why?"

"Well, you just said that the shamanism didn't work."

"If it didn't work the first time, it will the second," the goblin said with a shrug. "Working magic's no problem for these lads, they'll send some terrible monster with big teeth after us and then just disappear, as if they'd never even existed. The job's done, their Master's instructions have been carried out, they can hide away until the Nameless One comes out from behind the Needles of Ice."

"They don't have long to wait."

"That's what I'm saying. We need to get to Hrad Spein as quickly as possible and spoil the Nameless One's mood for another five hundred years or so."

Hallas came up to us.

"Listen, lads," said the gnome, taking his pipe out of his mouth and blowing smoke rings. "It's time to wake everyone up, or they'll sleep until the coming of the Nameless One."

"Well, let's wake them up then," said the jester, jumping to his feet and completely forgetting all his worries. "Don't happen to have a bucket of cold water handy, do you?"

The complete absence of wind promised a very hot day. Almost as hot as the day before, and the day before that, and the day before that, and . . . I could carry on for a long time.

No one was particularly surprised when at noon we found ourselves roasting in a charming oven.

I personally always anticipated that time of day with a shudder. Neither a wet rag nor the goblin's jokes and jingles were any help. But even so, everyone listened to the jokes and even laughed. Kli-Kli really pulled out all the stops in his efforts to demonstrate the skills of a royal court jester.

The group was complete once again and, despite the heat, we were in an exceptionally good mood . . . even me. Only every now and then a shadow of anxiety ran across Miralissa's face. Once, as I drew level with the elfess's horse, I heard a snatch of her conversation with Egrassa. She was still concerned about the shamans cooking up something horrible in their pots far behind us. From what she said it seemed that they wouldn't rest until they had completed their sorcery.

I trusted the elfess's intuition completely. The Nameless One's minions could send some kind of filthy garbage crashing down on our heads at any moment. As they say, the laws of universal beastliness always take effect just when you're not expecting anything.

That was why, to keep my nerves nice and calm, I kept glancing sideways at Tomcat in case he sensed anything in advance. But the overweight Wild Heart and failed magician of the Order remained serenely calm, even cheerful. And so the uneasy feeling that had overcome me gradually eased.

Hargan's Wasteland was a welter of tall grass and low tangles of heather. Sometimes the narrow line of the path was completely hidden under the grassy covering. Our ears were set buzzing by the chirring of thousands of crickets. When we rode into particularly thick grass the gray-green trilling insects cascaded out from under the hooves of the horses, complaining at our invasion of their kingdom.

After a while, we made our way between massive boulders of black granite, each the size of a small house, and came upon a rickety old hut. Honeycomb said that the scythe men who made the winter hay for the surrounding villages spent the nights in it. The long rows of mown hay lying across the grassy meadows confirmed what he had said.

"It's a long way to the next village; how long will they have to cart it?" Uncle asked in surprise.

"This is the best grass in the whole district. They come here from twenty leagues away," said Honeycomb. "And the scythe men come for the whole summer. There's plenty of hay for everyone and to spare."

"But no cart will get through here. Look how far they have to drive from the road. Half a day at the least," Uncle protested.

"Ah, it's plain to see that you're no country boy."

"You're the country boy here, graybeard. I spent all my young days in Maiding," said Uncle.

An hour after that, when the track completely disappeared and our group had to advance through the meadows of grass and mazes of bushes without being able to see the way, Loudmouth spotted a large herd of cows, about two hundred head. The animals were solemnly browsing on the juicy grass, flicking their tails lazily to drive away the buzzing clouds of midges hovering around them. We were seen, and a dozen shaggy, black-and-white herdsmen's dogs came dashing over, barking at the uninvited travelers.

Arnkh hissed through his teeth and reached for his crossbow, but a sharp whistle rang out across the meadow and the dogs ran back, growling in annoyance. Only the largest of them, no doubt the leader, stopped not far away from us and began observing our group with cautious interest.

"Just look at the way that beast is watching us," Deler muttered.

"Didn't you know they feed on dwarves?" Hallas chuckled, earning himself a dark look from his partner.

"You'll open your mouth once too often someday, longbeard. I'll take my favorite chair and belt you."

The gnome didn't even feel it necessary to respond.

The herdsman who had called off the dogs was also observing us, shading his eyes against the sun with one hand. He stared as if he was watching some kind of marvel, as if we were no ordinary horsemen riding by, but the twelve gods of Siala with the Nameless One in tow. The boy herdsman standing beside his older comrade had his mouth open so wide I felt afraid one or two hundred flies would go flying in.

The sight really was an amazing one for them. It's not every century that you come across an entire platoon of strangers from different races, all armed to the teeth, in the heart of a wasteland so far away from the nearest inhabited village that not even every shepherd would risk going into it.

Kli-Kli couldn't resist the temptation, and he stuck his tongue out at the young herdsman, frightening the boy half to death. It was obviously the first time the village lad had ever seen a goblin.

"Well now, Kli-Kli," said Eel, opening his mouth for the first time that day, "now there'll be talk all winter long. The boy will tell everyone he saw a live ogre."

"Who's an ogre?" the goblin said resentfully. "Me? Ogres roar like this!"

The goblin set up a miserable howling, frightening not only the little

herdsman and the dogs, who began barking again, but also half the
horses of our group.

"Quiet down, Kli-Kli!" Marmot said irritably. "You'll spoil Invincible's
appetite for a whole month."

"I was only showing how ogres roar," the goblin explained.

"Ah, come on. You're useless," Deler grumbled. "That's the way your
dear departed granny roars, not a full-grown ogre. Show him, Mumr."

Lamplighter, who was riding behind me, was only too delighted to
do as the dwarf asked, and he produced a sound that almost made me
fall off my horse. The herdsmen's dogs started howling in fright behind
our backs.

"Hey you lot!" Uncle shouted to our little group. "You dratted come-
dians! Stop frightening the crickets!"

"Oh, come on, Uncle," Deler shouted. "There's nothing else to do."

The sergeant just flapped his hand at us and gave up.

For the rest of the day nothing important happened to our party.

Another two days of riding across the wasteland flew by. We were crossing a huge area at the heart of Valiostr that people had never got around
to developing. The famous impenetrable forests were on our right.

"The day after tomorrow we ought to reach the highway," Honeycomb said on the third day of the journey.

"Eh, the sooner the better. I want some beer." Deler sighed. "I start to
get vicious without my beer."

The song of a lark trilled out in the sky.

"There's going to be rain," Tomcat said after a long silence.

Everyone looked round at the same time. There was a line of storm
clouds expanding along the horizon: dark violet, with occasional patches
of blue-black.

"Hoo-ray!" said Marmot. "The coolness we've all been waiting for is
on its way."

The ling on his shoulder livened up and twitched its pink nose excitedly. Obviously it could sense the approaching storm, too.

"I just hope we don't get caught out," Tomcat muttered, casting a
concerned glance at the black line of cloud.

It had already swollen up, like a goatskin filled to overflowing with water, and seemed to have moved a bit closer. This was not just rain coming toward us, it was a genuine tempest.

No one heard what Tomcat had said. Well, almost no one.

Deler set his hat dashingly on the back of his head and started singing:

If you have a rope on your neck—there will be treason under the mountains.
If you tread clay with your feet—you'll get a sharp knife in your back.
If you fall asleep in disgrace—your dreams will be shattered by an arrow.
And you will not forge strong fetters for holding your friends or your enemies!
If you do not wish to enter the world of shadows—strike first and kill if you can!
Strike first and kill if you can!

"Why so gloomy?" Kli-Kli asked after listening to the dwarf's simple little song.

"That's the way it ought to be," Deler said solemnly. "That's the war march of the dwarves."

"It sounds better for marching to the chamber pot than against the enemy," Hallas said scornfully.

"Some connoisseur of war marches you are!" Deler retorted. "You bearded midgets don't even have any like that."

"Shut up! Right now!" Tomcat growled.

The gnome and the dwarf stopped arguing and gaped at him in astonishment.

"Oh, come on, Tomcat," Deler said, clearing his throat. "Nothing terrible's going to happen. We've already made up, haven't we, Hallas?"

Hallas nodded eagerly.

"It's nothing to do with you!" the tracker exclaimed, stopping his horse and staring fixedly up at the sky. The storm clouds were closer now; they had licked away a quarter of the blue sky. A distant rumble of thunder was carried to us on a light wind.

"What's disaster?" asked Loudmouth, who also had his eyes fixed on the horizon. He had been infected by the tracker's alarm.

"Shut up, will you!" Tomcat growled irritably, sniffing at the air.

Speaking for myself, I couldn't smell anything at all. So what if it did rain a bit and we got wet? What was there to get all alarmed and excited about?

"And the day started so well," Kli-Kli said dejectedly.

"Those bastard children of lowdown skunks did it after all!" Tomcat whispered. He dug his heels into the sides of his horse and hurried to catch up with the elves and Alistan, leaving us behind, bewildered, at the back of the group.

"Who was that he was swearing about?" Hallas asked, staring in amazement at Tomcat's wild gesticulations as he spoke to Miralissa.

Whatever it was that Tomcat had sensed, Miralissa and Markauz both looked alarmed. And Ell kept glancing at the advancing clouds.

"What did I tell you, Harold," Kli-Kli whispered.

"What?" I asked mechanically, trying like everyone else to see what Tomcat had spotted in the sky.

"Do you ever listen? I said the shamans would never stop until they managed to work their magic."

Meanwhile the tracker had finished explaining something to Miralissa. She looked at Alistan, and he nodded decisively.

"What's happened?" asked Uncle, barely able to contain himself.

"Let's go and ask," Arnkh suggested wisely.

During our journey a certain order of travel had been established. Alistan and the elves always rode at the front. They spoke about subjects that only interested them and made decisions for us about matters of importance for the group. The Wild Hearts kept company with each other, trying not to butt into the conversations between the elves and Markauz. There could be no question of simply talking to them on the road, without any special reason. The only exceptions were Eel's long conversations with Ell.

It wasn't that the men were shy or they avoided the leaders of our group, it was simply that they felt, clearly on the basis of many years as soldiers, that everyone should do his own job and there was no point in bothering the commanders with petty details. They'd call you if necessary.

And while we were on the road the Wild Hearts themselves were divided up into little groups. Either according to their interests, or simply on the basis of a natural liking for each other. But that's perfectly normal—on a journey it's very hard to travel as one big pack. Honeycomb and Uncle. Eel, Tomcat, and Arnkh. Hallas, Deler, Marmot, me, and Kli-Kli. Loudmouth and Lamplighter. Although Kli-Kli was also the only one who dashed from the head of the group to the tail and back on Featherlight, managing to talk to everyone at least a hundred times a day.

I personally couldn't give a damn for all these rules, but it just turned out that I found myself in a small party that included Marmot, as well as the gnome and the dwarf, with whom I had close connections from the fight in Stalkon's palace, so I stuck to their company.

Arnkh's suggestion that we should go and find out what was going on was not destined to be acted on. Miralissa rode back to us herself.

"Tomcat says that the advancing storm is artificial in origin."

"Can you put that more simply?" Loudmouth asked plaintively.

"What's so hard to understand?" Tomcat asked in amazement. "Someone conjured up these clouds, you thickhead!"

"Shamans?" Lamplighter asked with a reproachful glance at Egrassa.

Of course, Mumr felt that Egrassa hadn't done enough work with his bow in the forest where the servants of the Nameless One were trying to work their magic. If the soldier had been in the elf's place, he wouldn't have let slip the opportunity to swing his bidenhander a couple of times.

"Maybe shamans and maybe not," Tomcat said with a shrug. "But it's magic, that much I can guarantee."

"It has to be shamans, it couldn't be anyone else!" Kli-Kli sighed.

"Can we avoid it?" asked Markauz, tugging on his mustache.

"I can't do anything," said Miralissa, spreading her hands helplessly. "My skill's not great enough. I can't feel anything."

"It's weather sorcery. The element of rain is pretty unstable," Tomcat muttered.

"What's that?" Hallas said impatiently.

"We were taught . . ." Tomcat hesitated for a moment. "We were taught that the rain magic created by shamanism is unstable. It lasts for no more than four or perhaps five hours and is heavily dependent not only on the skill of the shamans, but also on natural phenomena. The wind, for instance."

"You want to try to get away from these clouds?" asked Ell, one of the first to grasp what Tomcat was thinking.

"Uh-huh. The wind now is blowing directly to the southwest, so we can gallop southeast. If we're lucky we'll part company with the storm."

"Oh, sure," Honeycomb snorted. "It looks like someone's driving it along. Just look how fast it's moving!"

I glanced involuntarily at the wild weather advancing toward us.

"And just what can that little cloud do?" I couldn't help blurting out.

"Nothing." Egrassa answered me instead of Tomcat.

"Then what are we planning to run away from?" asked milord Markauz, getting the question in ahead of me.

"From what that cloud is trying to hide," Miralissa answered him in an extremely dismal voice.

"That will be an ordinary rain cloud, with ordinary thunder and lightning," Tomcat said. "The worst it can do is soak us to the skin. And if the shamanism is really good, there'll be a really wild storm. But not directly aimed. That is, it won't try to destroy us especially. It will be an ordinary storm, just like hundreds of others. If anyone's hurt, it will be by accident."

"You ought to give lectures at the university in Ranneng. I didn't understand a thing!" Deler complained. "What about the thing the clouds are trying to hide?"

"A bank of rain clouds with thunder and lightning always covers up any other magic," Miralissa explained. "There isn't a magician in Siala, even if he's worth three of the Nameless One, who can see hostile magic inside a thundercloud until the sorcery is literally right there under his nose. Tomcat senses that the storm was created by shamanism, but he doesn't know what it might be hiding. The shamans could have hidden something that they don't want the magicians of the Order to see. Clouds make a magnificent screen."

"The nearest magicians are tens of leagues away, they needn't have worried," Arnkh growled.

"Then they must be hiding something that can be seen for tens of leagues," Kli-Kli disagreed.

There were more lightning flashes and rumbles of thunder, still in the distance, but much closer now.

"Enough idle talking! Tomcat, since you can sense the storm, you're

the one to get us out of this. Lead on!" said Markauz. He had no intention of waiting for the rain.

And our crazy game of tag with the weather began.

Tomcat took control with an assured hand and set the horses a pace
no worse than when we were hightailing it out of Vishki. The rumble of
the thunder kept getting closer and closer. The wind grew stronger,
bending the tall grass right down to the ground. The music of the crickets and the songs of the birds fell silent. Every now and then one of us
would look back to check how much farther we could gallop before the
rain hit us.

But I just kept looking straight ahead. In the first place, at such a furious gallop, I was afraid of falling off Little Bee, and in the second
place, the one time I did look round I got such a fright that I almost
yelled out loud. The cloudy sky that was dogging our heels was black
enough to darken a hundred worlds.

Even Eel had turned pale, and that was completely out of character
for the coolheaded Garrakan.

"The wind's changed!" Kli-Kli shouted. "To the east! The clouds are
being carried off to the side!"

I forced myself to look round. Now, no matter how hard the storm
tried, there was no way we could end up at the very heart of it. It had
shifted far to the east of us. But our group would still be caught by
the edge of the magical tempest, that much was certain. And though
the downpour might be less powerful, the rain would still be pretty
substantial—no one had the slightest doubt about that.

The menacing clouds blocked off the entire sky. A furious wind
tossed up handfuls of sand aimed at my face and I had to pull the hood
of my elfin drokr cloak up over my head.

Others suffered worse than I did. Deler screwed up his watering eyes
and swore nonstop until the sand got into his mouth. The wind flapped
Hallas's beard and the horses' manes. Mumr's hat was torn off his head,
but he didn't stop to try to take the wind's new plaything away from it.

A whirlwind of a thousand demons howled in our ears and the solid
wall of clouds advanced on us like a herd of cattle on the rampage.
Again and again the festoons of diamond-bright lightning flashes fused
together into broad sheets running across the entire horizon and lighting up the wasteland, which looked even more desolate in the dark. The

wind was like an insane cowherd, driving his rain-swollen clouds straight at us. The rain hadn't actually started yet, but soon, very soon, behind the rumbling of the thunder and the flashing of the lightning, streams of water would come cascading down onto the ground that was frozen in impatient anticipation.

There was a flash, and we heard an angry rumble on the wind.

Another flash.

"Now there'll be a real bang!" shouted the jester.

There was a right royal bang. The skies were split apart by the roaring of the gods, and the horses whinnied in fright.

"Forward!" Tomcat shouted from somewhere up ahead, trying to make himself heard above the noise of the wind.

An intense peal of thunder reverberated across the sky, hurtling past us like a wild stallion and blocking my ears for a moment. The thunderclap was loudest right above our heads.

I barely managed to keep my seat on Little Bee, and Loudmouth's horse reared up, almost throwing its rider. Deler was unlucky: He went flopping down onto the ground and if not for Marmot, who adroitly grabbed the dwarf's horse by the ear, the startled animal would have bolted. Deler showered the "stupid beast, unworthy to carry a dwarf on its thrice-cursed hump" with fearsome abuse and scrambled back into the saddle. We all had to make an incredible effort to calm our frightened horses.

"Forward!" Tomcat had no intention of stopping, and he set his horse to a gallop.

The group strung out into a line and followed the tracker.

The rain covered us with its wet wings, and the isolated drops were replaced by a roaring cataract cascading down from the sky. In the blink of an eye, everyone who wasn't wearing an elfin cloak was soaked to the skin.

The thunder and lightning, the cataracts of water and other attributes of any decent, self-respecting storm shifted farther east. The booming was more distant now, no longer threatening us.

But the rain had not gone away. The entire sky was shrouded in dismal clouds that poured water down onto the earth from their inexhaustible heavenly stores. Not a single blue patch, not a single ray of sunshine. Hargan's Wasteland was enveloped in a gloomy, autumnal atmosphere. The earth was soaked with water and thick mud appeared out of nowhere under the horses' hooves, completely covering the grass.

The weather was foul, cheerless, and cold, especially for men who had grown accustomed to constant heat. Hallas suffered the worst of all. He was soaked right through and shuddering with the cold, and his teeth could be heard chattering ten yards away. The stubborn gnome rejected Miralissa's suggestion that he should put on a cloak.

"Watch out, you'll fall ill, and I won't make a fuss over you," Deler muttered from under his cloak. "Don't expect me to spoon-feed you medicine."

"You!" the gnome snorted. "I wouldn't take any medicine from you. I know your lousy k-kind! You'll sprinkle in some poison or other and then I'll wheeze, turn blue, and k-kick the bucket. I wouldn't give you the satisfaction!"

"You're no good to me soaking wet," the dwarf said sulkily.

Hallas snorted and didn't say anything else. The group was no longer galloping headlong through the meadows of the wasteland; the horses had changed to a rapid walk.

In about three hours it would start to get dark, so we would have to stop for the night somewhere soon.

"Ah, when's this going to stop?" the gnome finally cried out in exasperation.

His lips had turned blue and his teeth were rattling out a tattoo that would have turned the orcs' drummers green with envy. "Not before tomorrow morning," said Honeycomb, casting a glance up at the gray sky.

"Tomorrow morning!" Hallas groaned.

"Definitely not before then."

As evening came on, the rain grew stronger. It had already completely soaked the ground, and now the meadows were transformed into vast puddles of water. The hooves of the horses stuck in this shallow marsh and the animals began to tire, even though we were moving rather slowly. But after two leagues of this, we left the meadows behind us and came out onto something like a track.

"These are the remains of the old road. The one that led from Ranneng to Avendoom," Kli-Kli declared from under his hood, as if he had heard my thoughts.

"It's incredibly well preserved," Marmot muttered. "Almost five hundred years have gone by, and it's only been overgrown by grass."

"Noth-thing surprising about that," Hallas grumbled. "It was b-built by gn-gnomes."

"Come on, you joker, pull the other one," Lamplighter said dismissively.

"I'm not p-pulling your leg. Th-this is our work. I can smell it. Deler, you t-tell him."

"Of course it's yours," the dwarf agreed amicably. "But you'd do better to keep quiet and get warm. You can't even keep your teeth together."

"Why makes you so concerned for my health?"

"If you die, I'll have to dig your grave."

Hallas wrapped himself more tightly in the cloak and didn't answer.

Despite the rain, mist started rising from the ground. The transparent white wisps trailed across the earth, insinuating themselves between the stalks of grass, enveloping the hooves of the horses. But as soon as a wind sprang up, the mist dispersed and retreated for a while.

Markauz rode up to us and reined in his horse.

"Hey, Tomcat! Are you sure about those dangers? You didn't get anything confused at all?"

"That's right!" said Loudmouth, supporting Alistan. "The storm passed over ages ago. We've been getting soaked for the last four hours, and we still haven't had any particular problems from the sky."

"Well, thanks be to Sagra, let's hope we don't have any for another hundred years," Uncle drawled.

"I can't understand what's going on myself," Tomcat replied, sounding bewildered. "I felt it before, but now I don't. There's nothing. I'm beginning to think I must have imagined it."

"What about Miralissa and Egrassa?" Mumr asked Alistan cautiously.

"No, they don't know anything."

"So it's passed us by then," Loudmouth said with a sigh of relief.

"Don't go building your hopes up too high," said Kli-Kli, putting on a sour face. "It'll pass us by all right, then turn round and hit us really hard!"

"You'll jinx us, saying things like that, you green dummy!" Honeycomb rebuked the goblin angrily. "You should just say it'll pass us by, and not think bad thoughts."

"Well, of course, I'm an optimist by nature, but traveling with Harold tends to introduce too much pessimism into my character."

Kli-Kli cast a significant glance in my direction. I replied in kind with a look that promised the goblin a wonderful life if he didn't shut up. The jester merely giggled.

A goblin's eyesight is about ten times keener than a man's. What looked to me like a gray shadow barely visible through the rain and the mist was an unexpected discovery to Kli-Kli. He cried out in surprise, whooped to his horse, and raced off to overtake the elves.

There was something rustling and crunching under the horses' hooves, something in the grass that had grown over the road, as if the horses were treading on a crust of frozen snow. I leaned down from my saddle, but I couldn't see anything except the tall green stems.

Little Bee's hoof came down on the end of some kind of stick, and as the horse stood on it I again heard the sound that had caught my attention. After another ten yards there was another stick. This time I could make it out quite clearly. Black, blacker than an I'ilya willow, irregular and lumpy. It was a fragment of a human shinbone.

I turned cold. The horses were walking over bones. We were trampling the remains of dead strangers. I heard that crunching and scraping first on one side, then on the other.

"May I kiss a frying pan," Lamplighter swore. "There was a battle here!"

Kli-Kli came back, and his little face was darker than the cloud that had been chasing us in the morning.

"And what a battle it was, my friend Lamplighter. The battle of Hargan's Brigade."

"That's impossible," Marmot objected. "In five hundred years bones sink deep into the earth. They would have disappeared completely, they couldn't just be lying here as if was only two years since the battle happened."

"I don't like it here," Loudmouth said slowly.

"The bones are as fragile as Nizin porcelain," Kli-Kli muttered. "And you're wrong when you say the remains aren't from the time of that battle, Marmot. The ravine that I told you about is just up ahead."

But the goblin didn't need to tell us, we could already see for ourselves the obstacle that had appeared in front of us. A deep gap in the body of the earth—the ravine was overgrown with tall grass, as high as a man's chest, with a stream swollen by the rain and babbling loudly—it must have been a truly formidable barrier for the attackers during the storming of the brigade's fortifications.

The light mist in the hollow of the ravine thickened, acquiring density and form and almost hiding the bottom. The walls were no longer quite as steep and abrupt as they had been before. In five hundred years the snow and the plants had smoothed them out.

I didn't even realize that everyone had fallen silent. No one said a single word. We simply stared through the increasing rain at the far side of the ravine, from where centuries ago hordes of orcs had come flooding across to confront four hundred men.

"There must be a lot of bones down below," said Honeycomb, breaking the silence. "You can see why a road like this was abandoned."

"Where there are old bones, there are gkhols," said Lamplighter, setting his hand on the hilt of his bidenhander.

"They're too old. Do you hear the way they crunch under the horses' hooves? There haven't been any gkhols here for a long time."

"It's grisly," Tomcat muttered.

"What is?" asked Lamplighter, jumping down to the ground.

"I mean it's grisly, them just lying there like that. Not buried. Imagine your remains not lying in the ground, but out in the open for centuries."

"It's a bit too soon for you to be thinking about dying. Better watch out in case Sagra hears you," said Lamplighter, trying to joke.

The joke was a failure.

"Dead men everywhere! It's wrong to be walking over the bones of soldiers. . . . Tomcat's right, this place has the whiff of death, there's something unnatural about it." Arnkh tossed away the grass stalk that he had been clasping in his teeth for the best part of an hour.

"Who told you the bones were human?" asked Ell, getting down off his horse. He rummaged in the mud and then tossed something black across to Arnkh. "Look at that."

Arnkh caught the object and started turning it over in his hands, then flung it indifferently into the ravine. I just had time to notice that it was a lower jaw with unnaturally large and long canine teeth. Just like the ones Ell or any elf had. Or any orc.

"Orcs?" Arnkh asked with a curious glance at Miralissa's k'lissang.

"Who else?" said the elf, and his golden eyes glittered. "There are some human bones, too, but a negligible number compared to the orcs. The Firstborn were mown down in large numbers here."

"Yes, they took a real lashing."

"There were more than just arrows here." Tomcat nodded to indicate signs that only he could spot. "There was magic at work, too. The walls of the ravine have been melted by heat. You see? Someone turned the place into an oven."

"Hey, Dancer in the Shadows!" Kli-Kli had come across to me. "What are you thinking about?"

"I thought I asked you not to call me that," I growled at the goblin, but the little shit didn't bat an eyelid.

Only now he wasn't looking at me, but at the road.

"Harold," Kli-Kli said in a very grave tone of voice, "as Loudmouth says, we're up the backside now. All the way up. They've outflanked us!"

And so saying, the goblin went dashing back, yelling as if a giant had stepped on his favorite little bell on his cap. I went dashing after the jester, afraid that he might have lost his mind. Those green creatures are very hard to understand, especially when they're in such a panicky state.

When they heard Kli-Kli's shouts, everyone started staring at him in bewilderment. At least, the expressions on Alistan's and Egrassa's faces reflected the same thought that I had had—the jester must have gone insane.

Meanwhile the king's jester reached them and began performing something like a dance by a flea high from smoking charm-weed, at the same time yelling all the while that Tomcat had been right about the cloud.

When I reached him, he was still howling, and the others were staring at him as if he had the plague.

"Harold!" Kli-Kli cried, turning to me. "You listen to me at least! The cloud!"

"What cloud, my friend?" I asked in the most ingratiating voice I could manage, the way they talk to crazy people.

"Open your eyes and look! Not at me, you idiot! At the sky!"

Arguing with someone who's sick in the head is more trouble than it's worth and so, under the goblin's keen gaze, I started looking at the rain clouds. Several other members of the group followed my example. But neither they nor I could see anything frightening.

Just the same clouds as an hour earlier: gray, unbroken, spewing rain down onto the ground.

"Mmm . . . They all look the same to me."

"That one there!" said Tomcat, pointing way off into the distance with one finger.

In response there was a flash of lightning on the horizon and immediately one of the clouds was lit up for an instant with purple fire.

Hallas swore quietly.

"I was hoping I could be wrong," Tomcat said bitterly.

The thing that the storm created by the Nameless One's minions had been hiding had finally reached us, even though it had been obliged to make a substantial detour along the way.

"Sagra save us!"

"What is that rotten garbage, Tomcat?"

"Everyone shut up!" Markauz roared above the others' howls and questions. "Tomcat, can you do anything about this?"

"No."

"Lady Miralissa, Tresh Egrassa?"

"We'll try."

Miralissa and Egrassa started drawing something on the soaking wet ground—a cross between an octopus and a star with a hundred light beam tentacles. The elfess whispered words rapidly. The lines of the form on the ground began pulsating with yellow flame.

I was really hoping that their shamanism would help us. Ell stood in front of the two working the magic, almost on the very edge of the precipice, holding his bow at the ready, although I didn't think arrows would be effective against magic. The others, including me, crowded together behind the elves and observed the approaching danger.

It was making straight for us at full speed. Somewhere inside that seething cloud, at its very center, a purple flame was being kindled, and the cloud was moving against the wind with only one goal in mind—to overtake us.

Miralissa stopped whispering and began singing in orcish. Every word seemed to hang in the air like a tiny, jingling bell, vibrating and humming, its sound reflected in the yellow shape drawn on the ground.

"What are those repulsive beasts?" Loudmouth gasped.

He was as white as chalk, and I'm sure that right then my face didn't look much better, either.

A winged creature dived down out of the cloud. Then another, and another.

And then there were ten of the long creatures with broad wings circling in a predatory dance, disappearing into the purple glow and then reemerging from it. Their flight was smooth and spellbinding, but just then I didn't particularly feel like admiring the creatures' fluent grace.

"What is that, may an ice worm freeze my giblets?" Honeycomb whispered, clutching his useless ogre hammer desperately in both hands.

"I don't know!" said Tomcat, staring fixedly at the creatures.

They were small and rapacious, absolutely unlike anything else. Their oily skin had a purple shimmer to it. And that was what I disliked the most.

"*S'alai'yaga kh'tar agr t'khkkhanng!*" Miralissa shouted out the final words of the spell.

Something yellow spurted out of the drawing on the ground and went shooting off toward the magic cloud with the speed of one of the gnomes' cannonballs.

Whatever it was, along the way it grew until it reached the size of a small house.

The yellow met the purple and burst straight into the body of the cloud, which shuddered as if it were a living being, and recoiled. There was a blinding flash inside it.

And that was all.

The cloud had eaten the elves' creation.

The magical purple glow with those creatures dancing in a circle stopped right above our heads. Then the circle broke up and the creatures attacked.

Six of the ten flyers soared past high above our heads and four dived headlong at us, moving so rapidly that we barely managed to react in time.

A bowstring twanged as Ell fired at the first creature. He hit the mark, but the arrow passed straight through the flyer and disappeared, without causing our enemy any harm.

The elf just barely managed to jump out of the way of his attacker, saved only by his natural agility. The monster rushed past him, skimming the top of the grass with its belly and shrieking in disappointment, then began gaining height again and joined the other six circling above the cloud.

"Look out!"

Deler fell to the ground and pulled down Hallas, who was brandishing his mattock belligerently, by the legs. The gnome gave a howl of protest as he fell facedown in a puddle and the second creature zipped past just above his head and then followed its predecessor back up into the sky.

The two other creatures attacked in unison, flying down simultaneously and coming straight at us, choosing their victims on the way. Everybody went dashing in all directions like quail facing an attack by a hawk, but the creatures had picked out their targets. The first was Tomcat, who froze at the very edge of the steep slope, and the second was me.

Click!

In the hourglass of the gods, time slowed almost to a complete standstill. I saw the purple creature fly-ing slow-ly toward me. Now I was able to get a look at its face. And it was a genuine human face, the face of a man who was not yet old, frozen so that it looked like a death mask.

Miralissa shouted something to us, but I couldn't hear, my gaze was riveted to approaching death. Somehow I knew that after an encounter with this thing, I would not see Sagra, there would be neither light nor darkness, but total, all-consuming nothingness, from which there would be no return.

Tomcat waved his hand slowly and a solitary blue spark flew out of his fingers. A desperate attempt to use something from the arsenal of weapons that the magician who never finished his training had been saving for a day like this. The spark touched the creature's face, tearing open the skin and the flesh to reveal the skull, but the creature felt no pain, it probably didn't even know what pain was, and it went crashing into its victim with a howl of triumph. In an instant it passed straight through the Wild Heart's body like a small cloud of purple mist and then soared back up to the big cloud, while Tomcat, his face completely drained of blood, began slowly tumbling over onto his side.

"Gaaaarret!" The jester's shout reached me through the dense jelly of time, and I looked back at the second creature.

"This is the end!" The absurd thought flashed through my head.

I realized I'd hesitated for too long. The creature was approaching very rapidly, and I still hadn't jumped aside to get out of its way.

"I'll help," a painfully familiar voice whispered inside my head.

And then the agony came. Hellish, unbelievable pain. My insides were seared with fire, something boiled and seethed up inside me . . . then it broke out and smashed silently into the creature, tossing me aside at the same time.

A piercing shriek.

The winged creature disintegrated like fog in the face of a hurricane.

The ground came rushing up to meet me.

Click! And time started speeding up again.

The impact of my landing knocked almost all the air out of my lungs. I was left cross-eyed from pain and wheezing hoarsely as I strained to restore my breathing. On both sides hands grabbed me by the elbows, lifted me up, and tried to set me on my feet, but my legs were too soft, as if I'd drunk too much young wine. Honeycomb swore as he and Loudmouth began dragging me away from the edge of the ravine.

"Valder! You son of a bitch," I croaked out loud. "You promised to leave me alone!"

Naturally, no one replied. The magician had gone into hiding, and I couldn't sense him anymore. Only when things had got too hot, had he surfaced out of the depths of my own self and saved my skin.

"Who's that he's talking to?" Loudmouth asked warily. "Are you sure that brute didn't touch him?"

"I'm certain!"

Meanwhile the other nine creatures were circling again, with the clear intention of continuing the attack. The speed of their roundelay continually increased until the creatures fused into a single blurred circle that burst like a soap bubble and they came diving down toward us.

"Curses!" Loudmouth let go of me and pulled out his sword.

With no support, I tumbled to the ground, overwhelmed by a sudden wave of weakness.

Along the entire line of the edge of the ravine the air suddenly trembled and vague shadows began appearing—human silhouettes armed with bows. With every heartbeat they became more clearly defined.

"Do you see that?" Honeycomb whispered, stunned.

I gave a bemused nod, but I don't think he noticed.

The purple creatures were still falling from the sky. In real time no more than two seconds had gone by, but it seemed like an eternity to us.

A voice rang out above the ravine choked with rain.

"At the enemy! Choose your target! Correction half a finger to the right! Fire, you whores!"

The gray shadows of arrows went soaring up into the sky to meet the death that was diving down at us. With a scream of horror and disappointment, the flyers broke apart, dissolving into the air, and the purple cloud groaned.

"Together, fire!"

I had heard that voice before somewhere a long, long time ago, probably in a former life or, perhaps, in a dream.

We couldn't hear the twang of the bowstrings or the flight of the arrows. There was only the rain rustling on the ground and the cloud constantly groaning like an expiring ghost. The flight of transparent arrows bit into its belly, leaving behind huge ragged holes.

The loud, lamenting wail of a doomed creature rolled on and on above the earth, farther and farther . . . I put my hands over my ears, the sound was so loud and so terrible. I think they must have heard it even in Djashla.

The phantoms fired a third time and the cloud flared up as bright as the sun, flooding the surrounding region with purple light. In less than a minute I had collapsed from exhaustion and been deafened and blinded. There was nothing left to do except to curl up in a ball and try to emerge from this appalling nightmare.

When I came round, it was all over. There were no more purple storm clouds in the sky, the phantoms had disappeared as if I had simply dreamed them, and even the rain had stopped. The clouds had disappeared, giving way once again to a clear blue sky. The sun was shining straight into my eyes, but the former suffocating heat had been replaced by warm summer weather.

I tried moving first one arm, then the other, and then tried my legs. I seemed to be alive. Squinting downward, I saw that I was lying on a blanket and someone's considerate hand had covered me with another one.

"Welcome back," a voice said above my head, and then Uncle's bearded, smiling face appeared in my field of view. "So you're awake now? We were thinking of singing you the funeral song of forgiveness."

I cleared my throat and tried to sit up. I managed it without any difficulty, which meant that I was already back to normal after the piece of magic that Valder had worked. Once again I tried mentally summoning the archmagician who had swapped the Forbidden Territory for a life inside my head. But as always, it didn't work. The magician had either hidden himself away and didn't want to answer or he had simply disappeared.

"How long have I been lying here?" It was evening when those purple flyers attacked us and now, if the gods hadn't changed all the rules while I was out of it, it was early morning.

"A little while," said Alistan, walking up to me.

"How long exactly?" I persisted.

"A little over a day."

Not bad going.

"How are you feeling?" Miralissa had come over with the count and now she put her hand on my forehead. Her skin was dry and her palm was hot.

"I seem to be in good shape. What happened?"

"We should ask you that," said Alistan. "What happened at the edge of the ravine, thief?"

"I don't know." I frowned. "I can't remember."

"Well try, Harold." Markauz's voice had an ingratiating tone to it and he even forgot to call me thief. "It's very important."

The entire group looked at me expectantly.

"First those creatures were flying at us, then Tomcat did something, but it didn't help, then I saw one of them getting close to me, and then something happened."

"Something?" Miralissa echoed, raising one eyebrow in surprise. "Do you really not know what happened?"

"I really don't," I said without the slightest twinge of conscience.

I genuinely didn't know what the archmagician had done to kill the flyer and toss me out of its path. So I hardly had to lie at all.

"In the hundredth part of a second someone created an attack spell of such great power that I thought my hair would burst into flames! Only a very experienced magician is capable of doing that."

Uh-huh. Someone like my friend Valder.

"Well, it definitely wasn't me who did it."

"Naturally," Alistan said coolly. "But we'd like to know who did."

I shrugged.

"And the phantoms? Who, I mean, what were they?"

"They're the spirits of the men whose bones lie on this side of the ravine," I said. "The soldiers of the Dog Swallows Brigade returned to our world when they sensed the shamanic magic at work."

Miralissa kept her pensive gaze fixed on me. I think she knew perfectly well that I wasn't telling her everything, but for some reason she didn't try to shake the truth out of me right there and then.

"What the Nameless One's shamans created could have awoken the spirits of the fallen."

"And what happened to that cloud?" I asked.

"It disappeared."

"And Tomcat?"

Everyone turned their eyes away.

"He's dead, Harold," Uncle answered eventually.

"What happened?" Somehow I couldn't believe in the death of the platoon's tracker.

"That creature, whatever it was, passed through him and killed him. That's all we know. Are you fit to sit in the saddle, thief?" asked Alistan.

"Yes."

"Good. We've lost a day and we need to get out onto the highway. Is everything ready, Uncle?"

"Of course, captain," the sergeant of the Wild Hearts said with a nod.

"Get up, Harold, we need to see a soldier off on his last journey."

They had buried Tomcat before I came round. He had found his final resting place under a young rowan tree with silvery bark and branches that spread out above the large gravestone. On the stone someone had traced the words TOMCAT. BROTHER OF THE WILD HEARTS. ?–1123 E.D.

"Good-bye," Uncle said for all of us.

"Sleep well," Miralissa whispered, passing her hand above the grave.

Kli-Kli was blinking rapidly, trying to hold back the tears. Arnkh was clenching and unclenching his fists helplessly. Deler and Hallas looked like twins now—both small, sullen, and somber.

And then Lamplighter launched into the song "Forgiveness." The song that the Wild Hearts sing over the bodies of their brothers, no matter whether they fell in battle or died of old age. It's a strange song, not really suitable for warriors. After all, how can warriors forgive their enemies?

But this song was as old as the Wild Hearts and the Lonely Giant, and it had been sung since such hoary old times that now no one knew who first sang it to see warriors off on their final journey.

Kli-Kli and Alistan and Miralissa and the elves and I listened to this strange song that semed so incongruous for soldiers, and yet wrung the heart in such bitter enchantment. After the first couplet all the Wild Hearts joined in.

When the song came to an end, only the chirping of the crickets disturbed the silence of the morning. No one said a word; no one wanted to be the first to break the silence of mourning.

Our group had lost a comrade. But would he be the last? No one knew who or what was waiting for us up ahead. We still had so many obstacles to overcome in order to reach the Forests of Zagraba, where the burial chambers of Hrad Spein lay concealed.

"That's it." Uncle's voice sounded like flintpaper. "Time to go."

"Have a good winter, Tomcat."

Kli-Kli turned away, trying to conceal his tears. I had a bitter feeling in my heart. As well as the pain of loss we all felt a violent, seething anger. If the creators of that cloud had been there then, I swear I would have torn them limb from limb with my bare hands.

The group rode almost all day long without talking. Hallas and Deler stopped arguing, there were none of those interminable little songs from Lamplighter's reed pipe, Kli-Kli forgot about his jokes and sniffed occasionally, with his eyes noticeably redder than usual. Marmot frowned dourly and stroked Invincible, who was frozen as still as a statue on his shoulder.

I rode apart from everyone else, immediately behind Uncle and Honeycomb. I was in a foul mood and didn't feel like talking to anyone. My solitude was only interrupted once, when Alistan rode up to me.

Somehow he appeared out of nowhere on my right and we rode together for several leagues. I didn't object to his silent company and was actually a little surprised when he broke the silence.

"You know, Harold, Tomcat's lying in a good place."

"Is he?" That was all that I could force out to express my surprise at his words.

"Beside the grave of heroes. He has good neighbors."

"For him, yes," I replied after a moment's pause. "But who will remember him in ten years' time? A grave in a wilderness. Perhaps one cowherd a year ever finds his way to that spot."

"You're wrong, thief, he'll be remembered in the force," said Uncle, who had heard our conversation. "Beside the slopes of Mount Despair, not far from the Lonely Giant, there's a graveyard. That's where all the warriors of the force rest, it doesn't matter if their bodies are in the graves or were left behind forever out in the snowy tundra. Tomcat will be remembered."

For the rest of the day we didn't exchange a single word.

After all the rain that had poured down on the earth, the unbearable heat seemed to have receded. In the days that followed we traveled in relatively warm and very pleasant weather. The meadows of luscious green grass and impassable thickets of bushes were left behind and the open wilderness was replaced by sparse pine forest.

The mood of the group was gradually restored. Tomcat's death was not forgotten, it was just that the problems of the day pushed it into the background.

Conversations sprang up, first on one side, then on the other. Deler and Hallas started bickering again because they couldn't agree on whether they'd seen poisonous toadstools or edible mushrooms growing in the little meadow where we spent the night before. Out of the kindness of his heart, Kli-Kli got Ell up in the morning with the help of Deler's hat, which was full of water. For this escapade the goblin very nearly caught it in the neck from the elf and the dwarf, but he managed to hide behind me in time, lamenting that no one appreciated his talent.

Several times during the journey I caught Miralissa's thoughtful gaze on me, but she didn't ask me anything, evidently waiting until we would be alone together. So I took pains to avoid her company.

Without knowing why, I didn't want to tell anyone about Valder and the help he had given me.

We lengthened our journey by traveling parallel to the highway and taking our time before riding out onto it. Day followed day, and I was already thinking I would never lay eyes on the main road that we had all been longing to see. However, on the eighth day of the journey, already well into the second half of July, Kli-Kli gave a howl of joy and pointed to a light strip that had appeared between the trees.

We had finally emerged from Hargan's Wasteland onto the highway.

And it was only then that I noticed what the goblin was holding in his hand.

"Where did you get that from, Kli-Kli?" I asked when I recovered the power of speech.

"What do you mean?" the jester asked, and then he followed my glance, understood, and said: "Ah, you mean this trinket? You'll never believe it! While you were lying there out cold, we started looking for a spot for Tomcat's grave, may he dwell in the eternal light. I walked away from the others a bit and I noticed this thing."

"You just noticed it?"

"This was lying on a stone that was covered with moss. There were even words written on the stone, but I couldn't make anything out."

"So you took it?" I asked.

"And why not?" the goblin said with a shrug. "You can see what a beautiful thing it is. Why should something that good go to waste? I'll be able to sell it."

"Don't sell it, Kli-Kli," I said in a soft, insinuating voice.

"You don't think I should?" The jester cast another curious glance at his find, then fastened the chain round his neck and hid the silvery, drop-shaped amulet under his cloak. "Miralissa told me the same thing. Are you two in cahoots, then?"

"No, just trust me. Perhaps someday it will save our lives."

Kli-Kli looked at me seriously. "You're full of riddles, Dancer in the Shadows."

"We're all full of riddles and mysteries, Kli-Kli. I am, and Miralissa is, and you are. It's true, isn't it?"

"Uh-huh," he agreed, then suddenly smiled and said, "So you don't object to my calling you Dancer?"

"What good do all my objections do? They don't stop you anyway. Call me whatever you like. In any case now I'm going to do everything I can to retrieve the Horn."

"And that's another of the prophecies of the shaman Tre-Tre that has come true," the goblin said triumphantly. "The Dancer in the Shadows has accepted his new name and decided to go through with things to the end."

"There you go again, you and your stupid book!" I flared up immediately. "What if somebody else takes the same name?"

"First you find me the idiot who would agree to do it," Kli-Kli said.

What a pity that the little wretch managed to dodge my hands and avoid a good solid smack!

Early on the twenty-eighth of July, the walls of a city emerged from the morning mist in front of us.

Our group had reached Ranneng.

Moscow 2002

Glossary

Annals of the Crown - the most ancient and detailed of the historical chronicles, maintained by the elves since they first appeared in the world of Siala.

Avendoom - the capital of the northern kingdom of Valiostr. The largest and richest city of the Northern Lands.

battery sword - a variety of sword with a midsized blade that can be wielded with either one hand or both.

Beaver Caps or beavers - soldiers of Valiostr, armed with heavy two-handed swords. Each soldier bears the title of "Master of the Long Sword" and wears a beaver-fur cap as an emblem to distinguish him from the soldiers of other units. These forces are used as a reserve striking force, to recover all kinds of difficult situations in battle. During military action the beavers are also accorded the honor of guarding the banner and the king, taking the place of the royal guard.

bidenhander - a two-handed sword with a blade that can be a yard and a half long. They usually are designed with a massive handle, a heavy counterweight that is usually round, and a broad crosspiece. Sometimes the armorers would add massive metal spurs to prevent the blade running right through the opponent.

Border Kingdom or Borderland - the kingdom beside the northern outcrops of the Mountains of the Dwarves and the Forests of Zagraba.

Borg's link - named after a general of ancient times who invented the chain formation, in which every single soldier plays an indispensable part in repelling an attack.

brother and sister swords - the names of the two swords in the special school of swordsmanship that is widespread among the nobility of Garrak. During combat the weapons are held at different heights in relationship to each other. The "brother," a narrow, double-sided blade held in the right hand, is used both for slashing and for thrusting. The "sister," a shorter blade with no cutting edge, is used only for thrusting blows. The weapons are either carried behind the back or in a double scabbard.

Canian forge work - weapons made from the steel mined in the Steel Mines of Isilia. The steel is worked in the famous smithies of the kingdom's capital, Cania. Following special processing and forging, it acquires a ruby color and a unique quality—on encountering steel of a different type it emits a melodic ringing sound like small bells, or a shriek of fury. For this reason Canian-forged steel is also known as Singing Steel, Shrieking Steel, or Ruby Blood.

Chapel of the Hands - the assembly of the supreme priests of Sagot.

Cold Sea - the northern sea of the Western Ocean. It washes the shores of Valiostr and the Desolate Lands.

Commission - the agreement that is concluded between a master thief and his client. The thief undertakes to supply the item required or, in case of failure, to return the client's pledge and a percentage of the total value of the deal. The client undertakes to make payment in full on receiving the article in which he is interested. A Commission can only be abrogated by the mutual consent of both parties.

Crayfish Dukedom - the only state in the Desolate Lands.

crayfish grip (coll.) - a grip from which it is impossible to escape. The expression derives from the common saying that the men of the

Crayfish Dukedom have a strong grip, and once they take you prisoner, you will never get away alive.

crayfish sleigh - in the Crayfish Dukedom, men who had been executed were transported to their graves on sleighs. Hence the meaning of this phrase—if the crayfish sleigh has come for you, death is at the door.

Crest of the World - the highest mountain chain in Siala. It runs from north to south across almost the entire continent. The crest is very difficult to cross and the lands beyond it are almost entirely unexplored.

Defender of the Hands - one of the highest positions in the hierarchy of the priests of Sagot.

Desolate Lands - the forests, stretches of open tundra, and ice fields in the far north. They have been settled by beings of various kinds, several of which constantly attempt to gain entry to the Northern Lands of Siala, and only the unassailable Mountains of Despair, the Lonely Giant fortress, and the Wild Hearts hold back their invasion of the world of men. Ogres, giants, svens, h'varrs, winter orcs, and dozens of other races and varieties of creatures inhabit these vast territories. People also live here, savages and barbarians who are subjects of the Nameless One. In all the Desolate Lands there is only one human state, the Crayfish Dukedom on the Crayfish Claw peninsula.

In the far north of the Desolate Lands, beyond the Needles of Ice, lies the dwelling of the Nameless One, whom savages captured by the Wild Hearts' scouts mention only in reverential whispers.

Disputed Lands - the lands lying alongside the Forests of Zagraba, between Miranueh and Valiostr.

djanga - a rapid, rhythmical dance, very popular in Zagorie.

Djashla - the kingdom of the mountain people that lies alongside the Crest of the World.

Djok Imargo or "Djok the Bringer of Winter" - the man who supposedly killed the prince of the House of the Black Rose. The Long Winter began as a result of this murder.

Doralissians - a race of goat-people who live in the Steppes of Ungava.

Doralissian horses - a type of horse bred in the Steppes of Ungava and valued throughout the Northern Lands for their beauty, speed, and stamina.

drokr - an elfin fabric that is proof against water and odors and does not burn in fire.

D'san-dor (orcish) or the Slumbering Forest - a forest that lies in the Desolate Lands, close to the spurs of the Mountains of Despair.

dwarves - the race of short beings living in the Mountains of the Dwarves. They are quite different from their near cousins, the gnomes. It is astonishing how their short, thick-fingered hands can create the most wonderful items, which are valued highly in every corner of Siala, whether they are weapons, tools, or works of art.

E.D. - the Era of Dreams, the final age of Siala. The events described in this book take place in the final year of the Era of Dreams. This age was preceded by the Era of Accomplishments (the age during which men appeared in Siala, about seven thousand years ago), the Gray Era (the age deemed to have begun with the appearance of orcs and elves in Siala), and the Dark Era (it is not known who, apart from ogres, lived in Siala in these distant times and what happened then).

elves - the second young race of Siala. The elves appeared almost immediately after their relatives, the orcs. After living in the Forests of Zagraba for several thousand years, the elves became divided into light and dark.

The light elves were dissatisfied with what they could achieve using shamanism and set about studying wizardry, basing their approach on the magic of men.

The dark elves, however, felt the light elves had betrayed the memory of their ancestors. They continued to make use of the primordial magic of their race, shamanism.

The names of all dark elfin women begin with *M* and the names of the men begin with *E*. If an elf is a member of the ruling family of the Dark House, then *ssa* is added to the name.

Empire - following the birth in the imperial family of twin boys, the Empire split into two states: the Near Lakeside Empire and the Far Lakeside Empire. These two kingdoms are constantly warring with each other to unite the Empire under the power of one of the two dynasties that trace their descent from the twin brothers.

Eyes of Death - when dice are cast and they show two "ones."

Field of Sora - the field on which the battle between the gnomes and the dwarves took place in 1100 E.D. Cannon and battle-mattocks clashed with poleaxes and swords. In this battle there were no victors.

Filand - a kingdom lying along the southern spurs of the Mountains of the Dwarves.

Forbidden (Secret) Territory or "the Stain" - a district of Avendoom created as the result of an attempt to use the Rainbow Horn to neutralize Kronk-a-Mor in 872 E.D. The Secret Territory is surrounded by a magical wall, through which almost no one dares to pass. Evil is said to dwell there.

Forests of I'alyala - these forests lie in the Northern Lands of Siala, beside the Crest of the World. The light elves moved here from the Forests of Zagraba following the schism between the elfin houses.

Forests of Zagraba - these evergreen forests cover an immense area. In some places beautiful, in others terrifying, they conceal within themselves a host of secrets and mysterious creatures. The Forests of Zagraba are home to dark elves, orcs, goblins, and dryads.

Garrak - a kingdom in the southern region of Siala's Northern Lands, powerful and thoroughly militarized. The Garrak nobility are regarded as extremely quick-tempered, dangerous, and unpredictable.

Garrak's "Dragon" - King Garrak's guard.

garrinch (gnomish, literally "guardian of the chests") - a creature that lives in the Steppes of Ungava. A trained garrinch makes an excellent guard for stores of treasure.

giants - one of the races that live in the Desolate Lands.

gkhols - carrion-eating scavengers. These creatures are usually to be found on battlefields or in old graveyards. If their source of food fails for some reason, gkhols are capable of hibernating for several years.

gnomes - like their larger cousins, the dwarves, gnomes appeared in the world of Siala immediately after the orcs and elves. Both gnomes and dwarves settled in the Mountains of the Dwarves, burrowing deep into their heart. Gnomes are stunted, quarrelsome creatures with beards. In the Mountains of the Dwarves their position was that of younger brothers. Gnomes are poor craftsmen, and they have never been able to produce such beautiful and delicate wares as the dwarves. However, gnomes are magnificent at working with steel and mining ore and other riches of the earth. They are good builders and diggers.

After living in the Mountains of the Dwarves for several thousand years, the gnomes finally left their old home following a decisive falling-out with their relatives the dwarves.

The race of gnomes found itself a new haven in the Steel Mines of Isilia. For the right to live in the mines they pay the kingdom an annual tribute and also supply it with steel. The gnomes invented the printing press, and then discovered how to make gunpowder (the dwarves claim that the gnomes stole the secret from a dwarf who was on his way home from a journey beyond the Crest of the World). The fierce battle that broke out between the estranged relatives on the Field of Sorna (1100 E.D.) was inconclusive. Both sides returned home having suffered immense losses.

The gnomes jealously guard the secret of gunpowder and sell cannon.

They have no magic of their own, since their last magician was killed on the Field of Sorna, and the gnomes' books are hidden deep in the Mountains of the Dwarves, in a safe hiding place that they cannot reach because of their enmity with the dwarves.

goblins - small creatures who live in the very depths of the Forests of Zagraba. The shamanism of the goblins is regarded as the most powerful after that of the ogres, but it includes almost no common attack spells.

Gray Stones - the most terrible and impregnable prison fortress in Valiostr. In all the time that it has existed, no one has ever managed to escape.

Green Leaf - one of the dark elves' most terrible tortures, which they only use on orcs (the one exception being Djok Imargo). Almost nothing is known about it, but rumors speak of the infernal torment of the victim. The torture can continue for years without interruption.

Grok - 1) the legendary general of Valiostr who held back the army of the orcs at Avendoom until the dark elves arrived to help in the final year of the Quiet Times (640 E.D.). A statue in his honor was erected in one of the central squares of the city; 2) the younger twin brother of the general Grok, who bore the same name, i.e., the magician who was dubbed the Nameless One.

hand - an orcish military leader.

Hospital of the Ten Martyrs - the Avendoom municipal hospital, founded by order of Grok on the precise spot where a detachment of orcs that had broken through the defenses of the human army was halted by ten warriors from the Avendoom garrison (640 E.D.).

Hrad Spein (ogric) or Palaces of Bone - immense underground palaces and catacombs, where ogres, orcs, elves and, later, men have all buried fallen warriors.

h'san'kor (orcish) or fearsome flute - a man-eating monster that lives in the Forests of Zagraba.

imperial dog - a type of guard dog bred in the Empire.

"Innocent as Djok the Winter-Bringer" - a common saying. Djok Imargo was the man accused of the murder of the prince of the House of the Black Rose. He was handed over to the elves, who executed him. After that, from 501 to 640 E.D., the dark elfin houses of Zagraba had no contacts with Valiostr. It subsequently emerged that Djok was innocent.

irilla (orcish) or mist spider - an emanation generated by the shamanism of the ogres. To this day no one knows for certain if it is an immaterial substance or a living creature.

Iselina (orcish) or Black River - this river starts in the Mountains of the Dwarves, runs through the eastern section of the Forests of Zagraba, crosses Valiostr, then forks into a left branch and a right branch, which both flow into the Eastern Ocean.

Isilia (orcish) - a kingdom bordering on Valiostr and Miranueh.

Isilian marble is mined in the southern spurs of the Steel Mines. Walking across this stone generates a powerful echo. It is generally used for protection against thieves, or to prevent the approach of assassins, or even simply for its beauty, despite the unpleasant sounds that have to be tolerated.

Jolly Gallows-Birds - former convicts, criminals, and pirates who have been recruited to serve as soldiers. On joining the ranks of the army of Valiostr they are pardoned for all previous transgressions. They perform the military functions of marines.

k'lissang (orcish, lit. "ever faithful") - an elf who has sworn an oath of fealty and engaged himself as a bodyguard to an elf of a more noble line for nine years. If the ever-faithful elf is killed during his period of service, his entire family is accepted into the clan of the elf whom the k'lissang was protecting.

Kronk-a-Mor - the shamanism of the ogres.

labyrinth - an ancient structure erected by the orcs, located in the Forests of Zagraba. The orcs release prisoners into the labyrinth and place bets on which of the unfortunates will survive longest.

languages of Siala - there are three main groups of languages in Siala. The first group is the orcish languages, spoken by orcs and elves. The second group is the gnomish languages, spoken by gnomes and dwarves. The third group includes all the human languages. There are also other languages and dialects, for instance, the languages of the ogres and goblins.

"Like looking for a smoking dwarf" - a saying based on the fact that dwarves do not smoke and they regard smokers with a certain degree of disdain, since the first beings to take up smoking were the gnomes. Following the gnomes, men also became addicted to the habit.

ling - a small animal that lives in the tundra of the Desolate Lands. Very like a shaggy-haired rat, but with much larger teeth and claws.

Lonely Giant - the fortress that closes off the only pass leading from the Desolate Lands through the Mountains of Despair to Valiostr.

Long Winter - the name given by the elves to a period of 140 years from 500 to 640 E.D. The Long Winter set in following the grotesque death of the elfin prince of the House of the Black Rose in Ranneng during festivities in the town. It came to an end in the final year of the Quiet Times (640 E.D.), during the Spring War, when the elves came to the aid of Grok and his men in the battle against the army of the orcs. Grok was presented with the Rainbow Horn to confirm that the Long Winter was over.

Lowland - the kingdom lying beside the Forests of I'alyala.

Lowland masters - master craftsmen from the Lowland, famous throughout Siala for the dishes and tableware they make from a special lilac-colored porcelain.

Market Square - a famous Avendoom square where theatrical performances constantly take place.

Master of the Long Sword - a title that is given to soldiers who have completely mastered the three techniques for using the two-handed sword (classical grip, single-fang grip, staff grip). The hilt of the sword is decorated with an embossed gold image of an oak leaf.

mattockmen - a name sometimes used for the gnomes. Their favorite weapon is the so-called battle-mattock, which combines a large cutting blade with a war hammer.

Mirangrad - the capital of Miranueh, a kingdom located beside Valiostr.

Miranueh - a kingdom bordering on Garrak, Isilia, and Valiostr. Constantly at war with Valiostr over the Disputed Lands.

Mountains of Despair - the low but unassailable mountains that separate Valiostr from the Desolate Lands. There is only one pass through them, and the Lonely Giant fortress is located on it.

Mountains of the Dwarves - an immense mountain chain, so high that only the Crest of the World compares with it. It runs from east to west through the Northern Lands, dividing them in two. Zam-da-Mort, or the Castle of Death, is the tallest and most majestic peak in the Mountains of the Dwarves.

Nameless One - the title given to a Valiostran magician after he committed treason in the final year of the Quiet Times (640 E.D.).

Needles of Ice - ice-bound mountains far away in the Desolate Lands.

obur - a gigantic bear from the Forests of Zagraba.

ogres - a race from the Desolate Lands. The only old race of Siala still remaining in this world. From the very beginning the ogres were granted a very powerful and destructive magic, Kronk-a-Mor. They are regarded as distant relatives of the orcs and elves. The elves say the gods took away the ogres' intelligence. If the ogres had remained as clever as they once were, they would have captured and destroyed the entire world of Siala.

Ol's Diggings - stone quarries lying at a distance of six days' journey from Avendoom. They were named after their first owner. The stone for the city's legendary walls was quarried here. Nowadays Ol's Diggings are abandoned.

orcs - the first new race of Siala. The elves regard them as their arch-enemies, although they are directly related to each other. The orcs say that they were here first and should rule the entire world, and all the other races are an unfortunate mistake made by the gods. In addition to the Forests of Zagraba, orcs also live in the Desolate Lands (the winter orcs).

Order of Magicians - there is an Order in every kingdom, the only exceptions being Zagorie and Djashla. Each Order has a council of arch-magicians and is headed by a master. Within the Order there is a strict division according to rank, and ranks are marked on the magicians' staffs: magician of the Order, one ring; elemental magician (master of the specific skills of several schools), two rings; magician with right of access to the council, three rings; archmagician, four rings; master, four rings and a small black figure of a raven on the top of the staff.

Purple Years - a period of time during which the dwarves and the gnomes waged a series of bloody wars against each other, and as a result the gnomes withdrew from the Mountains of the Dwarves.

Quiet Times - the period from 423 E.D. to 640 E.D., during which Valiostr did not wage a single war. These were times of prosperity when the kingdom flourished. They came to an end when an immense army of orcs from the Forests of Zagraba invaded Valiostr.

Rainbow Horn - a legendary artifact created by the ogres to counter-balance their own magic, the Kronk-a-Mor, if it should ever get out of control. The Horn was captured by the dark elves, who later gave it to men (in the person of Grok) as a token of their good intentions and the conclusion of an eternal alliance between the dark elves and Valiostr. Every two or three hundred years the Horn has to be saturated with magic in order not to lose its powers. Following the creation of the Secret Territory, the Horn was buried with Grok in the Hrad Spein. It is the Horn's magic that keeps the Nameless One in the Desolate Lands.

River of the Crystal Dream - a narrow little river in Avendoom. It runs through the Port City and falls into the Cold Sea.

Royal Guard of Valiostr - the king's personal guard. Only nobles are recruited to serve in it. The guardsmen wear the king's colors of gray and blue. The guard is commanded by a captain.

Royal Sandmen - the king's secret police, who defend the interests of the state and the sovereign. Their nickname is derived from their emblem, an hourglass.

Sagot - one of the twelve deities of the world of Siala. Patron of thieves, swindlers, rogues, and spies.

Sagra - one the twelve deities of the world of Siala. Goddess of war, justice, and death, and also patroness of soldiers.

Shamanism - the primordial magic of Siala. It was first used by the ogres, then the orcs, the dark elves, and the goblins. The magic of men and the light elves is derived from shamanism.

Shamar - the capital of the Border Kingdom.

Siala - the world in which the events of this book take place.

Silna - the goddess of love, beauty, and nature.

s'kash (orcish) - a sword with curved blade. It is sharpened on its inner, concave edge and usually has teeth like a saw.

sklot (gnomic, lit. "corkscrew") – a heavy military crossbow designed to puncture the heavy armor of warriors walking the front ranks of an army.

Soulless Huntsmen – units of the army of Valiostr. In times of peace they perform the functions of the police. They are employed in military actions, and also assist in suppressing revolts and conspiracies, as well as capturing and exterminating dangerous gangs and individual criminals.

Spring War – the war that began in the final year of the Quiet Times (640 E.D.). Men and dark elves fought on one side, and the orcs of Zagraba on the other. The War of Shame is the name that orcs use for the Spring War.

Stalkons – the royal dynasty of Valiostr.

Steel Brows – the heavy infantry of the Wild Hearts.

Steel Mines – the mountains and mines in Isilia that produce the finest steel in the Northern Lands. The race of gnomes lives here.

Steppes of Ungava – the steppes on the very southern edge of the Northern Lands.

S'u-dar (ogric) or the Icy Pass – the only route through the Needles of Ice from the Desolate Lands to the citadel of the Nameless One.

Sultanate – a state located far beyond the Steppes of Ungava.

svens or chanters – creatures of the Desolate Lands that resemble shaggy flying spheres. When the freezing conditions in the open expanses of the Desolate Lands are at their fiercest they appear, chanting a song that kills all living things.

Thorns – the soldiers of this detachment carry out reconnaissance work and raids deep into the territory of the Desolate Lands. The Thorns have a reputation as daredevils and swashbuckling desperadoes.

Tresh (orcish) - a polite term of address used by elves to an elf of noble birth. Sometimes used by other races when addressing high-born elves.

vampire - a creature of legend. Even today it is still not known if it exists in reality or only in the tales told by drunken peasants. According to the legend, only human beings and dark elves can become vampires. Vampires are credited with magical powers, such as the ability to transform themselves into a bat or mist. The Order of Magicians regards the existence of vampires as doubtful.

Vastar's Bargain - in 223 E.D. Vastar, the king of Garrak, concluded an alliance with a dragon so that the creature would assist him in attacking neighboring kingdoms. The agreement, however, proved worthless to the king: the dragon failed to engage the humans in battle and Vastar's army was routed. The term "Vastar's Bargain" signifies any similarly disadvantageous agreement.

Wild Hearts - the detachment of soldiers who serve at the Lonely Giant.

Wind-Jugglers - the name given in the army to experienced bowmen, no matter to what detachment they belonged. Even when there was a strong wind interfering with the flight of the arrow, the "jugglers" almost always hit their mark.

wizardry - the magicians of men and the light elves possess a higher magic, based on the earlier magic, or shamanism, of the orcs and dark elves.

Zagorie, or the Free Lands - the lands beside the southern spurs of the Mountains of the Dwarves. All who are discontented with the rule of the authorities or the laws of the kingdom flee here: peasants, younger sons, courtiers in disgrace, adventurers, and criminals. Such people can always find land and work in the Free Lands.

Zam-da-mort (gnomish), or the Castle of Death - the highest and most majestic peak of the Mountains of the Dwarves.